Dear Reader,

It has been said the Mexican-American War is the war that the US cannot remember and Mexico cannot forget. I first learned of this war as an undergraduate in my twenties. How I wish I had known earlier that the state I call home, California, was once Mexico, and that my native tongue, Spanish, was spoken here. Knowing might have lessened the trauma of growing up Mexican in a country that made me feel I didn't belong, and told me in subtle and not-so-subtle ways that I should go back to where I came from.

I wrote *A Ballad of Love and Glory* to learn more about this war—or invasion, as it is called in Mexico—a conflict that led to my native country losing half its territory. The research I undertook helped me better understand the US-Mexican border, la "herida abierta [the open wound] where the third world grates against the first and bleeds," as Chicana scholar Gloria Anzaldúa described it. It is my dream that *A Ballad of Love and Glory* will bring this defining moment in history to the forefront, a moment relegated to a mere footnote in the US.

Throughout my fifteen years as a published writer, I have written about immigration, mostly about my own experience. But this novel gave me the opportunity to explore another migration experience. At a reading in 2013, someone asked if I had heard of the Saint Patrick's Battalion, an artillery unit composed of mostly Irish soldiers who'd deserted the US Army to fight on the Mexican side. I hadn't. "You should write their story," this person suggested.

Out of curiosity, I googled the Saint Patrick's Battalion and learned about its leader, John Riley. As I read books by historians Peter Stevens, Robert Miller, and Michael Hogan, my fascination grew. I discovered almost half the US Army was composed of foreign-born soldiers, mostly Irish, German, and Italian. On April 12, 1846, Private John Riley deserted the US Army and ended up in the Mexican ranks as a first lieutenant. Later that year, Mexican general Antonio López de Santa Anna created the Saint Patrick's Battalion with Riley as its leader. Interestingly, the US denied the battalion's existence for several decades. Perhaps to downplay the high number of desertions during the war, especially by immigrants in its ranks mistreated by nativist officers. Perhaps to avoid drawing attention to the largest mass hanging in US history, which took place in September 1847 in Mexico City.

Not much of Riley's personal story is known since parish records in Ireland were destroyed in a fire. What *is* known is that he left a son behind in Ireland, and perhaps a wife. In the 1840s, the Irish were the least desirable group of immigrants, dehumanized and reviled—much like Latino immigrants are today. I realized I did have a personal connection to Riley, even if we came from different cultures and historical eras. So, one day, I wrote a scene from Riley's point of view. Then I wrote another. To capture his voice and honor his cultural roots, I did extensive research, read nineteenth-century Irish literature and diaries, and consulted with an Irish historian.

Eventually I came upon John Greenleaf Whittier's poem "The Angels of Buena Vista" about a Mexican woman named Ximena who tends the wounded from both sides on the battlefield. I was intrigued by her. Who was she? How did she end up on that battlefield? Who and what did she lose in this war? Because I had very little to go on, Ximena proved to be the most challenging character to render, and yet, her voice became the most important in the novel. It was through Ximena that I felt, in every fiber of my being, the gravity of the moment: the loss, the struggle to survive, the desire to defend home and country against unjust invaders, the fierce determination to save Mexico's Irish heroes from the gallows, especially the man she loves.

In the US, the soldiers of the Saint Patrick's Battalion were viewed as traitors and renegades, but in Mexico, they are heroes and martyrs. This novel is a song dedicated to these brave sons of Erin.

It is also a love song for Mexico, a country devoured. Thank you for reading *A Ballad of Love and Glory*, for joining Ximena, John Riley, and the Saint Patrick's Battalion as they fight for freedom, honor, and love.

Reyna Grande

Also by Reyna Grande

Across a Hundred Mountains

A través de cien montañas (Spanish)

Dancing with Butterflies

The Distance Between Us

La distancia entre nosotros (Spanish)

The Distance Between Us, Young Reader's Edition

A Dream Called Home

La búsqueda de un sueño (Spanish)

A
Ballad of
Love and Glory

— A Novel —

Reyna Grande

ATRIA BOOKS

New York   London   Sydney   Toronto   New Delhi

ATRIA
BOOKS

An Imprint of Simon & Schuster, Inc.
1230 Avenue of the Americas
New York, NY 10020

This book is a work of fiction. Any references to historical events, real people, or real places are used fictitiously. Other names, characters, places, and events are products of the author's imagination, and any resemblance to actual events or places or persons, living or dead, is entirely coincidental.

First Atria Books hardcover edition March 2022

ATRIA BOOKS and colophon are trademarks of Simon & Schuster, Inc.

For information about special discounts for bulk purchases, please contact Simon & Schuster Special Sales at 1-866-506-1949 or business@simonandschuster.com.

The Simon & Schuster Speakers Bureau can bring authors to your live event. For more information or to book an event, contact the Simon & Schuster Speakers Bureau at 1-866-248-3049 or visit our website at www.simonspeakers.com.

Interior design by Jill Putorti

Manufactured in the United States of America

1 3 5 7 9 10 8 6 4 2

Library of Congress Cataloging-in-Publication Data

ISBN 978-1-9821-6526-0
ISBN 978-1-9821-6528-4 (ebook)

In memory of

Patrick Antison	Gibson McDowell
John Appleby	James McDowell
John Benedick	Laurence McKee
Patrick Casey	Lachlin McLachlin
John Cavanaugh	John A. Meyers
Dennis Conahan	Thomas Millett
John Cuttle	Auguste Morstadt
Patrick Dalton	Peter Neil
George Dalwig	Andrew Nolan
Kerr Delaney	Francis O'Conner
Frederick K. Fogal	William C. O'Conner
Marquis T. Frantius	Henry Ockter
Parian Fritz	William Outhouse
Robert W. Garretson	Richard Parker
Richard Hanley	John Price
Barney Hart	Francis Rhode
Roger Hogan	John Rose
George W. Jackson	Herman Schmidt
William H. Keech	John Sheehan
Harrison Kenney	James Spears
John W. Klager	Henry Venator
Henry Longenhammer	William A. Wallace
Elizier S. Lusk	Lemuel N. Wheaton
Martin Lydon	Henry Whistler
Hugh McClellan	
John McDonald	And John Riley

Dedication TK

Speak and tell us, our Ximena, looking northward far away,
O'er the camp of the invaders, o'er the Mexican array,
Who is losing? who is winning? are they far or come they near?
Look abroad, and tell us, sister, whither rolls the storm we hear.

Down the hills of Angostura still the storm of battle rolls;
Blood is flowing, men are dying; God have mercy on their souls!
'Who is losing? who is winning?' Over hill and over plain,
I see but smoke of cannon clouding through the mountain rain.'

—From "The Angels of Buena Vista,"
John Greenleaf Whittier, 1847

Part One

Whither Rolls the Storm

1

March 1846
El Frontón de Santa Isabel, Gulf of Mexico

When the three steamships came into view, undulating on the shimmering open waters of the gulf, the villagers grew quiet and still, in the way Ximena had seen meadowlarks freeze when hunted by a hawk. Standing on the shore of the Laguna Madre, the water soaking into her skirts, she squinted from the glare as she watched the ships passing through the entrance of the inlet, the smoke rolling out of their funnels dark as storm clouds. She trembled inside. These vessels were not traders or merchants bringing goods to market.

The port of El Frontón de Santa Isabel, just north of the mouth of the Río Bravo del Norte, was a lifeline for the small settlements and scattered ranches in the area and the nearby city of Matamoros. Ximena loved swimming and fishing in the bay, the cool salt air and rolling waves, so whenever her husband went to the port to sell and trade supplies from their rancho—cowhides, tallow, wool, livestock, and crops from the last harvest—she eagerly joined him. As the steamships anchored in the harbor, she caught flashes of red and blue in the air and something glinting on the decks in the afternoon sunlight. Though she couldn't see clearly what they carried, an image formed in her mind: bronze cannons and blue-clad soldiers.

For eight months, she'd been hearing rumors of war, ever since US and Texas soldiers had been encamped in Corpus Christi Bay. But as long as they remained a hundred and sixty kilometers away, their presence hadn't disrupted her daily life. Three months before, in the last days of 1845, the Republic of Texas became the twenty-eighth state in the Union, and a dispute had erupted over this strip of land between the Río Bravo—or the Río Grande, as the norteamericanos called it—and the Río Nueces to the north. She, like everyone, knew it was only a matter of time before the Yanqui president, James Polk, would order his troops to march south to take possession of the disputed land. These warships, Ximena realized, were bringing an end to what little tranquility had existed in her region.

"We should go," she whispered, turning to her grandmother who was standing beside her in the water. Nana Hortencia's silver braids hung loosely at either side of her head, and although the years had bent and twisted her brown body like the limbs of a mesquite, her hands were firm and steady.

The old woman sighed with worry and said,. "Let us go find your husband, mijita."

The tolling church bells shattered the eerie silence that had descended upon the small community. All at once, mothers pulled their children out of the water and rushed them home, fisherwomen snatched up their baskets, and fruit and vegetable vendors hastily loaded their crates onto their carts. Out in the Laguna Madre, the fishermen were rowing their boats back to the wharf. Then bugles sounded the alarm and the handful of Mexican soldiers protecting the port hurried to their posts.

Ximena waded out of the water and guided her grandmother to the storehouses. Her wet skirts clung to her legs, her boots squished, but there was no time to change. She quickened her pace, but as Nana Hortencia struggled to keep up, she forced herself to slow down, to not panic. Clutching the old woman's hand, they wove through the throng of frightened villagers, her eyes searching for her husband, Joaquín. She sighed in relief when she spotted the ranch hands at a storehouse, rushing to finish loading the sacks of coal onto the carts. But Joaquín wasn't with them, nor could she find him inside.

"Stay here, Nana," she said and hurried back outside.

As Ximena whirled around into the street, a party of Texas Rangers rode into the plaza from the rear of the port, shouting their wild cries and shooting their revolvers into the air. The villagers screamed and ran for cover. The Mexican soldiers guarding the customhouse hastily fired warning shots, and the Rangers retaliated.

The grass-thatched roof of the customhouse had already begun to smoke, and then, suddenly, burst into flames.

"Joaquín!" Ximena cried out, pushing past the crowd, her heart flailing like a seagull trapped in netting. Seeing her husband run out of the building, she rushed to join him.

"Vámonos," he said, taking her hand.

The air reeked of smoke. Ximena could hear the crackling of the burning timber and thatch as the villagers' huts burned. Flames licked the rafters in the plaza church even as the bells continued to toll. People ran out of their homes with whatever they could carry. A fortunate few loaded their wagons and carts and fled. The rest followed behind on foot in a frantic pace, seeking shelter in the prairie beyond.

The Yanqui cavalry suddenly burst through the smoke, led by a peculiar old man dressed like a farmer and wearing a straw hat. They shot their pistols into the air, and in the shocked silence that followed, the man in the straw hat pulled his horse to a halt and held up one hand.

"My name is General Zachary Taylor, commander-in-chief of the Army of Occupation of the United States of America," he declared. "Do not be afraid."

No one waited to hear the Yanqui general say more. Joaquín handed Ximena her horse's reins, and as soon as Nana Hortencia sat safely on one of the canvas-topped wagons and the ranch hands took the reins, they rode out of the village, eluding the general and his mounted troops along with the Rangers.

They made their way across the broad plains, but encumbered by wagons and carts loaded with sacks of rice, wheat flour, coffee and cacao, crates of piloncillo and dried fish, and other provisions they had picked up at the port, they couldn't get away fast enough. As the gathering dusk gave over to the fireflies twinkling over the prairie, Ximena, struggling to see in the deepening twilight, wondered how long it would take to cover the remaining nine kilometers to the rancho. .

She glanced back at the village in the distance and saw it was covered in an orange haze.

"War is coming," she said.

"No, mi amor," Joaquín said. "They will negotiate. I'm sure it won't come to war."

He was only trying to ease her worries. But it was futile to try to shield her from what she had witnessed that day. What else could this be, if not an act of war?

She remembered that ten years before, when Texas rebelled against Mexico and declared itself an independent republic, it proclaimed that its boundary would then extend two hundred miles south to the Río Bravo, even though the Río Nueces had been the established border even before Mexico had achieved its independence from Spain. Mexico had never recognized Texas's independence nor its claim to the Río Bravo and the region between the two rivers, and it had warned the United States to keep its hands off its lands.

Looking to the sky, Ximena thought of the single star on the flag of the Republic of Texas, realizing that it was now part of the American constellation. If it was now ready to destroy everything in its wake, what would become of her and her family?

2

The next day, Ximena sat on her horse facing northeast, looking beyond the prairie teeming with wildflowers at the wisps of smoke rising over the remnants of El Frontón de Santa Isabel. They had arrived at the rancho before sunup, and though she was tired, she had been unable to sleep. So she'd gotten dressed to ride out to the prairie and offer up a prayer for the villagers. If the Yanquis weren't stopped, would El Frontón de Santa Isabel be the first of many Mexican villages to be burned to the ground?

The wind rippled through the zacahuistle grass. Specks of the windblown ash settled on her opened hand, and she licked them off her palm, tasting the bitter sorrow of innocent families displaced from their homes. What would happen to them now? Those who'd fled were most likely scattered about the bare prairie, unsheltered and exposing themselves to further dangers. But where could they go? Those who hadn't been able to flee were surely now at the mercy of their enemies, facing an equally uncertain fate.

As she turned her horse, Cenizo, to return to the house, she spotted another cloud rising in the west. This one was not from a fire. Mounted riders were kicking up dust as they sped toward the rancho, and that kind of haste meant trouble. Ximena galloped back to the stables, calling for the foreman's sons to fetch her husband and the wranglers who'd taken the horses out to pasture. The teenage boys dropped their pitchforks and hurried off, but the horsemen reached the main house before Joaquín. The barking dogs brought out Nana Hortencia and the three house servants, who waited fearfully under the ramada.

Hiding her escopeta between the folds of her skirt, her finger on the trigger and ready to shoot if she had to, Ximena stood by the front door of her house and waited, her heart pounding to the beat of the horses' hooves. It wasn't the dreaded Texas Rangers or the marauding Comanches, and yet she felt little relief once she identified the leader of the twelve riders. It was Joaquín's childhood friend Cheno, or more officially, Corporal Juan Nepomuceno Cortina of the Mexican militia the Defensores de la Patria.

"Cheno, what a surprise," she said, loosening her tight grip on her shotgun, though the worry in the pit of her stomach intensified. What was the militia doing here?

Cortina pulled up to the house and dismounted quickly. "Ximena. Sorry to show up like this, but I need your help." He looked toward Nana Hortencia, who stood behind Ximena, and said, "Por favor. He doesn't have much time."

One of Cortina's men was slumped over his horse, about to fall off, his blood dripping steadily onto the ground. "Bring him in," Ximena said. "¡Pronto, por Dios!"

She directed them to the rear room off the kitchen garden where she and her grandmother tended their patients. After clearing the wooden table of all the medicinal roots Nana Hortencia had been grinding, they laid the man upon it. She ordered the servants to boil water and bring clean rags. Her grandmother cut off the man's bloodied shirt, revealing a hole where a musket shot had gone through his shoulder.

Ximena turned to Cortina and asked, "Who did this?"

He took off his sombrero and wiped his sweaty face with the dirty red handkerchief tied around his neck. "The Yanquis. We came upon

Taylor and his cavalry and had a little skirmish. Took two of his dragoons prisoners."

"Taylor? You mean he's no longer at El Frontón?"

"No. He's taking his entire force to set up an encampment on the north bank of the Río Bravo across from Matamoros. But he's left behind some of his men in the village to build a supply depot and a fort. Our port has fallen into the hands of the enemy, and they won't be giving it up unless we force them to."

"Then let's get those pinches Yanquis off our land, Cheno!" Joaquín said as he stood in the doorway.

"Claro que sí, amigo." Cortina grinned, and the two men embraced. Ximena knew that, like her, Joaquín couldn't get the villagers' frightful shrieks from the day before out of his mind.

The men left the room, and Ximena followed behind them on her way to the kitchen garden to get the herbs she would need for the wounded man. While the rest of the militiamen made themselves comfortable on the patio, her husband sat at the table and poured a shot of tequila for his friend. At twenty-two, Cortina was eight years younger than Joaquín, and his family owned the largest land grant in the region—44,000 acres—as well as thousands of livestock. He had tried to recruit Joaquín into his detachment of irregular cavalry in the Mexican Army, composed of local volunteers who provided their own horses and equipment. But while several rancheros had joined him or the local guerilla leaders, such as Antonio Canales, in patrolling the countryside and defending the northern frontier, Joaquín had politely declined and instead contributed several horses to the guerilla bands. He was compelled to fight alongside them when Comanches and Lipan Apaches came to pillage the settlements along the Río Bravo. Joaquín's father and two uncles had been killed and most of their livestock stolen or slaughtered during a Comanche raid ten years earlier.

But now Ximena could hear her husband eagerly discussing with Cortina the militia's plans to pester the Yanqui general, plunder his supply wagons, and above all, do what the Mexican central government wasn't yet prepared to carry out—initiate hostilities.

"The Yanquis have taken control of our port, and the Mexican military allowed it to happen!" Joaquín said. "That port is vital to trade."

Although Ximena wanted to hear the rest of their conversation, her grandmother needed help. She cut some hierba del pollo and hurried back to the healing room, its adobe walls permeated with the scent of lavender and sage, candle wax, and copal incense. Nana Hortencia was washing the man's wound with an infusion of llantén.

"Will he live?" Ximena asked.

"He's lost a lot of blood, but the lead ball went through his body whole and didn't leave any fragments," Nana Hortencia said, rinsing the bloody towel. "Although, I see bits of his shirt in the wound, which must be taken out."

Her grandmother was the best curandera in the area and had saved many lives, including Ximena's. Nana Hortencia had been born with el don, the healing gift, and had been trained by her own grandmother, a medicine woman with deep knowledge of herbal medicine. A physician was a rare commodity in these parts, but Nana Hortencia was worth more than a dozen doctors combined. Week after week, the locals, especially the poor, showed up at the ranch to seek her healing.

Ximena turned the patient's hand over, palm-side up, and placed two fingers over his wrist artery. "His pulse is weak but stable," she said. She brushed the man's dirty hair off his forehead and wiped the sweat and grime from his face. He was young, no more than eighteen, with a whole life yet to live. As she crushed the herbs with her mortar and pestle to make a poultice, she prayed for God's mercy.

After they finished tending to their patient, Ximena and Nana Hortencia transferred him to a cot. The day was waning, and Joaquín and Cortina were on the back patio with the others. From the looks of it, Cortina and his men would be spending the night at the rancho. Chickens were broiling over the open fire, two of the house servants, Inés and María, were busy making fresh tortillas on the comal and reheating a pot of beans while Rosita handed out mugs of café, which the men spiked with the bottle of aguardiente being passed around. The men sat on pieces of tree trunk, wrapped in their sarapes, smoking tobacco cigarettes rolled in corn husk as they talked about the Yanqui invasion. Some of them lay on the ground using their saddles as pillows.

Ximena sighed, wrapping her rebozo around her shoulders, and went to sit with Joaquín. He put a sinewy arm around her. As she leaned her head against his shoulder, soaking up his warmth, she breathed in his musky smell of sweat and horse, vaqueta, and tobacco leaves. She closed her eyes, remembering the first time she'd met him four years earlier. Her horse had been bitten by a rattlesnake and died, and her father had brought her to Joaquín's rancho to buy a new mount. They'd been told by everyone in Matamoros that Joaquín Treviño's horses were the best trained.

When they arrived at the rancho, she saw him before he spotted her and her father outside the corral watching him. He was inside breaking a horse, a beautiful blue roan about two years old. Ximena was captivated by the way he stroked and patted the filly with a firm but gentle hand to get it used to human touch. He was not only a patient trainer but also compassionate, for not once did she see him mistreat the animal even after it repeatedly tried to bite him. By the time the drill ended, a change had come about in the filly. Instead of trying to hurt him, it gently put its head on him. From outside the corral, Ximena could sense the emotional bond forming between man and beast, and she found herself wanting to put her head on him too. Even before a word had passed between them, she'd trusted Joaquín. Loved him.

With reluctance, she listened to Cortina, who was sitting across the fire from her, recount his expeditions spying on the Yanquis while they were encamped at Corpus Christi. As one of the dozens of scouts serving the Mexican Army, Cortina was one of the first to learn of President Polk's orders for Taylor to advance south to the Río Bravo. Most of the cannons had been sent by ship and the bulk of the troops on foot.

"You know what infuriates me?" Cortina said to Joaquín. "That for a handful of lentils our very own compatriots—Mexican rancheros—

provided the Yanqui general the pack animals he needed to transport his supplies."

Joaquín shook his head and cursed. "They've betrayed our country helping those land-grabbing Yanquis get down this far."

Ximena thought of the hundreds of mesteños, wild mustangs, Joaquín had captured and broken through the years. Unlike other rancheros who continued to illicitly trade and sell livestock to the norteamericanos, she and Joaquín had stopped shipping their saddle horses, mules, and oxen to New Orleans as soon as Taylor's army settled in Corpus Christi. They now sold only to Mexicans and exported to Havana. Since the survival of their ranch depended on the profits their livestock fetched, it made life harder for them.

Cortina recounted his face-to-face confrontation with Taylor's forces at the Arroyo Colorado. Mexican scouts and the militia had read the Yanqui general a proclamation from the Mexican commander, warning him to advance no further into Mexican territory and to turn back. Of course, Taylor would not be stopped and responded with a threat of his own, pointing his guns at Cortina and his men. Being no match for the Yanqui forces, the Mexican riders were forced to back down in disgrace and return to Matamoros to alert the inhabitants and their commander that the Yanquis were on their way.

"It's a shame General Mejía was just bluffing, because the arroyo was the perfect place to attack the Yanquis and repel their invasion," Cortina said. "We should have welcomed the Yanquis with arms ready and matches lighted. But Mejía insists he doesn't have enough troops, and the reinforcements and supplies he was promised haven't arrived."

"Surely our government will send them soon," Joaquín said.

Cortina scoffed, turning the chickens on the spits so they could roast evenly. The grease dripped onto the fire, and it crackled and shot up flames that glinted on his angry face. "We norteños are of little concern to the caudillos in Mexico City, my friend. They are too busy fighting for power. Instead of using national troops for border defense, they use them for their never-ending insurrections and will abandon us to our luck, as they always have. It falls to us to defend our homes from the perverse intentions of the Yanquis. So, what do you say, Joaquín? Will you join us in driving back our enemies to the Nueces? Will you do your sacred duty to protect our frontier?"

As the questions hung in the air, Ximena wished Juan Cortina hadn't come to the ranch. She wanted her husband home where she knew he was safe, or at least safer than sneaking around in the chaparral, spying, plundering, and killing. Waging guerrilla warfare on the Yanquis would only invite trouble. And where would that lead? Would he come home one day bleeding and tied to his horse? Or worse? She shuddered at the mere thought. She had already lost so many loved ones. She couldn't lose her husband too.

Ximena took Joaquín's hand and interlaced her fingers with his, hiding their locked hands in the folds of her skirt. *The thought of you out there risking your life terrifies me*, she wanted to say. *And you becoming a murdering guerrillero, what would it do to your soul, to your gentle spirit? Will it lead you down a path I cannot follow, Joaquín?* But Ximena couldn't say those words aloud. She didn't want to shame him by speaking her mind in front of the men.

She imagined them alone. She could speak to him then, saying what she wanted to express freely. She knew Joaquín would at least hear her out, even if he didn't heed her counsel. But now, as he avoided her eyes and gently tried to pull his hand away from hers while she refused to surrender it, she knew that neither her advice nor her blessing would be sought tonight. So she loosened her grip and let him go.

Joaquín rose and reaffirmed what he'd said earlier. "What are we waiting for, Cheno? Vamos. Let's get those pinches Yanquis off our land."

3

April 1846
Fort Texas, Río Grande

When the bugles sounded reveille at the break of day, John Riley was already buttoning his private's uniform. His tentmate, Franky Sullivan, barely turned over on the makeshift bed Riley had built to protect him from rattlesnakes. Riley shook him, and still, the snoring continued. The night previous, Sullivan took a drop too many despite Riley's warnings to leave liquor alone. In the seven months since he'd enlisted, he'd seen too many of his countrymen suffer all manner of punishments at the hands of the Yankee officers. Drunkards always fared the worst, but that didn't stop Sullivan—like so many others—from sneaking off at night in search of the liquor peddlers among the horde of camp followers.

Riley never indulged in the drink. It would mean fewer wages to send back to his wife and son in Ireland. God knew there was never enough for them to eat. Even before the rotten potato crop, life had been harsh enough. Besides, he liked being in control of his senses, his body. Irishmen needed their wits about them, always. Especially in this country. Especially in this army.

At the next bugle call, Riley shoved his tentmate clear off the bed, and Sullivan fell with a thud on the ground, even that didn't rouse him. With no other choice, Riley slapped him hard across the face. Sullivan finally bolted awake.

"You got five minutes, lad," Riley said. "And right well you know what will happen if you tarry." He shook out Sullivan's sky-blue fatigue jacket and trousers to check for scorpions and tarantulas and tossed the uniform to his tentmate, who stumbled to his feet.

"Och, I was dreamin' of my mam," Sullivan said as he slipped on his trousers over his dirty flannel underdrawers. "Sometimes, I start to forget what she looks like! But there she was, runnin' hither to me. I was comin' home in my dream, can ya believe it? I was comin' home."

"'Tis a fine dream, lad, but time to wake up now." Riley didn't let on how similar—and how bittersweet—his own dreams of Ireland had been r since he'd left three years before. "And be sure to shake your bootees," he said on his way out of the tent. "Best not let the poisonous vermin infestin' this place get ya."

Sullivan was a skinny young manwith wide green eyes as vibrant as grass after freshly fallen rain. His unruly red hair and the fuzz on his ruddy cheeks made him seem younger than his eighteen years. Riley himself had had that look once until he learned better. The lad was about the age Riley was when he first joined the British Army twelve years before. Riley had earned his sergeant stripes serving in the Royal Artillery and had high hopes back then of making something of himself, but in the military, as in everything else, the English treated the Irish like chattel. He soon discovered that a Connemara man like himself would never stand a fair chance of promotion on his merits. The English never let him forget that Paddies were great cannon fodder. Riley still remembered the hardships he'd undergone, and he wanted to spare Sullivan some of the heartaches that boyish fancies—and follies—could bring.

Under the command of the Yankee general, Zachary Taylor, Riley quickly learned that being in the US Army was no different.

He pushed through the worn-out canvas flap into the rosy light and took a deep breath of the fresh morning air. The change in weather was a blessing. Most of his service had been spent in the coastal village of Corpus Christi where he'd suffered blistering humid days under the scorching sun and keen, wet nights in a leaky tent. Here, on the northern bank of the Río Grande, he'd have to get used to the sudden changes in temperature. One day could burn as hot as living fire, and the next a bitterly cold norther could freeze a man to death in his sleep.

He made the sign of the cross and said a prayer before reporting for roll call. A gang of wild geese flew low above him. He followed their V-shaped line with his eyes south across the Río Grande where the red-tiled roofs and white buildings of the Mexican city of Matamoros peeked through the thickets. Hearing the church's bells echoing across the river, scarcely two hundred yards wide, Riley wished he were inside the warm walls, among the swirling scents of melted candle wax, incense, and flowers like the churches back home. The Yanks ridiculed the Catholic faith and spurned the Irish as savage fanatics, forcing Protestant services on Catholic soldiers. Their disdain for his religion made Riley's blood boil. He couldn't rightly remember his last mass, his last confession, and he longed for the words of comfort only a man of the cloth could give. He hoped prayers would be enough for now. *In nomine Patris et Filii, et Spiritus San—Áti.* He hoped Jesus and His Holy Mother would understand. *Amen.*

"*Anois*, Sullivan, what's keepin' ya?" he called out, putting on his cap. His eye was caught by what seemed another odd bit of weather—he mistook it at first for patches of snow, until he realized it was paper, hundreds of leaflets rustling about in the wind, flapping between the tents. As the soldiers emerged from their tents, they bent down to examine the leaflets, muttering among themselves. Riley brushed the dirt off one he found stuck on a nearby bush.

The Commander-in-Chief of the Mexican Army
to the English and Irish under the orders of the
American General Taylor:

Know Ye: That the Government of the United States is committing repeated acts of barbarous aggression against the magnanimous Mexican nation; that the Government which exists under the flag of the stars is unworthy of the designation of Christian. Recollect that you were born in Great Britain that the American Government looks with coldness upon the powerful flag of England and is provoking to rupture the warlike people to whom it belongs, President Polk boldly manifesting a desire to take possession of Oregon as he has already done Texas.

Now then, come with all confidence to the Mexican ranks, and I guarantee you, upon my honor, good treatment and that all of your expense shall be defrayed until your arrival in the beautiful capital of Mexico.

Germans, French, Poles, and individuals of other nations! Separate yourselves from the Yankees, and do not contribute to defend a robbery and usurpation which, be assured, the civilized nations of Europe look upon with utmost indignation. Come, therefore, and array yourselves under the tricolor flag, in confidence that the God of Armies protects it, and it will protect you, equally with the English.

PEDRO DE AMPUDIA
FRANCISCO R. MORENO
Adjutant of the commander-in-chief
Headquarters upon the road to Matamoros
April 2, 1846

Riley looked at the opposite shore. The Mexicans had labored all night, throwing up breastworks, extending trenches, adding more sandbag barriers and emplacements. They mostly worked under cover of darkness, unlike the Yankees who were building a fort upon this disputed land in broad daylight. Riley wondered why the Mexicans hadn't attacked the minute Taylor and his 3,900 troops marched into view. In their hesitation, they'd allowed the Army of Occupation too many advantages: control of their port at Point Isabel on the gulf, a foothold on land within striking reach of Matamoros, construction on a redoubt and a six-bastioned fortress, and the planting of the Stars and Stripes in soil they claimed was theirs. Peasants even brought provisions by the crate—eggs, milk, and cheese; fruits, bread, and meat—sold to the soldiers and officers who could afford them. Mexican civilians were helping the Yankee army become even stronger, providing other goods such as mules and horses. He had seen the local men wearing nothing but white pantaloons rolled up to their knees or simple breechclouts; the women with no bonnet, just a frayed shawl over their heads, homespun blouses that barely covered their bosoms and short, raggedy skirts that revealed their unstockinged legs; and children barefoot and without a stitch upon them—Riley wondered if their poverty made them behave thus. He had personal knowledge that for a hungry family, patriotism was a luxury.

Do not contribute to defend a robbery and usurpation . . . the Mexican general wrote in the leaflet. This brewing conflict wasn't just a border dispute. Riley had heard about the Yankees' territorial ambition beyond Texas, their desire for a bigger piece of Mexico's northern lands, such as Upper California and New Mexico. It was their destiny, the Yankees believed, a decree from Heaven to build an empire to the Pacific Ocean. So, unable to get Mexico to sell the coveted territory, here were the Yankees now, ready to take hold of the land by force.

"What's that yoke there?" Sullivan said as he finally emerged. Riley handed him the leaflet. "What's it say?" he asked, holding the leaflet upside down.

Many of the Irish in the army were humble tillers of the soil like Sullivan, men with no learning, who'd never held a musket before, only a miserable hoe or spade to tend their fields. These were the men the United States government was enlisting in its ranks by the thousands, fresh off ships arriving daily from Ireland and other impoverished and unstable lands.

"'Tis from the Mexicans." Riley surveyed the campground and didn't like what he saw. From the expression on the faces of the Yanks, he knew he ought to act quickly. "Toss it away,!" he told Sullivan, tearing the paper up and dropping it as if it had scalded him. "Don't you get caught with it. And for the love of Heaven, don't draw attention to yourself!"

As they scrambled to the drill field for morning muster, Sullivan struggled to keep up. Riley, at six-foot-two, easily outpaced his tent-mate, who looked like a child playing soldier. Around the campground Riley could see many of his countrymen and other foreign soldiers lingering in groups, clutching the leaflets in their hands. He wanted to tell them what he'd just told Sullivan, but knowing the price of late-ness, he kept on moving. So far, he was one of the lucky ones who'd escaped the punishments Yankee officers were keen on inflicting upon his kind, especially since desertions were on the rise.

Ever since their arrival a week earlier, men had been throwing themselves into the Río Grande and swimming across, some ending up in the Mexican ranks. After losing fourteen men in a single night, General Taylor immediately ordered his sentries to shoot anyone caught deserting. Those leaflets, enticing more men to desert, would fuel the distrust and hatred Yanks already felt for the foreigners in their ranks.

"What did that leaflet say?" Sullivan hurried to catch up, holding his government-issued musket as if it were a shovel.

"Bother yourself no more about it, lad. Focus on the day ahead and don't invite trouble."

"Arrah, just tell me! Everyone but me will know what's goin' on. The Yanks already treat me like a half-witted spalpeen."

Riley stopped and turned to Sullivan. He remembered his parish priest, Father Aidan, who had taught him to read and write. The Penal Laws imposed on Irish Catholics denied many, especially landless peasants, the opportunity for schooling, and if it hadn't been for the kindness of the priest, Riley would understand the Mexicans' procla-mation no better than his tentmate.

"As I said, 'tis from the Mexicans. They're keen on havin' us break our vows to the Yanks. Join their ranks."

"What they offerin'? Will they be kinder to us than the Yanks?"

"I wouldn't bet on it. Mexicans want trouble, that's all. And don't you forget that anyone caught desertin' will be shot on the spot. So, it doesn't matter what the offer be. 'Tis not worth the risk." Riley started off again.

"But, Riley—"

"Enough, lad!"

Nearer to the drill field, German soldiers were gathering up the leaflets and throwing them into a fire pit as Lieutenants Braxton Bragg and James Duncan shouted orders, hitting them with the flat side of their sabers. "Come on, sauerkrauts, make haste!"

Riley snapped a salute and was about to go on his way, but Bragg stopped him. "Where do you potatoheads think you're going?"

"To our rank, sir," Riley said.

"Not until you help pick up the leaflets, Mick," Bragg said. "Now!"

Riley glanced at the other soldiers around him, scrambling after the papers flapping in the wind, getting their uniforms full of dust and soot, which would surely earn them a punishment once they got to their ranks.

"Now, Mick!" Bragg yelled, striking Riley across his shoulder blades with the side of his saber.

Hiding any flicker of emotion on his face, Riley knelt to the ground, and Sullivan did the same. *Steady now.* As he gathered the leaflets, he stole a glance at Bragg's special-issue uniform and freshly polished shoes. Bragg and Duncan were artillery officers, members of the army's elite, second only to the engineers. They displayed the powder stains on their uniforms with arrogance and strutted around the campground yelling and insulting the immigrant soldiers in the infantry and the dragoons. Many of the officers were from the US Military Academy at West Point, and most had no more battlefield experience than the men they bullied and insulted. The worst of these loathly fellows was Bragg, who was a genius in the field but a monster in the campground. Too many of Riley's countrymen had been flogged or beaten at Bragg's orders.

Holding a leaflet in his hand, Riley felt the Mexican general's words tugging at him. *Come therefore, and array yourselves under the tricolor flag* . . . How much were the Mexicans willing to pay an Irish soldier seasoned in the British Army? Surely more than the Yanks. A year and a half before, Riley had been laboring in Mackinac Island in Michigan, but no matter how many hours he spent hauling timber and loading barrels of pelts onto barges, he couldn't save enough money for his family's passage to America. His employer had treated him well enough, but he'd been stingy with the wages, and Riley scarcely had enough to scrape by on. After hearing the blaring of the bugles and the pounding cannons during morning drills coming from the nearby Yankee military encampment, Riley had wondered if the army might be the surest way to fulfill his promise of sending for his family. American newspapers told of an impending war between the United States and Great Britain for control of Oregon and the Pacific Northwest, and the thought that this was his chance to fight against the British and thereby redeem himself for his years as a redcoat gave Riley that extra incentive to enlist. He had always felt guilty for joining the very army that kept Ireland subdued; fighting against them alongside the Yanks would have given him great personal satisfaction. To his dismay, the enemy he would be fighting had turned out to be not Britain but Mexico, a Catholic nation.

When he signed his name on the Yanks' muster rolls, Riley was promised that he would see his seven dollars in monthly wages increase with every promotion. By now it was plain the Yanks would never see him as more than a common soldier. Like with the English, he'd never be more than cannon fodder. Might the Mexicans see him differently?

He shook away those thoughts again. With a grin, he realized that the Mexican general knew what he was doing after all. The leaflets had put notions into his head, notions he needed to put right back out of mind to focus on the day ahead, just like he'd told Franky Sullivan to do. He threw the last of the leaflets into the fire Bragg was stoking. *'Tis not worth the risk.*

After the men fell into their ranks, Captain Merrill yelled at them about the leaflets. Half of Riley's unit, Company K of the Fifth Infantry, was composed of Irish, German, Italian, and Scottish immigrants—the very soldiers the Mexican leaflets were targeting.

"I better not catch any of you with those damn papers from the filthy Mexican greasers," Captain Merrill said. "And anyone thinking of deserting tonight will find their grave in the Río Grande."

Riley remained impassive to the insults Merrill hurled at them before moving on to the roll. Hollers of "aye" came after each name. "Maloney, James." Now silence followed. Riley glanced at Sullivan. His tentmate and Maloney, an older soldier, had gotten themselves half gone with whiskey the night previous. They would've kept at it longer if Riley hadn't stopped their drunken carousing and sent Maloney staggering back to his own tent. "Maloney, James!" Captain Merrill called louder, and when no one answered, he detailed two corporals to search the tents for him. Just as the roll ended, they returned dragging Maloney, passed out and clearly unfit for duty.

"Nothing but useless drunks, these red-faced foreigners," one of the corporals said. "Should we teach them a lesson, Captain?"

Captain Merrill looked at the pitiful sight of Maloney and poked him with his boot. *Wake up, ould fella,* Riley begged under his breath. Captain Merrill signaled his subordinates to tie Maloney's hands and feet. They dragged him across the drill field where a branding iron with the letters *HD*—habitual drunkard—was put into the coals to heat. The iron was destined for Maloney's forehead. Punishment for drunkenness was usually a mark on the hip or buttocks, but Maloney was an immigrant. Suddenly awake now, Maloney squirmed like a caterpillar. The corporals held him down on the ground while a sergeant brandished the red-hot iron close to Maloney's face, taunting him.

"Let me catch any of you drunk and your fate will be the same," Captain Merrill said.

"Shite, they can't do that," Sullivan said, taking a step out of rank.

Riley grabbed his elbow and pulled him back. "There's naught to be done."

Sullivan shook his head. "How can you stand aside and do nothin'?"

In dismay, Riley watched as Sullivan stepped out of rank and shouted, "Let him alone!"

"Get this insolent sonofabitch out of here!" Captain Merrill yelled. "Buck and gag him."

"Riley, do somethin'!" Sullivan pleaded as he was dragged away. Riley tightened his fists. *Do somethin'*? What could he do? Half of his unit were immigrants like himself—with the same anger in their faces, the same impotence. Like them, Riley remained silent. He wished that fool of a boy had known well enough to do the same.

It took all of Riley's willpower not to look as a piercing scream ripped through the ranks. The smell of Maloney's burning flesh drifted toward him. Riley felt his anger burning hotter. He thought of Nelly and their son Johnny. *For them, I'm doin' this for them.* Maloney's screams stopped suddenly, and finally, Riley turned to look. The pain of the branding overcoming him, the poor fellow now lay on the ground, immobile. At least for a little while, he would be at rest.

Captain Merrill ordered him carried to the hospital tent and then called everyone to attention. Riley made the sign of the cross for the second time that day. "Holy Saint Patrick, please give me strength."

After a breakfast of maggot-infested hardtack and pickled pork, which he downed with a pint of uninviting black coffee, Riley fell in for drill and spent hours under the broiling sunshine marching and learning maneuvers as they prepared for the approaching war. With his musket braced against his right shoulder and his head erect, Riley wheeled with his unit across the dusty parade ground. Flawlessly executed rotations and drills that usually gave him pride were marred today by the smell of burnt human flesh.

General Taylor sat side-saddle on his old mare surveying the troops, a straw hat on his large head, dressed plainly in linen trousers, a dusty green coat, and common army shoes. The sixty-one-year-old Taylor wasn't a typical general at all. He didn't put on airs, and Riley had often seen him laughing and chatting with various of his men, regardless of rank. More than once, the general had saved an immigrant soldier from being punished by a nativist officer. As a veteran of several wars, Taylor had the kind of wisdom that came only from the battlefield, but with none of the vulgar pride of the other officers, such as Braxton Bragg and James Duncan. Riley heard it rumored that the general hadn't supported President Polk's push to annex Texas and harbored doubts about the claims Texas and the president made about its boundary. But orders were orders, and Taylor remained true to his duties as the commander-in-chief of the Army of Occupation. Riley had admired General Taylor, up until his shoot-on-sight orders. The Articles of War clearly stated that desertion was not punishable by death when the country wasn't at war.

Sullivan and other soldiers were seated on the dirt throughout the campground, their legs drawn up and their arms tied around them, with a stick placed under their bent knees and a gag stuffed into their mouths. Other soldiers had been condemned to spend the day upon a wooden sawhorse with their hands tied behind their backs and irons on their feet. The poor wretches would fall off and be forced back on again and again until they wished they were dead. And some of them got their wish. Back in Corpus Christi, Riley saw a soldier fall off the "horse" and snap his neck. With his hands tied behind his back, the unlucky man had been unable to break the momentum of the fall.

Soon after setting up camp opposite Matamoros, Engineer Captain Mansfield designed a massive six-bastioned fort with ramparts, gunpowder magazines, and bomb-proof shelters, and construction of the stronghold was now underway. When finished, cannons would be placed on the arrow-shaped bastions and a ditch would surround the entire complex. Those on the fatigue detail had to excavate the dirt and haul it up to the scaffolds; others, like Riley, shaped the earthen walls while engineers bawled their instructions from down below. Sweaty and shirtless, his whole body caked in mud, Riley watched the fifteen-feet-thick walls slowly take shape while he and his comrades broiled under the sun.

Up on the scaffolds, he could at least enjoy the slight tang of briny air carried on the occasional breeze drifting in from the Gulf of Mexico some twenty miles distant, and he had a fine view of the open country. Beyond the dense chaparral were cultivated fields, fig and pomegranate orchards, patches of corn, and the grasslands dotted with horned cattle and shepherds with goats and sheep. Observing the Río Grande winding its way through the thickets, he realized it was the most crooked river he'd ever seen. It twisted and doubled-backed on itself so much that even a wagon could traverse the land faster than a boat. The winding path of its muddy waters created peninsulas that jutted out like fingers. General Taylor had chosen one of these long fingers for his camp, knowing they would be protected from ground assaults on three sides. But surely the location also had disadvantages—the river walled them in as much as protected them, making them vulnerable to a siege.

Riley turned away from the river to the fields where the Yankee artillery drills were taking place. With his collection of 6-, 12-, and 18-pounders, Taylor had at his disposal a magnificent artillery, especially of the lighter variety, what they called the "flying artillery," which could redeploy immediately to wherever they were needed. From the scaffolds, Riley spotted Bragg's crews and couldn't help but marvel at the dazzling speed with which the gunners and drivers could hitch the 6-pounder guns to their team of horses, move to a new position, unhitch, and fire with deadly aim at an astonishing range of 1,500 yards. The man was truly an excellent artillery officer. Riley was loath to admit how much pleasure it gave him to watch Bragg's gun crews at battery drill whirling the cannons around the field with such rapidity and precision.

He looked with disappointment at his muddy hands, knowing there was much more they were capable of besides shaping earthen walls.

When evening came, Riley called on Captain Merrill at his tent and, after saluting his commanding officer, said, "Permission to relieve Private Sullivan from the buck-and-gag, sir."

Captain Merrill looked at him intently from behind his desk. Riley held himself at attention, his face a blank. Any flicker of resentment, anger, or defiance would surely earn him his own buck-and-gag, or worse.

"You're a good soldier, Private Riley. Never given me any trouble at all. Perhaps you can convince your countrymen to do the same?"

"Aye, sir."

"Very well. Now go and show Private Sullivan how to be an exemplary soldier such as yourself. Dismissed."

"Sir!" Riley saluted his commander and left his quarters to rush to the drill field.

In the dim light, Riley could see the lad's face severely sunburned and his lips cracked and bloodied. It wasn't Sullivan's first time getting bucked and gagged, but Riley prayed it would be his last. Had he finally realized the folly of trying to be a hero? He removed the gag and gave him water from his canteen.

"Here, take a little sup," Riley said. "Easy, now."

Sullivan coughed from gulping it down too fast. He hadn't had a drink for ten hours. Just like the Yanks, the sun showed no mercy. Riley put water on his handkerchief and wiped Sullivan's face to offer him a little relief.

"*Go raibh maith agat,*" Sullivan said, then he broke into tears.

"No need to thank me, little fella. 'Tis over now," Riley said as he removed the ropes from Sullivan's hands and feet. He tried getting him to stand up. Sullivan dried his tears with his sleeve and allowed Riley to lift him. Riley was careful to go slow, but still Sullivan cried out in pain as he took a step forward.

"I can't," he said, leaning all his weight on Riley. "Can't feel my legs!"

"One step at a time, lad. I won't let you fall. Promise."

They hobbled toward the mess tent, Riley practically carrying his tentmate.

"And Jimmy?"

Riley remembered Maloney's screams, the smell of burning flesh. "He's in the hospital tent now. Perhaps we'll see him in the morrow. Don't fret about him. He's a tough bugger. But for the love of God, will ya stop gettin' yourself into a pickle, Franky Sullivan? Keep your eyes open and your mouth shut. 'Tis all you can do."

"You sound like my da," Sullivan said.

"Your ould fella is a wise man—"

"Wise?" Sullivan said, stopping to catch his breath. "Nay. I was reared by a coward, I was. Never stood up for his family. Just let those dirty English maggots take everythin' from us."

"Nothin' he could've said or done would've changed things. He was tryin' to protect his family. Just like I'm wantin' to do."

"Is that why you took the Queen's shilling? Why you became a traitor to your own people?"

Riley remembered the day he'd enlisted at a military garrison in Galway. He was about to turn eighteen, but he lied, saying he was nineteen. His son had just been born, and the only way to feed him and keep a roof over his head was to serve in the Royal Army and don the hated redcoat, even if it meant being looked upon as a traitor by his own countrymen. While Ireland lay prostrate at the feet of its English conquerors, the only two options Riley had were to tend the fields of an absentee landlord or become a soldier in the British ranks. He was serving the bastards either way, but at least in the military, he'd earn his bread while learning skills he could use when the day of future Irish rebellion finally came. He traded his scythe for a musket and made his choice.

"Everythin' I've done is for my family. Perhaps one day when you have your own babby you'll understand."

"I understand now, John, *a chara*. I know why you did it, why my da desired me to be quiet and do nothin'. But sometimes that isn't the answer."

After mess of half-cooked biscuits and boiled ham, which they ate with little relish, Riley and his comrades sat outside the tents smoking pipes and sharing stories of the old country. They lit a fire with the mesquite wood they gathered from the thickets. Some of the men roasted rattlesnakes and jackrabbits they killed earlier that day and passed around the flasks of whiskey they'd purchased from the sutlers. Riley, as usual, sat away from the group, burnishing the pewter metal buttons of his fatigue jacket until the American eagle stamped on each button shone brightly under the warm glow of the fire. He kept to himself, observing. Listening. Most of the men, like Sullivan, were landless Catholic peasants who'd suffered all manner of ill-treatment from the English, and knowing that Riley had been a redcoat, they treated him like an outsider, not one of their own. Except for Sullivan and Maloney, Riley didn't have any friends. And that night, with Maloney in the hospital tent, he only had one.

Sullivan sat near the fire. His comrades were freely passing him the liquor, thinking it would help, but Riley winced every time the lad took a drink. If they got Sullivan tipsy, he would have a tough time rousing him again. And what manner of punishment was the little fellow in for if he couldn't perform his drills? Riley thought of Maloney, of the smell of burning flesh, and just as Thomas Quinn was about to hand Sullivan another flask of whiskey, Riley, unable to stop himself, said, "Enough, lad. You'll go too far in the drink."

"And who are you to tell him what to do? Is it his master you are?" Quinn retorted.

"I have a need for a drop of comfort, John, *a chara*," Sullivan said.

"Let him be. The poor fella deserves it," Charlie Flanagan said. "You, John Riley, with the perfect soldierin' you learned as a redcoat, you've never been punished by the Yanks, have ya? Not like the rest of us." He pointed to the brand on his forehead, his entire sullen face illuminated by the firelight, and added: "You don't know how the lad is feelin', but I do."

Riley understood his comrade's anger. He knew that while living in the slums of Philadelphia two years earlier, Flanagan had barely survived the nativist riots that left many Irish Catholic neighborhoods destroyed. He'd enlisted in the US Army seeking protection from the wrath of Protestant mobs, only to encounter the same racist and religious rancor infecting the Yankee ranks.

"Here, Franky, ma bouchal, don't mind him. Have another drink!" Matthew O'Brien said to Sullivan, handing him his flask. "*Sláinte is táinte!*"

"*Sláinte is táinte!*" the other men said. Riley looked at his messmates, men who, like him, had been forced into military service by circumstance and necessity but who, unlike him, had no desire to do it right. He stood up to leave. He wasn't going to quarrel with his countrymen. If they wanted to drink their earnings instead of holding fast to them so they could provide for their families back home, that was their problem.

"Och, Riley, 'tis my last drop," Sullivan said after he downed the whiskey. "Stay here awhile, will ya?" Then as he had every night, he began to sing a patriotic air. Soon, the others joined in too.

Riley bethought himself of home. He remembered the hard but manful days working the land with his father and brothers, the stories and songs by the family's fireside, and visiting Saint Féchín's holy well with Nelly. What he wouldn't give now to spend a day with Johnny riding ponies down Omey Strand, to see his face lit up with boyish glee. He'd been obliged to walk away from them all because he and Nelly were fixed upon having a bit of land to call their own. But at what cost?

"A nation once again, a nation once again, and Ireland, long a province be, a nation once again!"

As they sang, Riley wondered if Ireland would ever free itself from the shackles of the British crown. Would he ever be able to return and live in the land where he was born and reared, instead of bringing his wife and son here to these foreign shores to start a new life in a country that didn't want them?

"Let's sing one more before the bugle sounds tattoo," Sullivan said. And, as if sensing Riley's melancholy and nostalgia, he chose a song that was not from the old country. Instead, he said, "Here's a ditty I made up today in honor of being bucked and gagged."

Come, all Yankee soldiers, give ear to my song,
It is a short ditty, 'twon't keep you long;
It's no use to fret on account of our luck,
We can laugh, drink, and sing yet in spite of the buck.
Derry down, down, down, derry down.

Sergeant, buck him and gag him," our officers cry
For each triflin' offense which they happen to spy,
Till with buckin' and gaggin' of Dick, Pat, and Bill,
Faith, the Mexican' ranks they will help to fill.
Derry, down, down, down, derry down.

The treatment they give us, as all of us know,
Is bucking and gagging for whipping the foe;
But they are glad to release us when going to fight.
They buck us and gag us for malice or spite
Derry down, down, down, derry down. . .

It didn't take long for the men to learn the ditty, and they asked Sullivan to sing it one more time so that they could join along. Riley, too, joined in. He looked across the fire, at his tentmate, only six years older than his son, and he realized that this skinny, wide-eyed country boy was the only kin he'd have for now, and this mesquite campfire his only hearth.

4

In the morning, word spread quickly—despite the harsh punishments the day before, or maybe due to them, more soldiers had deserted in the night, including men from Riley's own unit. As he walked to the field hospital detailed by his commander to retrieve Maloney, Riley saw many more foreign-born soldiers bucked and gagged or made to ride "the horse." He sang Sullivan's ditty under his breath. If the Yankee officers kept it up, they'd end up actually helping the Mexicans fill their ranks with deserters.

He found Maloney sunk in peaceful slumber on a dirty cot. Riley looked around at the dozens of soldiers, ill from the wretched diarrhea, fever, pneumonia, snakebites, or other maladies. He crossed himself and asked Jesus and his Holy Mother to watch over them. He smiled bitterly as he recalled the recruiting officers of the US Army promising their enlisted men a wholesome diet, comfortable quarters, and the finest medical care.

Maloney's branded forehead was violently inflamed, his usually mirthful face now wan and blanched of its good-natured color. How could he disturb the poor man's dream where there was no pain and suffering? *Captain Merrill be damned.* He quietly pulled a stool up to the old man's cot. He took out a letter he received at mail call two days earlier, though his wife had sent it more than three months before. That morning he'd woken up long before reveille sounded to read and reread Nelly's words, admiring her effort to write a good hand.

26, Dec' 1845

Dear husband,

I pray to God that whin you receive me letter you're good of health and spirit. Johnny and I pray for you every night, and we fancy the day when we can finally be together. I received your letter and your remitance, and my heart lep to me throat wid delight to know you have not desarted us, John, darlin. We've had many a dark day to be sure, but this Christmas was darker than most because you weren't here with us in these unsartin times. I miss you terribly, John. How many more Christmas holidays will we be apart? Nothing grieves me more than being separated from you. I'm afeard of what's to come if our next harvest fails again. The commissioners can't figure out why the potatoes rotted undher the ground. Was there something evil in the fog that rolled over our potato gardens? Did the English lay a curse upon our soil to starve us out? Is it a punishment from the heavens above? My heart longs for you so much, a stór, sometimes I think it will rot widin me, just like our praties. Please, my love, all I ax is that you do what you can to send us the means to ship off. Let nothing prevint you from sending for me and Johnny and me parents. Every night I lie awake, fancying myself riding on the waves of the Atlantic and into your arms.

Your wife who loves you deeply,
Nelly

He knew well enough that she was right to worry. If the potato crops failed at the next harvest, Ireland would once again be faced with the scarcity it had repeatedly witnessed in times past. Hadn't he been born in such times? He still remembered the hunger and the stench of death that overtook his hometown until the potato once again returned, keeping his people fed, but never satisfied. As a lad, hearing the stories of Irish heroes that Father Aidan would tell him, or seeing heroes like Daniel O'Connell, or even rebel groups such as the Ribbonmen fighting on behalf of Ireland, had made him hope that one day he would be a hero, too, and save his country. But then he became a father and realized that heroism doesn't feed your family.

He needed to get them out of Ireland, that much was clear. But Nelly wouldn't leave without her parents, though he feared they were too old to bear the voyage. And where would he get the money to send for them all?

"What troubles you, John Riley?"

His comrade's voice startled him. He folded the letter and put it in his pocket. "How are you keepin', ould rascal?"

"Never mind me," Maloney said. "I asked you a question, I did. I know 'tis no music to a man to recite all his woe, but you can't keep it all inside, hurtin' ya. Go on, then. You can tell me, you can."

Riley felt ashamed at seeing the concern in the older man's face, that even after the brutal punishment inflicted upon him, he was more worried about what troubled Riley. *No, what right do I have to unload my sorrows on my comrade, especially when the old man has just suffered more than he ought?*

Riley shook his head. "Don't distress yourself about me none. I've nothin' to tell. I'm here to fetch ya. Captain Merrill said 'tis time."

Maloney cursed under his breath. "Is it wantin' to kill me, he is? I'd rather be a deserter, a turncoat, than remain here a blessed minute more."

"Hold your tongue, you fool!" Riley said, wondering if anyone had heard him. Didn't he know that would only make things harder for him?

"See here, boy, I watched my missus and daughter ravaged by disease in that rat-infested ship that carried me here. When their bodies were thrown overboard with the rubbish into the Atlantic, I wanted to join them in their watery grave. But suicide is a sin, so, in faith, I remained alive. And all for what, to end up in hell all the same?"

Riley looked at Maloney's graying hair, his face as wrinkled and sunken as a dried gooseberry, though at least his eyes had not grown dim with age and he still had all his teeth. At sixty-five, his comrade should know better than to disobey orders, to neglect his soldier's duty. "I ought to remind you of the words you pledged, the contract you signed? We're bound to this country, whether we like it or not. Bein' a turncoat would be a disgrace to you, to your f—" he caught himself just in time. He was going to say family, but Maloney had no one. "To your countryfolk," he said instead.

Maloney pointed to his branded forehead. "To perdition with the contract! They made pledges to us, too, didn't they?" He pointed at a soldier a few cots away. "That German fella had his skull laid open with a sword because he's ignorant of the English tongue and didn't understand his commander's orders. That Irish laddie is out of his senses, lashin' on his bed because an officer bound him hand and foot and threw him into a filthy pond till he was nearly drowned. The Yanks won't abide by their oaths, so why should we?"

"Because we need to be better than them. Because our vows ought to mean somethin', and we must go through with what we've under-taken."

Maloney spat on the ground. "I can honor the ones I make to Jesus and Saint Patrick then, eh? But the Yanks can kiss my arse. 'Tis a thousand pities I cannot swim a stroke, for if I could, I would be a Mexican soldier by now. And you, John Riley, you were once faithful to the sassenachs, and where has your obedience got ya, eh? What a misguided creature you are. Maybe one day you'll learn where you belong."

Riley stood to leave. "'Tis folly to think it'll be better over yonder, ould fella. I ought to know. As you say, I've been in two armies now, and they're both the same. What in blazes makes you think 'twill be different with the Mexicans? I've not the least notion to trade what little I have now for a fate less certain. Now get yourself dressed. Captain Merrill expects ya for duty. And mind that you do it right this time."

He'd been so distracted helping Maloney back to his tent that Riley didn't see Lieutenant Bragg and his companions heading toward them from across the camp until it was too late.

"Privates," Bragg said. "Is there a reason why you didn't salute your superiors?"

"Beggin' your pardon, sirs. We didn't see ye, sirs," Maloney said, as both he and Riley stopped and saluted the officers.

"You didn't see us?" Bragg said.

"The swellin' on his face has affected his eyesight, sir," Riley said.

"And what's your excuse, Mick?" Bragg stood closer, his spit on Riley's chin. Riley was thankful to have the advantage of the lieutenant in height, hence it was Bragg who had to look up at him, not the other way around.

"Shall I teach you to pay attention?" Bragg turned to his companions, Duncan and two other artillerists, who immediately grabbed Riley's arms and twisted them behind his back. Riley tried to break free from their grasp. "Stand down, Mick!" Bragg said, hitting Riley in the stomach with the hilt of his sword. "And not a word of insolence from you, if you know what's good for you."

Riley doubled over, gasping for breath. Maloney rushed to his side to help him stand up, but Riley shrugged him off. "Don't ya meddle in this," he whispered, knowing Maloney was in no condition for more punishment. The old man reluctantly retreated into the crowd that had gathered around them. Riley looked at the soldiers huddled in a circle, witnessing his humiliation. He was a seasoned veteran, not a young fellow like Sullivan, or an old drunk like Maloney, yet there was naught he could do to prevent this bullyragging and keep his dignity as a soldier from being trampled upon. He held himself together and checked his anger. Just then, he caught sight of a piece of paper by Bragg's foot. The letter from Nelly. It'd fallen out of his pocket. Bragg followed his gaze and spotted the paper. He bent and picked it up.

"What's this? Still carrying around the leaflets from the greasers, are you? After I made you burn them." Bragg nodded to his companions. "Strip him!"

" 'Tis not a leaflet! I'm no traitor, sir," Riley said as he struggled against the artillerists' grasp. "I'll take whatever punishment you want, but give it back."

Bragg snickered as he held the letter between his hands, and in that second, Riley knew he was about to tear it to pieces. One of his arms broke free from Duncan's grasp, and Riley lunged at Bragg. The officer staggered back just in time and jabbed his saber at Riley's breast. "Insolent fool, how dare—!"

"What in God's name is going on?" General Taylor's voice boomed suddenly from behind Riley. He turned to see the general dismounting his mare. Next to him, his second-in-command, General Twiggs, watched from atop his horse.

"This scoundrel here has given me impudence, sir," Bragg said. "He even dared to physically attack me."

Riley remained silent, but he stood straight and held his head high. He was going to be punished, he knew that. There was no point in defending himself, but he wasn't going to be defeated.

"Is this true, Private?" General Taylor said. "You attacked a superior officer?"

"Aye sir, 'tis true sir. But—"

"He's carrying a leaflet from the Mexicans," Bragg said, waving the paper around.

"'Tis no leaflet, sir! But a letter."

"He's lying," Bragg said, about to tear it to pieces.

"General Taylor, sir!" Riley said, his voice urgent. "If you please, sir, may I have it back?"

"What's all the fuss?" the general asked. He put out his hand, and Bragg handed it over. As he read it, the expression on his weathered face changed, and somehow the compassion in the general's eyes made Riley's anger return.

General Taylor handed Riley the letter and then got back on his horse. "Lieutenant Bragg, let the private go on his way."

"But, sir!" Bragg said.

General Twiggs looked at Riley, his face puckered and annoyed. "Should we not make an example of him? Have him court-martialed for disobedience and disrespecting an officer. If you don't, his country-men will be following his example."

"We need every soldier we have to win Mr. Polk's War. Don't you agree, General Twiggs?" General Taylor said. " But Private, another instance of disrespect and I will oversee your punishment personally. Understood?"

"Aye, sir, I do, sir."

Taylor mounted his old mare and turned to leave, Twiggs following behind him, fuming. Riley stood still, his eyes on Bragg.

"Watch out, croppie." The West Pointer cursed under his breath. "This isn't over yet."

Riley and Maloney watched Bragg and his companions follow General Taylor and General Twiggs to the officers' quarters.

"Och, all the turf in the bog couldn't warm me to the likes of him," Maloney said, spitting on the ground. "Don't let him nettle you, lad. Every dog is bold on his own doorstep." He turned to Riley and grinned. "As for the general, though . . . just did you a bit of a favor, he did."

"What gave you that foolish notion?" No, General Taylor had done him no favor. Bragg would follow through on his threat, and Riley needed to be ready.

Throughout the following days, gunshots were heard at all hours. De-serters were steadily bolder, no longer waiting for darkness to brave the river. *Seeking what?* Riley wondered. *What do they think they'll find?* He held no romantic notions of life on the other side. But he seemed to be in the minority. Some deserters didn't make it across, but the ones that did would wave and shout at them from across the river. As Riley toiled under the brutal sun to build the fort, he recognized his comrades, not two hundred yards away.

"Come join us, fellas!" they yelled. "The Mexicans are treatin' us as friends!"

The Yanks raised their muskets, but Taylor had ordered men shot only in the act of desertion, not after. So they focused their anger on the foreigners in their ranks—the punishments escalated, and, in turn, so did the desertions. The Negro slaves the Yankee officers had brought to cook and wait on them soon joined the trend to swim south. Mexican abolition laws made them free as soon as they set foot across the river.

General Taylor ordered round-the-clock work on the field fort, and Riley and his team on the fatigue details, labored day and night. When the redoubt was finished, the walls held four cannons, 18-pounders, which gleamed in the sunlight as they aimed at the city. One gun pointed straight at the Mexican general's headquarters.

Ignoring his sore limbs and sunburned skin, Riley carried on. But Engineer Captain Mansfield's grueling orders pushed some to the brink. Five of the men on the fatigue details, driven by exhaustion, deserted in broad daylight. They tossed their shovels aside and threw themselves into the Río Grande. Before the pickets could raise their muskets to shoot, four were pulled underwater and didn't surface again. The fifth was shot down as soon as he emerged on the other side.

Riley saw Maloney and Sullivan's eyes widen in horror as they worked a few paces from him up on the parapets of the fort. Riley wanted to say, *You see the danger now?* He took his eyes off the dead man and studied the additional sandbag barriers and earthworks the Mexicans had thrown up the night previous. By now, their emplacements contained several cannons that pointed straight at the camp. But thus far, their guns had remained silent. A rumor was afloat in the camp that the Mexicans were waiting for reinforcements. If that was true, Riley realized they were losing their opportunity since the Yankee army grew more entrenched with each passing day, and General Taylor had plenty of time to strengthen his ranks.

Riley was surprised when Mexican soldiers appeared on the other side of the river accompanied by a priest and proceeded to bury the deserter who had been shot down. "*Fidelium animae, per misericordiam Dei, requiescant in pace. Amen . . .*" The Latin prayer was carried over to him by the breeze, and he savored the familiar words. The proper burial heartened him too.

"The Mexicans are our Catholic brethren," Maloney said, coming to stand next to Riley. "If we die here, we will die as heathens. If we die there, we'll at least die as Catholics."

"And as traitors," Riley said.

"Or hcroes," Sullivan shot back, coming to join them.

Riley glanced up the river at the Mexican colors flying from their commander's headquarters. In the two armies he'd served, officers had never treated outsiders as friends, much less as equals. Why would the Mexicans be any different?

"Quiet, Micks. And back to work!" Captain Mansfield yelled from down below.

Riley did as he was told, but he pondered what Sullivan said about heroes. He remembered his uncle back home, who'd joined the Ribbonmen, a secret society that fought against the Irish tenant farmer's miserable conditions. Riley remembered the day the redcoats captured them and hanged them from the gallows. He had been only nine when he gazed up at his uncle dangling from the rope, raindrops sliding down him like tears. *That's what happens to heroes*, Riley thought.

5

The village was burning all around them, yet she wouldn't leave. Though the smoke stung her eyes, and her lungs screamed for air, she remained by his side watching as he took his last breaths. She tried pushing down on his chest to stem the flow, but his blood seeped through her fingers, an unstoppable river of red. Fire, blood, fear, all choking her. Don't die, Joaquín, don't leave me! *A building collapsed nearby, then another, and soon his body succumbed as well. In his lifeless eyes, she could see across the months, the years, everything that was to come.*

"Mijita, wake up, wake up."

Ximena bolted awake drenched in sweat, choking down a scream. Nana Hortencia was shaking her, pulling her into her arms, soothing her. The old woman smelled of raw earth, of wild herbs and sweet acacia blooms quivering in the balmy breeze, her voice as soft and gentle as the murmur of an arroyo. Ximena clung to her grandmother and breathed her in. Closing her eyes, she listened to the thump-thump-thump of her own heart. She concentrated on taking a deep breath, and then another, until slowly the pressure in her chest subsided and the acrid smell of smoke and blood faded away.

"Was it the same dream?"

Ximena nodded, still feeling the weight of her dead husband in her arms. She'd been having the same dream for several nights now, ever since Joaquín had gone off with Juan Cortina. But never before had the image been so vivid, the blood so real.

"It's the susto you got from seeing the village burn," Nana Hortencia said. "I will give you a limpia later today to cure you of your fright."

"Why isn't he back yet, Nana?"

She'd ridden out to the road each day, scanning the prairie for any signs of riders, as she awaited his return. The day before, the wounded guerilla had been well enough to leave and rejoin Cortina's band, and she'd asked him to implore Joaquín to send her word of his whereabouts. For now, though, she had nothing to reassure her he was safe.

The roosters announced the break of dawn. She could see through the window the sky tinged crimson with the morning's first glow. Nana Hortencia grabbed a brush and set to work on braiding Ximena's black waist-length tresses. Once again, Ximena closed her eyes, haunted by her earlier visions. The remnants of her dream clung to her mind like sandburs—her husband in her arms, blood blossoming on his chest. Screams, the deafening sounds of a cannon. And she herself standing in the middle of a battlefield in a cloud of burnt gunpowder. Death everywhere.

When she was done getting dressed, Ximena followed her grandmother to the stables, and together they rode out to forage for medicinal plants to replenish their supplies—prickly poppy, camphorweed, wild lettuce, purple sage, toloache. With walking sticks in hand, they scouted the terrain, keeping a vigilant eye out for rattlesnakes coiled in the grasses. Drops of dew still clung to the plants, glistening under the blessed light of the sun, and the golden clusters of the agarita and guajillo perfumed the morning air.

Ximena loved the time she spent with her grandmother, learning about curanderismo and the healing power of plants. She liked the stories her grandmother told of the old ways, of her ancestral tribe, the Pajalat, who had been displaced from their homeland when the Spanish arrived, stories of Nana's childhood in the mission along the Río San Antonio, of her forced marriage to a Spanish soldier when she and her family had tried to run away from the missionaries. But Nana Hortencia didn't linger on the sadness of those moments. Instead, she taught Ximena to focus on the wonders and magic all around her. How to listen.

There were times when Ximena's mother accused her of loving her grandmother more than her. Ximena couldn't explain to her mother that Nana's ways were simpler, her love unconditional. Ximena's mother, a light-skinned mestiza born in San Antonio de Béxar, had expectations of what kind of woman Ximena should grow up to be—a Tejana belle with many suitors falling at her feet, who went on to marry into a well-to-do family—expectations she'd never lived up to. Unlike her two older brothers who, with their fair skin and copper hair, took after her mother, Ximena's features were more Indian than Spanish. She took after Nana Hortencia, including her need for still-ness and quietude, her reverence for the earth and open skies, for the blessing of the Spirit, and for that, her mother resented her until the day she died.

Ximena was twelve when the cholera epidemic swept through the regions in 1833. Her mother and brothers perished, but Nana Hortencia managed to save Ximena and her father from death's clutches. Would she be able to do the same when the time came to save Joaquín? What if her grandmother's teas, salves, and poultices weren't enough this time? How could she protect him from what was to come?

"Mijita, you know he won't listen," Nana Hortencia said as if read-ing her thoughts. She was carefully harvesting the seed pods of a white prickly poppy and placing them in a leather pouch. "Your dreams alarm him, but he will not give heed to them."

Ximena knew her grandmother was right. Joaquín wouldn't change his mind. He found her dreams disturbing, frightening even, and pre-ferred to not discuss them with her. She'd had these strange dreams ever since she almost died from cholera, visions of things to come, though they didn't always come to pass. Her grandmother said the dreams that helped her foresee were part of her healing gift. But to Ximena, sometimes they felt more like a curse.

The year before, she had dreamed that the baby she carried in her womb wouldn't survive the birth. When she told Joaquín of her vision, he brushed aside her fears in his excitement, hoping it would be a boy. A boy it was, but his weak heart had stopped beating and his life had set with the sun that same day. After that, Joaquín forbade her to speak of her dreams. It was as if he blamed them. Ximena blamed herself. No matter how many times her grandmother, who'd lost children herself, said that it was the Creator who had called her baby's spirit to return to Him, she couldn't let go of the feeling that she had failed in her sacred duty as a mother to keep her child safe. And what good were those visions from God if there was nothing she could do to stop what she had been shown? If all they did was to prolong her pain?

"I can't lose Joaquín, Nana. If anything happens to him—"

"Your husband knows the risks. And he is willing to make sacrifices to do what must be done to protect his home. Would you have him do otherwise?"

She sighed. "I would rather he stay with me and be a coward than a dead hero. My father once played the hero, remember?"

Ximena was living with her family in San Antonio de Béxar, which was part of Mexico back then, when thousands of norteamericanos began pouring into the province after the Mexican government gave Stephen Austin permission to settle a colony. First farmers and cotton planters came to exploit the land with slave labor, despite Mexico's abolition laws, and then restless adventurers, squatters, and armed desperados swarmed into the region looking for a fresh start. As soon as the whites outnumbered the local Mexicans, everything changed. They took over, and then they rebelled against the Mexican central government in 1835. This was two years after her mother and brothers had died.

Ximena still remembered when the mayor of San Antonio and a commander in the Texas Army, Juan Nepomuceno Seguín, came to their house to convince her father to join the norteamericanos—or Texians as they liked to be called—in their armed rebellion against Mexico, and to force President Santa Anna to reestablish the liberal constitution that he'd abolished and restore the states' rights. After seven months of fighting, the Texas revolt turned into a war of secession—the Texians wanted Texas to be completely free of Mexican rule—forcing her father and the other Tejanos to choose between remaining in the fight against Mexico, or renewing their loyalty to the Mexican government. Her father chose to side with the Texians, not knowing he would regret doing so until the day he died.

After the Texas Revolt, things were never the same between the Texians and the Tejanos. Anyone of Mexican origin was suddenly viewed with suspicion and even hatred. A whole town was razed, others threatened with violence, and hundreds of Tejano families had to flee their homes. Eventually, even her own family packed up and headed south. A few months later, they lost their lands to white squatters. Thus, they were forced to remain in Matamoros, where she met and married Joaquín. Her father died soon after her marriage, undone by grief that his service and loyalty to the Lone Star Republic had been repaid with suspicion, exile, and ruin.

Her life with Joaquín had given Ximena new hope. Alongside him, she had come to believe that she could grow new roots and build a home with him and for the children they'd hoped to have. But now the Yanquis were threatening to take everything away from her again.

"It's going to be worse this time, Nana. Much worse."

"Even you cannot know what God has planned for us," Nana Hortencia said.

"But Nana—"

"Look at this beautiful gobernadora, and our salve has run out," Nana Hortencia said and busied herself plucking the waxy dark-green leaves of a creosote bush. Exasperated with the old woman, Ximena turned toward the road, straining to see beyond the high brush fence and the groves of huisache glowing golden in the sun. No one was coming.

That night, she drifted in and out of sleep, afraid to succumb to the dreams that would surely reappear as soon as she surrendered to the darkness. As she reached for the sheepskin blanket that had slipped off the bed, she saw him. He was standing by the window, gazing out as if it were daylight. He was admiring the beauty of their ranch, open land stretching as far as the eye could see. At hearing her stir, he turned around. There was a look of such pain on his face, perhaps of what was to come.

"Ximena," he said. Blood began to bloom on his chest, a bright crimson hibiscus flower. He pressed his hand against his heart and gasped at the sight of his bloody hand.

She screamed his name, and he disappeared into the moonbeams piercing through the curtains. The dogs began to bark, and soon after, there was a pounding at the front door that jolted her awake. Fighting to catch her breath, she could hear hurried footsteps amid the continued pounding. She rushed out of her chamber and bumped into Nana Hortencia.

"Is Joaquín—?"

Her grandmother placed a loving hand on her arm. "Rest easy, mi niña. He has returned to you." Together they went into the kitchen and there was Joaquín sitting on a chair, his caporal, Ramiro, by his side, their eyes haggard from want of sleep. Then, spotting the dried blood on her husband's shirt, she ran to him and fell into his open arms.

"Joaquín!"

"No llores, querida," he said, reaching to wipe her tears.

She hadn't even realized she was crying. "Where are you hurt?" She patted his chest, searching for the wound.

He turned his gaze away from her. "It isn't my blood."

"Tell me what happened," Ximena implored, looking at the men.

"We've killed a Yanqui." Joaquín looked at the orange blossom tea Nana Hortencia had placed in front of him. He banged his hand on the table and tea spilled out of the mug. "A colonel. ¡Maldita sea!"

"We came upon Ramón Falcón and his guerillas," Ramiro said. "Falcón told Cheno that the Yanqui was out riding alone five kilometers from his camp. He wanted us to go with him on an ambuscade. We found the Yanqui and dragged him into the chaparral."

"We were going to deliver him to General Mejía in Matamoros, make him a prisoner!" Joaquín added. "But Falcón decided to rob the colonel and killed him with a blow to the head. He took his watch, his pistols—"

"His life," Ximena added.

Joaquín looked away in shame.

"Where's his body?" Ximena asked.

"Hidden in the brush," Joaquín said. "Falcón said to leave him to the buzzards. You know how he is, as mean as a rattler in mating season."

"And that's someone whose company you keep? You want to become like him?"

"No, Ximena. But as long as our government does nothing, what choice do I have? Would you rather I gather some pecans and hide in the house while the Yanquis invade our land?"

Ximena grabbed her husband's hands. "Are you really willing to compromise our future with all this violence, Joaquín? To risk everything we're working for?"

He stared at the floor, and she could tell he was thinking about what she'd said. Then he looked up. "You were right, Ximena. War *is* coming. And I'll be damned if I let the gringos take it all like they did to your father."

The following morning, Ximena awoke to Joaquín caressing her. She smiled and gathered him into her arms. Usually in the mornings, when she awakened, he'd be already gone, his side of the bed cold and empty. So now, as he placed himself on top of her, she clung to him and breathed him in, the sweet and earthy smells of chaparral mingling with tanned leather. It helped her forget the fear that was slowly suffocating her, squeezing her like a frightened jackrabbit caught in the talons of a hoot owl.

As if sensing her troubled state of mind, he whispered her name in her ear, said sweet nothings to her as he touched her, stroking and coaxing her tense body to relax, to give in to pleasure, to anticipate only the sweetness of release.

We will get through this. We have to.

Afterward, as she lay in his arms, basking in the warm glow of their lovemaking, he invited her for a horseback ride around the ranch. Though she hated the thought of getting out of bed, of this intimate moment coming to an end, it had been a while since they'd gone on a ride together. She roused herself from bed and got dressed to join him.

Before long, she was guiding Cenizo out of the stables and into the approaching dawn, as the last stars faded and the grays gave way to violets then golds and reds. She and Joaquín watched as the sun peeked over the prairie and its first rays fell over their house, the huts of the ranch hands, the wells, the barn and stables, the corrals, the pigpens, the grove of pecan trees, the fruit trees and the cultivated fields, the open range, and the river beyond—then suddenly the entire ranch was illuminated, their land, their home. Bathed in the morning sunlight, Ximena prayed for God to bless her with more children. She prayed for the day when she and Joaquín could take their sons and daughters on a ride like this one, where they could all listen to the raucous calls of the chachalacas nesting in the huisaches bursting in vivid yellow blooms, and inhale the crisp fragrance of the warm, dewy morning as they watched the prairie quivering with life. She imagined their children riding along on their bay ponies. She would point out to them the doe and her twin fawns grazing on the white flowers of a blackbrush, the bees burrowing in the violet flowers of a guayacán, the prairie chickens chasing fluttering grasshoppers.

"You knew it was a bad idea to get involved with the guerillas," Joaquín said, breaking her reverie. "I should have discussed it with you first, I'm sorry, mi amor."

She took her eyes off the turkey vultures circling in the distance and turned to look at him.

"I was wrong. But, Ximena, please understand that I'm not the one putting our future at risk. That happened the minute the Yanquis arrived. You, more than anyone, know what will happen if their invasion succeeds. We will lose everything. What kind of man will I be, cariño, if I don't at least try to protect what's ours?"

She thought about her dream, of the battlefield, the booming of the cannons, the smoke as menacing as storm clouds. "But there's nothing you can do to stop what's coming, Joaquín. Neither of us can."

His face paled, and for a second, his eyes flared like hot coals. He put spurs to his horse and started off without her to the fields. She watched him go, and then, suddenly he pulled on the reins.

She caught up to him and saw something her dreams hadn't warned her about.

Among the recently planted fields, some of the foot-high corn stalks and beanstalks had been flattened or uprooted, the soil trampled by horses that had evidently ridden over it in circles. The stench of blood reached them, and she and Joaquín galloped on, past the brush fence, following the scavenging birds to the prairie where the branded cattle had been grazing the day before. The grasses and wild rye were speckled red with blood. Some of the cattle had been slaughtered and were being feasted upon by turkey vultures and caracaras. The rest of the herd was missing, either wandered off from home or taken.

"Comanches?" she asked.

Joaquín shook his head and said, "No. Los Rinches."

"Rangers? Here on our land?"

"I didn't want to worry you. But the Texas Rangers who've come down with Taylor have been roaming wild, destroying property, violating women, killing innocents. The Texians have volunteered in the US Army, coming in that guise to seek out personal revenge."

"Revenge for what? Haven't we hurt each other enough?"

Joaquín looked at her, impatient with her question. And then she realized he was right. The Alamo, Goliad, Mier . . . The Texians would never stop trying to avenge the deaths of their friends and relatives.

"Make no mistake, mi amor," Joaquín said, reaching for her hand. "Texas knew what it was doing when it gave up its rights to govern itself. Under the flag of the United States, the Texians are hoping to settle old scores—and get rid of us once and for all."

"And no matter how many of us they kill, it will never be enough," she said.

6

On April 11, there was a commotion across the river in Matamoros. The church bells rang over the city, and a cannon roared in salute. General Pedro de Ampudia and his troops had arrived. From the parapets of the bastioned fort, Riley caught a glimpse of the Mexican troops and civilians lining the streets and rooftops, greeting their new commander and long-awaited reinforcements with patriotic music and cheers. The Mexican tricolor flag undulated in a warm southeast wind. Riley's view was limited by the thicket of trees, but he saw enough to be impressed.

"He's here," Sullivan said, coming to stand beside him. "I reckon it can't be much longer the war's about to start. Maybe even tomorrow?"

"Aye, with General Ampudia here and Cross gone, that's true enough."

The morning before, General Taylor's quartermaster, Colonel Cross, had failed to return from his usual horseback ride. Taylor dispatched several patrols, but rumor had it the colonel was captured or murdered by Mexican irregulars.

"And what are they bickerin' about? This muddy river?" Sullivan asked.

Riley explained to his tentmate what he knew about the dispute over the Río Grande boundary and how the Americans were look-ing to start a fight with Mexico so that they could take what they desired.

"So that's why they're goin' to war, for this crooked river and land with more rattlesnakes than people?" Sullivan shook his head.

"'Tis not that simple. The Yanks see this land as part of their des-tiny. And the Mexicans see us as invaders, do they not?"

"Destiny? 'Tis English greed runnin' through those veins of theirs, as thick as buttermilk," Sullivan snickered.

"And a bad dose of superiority they've inherited," Riley added. He thought about the English, of how they'd conquered territories all over the world to fill the royal coffers, and the way they'd plundered and raped and killed to prove their dominion. The United States was Eng-land's child after all. Even though the Yanks had rebelled against the English and defeated them in battle seven decades before, the insa-tiable lust for power and egotism of their forefathers had already been bred into them.

The Yanks spoke of the Mexicans as being nothing more than ig-norant, filthy, semisavages, a miserable mongrel race. Riley had heard this before about his own people, descendants of kings and chief-tains, but Ireland was a conquered land after all. He looked across at Matamoros and wondered if Mexico would soon face the same fate. "'Tis Mexico's bad luck to have the United States as its neighbor," he said. "Just as 'twas our bad luck to have England looming across the Irish Sea."

Not wasting any time, General Ampudia sent one of his officers with a parley flag and an order for General Taylor to decamp his army, withdraw from Mexican territory, and return whence he came. He gave them a day's notice. General Taylor's orders were to stay put, and if Ampudia commenced hostilities, the war would rest on his shoulders, not Taylor's. He then ordered the navy to blockade the port and to seize any vessels carrying supplies for the Mexican troops. News of the standoff filled the camp with anxiety over the Mexicans' next move.

Talk around the campfire that night turned to the deserters. Not the unhappy wretches who didn't make it, but the ones who did.

"I heard the Mexicans pay good wages," O'Brien said. "We might not have to wait donkey's years before we see our relations again."

"And they treat the Irish as equals, not cattle," Maloney said, touching his forehead. "And don't we Irish know how it feels to be driven forth from our land by Protestant invaders?"

"The Mexicans are Catholic," Flanagan said. "'Is it shootin' our Catholic brethren, are we now?"

" 'Twill soil our souls right enough," Quinn said.

"How many more buckin' and gaggings? How many more brandings ought we to put up with?" Sullivan asked.

Riley listened quietly, contributing no opinions. When he finally stood up to turn in for the night, Maloney called after him.

"Unholy war is nigh, John Riley. Which side will you be on when it starts?"

"I saw you, brave fella," Quinn chimed in, "standin' up to that dirty li'l maggot, Lieutenant Bragg. Seein' ya put the blaggard in his place made my day. If not for the general, I bet you would've knocked the bejabbers out of him."

"Faith, you've knocked a grinder or two at least!" Flanagan said laughing. "Look here, John Riley. I know I was wrong about you, I was. If you lead us in the crossin', I'll follow ya. We all will, won't we, boys?"

"Aye, aye," the men said, nodding.

Riley glanced at his countrymen and wondered which of them would be gone the next day. "I won't be castin' my lot with Mexico. I'm stayin' here with my regiment, but ye areall free to make your choice." He sensed their disappointment and added, "May Saint Patrick protect ye. *Oiche mhaith*." He thought of the oath that bound him to the US Army, of his duties as a husband and father—promises made before God.

A soldier obeys orders, hadn't he learned that already in the British Army? How many times was he obliged to do things he didn't approve of? Despicable things that stained his soul, that no amount of Paternosters or Ave Marias would ever serve to absolve him. He still remembered the utter shame he felt at going up and down the Irish countryside with the redcoats to make sure that his countrymen obeyed the whims of their English landlords, helping to reinforce the police and bailiffs as they evicted the poor tenants, tore down cottages, tossed entire families out to the high road for a life of beggary and ruin. He still remembered that brutal episode in Clare a year after he'd joined the army when a group of tenants was driven off their land to make room for cattle. They'd protested and beaten back the constabulary. He'd been part of the division called in to quell the disturbances. Taking their marching orders from the local landlord, they burned out the farmers and shot two men who had resisted. And these were his people. Poor men and women who were just like his family and friends from Clifden.

He, John Riley of the unhappy county of Galway, had worn the red. Now he wore the blue. And soon, he would go into Mexico and help the Yanks bespoil the Mexican people of their lands and bring them into submission.

But wasn't life like that? A powerful nation will always hunger for more power. And they will always find men like himself—starving wretches, so far from home and country and desperate to do right by their families—to do the dirty work.

Sitting on his cot, cleaning his smoothbore flintlock musket for the next day's inspection, Riley heard whispers and spurts of merry laughter from outside. Were his comrades laughing at him? They could mock him all they wanted. He had nothing to prove to them. He owed them nothing. If they wanted to risk their lives swimming across the river—not even knowing if things would be better yonder—that was on them. The bugles sounded tattoo, and Sullivan came into the tent as the others dispersed. Usually, they would spend the last few minutes before lights-out talking about their dreams for the future, but that night Sullivan crawled under his blanket with nary a word from his lips. Riley reckoned he was cross with him again. *Just as well*, he thought. He was tired of trying to make the little fellow understand how life truly worked.

Just then, sharp yips—like the bugles of the Mexicans—made Sullivan sit up on his cot, clutching his musket.

"Don't be alarmed," Riley said. " 'Tis only a coyote."

Sullivan nodded but didn't lie down. In the mellow ray of a tallow candle, he perused the leaflet he pulled out from under his bedroll.

"Is it mad you are? Didn't I tell you not to carry that around!" Riley said.

Sullivan looked at it intently, as if he had suddenly learned how to read, but then handed it to Riley. "Will ya read it to me?"

Holding its faded words close to the candle, Riley read the leaflet slowly but softly, wary of anyone lurking about. Tonight, extra sharp-shooting guards stood alert to catch deserters—with orders to fire on sight. When he got to the last paragraph of the leaflet, he felt compelled to read it twice. *Separate yourselves from the Yankees, and do not contribute to defend a robbery and usurpation . . .* Had he joined an army about to attack a Catholic nation? Would the Yanks do to the Mexicans what the English had done to his people?

He handed the pamphlet back to Sullivan and blew out the candle, his thoughts churning in his head.

"The Yanks promised me adventure full of fun and frolic and plenty of fine whiskey," Sullivan said a few minutes later. "They promised me roast beef and pretty black-eyed señoritas," he continued, with a bitter laugh. "But they're the biggest liars on this side of perdition! I didn't leave Ireland and my family to end up in this Yankee pisshole."

Riley had his own version of the Yanks' false promises. He could "earn back his sergeant's chevrons," they said. Rise through the ranks. Obtain US citizenship and good wages to pay for his family's passage through the golden door. He thought about his wife and son. It'd been three years since he'd seen them. Johnny was already thirteen and would soon be a little man, yet Riley wasn't there to guide him and teach him all he ought to know. That thought gave him the most sorrow. He closed his eyes and willed himself to sleep.

He was drifting off when he heard a rustling in the dark. Franky Sullivan was getting dressed. "Don't do it, lad," he said in the darkness.

"Come with me," Sullivan said softly, kneeling beside his cot. "We can do it together. Look out for each other!"

"I cannot."

"Those miserable sinners told us false. How can you stay?"

Riley didn't answer.

"Very well then. I'm goin'. Will ya give me your blessin'?"

"I need scarcely remind you that there are pickets out there ready to shoot anythin' that moves," Riley said instead. "How far d'ya think you'll get? And if they don't get ya, the river will. 'Tis a mighty current and will pull you under when you least expect it."

Sullivan sat back down on his bunk with a sigh. "I can't do this no more."

"Don't let your passion lead you astray, lad. These sonsabitches are all strung up, itchin' for the war to start, so they've nothin' better to do but to amuse themselves with us. We'll prove our valor soon enough, and by-and-by they'll realize their ignorance of us Irish. They'll see we're damn good soldiers, better than those West Point *amadáns*."

"I'm just a farmer," Sullivan said. "And I wasn't even good at that. If I was, the hunger wouldn't be hard upon my poor parents now."

" 'Twasn't your fault the potatoes rotted, was it now? God willing, the upcomin' harvest will be plentiful enough for our people to get by." He heard Sullivan laying back again on his bunk and settling in with a sigh. "Be patient, Franky, *a chara*. I promise I'll keep ya under my eye, and I'll see to it you get your share of glory and honor."

When Sullivan finally closed his eyes, Riley stayed alert to the murmur of the Río Grande, the clamor of toads, crickets, and hoot owls echoing in the dark, the barking of dogs in the sleepy city across

the river, the melancholy howls of a solitary wolf beyond, and the wailing cry of a jaguar. Then finally Sullivan's snores joined the chorus, and
Riley surrendered at length to his own fatigue.

Scarcely had he closed his eyes that he was roused suddenly, not by
a bugle call but by musket shots. Seeing Sullivan's bunk empty, he
scrambled to his feet and rushed out of the tent, bootees unlaced. The
camp was in an uproar, drummers beating the long roll, soldiers running in all directions, muskets at the ready, thinking the Mexicans
were upon them. But Riley knew better. He ran to the river, his heart
squeezed tight inside his chest. He heard what might have been the
squealing of geese, though it was a human voice, high-pitched and
laced with fear.

"Stop, please, I beg ya!"

Day was just breaking, and it was hard to see clearly through the
wreaths of mist, but he knew without seeing that it was Franky Sullivan. Riley pushed his way past the crowd, and through the rushes,
he watched that fool of a boy struggling to swim back to the camp
after getting himself caught deserting. On the riverbank, a sentry was
pointing his musket right at him.

"I made a mistake!" Sullivan said as he struggled to pull himself out
by grabbing on the rushes. The sentry lowered his musket, and Sullivan began to wade out of the river. Just then, General Twiggs pulled
up his horse beside the sentry and said, "Do your job, soldier!"

"But General—"

"I said do your job!"

The sentry raised his musket again, and with a click of the trigger,
discharged his load of buck and ball. Riley watched in horror as Sullivan dropped to his knees, the water around him tinged with red. Soon
he was floating downstream, and moments later, he got pulled under,
disappearing from sight.

"Who's next?" General Twiggs said as he surveyed the soldiers
from atop his horse.

Riley took a step forward, feeling his blood boiling inside him. Twiggs had Sullivan shot down even though he'd begged for mercy.

"Easy, now," Maloney said from behind him. He put a firm hand on Riley's shoulder and steadied him. "When the proper time comes, we'll cut their sinnin' souls out."

"Get to your ranks and be prepared for a hard day's work!" General Taylor shouted as he approached the crowd on his mare. "Ampudia is here in Matamoros. War is now upon us, and I want this fort finished once and for all."

7

April 1846
Fort Texas, Río Grande

Riley spent the next rainy Sunday poring over Franky Sullivan's meager belongings. There was no one to send them to. In the months since they'd shared a tent, the lad had never received a letter from his relations.

The bells of the church in Matamoros began to toll. Riley turned toward the sonorous sound and felt his heart aching. Gathering up Sullivan's things, he hurried to the riverbank. He'd loved coming here before General Taylor ordered shoot-on-sight. He missed watching herons, snowy egrets, and geese and ducks alight along the low banks to play in the shallows. The sight of the Río Grande was now forever changed by the heartless punishment of a boy's blunder.

A soft mist clung to the towers of the church on the other side, and Riley imagined the priest inside preparing for mass. For a moment, he fancied himself there, safe in God's home. He bent down to the muddy ground and quickly dug a hole, putting all of Sullivan's things inside, except for a crude wooden shamrock the little fellow had whittled himself. A token to remember him by, Riley decided. He said a prayer before throwing the clay back into the hole.

"Thou art dust, and unto dust thou shalt return."

"Hey, move away from the river!"

Riley turned to see a sentry walking toward him, pointing his musket.

"You know what happens to deserters, right?"

"Aye, right well I do," Riley said, taking a few steps away from the river. He glanced at the church. If only he could find a way to get there.

"Get on with you then, Mick," the sentry said, "if you don't want to end up like the rest of your traitorous kind."

With one last glance at the church, Riley turned around and hurried back to his tent as the rain began to let up. Along the way, something caught his eye. A man hanging by his thumbs from a tree limb. He rushed over to find it was Maloney. He reached for the rope, and the old man jerked out of the way, crying in pain as he did so. "Stop! You'll get punished, you will."

Riley glanced at the patrolling sentries. One would surely look toward them, in only a matter of time.

"But why?" Riley asked, immediately regretting it. Did it matter why?

"Duncan got into a passion because I didn't salute him proper," Maloney said through clenched teeth. Sweat dripped from his face, the letters branded on his forehead were scabbing and stood out hideously. He glanced at the river and said, "If 'twasn't for my ignorance of swimmin', I'd do it, you know? I'd be long gone by now."

"And end up like Sullivan?" Riley asked.

Maloney nodded. "Aye, even the bottom of the river is better than here. Look, lad, I know honorin' your oaths is important to ya, and I may be an ignorant spalpeen that knows more about pickin' spuds than military laws, but I do know well enough that a contract binds both parties. Won't you at least go see for yourself what the Mexicans are all about? For Franky?"

The sentries drew nearer. "God give you strength, Jimmy, *a chara*," Riley said, before quickly parting.

"You'll come back for me, won't ya? I'll fight with you through sunshine and storm. 'Tis a promise!" Maloney shouted after him.

Up ahead, Braxton Bragg, James Duncan, and other West Point officers swashed across the campground. Something Bragg said roused laughter. Riley's face heated, his jaw clenched. When Bragg fixed his spiteful dark eyes upon Riley, and his lips curled with insolence, Riley knew the West Pointer meant mischief. What if Maloney was right? He ducked behind the tents and headed straight to his commanding officer's quarters.

After a proper salute, he asked for permission to speak. He knew that the Yanks looked down at his religion, but it was the best lie he could come up with at the moment.

"Permission to leave camp, sir," Riley said. "Word is a priest will be holdin' services yonder north at a local farm. I'd like to ask a prayer of him for my dead tentmate." Riley held himself straight and still as if frozen inside his American blue uniform. Lying to his commander made his body itch, worse than if he'd just gathered a field of fuzzy corn. He looked straight ahead at the wall behind Merrill, lest his eyes betray him.

"General Taylor was clear about the consequences of deserting, was he not?"

"Aye, sir."

The captain studied Riley for a few seconds. "You're a good soldier, Private Riley," he said at last. "What a pity that your countrymen cannot see the error of their ways."

Riley thought of Maloney hanging by his thumbs on that tree, of Franky Sullivan at the bottom of the river, of the church and the bells that called to him. He clenched his fists and unclenched them. *Steady*, he told himself. *Steady*. He held his breath as he watched Merrill sign the paper that would get him past the guards.

"Don't disappoint me, Private," Captain Merrill said, handing him the pass.

Dismissed, Riley headed through the rain to the perimeter of the camp, the pass tucked safely in his pocket. He quickened his pace, feeling Merrill watching him from his quarters. There was no priest giving mass at any nearby farmhouse, and his lie would be found out soon enough. He passed by tents, the parade grounds, the cannons that pointed at Matamoros. When he reached the perimeter, he took out the pass and handed it to the sentries.

Taking in the landscape outside the camp, he remained alert for any movement. Sentries were on the lookout for deserters, and maybe even Bragg or Twiggs was out there, looking for a little diversion. The Río Grande roared below as he struggled through a thick tangle of shrubs and cane near the water's edge. His uniform was soaked with rain, but no matter, he would be in the river soon. Still, his heart palpitated so hard he could feel it. He turned to see the pickets farther away, pointing their muskets at a flock of honking geese that had suddenly taken off into the air, as if to give Riley a chance. With a quick sign of the cross, he plunged into the river. With all the strength he could muster, he began to swim across. The current was strong, but his determination was stronger. Through the water's noisy roar, he thought he heard shouting, then musket fire. He stopped for nothing till he gained the other bank.

Water pooled at his feet. Two Mexican soldiers approached him, muskets raised. Riley didn't speak the Spanish tongue and didn't know if the soldiers spoke English. Not that his Irishman's brogue would be easy to understand.

With their muskets, they motioned for him to follow. Flanked by a soldier on either side, Riley walked down the muddy street that turned to cobblestone as they reached the heart of the city. Rectangular houses made of unbaked brick lined the streets, stretched as far as he could see, their roofs bright with red tiles or thatched with palm and cane. Their facades were plastered with white lime and bore sturdy double doors and tall iron-barred windows.

As he sidestepped the muddy rain puddles and animal droppings, Riley could feel the stares of the local people as they hurried by on foot or atop donkeys and oxcarts. A woman poked her head out the window of a dry goods store to stare at him with rude curiosity. She took in his Yankee uniform and spat as he passed. He kept his eyes ahead, grateful when the rain suddenly stopped, and sunbeams pierced through the clouds. He wondered how much time he had before he was missed at the camp.

They passed by the church fronting the public square. It was a fine old church and higher than most of the buildings. Riley pointed to it, and said, "Ecclesia," hoping the soldiers could understand his Latin, but they shook their heads and kept walking. They took him directly to the general's headquarters, where Riley found himself standing before the commander-in-chief of the Mexican Army and an assortment of other officers. Though the general seemed unfazed by his appearance, Riley wished he looked less like a cur dog left out in the rain. He towered over the general, and yet he felt small. In his early forties, General Ampudia stood proudly in a brilliant blue uniform adorned with golden epaulets. From beneath his thick dark brows, he examined Riley from head to toe while twirling his long mustache, as if trying to guess his intentions. Another general drew near and General Ampudia said something to him in Spanish. Then both turned to Riley.

"I am General Mejía. My commander welcomes you to Mexico, Private. Who are you and why are you here?"

"Private John Riley, sir," he said, snapping a salute. He spoke slowly and carefully. "I'm here to seek consolation in your church, if you grant me permission to do so, sir."

General Mejía translated and exchanged glances with General Ampudia. "The doors of our church are open to anyone who seeks the comfort of our Lord and Savior," General Ampudia said, through Mejía. "I'm well aware the Yanqui heretics don't allow you Irish to practice your faith."

"I'm much obliged, sir," he said. And then, the voice of Franky Sullivan pleading for mercy, his body bobbing in the water, rose up in his mind, and he decided to speak plainly about what else drove him here.

"If I may, I desire also to meet the man who wrote the leaflet. I wish to know if he speaks in earnest."

General Mejía translated his words and General Ampudia motioned for Riley to take a seat. This was a new experience for him, being invited to sit and have a conversation with his superiors. Usually, his commanding officers in both the British and the Yankee armies simply issued commands for him to obey.

"The commander meant every word in that pamphlet," General Mejía said. General Ampudia pulled on his thick goatee, observing him through keen eyes.

Riley nodded. "Too many of my countrymen have perished in the river. My tentmate was shot and killed whilst tryin' to come here. I must know that he didn't die in vain."

"I can assure you, Private Riley, that the deaths of your countrymen do weigh on me," General Ampudia said. "The young man you speak of would have made a great soldier in our ranks, I'm sure of it. May he rest in peace, along with all who have perished trying to swear their allegiance to Mexico.

"President Polk has made it quite clear how much he covets Mexico's rich lands and ports in its northwestern territories. That's how he won the presidency, did he not? He'll go to any lengths to reach his objective of westward expansion and continue the abhorrent institution of slavery. Mexico is a young nation and not as wealthy as the United States, but we will do everything in our power to maintain its territorial integrity!"

Noticing General Mejía's lack of breath from having to translate his tirade, General Ampudia paused and cleared his throat before continuing. "Enough about that. Let us now talk about you, Private Riley. You strike me as a man who does not belong in a private's uniform. What type of military experience do you have?"

"I was a sergeant in the Royal Artillery, sir."

Ampudia's eyes lit up.

He told Riley that he had been an artillery officer in the campaigns during the Texas Rebellion. He'd been in Mexico's service for twenty-five years, and before fighting the Texians, he'd helped Mexico gain its independence from Spain and had protected it against French invaders as well. The general went on to ask Riley about the artillery tactics he'd acquired under Her Majesty's service, and Riley knew the questions were meant to test him. He answered carefully and the general seemed pleased.

"I've never been to England," General Ampudia said, "but the British certainly know how to fight a war."

"Aye," Riley affirmed, but he thought of Braxton Bragg, the man he both hated and envied. "Is the general familiar with the Yanks' flyin' artillery?"

"It has been brought to my attention. And we suspect our artillery cannot rival the enemy's! But one can never be sure. What are your thoughts, Private?"

After Riley finished describing in detail his observations of the Yankee's artillery, the Mexican commander became pensive. Suddenly, he stood up, and Riley did the same. General Mejía got to his feet as well and listened attentively as his commander spoke to him. General Ampudia seemed excited about something and did not take his eyes off Riley while his interpreter translated his words.

General Mejía looked at Riley and said, "General Pedro de Ampudia, commander-in-chief of the Army of the North, would like to offer you a commission as first lieutenant in the Mexican ranks. Do you accept, Private Riley?"

Riley was taken aback. First Lieutenant? He hadn't heard of any deserter who had joined the Mexican ranks being given a commission. Were the Mexicans making a jest of him? He peered into the general's eyes to see if there was mockery there. But he could see plain the general's admiration as he looked upon Riley with keen interest.

"Here you will find that even though you are a foreigner, Mexico will welcome you with open arms. Just look at me," General Ampudia said, puffing out his barrel chest. "Cuban by birth and yet here I am as the commander-in-chief of the Mexican Army of the North! Here in Mexico, you will find what you've been searching for, Private Riley. Well, what do you say?"

Just then, the church bells started ringing, announcing the noon hour. Riley listened to the bells, never taking his eyes off the men before him. Perhaps the general was right. Perhaps he was not. Either way, Riley needed time to think. And to get to church.

"With your leave, sir, may I go to church before giving you my reply?"

"Of course," General Ampudia said, motioning to the soldiers by the door to escort Riley out. "May you find the peace and comfort you seek, Private."

When Riley stepped outside the headquarters, the day had turned bright and sunny, with no sign remaining of the morning showers. His uniform was still damp, but by the time he reached the church, the hot Mexican sun had done its work. The soldiers escorted him to the doors and then waited there while he went inside.

He took a deep breath, savoring the serene quietude. The church was much bigger than the one back home, grander and more splendidly decorated, but just as welcoming. His eyes adjusted to the dimness inside and he felt thankful for the absence of bright light. He had never gotten used to the glare of the sun in this land of suffocating heat.

Hundreds of candles burned against the cold walls, illuminating paintings and life-size wax figures of the Savior and saints standing on pedestals, the silver embroidery and beads of their garments glimmering in the candlelight. Sunlight streamed through the stained-glass windows and fell upon the walls in colored patches. He knelt at the feet of the Holy Mother and made the sign of the cross. The tears for Franky Sullivan finally gushed forth. If only he'd given the lad his blessing. If only he'd come with him like he'd asked, perhaps the poor boy would still be alive. From his pocket, he took out the shamrock Sullivan had whittled and rubbed it with his fingers. *You were right, Franky,* a chara. *Here, you would've been a hero.*

A priest came into the church from the back door and entered the confessional. Riley recognized him as the priest that had prayed over the dead deserter. He stood and dried his eyes and followed after the priest. He knelt and made the sign of the cross.

"*In nomine Patris, et Filii et Spiritus Sancti. Amen,*" the priest said.

"Bless me father, for I have sinned. It has been over seven months since I confessed." He wondered if the priest spoke English and if he would be able to understand him at all.

"Speak my son, God listens," the voice inside the confessional said in soft careful English. Riley sighed in relief.

"I am guilty of lettin' my friend die, for I wasn't there to protect him and keep him safe." He closed his eyes and told the priest about the previous morning, the fear in Sullivan's voice. His own impotence.

"You no blame for he dying, son. He is with God now."

"He was scarce eighteen, Father, with his whole life ahead of him."

"Your friend in a better place, and he watch you now, like you watch him before."

Riley wiped the tears from his eyes. If only he could give faith to that.

"You more troubles, son? Speak. Here is house of God."

"I have been offered a commission as first lieutenant in the Mexican ranks. If I accept, I will become a deserter. I will become a man who betrays his oaths. I don't want to be that manner of man, Father. God knows I've already broken enough vows."

"The Yanquis no treat Irishmen good. The heréticos protestantes deny you practice your faith! Remember, son, the one true promise is to God, no to Yanquis."

Riley remained quiet. He thought about what Maloney had said. The Yanks had made an oath to them, and they were the first to break it. If there was no sanctity to their oath, no validity, was Riley then no longer bound to observe his own?

"If promise is no good, it no can bind you. What your heart say to do, son? In your heart you find God's will. Listen, make right choice."

"Thank you, Father. Will you say mass in honor of my friend? His name was Sullivan, Franky Sullivan."

"Yes, son. Go in peace. *Ego te absolvo a peccatis tuis, in nomine patris, et filii, et spiritus sancti. Amen.*"

"Amen." Riley finished making the sign of the cross and headed out of the door. The soldiers followed behind him. He could hear the burbling of the Río Grande and that was where he headed. He stood by the bank, the water rolling beneath him, and looked across at the camp. He could see the Yanks going about their day. Had his absence been noticed by now? He turned back to look at the Mexican soldiers who were waiting patiently and wondered if they'd been instructed to shoot him if he decided to swim back to the camp. But he wasn't a prisoner. He'd come here of his own free will and would leave the same way he came. He could return to the camp, to his tent, to his unit, and continue on as if nothing had happened. No one would be the wiser. Only he would know he'd swum across the Río Grande twice, and naught else had come of it. But was that what he wanted?

He took out the pass Captain Merrill had given him that morning. It was a little blurry, but still legible enough to get him past the guards and into the fort. He walked to the river's edge and glanced once more at the Yankee camp. He remembered when he'd left Galway, fired by an ambition to give his family a life of dignity and prosperity without having to sell his soul to the British Army. To finally earn enough money to buy his own piece of land and never again be answerable to the whims of a landlord. He'd crossed an ocean then to cast his lot on this side of the Atlantic. In Canada, he'd not found what he was looking for, and he'd crossed a lake to search for opportunities in Michigan. Now, he had crossed a river, and the dreams were still there, just beyond his grasp, waiting to be realized, waiting for him to make his choice.

Riley let the pass fall from his fingers and watched as the bold sweep of the current carried it away, just like it had Franky Sullivan. His decision now made, he walked back to the general's headquarters to accept his commission as first lieutenant in the Mexican Army of the North.

8

The pecking of raindrops on the chipichil roof roused her. Joaquín's side of the bed was empty. In the darkness, she spotted him puffing on a cigarette by the opened window, the white curtains and smoke billowing about him as if he were half man, half specter, and she wondered if she was dreaming. A gust of wind filled the room with the scent of spring rain—sweet grasses, mud, wet hay. She breathed it all in, her mind now fully awake.

She heard Joaquín sigh in resignation. She went over to him and peered outside. Far into the wet darkness, in the direction of the west entrance to the rancho, she could see lights flickering on and off, in a pattern she couldn't understand but knew was not random. These were signals guerillas used to communicate with each other. Torchlights by night, smoke signals by day.

Joaquín turned to get dressed.

"What do they want?"

"Tú sabes," he said. He put on his boots, strapped on his spurs, and came to kiss the top of her head. "I must carry out my sacred duty to protect our frontier," he said, repeating Juan Cortina's words.

She wrapped her arms around his waist and looked up at him. "Whatever happens out there, there will be no turning back."

"Así es, mi amor. But what choice do we have?" He bent to kiss her, soft and gentle at first, but then, he pressed her against him and his kiss deepened. Urgent. Pleading. She reached for him, but he groaned and tore himself away. "Go back to bed, cariño. At least one of us should get some sleep." He turned and headed to the door.

"Joaquín!"

He stood in the doorway holding his escopeta, knife, and tobacco pouch.

She lowered her gaze. "Be careful," she said simply.

He returned to her side, stroked her hair, and held her while she rested her head on his chest.

"I will come back to you," he whispered. Then he pulled away.

Minutes later, in the faint light of the indigo dawn, she could barely make out the solitary figure of man on horseback braving the storm as he left the rancho. There was a knock on the door, and Nana Hortencia came in carrying a tray of yaupon tea. "He wouldn't have stayed, even if you had told him what you saw in your dreams," she said, matter-of-factly.

Ximena realized her grandmother had seen Joaquín leaving their chamber.

Nana Hortencia looked out the window, at the pouring rain, and said, "Whenever a storm comes, the cattle turn their tails to the storm and try to outrun it. But the mighty buffalo faces the storm and runs straight into it. Your husband is trying to do as the buffalo, mijita. It takes courage to do so."

Her grandmother took the brush and ran it through Ximena's abundant hair. While she sipped her tea, Ximena thought about Nana Hortencia's words and shook her head. The buffalo could do what it damn well pleased. She wanted Joaquín by her side, so they could both run away from the storm.

When the old woman began to braid her hair, Ximena stopped her. She wanted her hair loose today so she could hide behind it.

"Come now, we must get ready for our patients," Nana said. "Giving of ourselves, our gifts, is how we overcome the distress in our spirits."

"I'm sorry, Nana. But I cannot accompany you today. Pardon me."

Nana Hortencia patted her head in understanding. "Don't let your worries take possession of your soul, mijita," she said and left Ximena to her solitude.

For the rest of the day, the sky was bruised with storm clouds. The rain stopped and started in intervals, and the earth soaked it all in. The sun struggled through the watery clouds, and a few rays of sunshine broke forth at times, illuminating the rancho with golden beams. Ximena's breath caught in her throat at the beauty before her. How could she blame Joaquín for fighting to protect the spirit of these fertile plains? Their sanctuary. To keep it from falling into the hands of invaders, these white "men of vision" who would come to desecrate the soil with their cotton plantations and machinery and their tortured slaves, ambition-driven men who would exploit the land with wantonness and violate its soul with their technological "advances" while they profited from it. Vultures coming to feast upon Mexican lands.

Joaquín returned in the evening. Ximena could barely see him trudging along the muddy path back to the rancho, his head drooping like a flower pelted by rain. When he came in, he was so disoriented, he didn't even take off his boots and chaparreras and tracked mud all the way into their chamber, his spurs jiggling like the iron chains of a condemned man.

"Ximena," he said, the rain dripping from his sarape onto the floor. He smelled of wet earth and sagebrush, laced with something else. Blood.

"Válgame Dios, ¿pero qué has hecho, Joaquín?"

There was a savage look in his eyes. And instead of telling her what he'd done, he fell upon her, his mouth crushing hers. He tore at her blouse, lifted her skirt and petticoats, and pressed her against the wall, taking her from behind so that she couldn't look at him. Couldn't see the wild, feverish look of a man who had just killed someone. Then suddenly he burst into sobs and crumbled to the floor.

"I'm sorry," he said. "I'm sorry."

She knelt down and gathered him onto her, rocked and cooed to him as if he were a babe in her arms.

Joaquín came down with chills and fever and spent two days delirious in bed. The healing teas and spiritual cleansings Nana Hortencia gave him finally cured him, restoring enough of his strength that he could go outside for some fresh air and to soak up the sun. He insisted on taking a morning ride with Ximena, and it wasn't until they were almost back at the house that he began to tell her about the man he'd killed. A patrol of Taylor's soldiers, probably looking for the missing quartermaster, had come upon him and the other guerrilleros hidden in the chaparral spying on the enemy camp. Weapons were drawn and fire exchanged. Joaquín's gunpowder was wet from the rain. With his escopeta rendered useless and the Yanquis shooting at him from behind, Joaquín hurled his knife over the shrubs at the lieutenant aiming his pistol at him. When the Yanqui fell off his horse with the blade buried in his gut, Joaquín fell on him and plunged his knife into him again and again. The other Yanquis dispersed and left their fallen officer behind.

He looked at his hands. "What have I done?"

"You're trying to protect your home. There's no shame in that," Ximena said, grabbing his hand. "But if you must fight, mi vida, wouldn't it be best to face the Yanquis on the battlefield, not hiding behind the chaparral?"

"They must still be scouring the country for him," he said.

A short while later, as they were approaching the stables, a cloud of dust appeared in the distance, and the sound of the horses' hooves striking the earth shattered the silence. Riders were heading in their direction at high speed. Joaquín and Ximena looked at each other. The color drained from his face. "Get in the house and hide yourselves!" he said. "And don't come out until I tell you it's safe."

She did as she was told, first calling out to Ramiro and the other ranch hands to join Joaquín. She ran into the house and gathered Nana

Hortencia and the three house servants. They locked themselves in the healing room, barring the door. Peering out the window, Ximena had a view of the stables and men running in all directions. She heard Joaquín's muffled voice as he issued orders.

"What's happening out there?" Inés asked, holding on to Ximena's arm.

"Los Rinches are here," she said. "They've tracked him to the rancho."

Gunshots rang out, followed by Joaquín's angry voice and the voices of strangers. Then the stables burst into flames. They were too far for the smoke to reach them, and yet Ximena's lungs choked up. She could feel the intense heat of the fire burning—not outside of her, but within. Her dream came back suddenly. The fire. The smoke. The blood.

"I need to help Joaquín!" She rushed to remove the bar from the door.

"Mi niña, do not go out there. We must stay hidden!" Nana Hortencia pleaded, hurrying to her side.

"They're taking the horses!" María said, looking out the window.

"Let me leave, Nana," Ximena begged, trying to get past the old woman. But Nana Hortencia grabbed her arm with a strength that surprised Ximena.

"They will hurt you and these innocent creatures if they see you," she said, pointing at the young women. "You know how the Rinches are. Come, do nothing foolish. Let your husband and the ranch hands handle it."

"Nana, please."

"Patrona, I'm scared."

She turned to see Inés cowering in the corner, with her hands over her eyes. She rushed to her and held her. "Don't be afraid."

"Stay with us, señora Ximena," Rosita pleaded.

Ximena nodded. Her grandmother was right. She was responsible for the safety of these women. She looked around in resignation and spotted the pile of calendula flowers Nana Hortencia had picked that morning to make a salve. She took some of the flowers and sprinkled the orange petals on the altar in the corner, then lit fresh candles to the Virgen de Guadalupe. Removing the rosary she wore around her neck, a gift from Nana Hortencia made with bright red mescal beans, Ximena told the others, "Come pray with me." They got on their knees, and in the pauses between their prayers, Ximena could hear the commotion outside, horses shrieking, men screaming, gunshots punctuating the chaos. Then suddenly all the sounds were gone and only the women's soft chanting was heard. She opened her eyes and the prayers came to a stop.

"Stay here. I will return for you when it is safe," Nana Hortencia said, getting to her feet. She left the room, and Inés slid the bar back.

Ximena stood to look out the window, but only the stables were in plain view, engulfed in flames. There was no sign of Joaquín, or of anyone. Smoke began to curl into the room through the gap in the door. The main house was on fire.

She yanked the bar from the door and said, "Out. Now!"

"But the Rangers—"

She pulled the three women from the window and hurried them to the door. Just then, Nana Hortencia returned. "They are gone now. But—"

"He's hurt, isn't he?" Ximena said. She looked around the healing room, and her eyes fell on the calendula flowers on the table. She scooped them up in her arms and took off running, rushing past the burning house, the stables. Even before she reached him, she knew that her dream had come to pass. He was sprawled on the ground, shot through the breast.

"Joaquín!" She stuffed the calendula under his shirt, pressing them on the wound to staunch the flow, but the blood seeped through the petals, through her fingers.

"Ximena," he gasped, clutching her hands, his lips bloody. "You need to leave. It isn't safe—send for Cheno. Tell him . . ."

"Joaquín! Don't leave me!"

The stables collapsed just as he began choking on his own blood. Ximena held him while his body spasmed and then grew still as his heart stopped beating. His lifeless eyes stared at her, the orange petals all around him stained red.

9

April 1846
Rancho Los Mesteños, Río Bravo

Even as a young girl learning the healing arts from her grandmother, the sight of blood had never troubled Ximena. But now, inside the healing room, as she washed the wound on her husband's chest with lavender-scented water and watched the red rivulets running down his torso, she had to control the queasiness in her stomach. This was Joaquín's blood. This cavity in his flesh was where his life had seeped out.

She remembered how, a few months before, while returning from a day of fishing at the river, they'd been overtaken by a sudden thunderstorm. The crashing got louder and lightning struck nearer as they held onto their horses, spurring them hard across the fields. Then lightning struck in front of Joaquín with such force it knocked him off his saddle, and he fell to the ground. In the flickering lightning, she saw him lying there, unmoving, and she thought that he'd left her to the mercy of the world. But then, illuminated by another flash above her, she saw him open his eyes and smile at her. He was unhurt, just slightly stunned and disoriented.

Now, as she gazed at him lying motionless on the table, she willed him to move, to open his eyes and smile at her once more.

"Let me do it, mijita," Nana Hortencia said, placing a warm hand over Ximena's. "I can finish."

Ximena shook her head. "Gracias, Nana. I want to do this." She took a deep breath and plunged the bloody towel into the warm water. Watching the blood swirl in the bucket, she began to have trouble breathing, as though she were sinking under an unbearable weight that would strangle her. She resolved to remain strong, to not allow the mounting pressure inside her to prevent her from performing this sacred act. She squeezed the towel and continued washing her husband's body, then she gently patted him dry. Nana Hortencia had washed, mended, and pressed his bloodied shirt and now handed it to her. His body was stiffening, and it was difficult to put clothes on him. She wished she could have dressed him in his favorite outfit—buckskin pantaloons and a jacket embroidered with silk thread and ornamented with silver buttons. She would have tied the silk bow around his neck in the shape of a butterfly, just as she'd done the day he'd married her in that suit. But it was ashes now. Only the blackened limestone and adobe walls and the caved-in roof of the main house remained.

When they were done, Nana Hortencia gathered the soiled towels and the bucket of tainted water and then excused herself. Ximena was alone now with Joaquín to sit vigil beside him until he was buried out in the consecrated plot in the grove of pecans, next to their son. She was grateful for the time she could spend with him, to honor his body, to pray for his spirit. Here, she could let the tears she had been holding back flow freely. But they didn't come.

She placed a pillow under his head and ran her fingers through his wavy hair. She caressed his cold cheek and leaned over him, resting her head on his unmoving chest.

"Do you remember that yearling calf after the gulf storm swept across the prairie?" she asked him. "Remember how she fell into a mudhole and no matter how hard she tried, she couldn't get out?"

The animal's bellowing could be heard all the way to the house, and Joaquín and the vaqueros had spent an entire day freeing her.

"Now I know how that calf felt," she said. Alone, frightened, trapped. And the more she struggled, the more her grief sucked her into its suffocating darkness.

There was a knock on the door and Juan Cortina came in, out of breath. "I came as soon as I got your message. I'm so sorry, Ximena."

At the sight of Cortina, her grief turned to anger. He'd gotten Joaquín into this mess, turned him into a murderer. Got him killed. Cortina tried to comfort her, but she turned away. Then, she heard his sobs, and saw his body convulsed with his own sorrow.

"¡Maldita sea!" he said. "¡Esos malditos diablos! God damn their souls! I'll make them pay for this!"

She motioned for him to come closer so that he could pay his respects to Joaquín. He stood beside his friend's body and shook his head. "It's my fault. I shouldn't have encouraged him to join us."

Hearing him echo her thoughts, Ximena wondered if she was wrong to blame him. She thought of what Nana Hortencia had repeatedly said to her, and she finally understood. "No, Cheno. Joaquín did what he felt was his duty, to defend his home and country against the invaders. He knew the risks."

Cortina was silent, contemplating her words. He nodded and said, "He was a good son of the frontier who offered his country his blood, and it will not be in vain." Then he turned to her and added: "But we have to think about you now. Come with me to Matamoros. I hear Joaquín's sister will be leaving in a few days for Saltillo, away from the impending battle. It'll be safe there for you too."

"I won't leave, Cheno," Ximena said. "This is where Joaquín would want to be buried."

"And here he will remain, but not you. Not now."

As she looked at her dead husband lying on the table, she felt a dull ache in her heart, and she felt tired, so tired. She wanted to curl up against Joaquín and go to sleep. "I wish they'd killed me too," she whispered, realizing too late she'd spoken aloud. She'd not meant to confess to Cortina the yearning of her soul. To admit that it hurt too much to live.

"No digas eso. No, never think that. When the battle is over and we have won, you can return to your home and begin a new life. In the meantime, I promise I'll do my best to protect you—"

"The way you protected my husband?" The accusation was out of her mouth before she could stop it. Her anger returned and swirled inside her, and she wanted to let it grow, let it turn dark and menacing, like the howling blue norte that lays waste to everything in its path. The hailstones that beat the tallgrasses into the ground. The raging wind that strips the bark off the mesquites and leaves them naked and exposed. The lightning whose fury gouges holes in the earth. She wanted to hurt something. Someone.

She took a deep breath, looked at Cortina, and said, "I don't need your protection. But I do want one thing from you. That you tell the Yanqui general where to find his dead men."

His eyes were on Joaquín, not on her when he said, "I don't know where he left Lieutenant Porter, but I do know where Falcón left Colonel Cross."

"I don't want them left to putrefy in the chaparral, Cheno," she said. "If their souls are left to wander, so might Joaquín's. Will you promise, then?"

"Sí. Te lo prometo."

At daybreak the next morning, they rode out from the rancho in silence. Cortina and his men up front, Ramiro and the few remaining ranch hands in the rear behind their families riding in the wagons. Ximena was seated on the extra horse Cheno had brought and did not speak to any of them. They respected her need for silence, even Nana Hortencia, who secluded herself in the carriage with the house servants, leaving Ximena to her thoughts. She kept her eyes looking ahead and did not turn back to see the smoke and ruin behind her.

The route to Matamoros was a well-traveled and hard-packed dirt road. As they traversed the open plains, the road was wide and the sights were beautiful—the prairie alive with the swaying of luxuriant grasses as the wind whispered through the blue-green blades, salvias and lupine, golden Zizia, Herbertia, and globe mallow pulsing in a wave of colors under the sun, the air radiant with butterflies. In other times, Ximena would have wanted to stop and immerse herself in the beauty around her, to say a prayer of gratitude to the earth for its blessed gifts, but now, neither the wildflowers, nor the singing of the green jays from the thicket of blooming huisaches, nor the clamorous calls of the whooping cranes wading in the water holes could lift her spirits. A small herdof wild mustangs roamed in the distance, and she thought of Joaquín, of how if he'd been here, he would have given them chase. But now he was gone. As was their house. What would become of her and her grandmother?

As they neared the river, the chaparral began to take over the prairie, becoming thicker and thicker as they continued on the road. A family of javelinas wallowed in a shallow resaca, grunting in contentment. Ximena could hear the *chip-chip-chip* of the quail feasting on the blackberries of the crown of thorns. The ground cuckoos nesting within the thick spiny shrubs greeted them cheerfully with their *cuc-cuc-cuc*. How could these birds find any joy living among thorns? But then she latched on to another sound. A solitary Inca dove perched on a drooping paloverde branch called to her, its melancholy coos echoing the mourning of her soul. *No hope, no hope, no hope.*

They came upon General Antonio Canales and his guerilla band, who were also on their way to the ferry crossing. "We heard what happened to Joaquín Treviño," Canales said to Cheno after the men greeted each other. He turned to Ximena and said, "Lo siento, señora."

She nodded but didn't feel like conversing with the guerrilleros Joaquín had become involved with. A few years earlier, Canales had persuaded more than five hundred rancheros to join him in rebelling against the Mexican government to establish the Republic of the Río Grande, carved out of the states of Coahuila, Nuevo León, and Tamaulipas. But unlike the Texas Rebellion, his insurrection had been squashed by the Mexican forces, and now here he was, serving as a spy for the Mexican general. Ximena had even heard rumors that while

Taylor was camped in Corpus Christi, Canales offered his services to him in exchange for help in making his dream of the Republic of the Río Grande into a reality. Taylor had refused his offer, or at least that was what the rumors said.

She glanced at Canales and wondered if he was double-crossing the Mexicans. If so, he was in for a big surprise. The Yanquis cared only about their own dream. In helping the enemy win the war, Canales would only ensure his own displacement. The same had happened to her father. Just like Juan Seguín and other Tejanos, he'd made friends with some of the norteamericanos who'd settled in Texas. He'd admired their industry and advanced machinery, and with awe had watched as San Felipe de Austin and other Anglo settlements flourished while San Antonio stagnated. As young as Ximena was at the time, she had understood something her father had not—that the economic success of the white villages was thanks to enslaved labor. She, unlike her father, had no admiration for the Anglo colonists. But her father had even hired a tutor to teach him and his children English, though Ximena turned out to be the better pupil. In the end, her father's admiration and friendliness to the norteamericanos would prove his undoing.

They traversed the dense chaparral in silence, squeezing through the narrow, winding passage in single file until it eventually widened as they neared the El Paso Real crossing, where the ferry would take them to Matamoros. They could see the perimeter of the Yanqui encampment at a bend on the northern shore, and the cannons pointed directly at Matamoros. But even more menacing than the cannons was the flag of stars and stripes rising over the newly built fort, a blatant proclamation of possession and ownership of a land that was not theirs to claim.

Cheno pulled up alongside Ximena to observe the enemy's flag. "They're here to provoke a war," he said. "And if it's a war they want, then it's war they'll get."

"Didn't we learn anything from Texas?" she said, incensed. "Mexico lost Texas long before its rebellion, from the time our government first allowed them to immigrate to the region. And now here we are again, conceding another Yanqui invasion."

"We should have fired at them the moment they came in sight," Cheno said.

As they waited at the ferry crossing, Ximena looked at the US flag waving on one bank, and the Mexican flag on the other, with the Río Bravo/Río Grande rushing wildly between them. This restless river with its twisting course would soon run a vivid red, like a gash across the heart of the land. Would it become a festering wound that never healed?

As if reading her thoughts, General Canales said, "This battle will last but a day. General Arista and his troops are on their way now. With them plus the two thousand men General Ampudia brought with him, we'll have the Yanqui trespassers wishing they'd never set foot on our land."

They boarded the ferry, and when it docked in Matamoros, the ranch hands and their families dispersed, some to find work at Cheno's mother's ranch, nine miles upriver, others to join relatives living in the south, as far from the Yanquis as they could get. After their sad farewells, and as she watched the men, women, and children who were like family to her disperse like dandelion seeds, Ximena felt that the disintegration of her home was final.

With reluctance, she and Nana Hortencia continued on to the house of her sister-in-law, Carmen. Up and down the street, she saw families packing their belongings and loading them onto their carriages. Feeling the tense atmosphere in the city, and sensing the people's fear, Ximena's anger returned. Why were the Yanquis being allowed to occupy their territory and fly their flag in defiance while innocent families were being displaced from their homes?

The following morning, the locals and the Mexican troops celebrated the arrival of General Arista in Matamoros. The church bells rang joyously, and the people lined the streets, crowded their balconies, and climbed on their rooftops to cheer for the newly arrived general. From the balcony of Carmen's house, Ximena had a good view of the troops gathered in the plaza.

General Arista addressed his men from atop his horse. She was too far away to hear him clearly, but by the sound of the cheers, she knew the general's words had everyone's approval. "Viva el general Arista!" the people shouted as the band broke into another lively tune.

Carmen came out to the balcony to join her. The day before, she had not wanted to talk about Joaquín's death with Ximena. She'd simply said that Joaquín had brought it upon himself by joining the guerilla and should have let real soldiers handle the Yanquis. Ximena had no wish to antagonize her sister-in-law and had kept her thoughts to herself. The two of them had little in common, but being Joaquín's older sister, Ximena had always treated her with respect.

"It's a relief to see General Arista here," Carmen said, fanning herself with a Spanish fan decorated with mother-of-pearl and lace. Her husband was a successful merchant and always brought her expensive gifts from his trips. "Arista is the best general we have. When we heard that Ampudia had been named general-in-chief and was on his way to Matamoros, everyone dreaded his arrival. The man is unbearable. Thank God that President Paredes replaced him with Arista."

Ximena had heard of General Ampudia's excesses, such as what he did to a former governor of the state of Tabasco, who'd been sentenced to death for treason. It hadn't been enough to execute the poor man, but Ampudia had had him decapitated, fried his head to preserve it, and displayed it in the town's central plaza to serve as a warning to the tabasqueños and prevent another insurrection.

"With General Arista in charge, we will defeat our enemy," Carmen said. "My brother's death shall be avenged. And life will be safer for us all once the Yanqui invaders are gone."

As Ximena scanned the troops, she didn't feel as confident as Carmen. As was usual in the army, most of the generals and officers were criollos, of "untainted" Spanish blood, but the foot soldiers were Indian or mixed-blood conscripts, poor peasants who knew nothing about soldiering. They were haggard and grimy, their brown faces showing the toll of the brutal march to Matamoros. As they stood in formation near Carmen's balcony, Ximena could see their old and unkempt uniforms. Some didn't even have uniforms but wore the typical peasants' attire: coarse white trousers rolled at the knees, colorful sarapes, and wide sombreros. Many didn't have proper army shoes either, wearing leather huaraches instead. But what most surprised her was that many carried only a machete or rawhide slingshot. Where were the muskets, the pistols, the rifles, the bayonets that would be needed to defeat the enemy? The only ones who looked well prepared were the mounted soldiers of the cavalry, the flower of the Mexican Army composed of criollos and a few mestizos who were clad in brightly colored uniforms and had long flowing plumes sticking out of their helmets.

She noticed a group of soldiers who were neither Indian nor mestizo. In fact, they didn't look Mexican at all. The troops were too far away for her to make out their faces clearly, but she could see that most of them had fair skin and fiery hair that reminded her of the red feathers on the heads of cactus woodpeckers.

"Are there foreign soldiers in our ranks?" Ximena asked.

"Yes, the Irish, of course," Carmen said. "And some Germans and Poles. They've been deserting the enemy's ranks to join us. Do you see the lieutenant there with dark hair? That's their leader, teniente John Riley."

Ximena looked at where Carmen pointed. She saw a tall man—taller than most—with a confident stance, a hand on the hilt of his sword. He was dressed in a dark blue uniform, the trousers trimmed with a scarlet stripe running down the sides, and the coat with a scarlet collar and cuffs and a row of brass buttons down the center. On his head he wore a black leather shako with a red pom-pom . "And what would happen to them, if they're caught by the Yanquis?"

"They would be executed, I assume," Carmen said.

As she followed Carmen back into the house, Ximena turned to glance at the plaza once more, wondering about those foreign soldiers who were willing to risk their lives to help her country.

10

Just as morning's review ended, the new Brigadier General summoned Riley to his headquarters. In the last twelve days since he'd joined their ranks, Riley had been busy helping train the gunners not just to operate the cannons but to maneuver them around the field. Unfortunately, the cannons in the Mexican arsenal were twenty-year-old relics, and some were obsolete. The round shot used was inferior and its range too short. But the most pressing problem was that the Mexicans didn't have heavy caliber guns, their biggest being 12-pounders. He knew that the walls of the Yankee fort, which he helped build with his own hands, could not be penetrated by the cannons the Mexicans had at their disposal.

As he made his way to meet General Arista, Riley thought about how familiar Matamoros was to him now. The city was laid out in blocks, and General Ampudia had marched the troops in long parades up and down the streets to fool the Yankees into thinking the Mexican force was more massive than it actually was. This was how Riley had come to learn his way around the city.

The outer fringes of Matamoros had dirt streets and crude huts made of tall cane and thatched roofs, with frail walls and no windows, not unlike the wretched cabins of Irish peasants, except that instead of the potato garden and cabbage patch, here they grew beans, tomatoes, and maize for their tortillas . The inner part of the town, where the higher classes lived, had cobblestoned streets, houses made of sun-baked clay bricks, which the Mexicans called adobe, with tiled roofs as red as the sunset. The whitewashed buildings near and around the plaza had massive walls with large windows grated top to bottom with ironwork, all of it woven with red bougainvillea.

The air smelled of the noon meal, and Riley caught a whiff of beans and frying meat, handmade tortillas, and the pungent peppers so relished by the Mexicans and used too generously in their cooking. His throat spat fire like the barrel of a cannon whenever he tried their salsas. The Mexican Army had no mess tents. Soldiers nourished themselves thanks to the civilians selling food from doorways—tamales, enchiladas, tacos—home-cooked meals, freshly made. He walked past the tree-lined central square and the church, Nuestra Señora del Refugio, Our Lady of Refuge, a title that aptly captured how he felt attending mass there. Their pronunciation of the familiar Latin mass differed, but their humility and devotion for the Creator matched that of his own people, he thought.

The general's headquarters were located at the best hotel in town, with elegant arches and a red-tiled roof. The guards standing at the entrance stepped aside to let Riley enter. He was escorted across a brilliant courtyard full of lush green plants, cheerful fountains, and canaries chirping merrily in cages. Riley liked the design of the buildings in Spanish fashion. Nothing but high walls could be seen from the outside, but the inside was protected and safe, a private Eden that closed the doors on the outside world.

General Ampudia looked entirely out of humor as Riley entered. He made no effort to hide his displeasure at being replaced as commander-in-chief by General Arista, regarding his demotion as a personal affront. Riley didn't know why the Minister of War had made this decision, but the transfer of power at this crucial time had further delayed their assault on the Yankees, and time was on Taylor's side. Discord and rivalry among the Mexicans could only increase that advantage.

"Lieutenant Riley, please come in," General Mejía said. "May I introduce you to our new commander-in-chief, Major General Mariano Arista?" As Arista's new deputy, Mejía seemed pleased with the new change in command.

"An honor, sir," Riley said after snapping a salute. He had heard that Arista had distinguished himself in the War of Independence as one of Mexico's best cavalry officers.

"At ease, Lieutenant Riley, I'm pleased to meet you. Both General Ampudia and General Mejía say we can trust you," General Arista said in accented English, and Riley remembered hearing that the forty-three-year-old general had lived in the United States for a time before returning to serve in Mexico's military. What surprised him most was the general's freckled complexion and red hair. If it weren't for his Mexican accent, he could pass for an Irishman.

"'Tis an honor to serve the great Republic of Mexico," Riley said.

"We are going to war, Lieutenant," General Arista said. "We are going to run the Yanquis off our land once and for all."

"Aye, sir," Riley said. "That we will."

General Ampudia approached Riley with a pat on the back. He said something in Spanish, and General Mejía quickly translated.

"General Ampudia says that you have improved our artillery and have been of great service to our country."

"I'm only doing my duty, sir," Riley said. He didn't want to say anything about the state of their weapons.

As if reading his thoughts, General Arista said, "The Yanquis, despite their flaws, have a magnificent army to be sure, and the latest weapons of war. Our training may be insufficient and our weapons in need of replacing, but we Mexicans fight like devils when aroused, and make no mistake, Lieutenant Riley—the presence of the Yanquis on our own land has more than provoked us."

Arista beckoned for Ampudia to hand him the pile of papers sitting on his desk and then turned back to Riley again. "Now you must be wondering why I've summoned you. Since you have served in the ranks of the enemy, your keen observations and recommendations are of utmost value to us, and we will do our best to take your counsel into account. But now, we require your assistance in another matter." He handed Riley one of the papers and said, "General Ampudia had great success when he penned a pamphlet addressed to your countrymen. As a result, I'm employing the same tactic. There's widespread discontent in the American ranks, and I aim to exploit that. You're to deliver these pamphlets tonight to your countrymen and all foreign soldiers in the Yanqui ranks. They must make their choice before we attack."

All three generals keenly watched Riley as he read through the pamphlet General Arista had given him. It was a fine letter, urging the Irish and other immigrant soldiers to abandon their ranks, and promising them land grants based on their rank, of three hundred and twenty acres or more. He thought about Maloney, Flanagan, O'Brien, and the rest of his countrymen who shared the same dream as he—to have a piece of land to call their own. Was it possible that it was finally within reach?

"By this time tomorrow hostilities shall be underway," General Arista told Riley after he had finished reading.

The general went on to inform him of the plans he'd set in motion even before reaching Matamoros. A few days before, he'd given the command for a covert crossing of the river, whereupon General Torrejón led 1,600 of the Mexican forces—cavalry and infantry—across the Río Grande upstream from the Yankee camp completely unnoticed, with the ultimate goal of disrupting communications and convoys between Fort Texas and its supply depot at Point Isabel. By the time rumors of the maneuver had reached General Taylor, the Mexican troops were safely resting on the north shore. Arista's spies alerted him that Taylor was set to dispatch two cavalry patrols that evening to find evidence of the crossing and intercept the Mexicans. Now Riley understood why he must hasten to deliver the pamphlets. By this time the following day, if blood was shed, the war would have commenced.

"I wish to see your countrymen fighting alongside us, as our Catholic brethren, and not on the receiving end of our guns," General Arista said.

"I will call upon my countrymen," Riley said as he looked at the three generals. "And personally oversee the safe passage across the river of those who choose to come with me."

"Very well, Lieutenant," General Arista said. "Tonight then, you shall be our messenger."

"May I offer a suggestion, sir, by your leave?"

"Of course, Lieutenant, you have my permission to speak freely."

"Would the general consider forming the deserters into a company of gunners? 'Twill give them an extra enticement to come."

"An excellent suggestion!" General Arista said.

"Indeed, it is," General Mejía said. "You and I can train anyone who follows you across the river to man our field pieces."

"Now, Godspeed, teniente Riley," Arista said. "Bring all your countrymen to us. Tell them we will receive them with open arms."

After he was dismissed, Riley returned to the barracks to seek out the men—deserters like himself—to tell them of the plans. He chose three of them, John Little, James Mills, and John Murphy, to accompany him.

He never thought he would don the hated Yankee uniform again, but that evening found him buttoning his old army jacket. Maybe Saint Patrick had prevented him from tossing it in disgust, as he had been inclined to do upon receiving his new Mexican uniform, for clearly, its usefulness hadn't ended.

"Faith, you look like a Yank," Murphy said as Riley approached them, clad in American blue.

"Let's hope I don't get caught," Riley answered. He was glad the men were ready for action.

" 'Tis a dangerous thing you're doin', Lieutenant," Mills said. "Let us accompany you. I know my way around the camp as if it were my own potato garden."

"And I can be as quiet as a fox stealing hens," Murphy said.

"Faith, the fox might be quiet, but the hens certainly won't be!' Riley said good-naturedly.

"I'm a fair swimmer," Little said. "I can carry two fellas on my back if need be."

Riley shook his head. "*Nil*, I need ye on this side, boys, waitin' by the river to help the ones who swim across."

Two Mexican soldiers escorted them from their barracks toward the edge of the river. As night gathered around them, they traversed the streets, and he could hear families inside their homes, their merry laughter ringing out through the opened windows as they shared their evening meal. He wondered how soon it might be his turn to partake of such moments with his family.

The aroma of meat and tortillas wafted toward them as they passed a small adobe house where a señora was selling food from her doorway. Behind her, an old woman knelt before a hot flat stone, patting tortillas into shape. Riley's stomach rumbled. He thought of his new favorite meal, tamales, a kind of meat pie wrapped in corn husks. As they passed another house, his mouth watered as he smelled the buñuelos a woman was frying, and the tantalizing whiff of cinnamon made him almost stop to purchase one. He regretted that his preoccupation with the night's plan had kept him from supper. With one deep breath, he set aside his cravings as he veered toward the river. On the northern bank, the Yankee encampment was settling in for the night, and he sensed that his timing was right. He was taking a great risk going at this hour, before tattoo, when everyone was still awake, but he needed his former messmates gathered together. It would do him no good to sneak into the camp when they were all sleeping in their tents.

Riley scanned the darkness for the right crossing. Sharpshooters were out there with instructions to shoot first and ask questions later.

"May the Virgin Mother keep and guard you," Murphy said. "Tell our countrymen we'll be here, ready to help them."

"Keep your eyes open and your ears alert, boys," Riley said as he stepped into the water. "And pray Saint Patrick is lookin' out for us tonight."

One of the Mexican soldiers handed him the sack with the freshly-printed leaflets wrapped tightly in oilcloth, and he put them in his knapsack. *Be wise then, and just, and honorable, and take no part in murdering us who have no unkind feelings for you,* the general had written. *Throw away your arms and come to us, and we will embrace you as true friends and Christians.*

As he stood at the banks of the river, Riley thought of the generosity of fifty-seven dollars a month, and the acres of land the Mexicans were offering him for his allegiance—how it would help him reunite with his family. Once again at the edge of this fierce river, a familiar fear arose. But he had never been surer that a life of dignity and prosperity awaited his countrymen. Eager to deliver those tidings, he threw himself into the currents and swam hard and fast.

11

April 1846
Fort Texas, Río Grande

Hiding amid the cane on the other side, Riley shook off the water as best he could. The pamphlets had been wrapped well enough in his knapsack to stay dry. As he pushed through the foliage, his thick woolen uniform clung uncomfortably to his body. Glancing with gratitude at the cloudy sky that kept the moon hidden, he made his way to the camp's dwindling fires. The air smelled of smoke and roasting corn and scattered laughter rang out. One of the regimental bands was playing "Oft, in the Stilly Night."

"Who goes there?" a deep voice challenged from the other side of the thickets.

Riley stopped walking and cursed under his breath as he reached for his knife. An old man emerged from behind the twisted mesquite branches and into the dim light. Dressed in disheveled trousers and a white linen shirt, one would mistake him for a bootlegger, but in another second Riley realized it was General Taylor. "Who are you?"

Riley wondered what in blazes the general was doing at this late hour walking around the camp by himself.

"Lieu— Private Sullivan, sir." Would the old man remember him?

"And what do you think you're doing, Private, fumbling about in the dark?"

Riley didn't know what to say but was relieved to see no recognition of him, one of thousands in his ranks surely.

"Not deserting are you?" the general said, spitting out his chewing tobacco.

"No, sir."

And then, perhaps realizing that Riley was heading toward the camp, the general said, "Oh, I see. I see. Snuck off to see the wenches, didn't you?"

Riley remembered the camp followers, the whores, and liquor ped-dlers always near, enticing soldiers to spend their wages on pleasure and vice. "Beggin' your pardon, sir," Riley said, relieved at the general's assumption. "The nights are long and lonely."

"But that's the soldier's lot, isn't it?" Taylor looked up at the bright piece of moon that was now peeping forth through the clouds. Riley wondered about the general's wife, the family waiting for him at his plantation in Louisiana. Surely the old man got lonely as well. "Ah," the general said, looking keenly at him, "Now that I can see your face, I reckon I know you. You got into a scuffle with Lieutenant Bragg, didn't you?"

"Aye, sir," Riley clutched the knife tighter. He didn't want to use it, but he would if he had to.

"Well, I trust you're staying out of his way, Private," the general said. "Now get on with you. It isn't safe for you to be out and about. You might be mistaken for a deserter, and you know what the conse-quence of that would be."

"Aye, sir. I know it right well." The image of Franky Sullivan sud-denly returned to him, along with the old anger. He turned on his heel and proceeded toward the tents, not even bothering to reply to the general when he wished him a good night.

Maloney spotted Riley first as he neared the gleaming light of the campfire. "Bejesus!" he said. "Look who's come back—?"

"Whist, whist!" Riley urged hastily as he rushed to join them. "You'll give me away, shriekin' like a banshee."

Realizing his folly, Maloney beckoned everyone closer in to block Riley from view. Soldiers passed by now and then, and Riley was ill at ease thinking that one of them might be from his own former unit and go running to Captain Merrill. He scooted closer to the fire, thankful for a bit of heat on a still-wet uniform.

"I didn't expect to see ya," Flanagan said.

"And what are you doin' here, John Riley? Riskin' your life to come back here. Not joinin' the Yanks again, are you?" O'Brien said.

"Never!" Riley said. "I brin' ye good tidings, boys. There's a better life to be had yonder across the Río Grande, and I've come to brin' ye with me." He took out the pamphlets from his sack and handed one to each. Then remembering that most didn't know how to read, he quickly told them what was written there.

"Holy Mother of God," O'Brien said. "Up to three hundred and twenty acres of land? You speak in earnest, my boy?"

"Fancy that? Me, a landowner, for the first time in my life," Quinn said.

"Aye. . Every single one of ye fellas could be landowners," Riley said. "All your days of drudgery will be behind ye. There'll be no more absentee landlords, no more redcoats and police comin' to tumble your roofs and turn you out of your fields, no more Yankees to mistreat and make ye rue the day ye crossed the Atlantic. You'll have land and can practice your faith as you will."

"Tell us about the Mexicans. Have they shown themselves better Christians than the Yanks?" Quinn asked.

"Aye," Riley said. "They've offered me friendship and their confidence. They appreciate my skills and recompense my hard work and insight. The Mexicans treat me like a brother, I tell ye. And if ye come with me, that's how ye shall be treated as well."

"'Tis a big risk," Flanagan said. "And if we're caught, the Yanks will show us no more mercy than they showed Franky Sullivan."

"The Río Grande is a graveyard now," O'Brien said.

"Listen now, boys," Riley said. "The war's upon us, and I don't want ye on the other side of my guns but beside me in the Mexican artillery.

I cannot bear the bitterness of my soul at the thought of spilling your blood! The Mexicans have agreed to let me train ye all as battery gunners. Ye won't be common foot soldiers but artillerists!"

The men looked at one another and said nothing.

"By the holy fists of the blessed Saint Patrick, mind what I'm sayin', eh? Ye all can die here, too, in infantry blue. Ye'll have a better chance with the Mexicans. Beyond on the other side of the river, ye'll be surrounded by people who'll treat ye with respect, who'll offer ye friendship and call ye brothers and Catholics. Not savages. Not Micks or potatoheads. Not deserters or traitors."

Riley stood up. He still had to distribute the pamphlets around the camp, but he needed to wait until everyone settled in for the night. "Meet me by the river in one hour. Upriver, near the ferry crossin' by the Mexican fort. My Mexican friends will be waitin' with my men on the other side, ready to help." He looked at Maloney, who'd said nary a word the whole time. "And you, ould fella, you told me to come back for ya, and I have. Sunshine and storm, remember?"

"Aye. I know well enough you're here for me." Maloney took a swig of whiskey, looked at the fire and said, "But Riley, this poor ould creature of five and sixty hasn't—"

"—lost his mettle yet," Riley finished for him. "I'll meet you at the river then, eh?"

He retreated into the shadows to wait until the bugles sounded their call to quarters and watched his former messmates retire to their tents. The camp was soon still but for the night patrol. He was a tall man, an easy target, but Riley was quick on his feet and he made no sounds as he went from tent to tent. He carefully placed short stacks of leaflets on the ground in front of the tents as he went. He'd let the wind do the rest.

When he was finished, he retreated to the riverbank. It was harder to see where he was stepping, but he listened to the roaring of the river and followed the sound until finally, his feet were on the shore. At first, he saw only the deserted shoreline. Had he convinced no one?

"Riley, over here!" someone whispered. He turned just in time to see eight of his former mates step out of the tall cane where they'd been hiding. Flanagan, and Quinn, O'Brien, and a few others. But no Maloney.

As if reading his thoughts Quinn said, "The poor creature is in terror of the river."

Riley didn't say anything. He guided them down to the riverbank, his eyes straining in the darkness. Were sharpshooters watching them right now, just waiting to shoot them as soon as they started swimming?

"Swim as hard as ye can," Riley said. "The river is calm from above but mind the strong undercurrents. Don't look back. Don't hesitate. Our friends await ya on the other side. Understand?"

"Aye," the men said.

He watched as one by one the men entered the river and started swimming across. *Preserve them, holy Saint Patrick.*

With the last of them in the river, Riley turned quickly back toward the camp. He knew where Maloney's tent was. He also knew that he had befriended his tentmate, a German immigrant, Private Kirsch, a veteran of the Napoleonic Wars. Like all Germans, he received the same bad treatment from the Yanks. Riley would take them both across if Kirsch would follow.

As he neared Maloney's tent, four sentries marched past it, their muskets at their sides. Riley barely had time to throw himself on the ground. Once they were far away he continued cautiously, but he hadn't taken but three paces when he tripped over something heavy. It took him a moment to realize it was a slave sleeping on the dirt outside of his master's tent. The young man stared at Riley, too scared to make a sound.

Finger to his lips, Riley motioned for him to follow him out of earshot of his master. He handed him a pamphlet, but suspecting the man couldn't read, he whispered its contents. "You'd be a free man," Riley said, pointing to the river. "The Yanks don't allow your kind into their muster rolls, but the Mexicans will. Freedom and glory await you on the other side if you join us."

The young man looked toward the river and nodded in understanding.

Riley made haste to his task. Once safely inside Maloney's tent, he breathed a sigh of relief. He shook Maloney violently to rouse him from loud snoring.

"Wake up, you foolish spalpeen."

Maloney still snored.

"Wake up! Did you truly believe I would leave without ya!" Riley heard the sound of stirring in the other cot. He thought to wake up the German first but was startled to turn and find him already awake and lighting a candle. A glow was enough to see that it wasn't Kirsch at all.

"Who are you, and what are you doing in this tent?" the soldier said in perfect American English.

Riley inhaled sharply. Of all the worst things that could happen, for Maloney to be stuck with a Yank for a tentmate. "Don't be alarmed," Riley said. "I'm just here for the ould fella, that's all." He shook Maloney harder, urging him to wake up.

"What the dickens? Riley is that you?" Maloney said as he opened his eyes.

"You told me to come back for you, and I did," he said. From the corner of his eye, Riley watched the Yank moving steadily toward his musket.

"Och, I beg pardon for lettin' you down, lad. But in Heaven's name, didn't you know I'm sleepin' with the enemy!"

"He's a deserter, isn't he?" The Yankee said as he grabbed his musket. He extinguished the candle and plunged them into total darkness.

With a quickness Riley hadn't expected, Maloney leaped to throw himself atop his tentmate. Riley wrestled the musket away, though once he had it, he couldn't see well enough who was who. "Quiet, or I'll shoot!"

"And wake up the whole camp too," the Yank said. "Go on then, give yourselves away."

He broke free of Maloney and threw himself against Riley, scream-ing as if to wake the dead. Riley punched him in the gut. The Yank fell and doubled over, gasping for breath.

"Do it, lad," Maloney said.

Riley shook his head. "Hold him!" He snatched Maloney's sheet and tore a large piece of it and rolled it into a ball, which he stuffed into the soldier's mouth. Then he tore off another strip and tied the soldier's hands and feet. "We'll have his life, but on the battlefield," Riley said as he stood up, wiping his forehead. "I have no relish for murder."

He poked his head out of the tent. Sentries were at the other end of the row, far enough for him and Maloney to move on, as long as they hid in the shadows. "Come on then. Follow me."

Maloney emerged from the tent carrying a bundle and handed it to him. "I took them from your tent afore the Yankees realized you were gone."

Riley took the letters from Nelly and wrapped them in the oilcloth that had covered the leaflets. "I never thought I'd see them again!" he said. "*Go raibh maith agat.* I'm indebted to you."

"*Níl*, you came back for me, you did."

They made it safely back to the river, to the spot where the others had crossed. Maloney stood to the side, watching the water with terrified eyes. Riley put an arm around him.

"The river puts me in a tremble. Wish I had another drop in me. I'd be braver if I was tipsy, to be sure."

"Nay, better to have your wits about ya."

"Ever since my missus and daughter died, my heart's been as mirth-less as an empty bottle of whiskey. I reckon if I drown tonight, at least I'll finally be with them again."

"No one's drownin' tonight, ould fella," Riley said.

Together they entered the river. The moon was swallowed up by the clouds once again and the darkness deepened. Maloney clung to

Riley with astounding strength. "Here we go," Riley said as he stroked through the black waters, shuddering at the sudden cold.

"Jesus, Mary, and Joseph, and all the Holy Martyrs, please preserve us!" Maloney said under his breath.

Riley battled the current while Maloney pressed all his weight on him. Riley could barely keep his head above water. He wanted to tell Maloney to let his body float, but opening his mouth meant taking deep gulps of water, hence he kept his lips closed and focused on his strokes.

"I can still see it," Maloney whispered, "I can see the waves partin' for them and then closin' in on them forever!" Terrified, he tried to climb on top of Riley, plunging him deeper still. He struggled to get loose from Maloney's hold on him, but the old man held on with the grip of death. Riley kicked and labored madly to get to the surface, his lungs screaming for air, but Maloney was a dead weight. The current pulled them along, and Riley knew that the sentries were down river and he needed to swim harder, or they'd be caught. As they both sank into the water, with one last effort, he pushed Maloney off him so he could breathe, but when he returned to the surface, he was barely holding on to Maloney's hand.

He took deep gulps of air and tried to get a better grip on his friend. "Don't let go."

"I can't do it. I can't!"

Then the river tore them asunder, and Maloney disappeared back into the black water. Riley dove underwater after him, but he couldn't see a thing.

He heard gunshots farther downriver and swam until he got ashore and crawled on his knees on the gravel, hiding amid a patch of rushes. He struggled to catch his breath, shivering in his wet clothes. Shame overcame him and soon tears burned in his eyes. *I've let the river bear him away. May God have mercy on my soul.*

12

April 1846
Matamoros, Río Bravo

"I miss him terribly, Nana," Ximena said, as she and her grandmother walked arm in arm out of the Catedral de Nuestra Señora del Refugio into the morning light. It was here, in this temple, where she and Joaquín had married. But now, she had been forced to sit through a different kind of service—a mass for the repose of his soul. This wasn't the future she'd imagined for the two of them when they promised to love each other until death tore them apart. "I should have tried harder to stop him."

"He would have resented you for keeping him from doing what honor demanded of him," Nana Hortencia said, wrapping her rebozo around her shoulders, her silver braids shining as bright as two moonbeams. "He was a good man and a good husband. But just because he isn't with you in the flesh doesn't mean he isn't still with you, mijita. His spirit will always live."

Ximena stared at the ground and said nothing. Her grandmother gently raised her chin and looked up tenderly at Ximena. "Let God help you to let go of your sorrow, mijita. Accepting loss and grieving what is no more takes time, but you have the strength to heal. You always have."

"I wish I could believe as you do, Nana."

"One day you will. Right now, you must work through your grief."
Nana Hortencia hugged her tightly and said, "Come, let us gather
some estafiate by the river, and I will give you a limpia to lift the sorrow from your heart and restore your harmony."

As they started down the steps, Ximena noticed the Irish lieutenant leaving the church behind them. He seemed deeply preoccupied.
When he glanced up at her and their eyes met for a second, she
could feel a negative energy in him, his troubled aura. Inside the
church, she'd seen him lighting a candle to Saint Jude, the patron
saint of desperate cases. Now, as he hurried past them with urgent
steps in the direction of the river, Ximena wondered what was dis-
tressing his soul.

They followed a group of peasant women carrying empty earthen
jars to collect water. Despite the enemy's encampment directly across,
the river was busy. Several women were washing clothes and bathing
themselves or their children. Ximena observed the Yanqui soldiers up
in their fort, gaping at the young women splashing playfully in the
water, naked to the waist. The soldiers whistled and called out to them,
"Little bonitas! Beautiful señoritas! Can we be friends?"

As she guided Nana Hortencia along the banks, they admired the
willows and tepehuajes, which threw their shadows upon the river.
Then the old woman pointed out the clear amber sap on the honey
mesquite trees, warmed by the sun, and lamented not having a pot to
collect it.

"The trees look as if they're crying," Ximena said.

Nana Hortencia patted her shoulder and said, "There's no shame in
crying, mi niña. Even the trees know that."

Ximena wanted to tell her grandmother that it wasn't that she was
ashamed to cry. It was that she couldn't, as if her tears had hardened
inside her.

"You can't let your suffering overwhelm you, mijita. Nor your anger.
Don't let them darken your soul. Release them through your tears,
your prayers. It is true that the path God has chosen for you is one full
of thorns. But to despair is to turn your back on Him."

From the banks, they observed a patrol of Mexican mounted militia boarding the ferry from the opposite shore to cross to the southern bank. When the vessel approached, Ximena looked at the men's faces, wondering if Cheno might be among them. Instead, she recognized another face.

"Nana, is that who I think it is?"

"It's Juan Seguín," her grandmother replied.

The man on the ferry was the commander who had once convinced her father to take up arms against Mexico during the Texas Rebellion. she remembered how, six years later, in March 1842, when the Mexican Army tried to retake San Antonio de Béxar, the attack fanned the distrust the Texians felt for anyone of Mexican descent, and reprisals against defenseless Tejano families soon followed. Even Juan Seguín—the town's mayor and a hero of Texas Independence—was a victim of a conspiracy to ruin him. After being physically attacked, he had no choice but to flee south to Laredo for fear of his life after being accused of disloyalty. But he was captured by Mexico and forced to join the Mexican cause so as not to be executed as a traitor to the motherland. This is why, in September 1842, when the Mexican Army attempted to reclaim San Antonio once again, among their commanders was none other than Juan Seguín.

At the sight of him, Ximena's father had said, "The Anglos see us as traitors, but so do the Mexicans. So where does that leave the Tejano? Mark my words, Ximena, as soon as the Mexican troops leave, the Anglos will come for us seeking revenge. But we won't be here when that happens."

And so, when the occupation of San Antonio ended, Ximena, her father, and Nana Hortencia, along with two hundred other families, loaded what possessions they could into carts and followed Seguín and the Mexican troops south to the Río Bravo.

Ximena had once resented him for pulling her father into the rebellion and allying himself with the Texians, but her father was gone now and this Tejano was her one connection to her past in San Antonio de Béxar. So when the ferry finished the crossing, and the steersman jumped off at the landing to tie the ropes and allow the riders to disembark, Ximena rushed to intercept the group. He was the last one off the ferry, and as he was paying the ferryman, she called out his name.

"¡Don Juan!"

He turned to look at her, his face registering surprise. "Ximena, ¡pero qué sorpresa!" He turned to his men and said, "I'll meet you at the cantina." "You're still serving the Mexican government, I see," she said.

"It's the only choice I have, for now."

A scream startled them both, and they turned toward the riverbank, Seguín's hand on his escopeta. Yanqui soldiers had plunged into the river to bathe under the watchful eyes of the sentries, and they and the Mexican women were splashing water at each other, shouting and squealing in delight. Ximena's concern turned to relief and then anger. How could those women be playing and flirting with the enemy? Couldn't they see the Yanqui cannons pointing straight at their homes?

To escape the commotion, she and Juan Seguín began to walk away, farther down the riverbank where Nana Hortencia had gone ahead until the only noise they could hear was the raucous chattering of the green parakeets in the trees. Ximena had last seen Seguín two years earlier when he'd come to pay his respects at her father's funeral.

"Do you think you'll ever return home?" she asked.

Seguín sighed. "I will serve Mexico loyally and faithfully, but one day, I will return to the land of my birth to reclaim my property and clear my name or die trying. And you, have you been happy here with your husband and the ranch? Have you made a good life for yourself?"

Attempting to disguise her pain, she fixed her gaze on a nearby buttonbush where swallowtails fluttered over its white pincushion-shaped flowers. But it was no use. She gazed back at him and said, "My husband is dead, don Juan. The Rangers who came down with Taylor murdered him, burned our house, plundered our stables. I'm not sure what I will do, but I know this much—I can never return to Béxar. There's nothing for me there. Just like there may be nothing for me here."

He put a hand on her shoulder and squeezed it. "I'm sorry, Ximena, I'm sorry to see you suffering. I wish I could help you, but I'm as destitute as you are at the moment. Still, as long as we have hope, then all is not lost. War is about to commence, and right now, all we can do is survive it."

"Don't you think we fought on the wrong side, don Juan? Could this war have been prevented if Texas hadn't rebelled against Mexico, if *we* Tejanos hadn't helped the Texians win? Could this war allow Texas to return to the Mexican nation? To us?"

He smiled and shook his head but didn't answer her questions. He stared off into the distance, and Ximena began to feel foolish for speaking with such naivete. But she desperately wanted to believe that the opportunity to take back Texas from the Yanquis hadn't yet passed. The thought of her homeland being turned into a slave nation sickened her.

"Don't torment yourself with such thoughts, Ximena. What's done is done," Seguín said at last. "It's true, once the smoke cleared after the rebellion, we Tejanos became foreigners in our own land, and I, like your father, had to leave Texas and abandon all for what I had fought to become a wanderer. But you know as well as I that the Mexican central government has never had our best interests at heart. With one political uprising after another in the capital, there has never been stability or progress, especially here in the northern frontier. Then that vile caudillo, Santa Anna, rose to power and threatened our rights of self-government, and what else could we Tejanos do, Ximena, but to defend our homeland from his tyrannical government?"

He stopped walking, and grasping her shoulders firmly, he turned her to face him.

"You wish to return to that? No, querida amiga, no. Béxar—all of Texas—deserved its freedom, and I shall never regret playing a part in its independence. Even if by doing so, I—we—paid the price for its liberty." He released her and kissed her hand tenderly, then mounted his horse. "I'll be scouting for General Arista, so you might not see much of me. But if you need me, send word with my tocayo, Juan Cortina. You know him, I assume?"

She nodded and bid him farewell.

"We'll get through this," he said. "And when I'm back in Béxar, if you wish to return home, know that you'll have a friend there."

She watched him ride away, thinking about his words, more certain than ever that she could not return to San Antonio de Béxar. But she was Joaquín's sole legatee and had a full claim to his rancho here in these beautiful river delta. Though the Rangers might have destroyed their house and stables, the land was unharmed, and as long as it was alive, Ximena and Nana Hortencia could survive, even if their home was a humble jacal made of carrizo cane and thatched with palm leaves. She refused to let those vile men prevent her from seeing the sunrise over her home, to behold the changing colors of the prairie through the seasons, to taste the wind sweetened by wildflowers. But if Mexico lost the war, would history repeat itself? Would she once again find herself dispossessed?

She quickened her pace to catch up to Nana Hortencia, who was picking and eating the berries of an anacua tree. Ximena joined her and reached to pull down a branch. Just then, something blue caught her eye. At first, she thought it was the iridescent wings of the bluewing butterflies puddling in the mud. But as she peered through the shrubs and reeds at the water's edge, she could see a soldier in a blue uniform tangled up in the branches of an uprooted tree at the edge of the bank.

"Nana, can you see that man or am I imagining him?"

"I see him, but I'm not sure if I am looking at a dead man or a live one," her grandmother replied.

He was wearing a Yanqui uniform, and Ximena wondered if he might be one of the foreign soldiers in Taylor's ranks who were deserting. Had this poor man died crossing over to join her country's army?

"Nana, go find help! Pronto, ¡por el amor de Dios!"

While Nana Hortencia hurried away, Ximena made her way down the sloping bank, sending the hundreds of bluewings fluttering into the heavens like a shimmering prayer. *Please, God. Please.* She waded into the water, holding onto a tree limb as she got deeper. Battling the current, she managed to reach the soldier whose hand was clutching a branch. He had pulled himself halfway onto the tree trunk, and his head and torso rested on it, but his lower body was still immersed in the cold water. On his forehead, she could make out two letters: HD. Who had branded this poor old man and why?

His hand felt cold and limp, and she wasn't able to find a pulse. She grabbed him by his collar and shook him, already fearing the worst. "Hello? Can you hear me?" she said in English as she shook him harder. "Hello?" Finally, the man coughed faintly.

She heard a sudden splashing behind her and turned to see the Irish lieutenant swimming toward her. "Is he alive?" he yelled. "Tell me, does he live?"

"Yes! Hurry, please. Hurry!"

13

April 1846
Matamoros, Río Bravo

Together, they pulled the man from the river and transported him to Carmen's house. She begrudgingly allowed them the use of a room, where Ximena and her grandmother immediately took over his care. The lieutenant seemed to know the man and refused to leave his side.

"Will he recover?" he asked when Nana Hortencia left the room to gather her supplies.

Ximena wanted to reassure him without giving false hope. The old man had now begun to thrash in the bed, and she turned to soothe him. He was burning up with fever.

"Riley, don't let go of me," he cried. "Help me, lad! Help me!"

"Shhh. We are here," Ximena said in English. "You are safe. Shhh."

"'Tis my fault," teniente Riley said. "I was aiding him in crossin' the river to bring him over to our ranks, and I, well, as you can see, my folly endangered his life."

"Is why you go to the river this morning?"

He nodded. "I was hopin' against hope . . ."

She looked at him, wishing to put a comforting hand on his arm, but it wouldn't be appropriate. "My grandmother, she will cure him. No worry." She touched the patient's forehead, tracing a finger over the letters *HD*. "Who did this?"

"The Yanks. Punishing my countrymen is a favorite amusement for them."

"They pay one day for this!" she said and saw the same anger blazing in his blue eyes.

"Aye, we'll make them regret it," he said.

"Dile que se retire," Nana Hortencia said as she returned with the needed items.

"Please, we must work now," Ximena told him.

"I'll go," he said, "but pray do send for me at the barracks as soon as he wakes."

As she escorted him out of the room, he turned to her and said, "I beg your pardon, lass, but I do not know your name . . ." His voice trailed off, and the color in his cheeks deepened. He towered over her by a head, but for some reason, he didn't make her feel small.

"My name is Ximena Salomé de Benítez y Catalán, widow of Treviño." He coughed at hearing her long name, and she felt her lips twitch with suppressed laughter. "But please, call me Ximena."

"Hee-meh-na," he repeated, drawing out each syllable as if tasting her name on his tongue. "I'm teniente John Riley. And that's James Maloney."

She nodded. "I see you tomorrow, teniente Riley."

After treating the fever with white willow bark, Nana Hortencia lit the copal incense in her sahumador and asked God for his presence. She was about to perform a limpia on their patient to rid him of the susto from the trauma of nearly drowning. As Ximena watched her grandmother sweep their patient's body with her sacred eagle feather and then with fresh sage, she knew retrieving the piece of his soul that had remained in the river would require several spiritual cleansings. Her grandmother wouldn't give up until she persuaded that lost piece of soul to return to his body, and so she whispered his name in his ear and called him three times.

When Nana Hortencia was finished with the ceremony, Ximena sat vigil through the night. The man would say words in the Irish tongue, and when he woke, he would grab her hand and call her by a name she couldn't understand. "*A ghrá*! *A ghrá*!" She knew he was call-ing for his wife. And she knew, without being told, that his wife was dead. Each time he cried out in his fevered delirium and insisted on going home, Ximena saw his pale, sorrowful countenance contorted by the visions of his fevered brain. Suddenly, she felt something loosen inside her, and her own tears finally gushed forth. She found herself crying along with him for the loved ones they'd both lost. For the home neither of them would ever see again.

"Mi niña, there's someone here to see our patient," Nana Hortencia said the next afternoon as she came into the room trailed by the tall, broad-shouldered Irishman. The light streaming in through the open window made his eyes glow like a field of blue lupines.

Ximena moved aside to let him see the sleeping patient. "I'm sorry we no send for you before, teniente Riley, but he had fever and . . ." she pointed to her head, trying to get him to understand his friend had been too delirious, but she couldn't think of the words in English. She wished she could speak the language better. The words got stuck in her mouth. It had been so long since she'd practiced with her tutor. Still, it was better than nothing. "His fever is now away. He wake be-fore. Eat a little soup."

"Will he live?"

Upon hearing his voice, Maloney woke up. "Riley, is it you, lad?" His voice was a mere whisper, and Ximena leaned closer, taking the old man's hand in hers. It was limp, but his pulse was much stronger than the day before and his color had improved. She was sure he was going to pull through. She watched the shock on the lieutenant's face turn into utter felicity.

"You're awake! I'm here, Jimmy, *a chara*. How do you find yourself?"

"I thought I'd never see the blessed light of Heaven again," he whispered. "But I was saved by Saint Patrick himself! A miracle if I ever saw one."

"A miracle?"

"A fallen tree. Put there by Saint Patrick. It caught me in its limbs."

"You sit with your friend? I come back later," Ximena said, pulling up a chair for him.

Teniente Riley nodded. "Much obliged, lass."

"I come with a little chicken broth for you," she told Maloney.

"God reward you, jewel," Maloney said.

"I'll see you out," teniente Riley said. At the doorway, he added, "A thousand thanks for what you've done for my friend."

"It was noth—"

"No, it means a lot to me. Truly, it does."

The guilt in his voice told her he was still berating himself for what had happened.

"He fight with you now, for my country, ¿sí?"

He smiled at her, and then went back inside the room. Ximena stood in the doorway for a moment.

"It's good to see you alive, Jimmy," he said. "I need you on the battlefield with me. Welcome to the Mexican Army of the North."

"Thank you, Lieutenant," the old man said with pride. "'Tis an honor to fight by your side."

A few days later, Ximena watched, along with the townspeople and the troops, as General Torrejón and his lancers made their way into Matamoros escorting the Yanqui soldiers they'd captured in the altercation upriver at Rancho de Carricitos with a party of Taylor's cavalry. They'd killed eleven Yanquis and injured many. The crowd cheered at the sight of the prisoners, and everyone knew full well what it meant.

Hostilities had commenced.

That afternoon, at Ximena's request, Cheno brought a uniform for her patient, who insisted he was well enough to join his friends in the barracks.

"How do I look, lassie?" Maloney said as he came out of the room, dressed in his new Mexican artillery uniform.

After his near-death experience, the man had become as skinny as cattle after a winter's blight, but his eyes looked alive again and shone with the deep gray-green of moss-coated rocks. She smiled and said, "¡Como un soldado valiente! Like a brave soldier."

In the morning, she took him in the carriage to the outskirts of the town, where teniente Riley and his artillery crew were practicing their drills. Maloney wanted to surprise them. Seeing him, they all rushed to embrace him, picking him up onto their shoulders and cheering for him. Maloney laughed and burst into an Irish song. "*Óró, sé do bheatha bhaile. Óró, sé do bheatha bhaile. Óró, sé do bheatha bhaile. Anois ar theacht an tsamhraidh . . .*" His comrades joined him and soon all their voices rose in unison, everyone except teniente Riley, who stood removed from the group. Guilt and shame seemed to be permanently etched on his amiable face. He needed a good spiritual cleansing like the ones Nana Hortencia had given Jimmy Maloney to rid him of all that tormented him. He caught her watching him and touched the visor of his black officer's shako in salutation, then called his crew to attention in order to resume the drills.

She seated herself in the carriage but did not yet leave, remaining with the other onlookers, mostly local boys who'd come out to watch the foreign gunners manning the Mexican cannons. It was arduous work, the sun beating down on them relentlessly. Teniente Riley had separated the men into crews, and Maloney now joined one of them. She worried the old man was not yet strong enough to perform his duties. The lieutenant seemed to have known this as well because he gave Maloney one of the least strenuous jobs—lighting the charge with a long match, except they weren't firing for real yet, but rather going through the steps, too many steps for her to keep up with. And she wasn't the only one struggling. The gunners were clearly beyond fatigued from having to push the heavy pieces into position and haul the ammunition. Teniente Riley shouted the orders as he walked the crews through each of the steps involved. Aligning, swabbing, loading, pricking, priming, and finally firing.

"¡Fuego!" the spectators shouted along with teniente Riley. But when the cannons remained silent, the local boys shook their heads in disappointment.

"Why won't they fire for real?" they asked.

"Because first they have to learn the steps so well they can do it with their eyes closed," she told them. "And because gunpowder is expensive and cannot be wasted blasting away the shrubs."

Finally, in the last drill before the crews were dismissed, the boys' patience was rewarded when the cannons roared to life and spewed fire out of their mouths. Ximena covered her ears as the shots boomed. The diabolical sound made her tremble, but the boys cheered and clapped, clamoring for more.

"Fair play, fellas!" she heard teniente Riley say. The smoke hovered over the crews, and the stench of burnt gunpowder permeated the air. Through the haze, Ximena looked at the foreign soldiers, at Maloney and teniente Riley, and gave an involuntary shudder. She thought of the atrocities she'd witnessed first hand during the rebellion in Texas. She remembered the Battle of the Alamo, the cannons blasting, limbs strewn about, the rubble and chaos. *This is what awaits these Irishmen*, she thought. *Carnage and bloodshed, mutilation and suffering, all for fighting a war that isn't even theirs to fight.*

If only this despicable war could be avoided. But how? The Yanquis were already there, right across the river. And the conflict had begun. The boundary line was already being drawn with blood and gunpowder.

Juan Seguín was right. The only thing they could do now was to try to survive it, and she couldn't do it while wallowing in grief. But she couldn't give in to her anger, either. So she had to turn to the only thing she knew would give her comfort and solace—her God-given gift of healing. Ever since she was a little girl, this is what she had wanted to be, a curandera like her grandmother. She would act upon the sacred calling to help the suffering. And by doing so, perhaps it would help her ease her own.

This time, Ximena would make sure not to be on the wrong side of the war. This time—to honor Joaquin's courage and to absolve her father—she would stand with Mexico.

"Surely you must have lost your senses," Carmen said that evening when Ximena told her what she had decided to do. All around them, the servants were rushing to finish packing up the house. "Have you told Cheno about this?"

"He was the one who told me the army has hardly any medical staff. He agrees I should help." Ximena thought of the soldaderas— the soldiers' wives, mothers, and daughters who had followed the men to battle to provide an invaluable service to them as laundresses, cooks, nurses, and sometimes, when the need arose, even took up arms with the men. "He also suggested I could train the soldaderas to make herbal remedies and better care for the troops."

Carmen scoffed, shaking her head again, waving Ximena's words away. "This is madness. A battle is no place for us women."

Ximena looked across the table at Carmen. She knew Joaquín's sister wouldn't understand her desire to stay in Matamoros and contribute to the war effort. In her sister-in-law's condescending attitude, Ximena saw her own mother, the way she'd objected to Nana Hortencia teaching Ximena the healing arts. She'd accused the old woman of filling her little girl's head with talk of plants and spirits, rituals and ceremonies. And how could her daughter one day be a desirable young lady if she was running around the countryside digging up roots with her bare hands?

"We have no medical facilities, no medication and supplies, no experienced nurses," Ximena explained to Carmen. "My grandmother and I can help with that."

"And what about Saltillo?" Carmen asked.

Ximena couldn't bear the thought of going to Saltillo and sitting with Carmen in her parlor, sipping hot chocolate and eating buñuelos while her country was under attack. She couldn't do it. She looked down at her hands. They weren't meant to be wrapped in white-laced gloves while fanning herself with expensive fans from Spain. Her hands were meant to heal.

"The war is here and the soldiers need us," she insisted. "How can we run away?"

"A woman does not belong in a field hospital," Carmen repeated. "At least, not any woman of our station. My children, my husband, and I will leave for Saltillo tomorrow. You do what you want. Become a soldadera if that is what you wish. But if my brother were here—"

"He would give me his blessing," Ximena said. "Joaquín didn't run from the storm, and neither will I."

14

May 1846
Matamoros, Río Grande

15, Feb' 1846

Beloved husband,

I received your letter and remitance. It soothes the hurt in my heart to know you are in good health. God continue to bless and presarve you, a stór. It has been sich a hard winter here in Clifden. Since the blight killed almost half of our lumpers from last year, we had no choice but to eat our seed potatoes. I'm afeard there isn't much left to plant. But we'll soon put in the ground what remains and pray that the rot will not return again this year. Otherwise, we'll be slaving at the spade for naught. Some of our nabours who have the means have had enough and spake of going out to America. But most of our parish are too poor for that, as you well know. I'm afeard there will be hungry months until the next harvest, but we have survived bitther bad times in the past and with the grace of God things will improve. Johnny, Mammy, and Daddy all send you their blessings. You would be proud of our Johnny. He is a strong boy and he loves the horses like yourself. We are looking forward to the time we can make the crossing to be with you. I know you're working hard for us. Plase send us word of how you are keeping.

I send you all my love,
Nelly

Nelly's letter had arrived after Riley separated himself from the Yanks, but at mail call Maloney had lined up for him. The Mexican northern frontier seemed so far away from her and everyone he loved, and hearing her need for him was all the more painful. But return to Ireland was impossible. What else to do then but to stay and earn his lieutenant's wages? He picked up the writing materials he'd purchased and finished his letter in reply to her: *Any day now the war will start. When Mexico is victorious, I will send for you and Johnny and your parents. In this country we'll begin a new life as proud landowners. Can you fancy that, my dearest one? It shall be so. I promise you. Please, remember me to Johnny. Tell him when he gets here, I will have a fine horse waiting for him.* He urged her to write back to him, though he wasn't sure where he would be in a week, let alone, six months hence.

When he was done, he walked over to the church. Mexican postmasters were unreliable with mail within the republic, let alone from another country, and he could not risk losing his wife's remittance. Thanks to the parish priest, he learned a better way was through the Catholic Church. Addressed to Father Aidan from padre Felipe, it would be nigh on three months before his wife would receive it at the chapel, but it was the surest way.

"Tell me, my son, you have troubles?" padre Felipe said as he stood outside the door of the sacristy, watering geraniums in the flowerpots. He set down the watering can as Riley approached.

"Good afternoon, padre," Riley said as he climbed the steps. He removed his shako and kissed the priest's hand. "I am trying to escape gloomy thoughts, but alas, they've taken possession of me. I think of my wife. If anythin' happens to me in the upcomin' battle—"

"God will protect you," padre Felipe said. "You, John Riley, are here to defend a Catholic nation from protestantes bárbaros. Our Lord and savior, Jesus Christ, watch you."

"Thank you, padre," Riley said as he handed over the letter. "If God has other plans, will you write to my wife and inform her of my fate?"

The priest shook his head. "When battle over, you write to your wife and inform of our victory."

"Would you give me your blessin', padre?"

Riley knelt down, hoping the priest's prayer would give him the strength he needed to face whatever fate awaited him.

On the banks of the river the following day, Riley watched the Yankee forces form ranks. The reinforcements and equipment General Arista requested from the capital had yet to arrive, but unable to wait any longer, he'd taken 4,400 troops with him to cross the river farther downstream and cut off Taylor on the road to Point Isabel. The balance of his troops, including Riley's battery, had remained in Matamoros under the command of General Mejía to guard the ferry crossings and to man the defenses along the river.

At the council of war, Riley had proposed that the best course of action would be to surround Fort Texas while Taylor and most of his forces were still inside. But General Arista believed it was too great an undertaking now that construction on the fort had been completed. Its high sturdy walls and deep moat prevented the Mexican infantry and cavalry from infiltrating it. They could besiege the fort with cannon fire, but as Riley had pointed out, the Mexican cannons couldn't penetrate the walls. In an effort to protect Matamoros from Taylor's 18-pounders, Arista had decided instead to lure the Yankee forces away from the city and attack them out in the open field. And so General Arista had forced Taylor out of Fort Texas by blocking his supply line. Short of needed rations to feed his troops, the Yankee general was now marching away from his camp and heading east to his depot.

Arista had put all his faith in his cavalry. The Mexican mounted troops had equestrian skills unlike any Riley had ever seen, to be sure, especially with their lassos. In addition to their carbines and pistols, they also carried long lances, which though outmoded, they used quite effectively. But confronting the enemy in an open field might prove disastrous. Recalling the artillery drills he had witnessed from the scaffolds of the Yankee fort, Riley feared that once in the open, the

Yankees would have all the space they needed to execute the drills they'd been perfecting for months with their highly maneuverable batteries. Containing the Yankees in one place and storming the fort with all of them inside might prove to be a missed opportunity they would come to regret.

Through his field glasses, Riley observed the small garrison Taylor had left behind to man Fort Texas. He spotted Engineer Captain Mansfield, rubbing his chin as he inspected the fort he had designed. Up on the redans, Major Brown and Lieutenant Braxton Bragg were checking the cannons and taking the range of the Mexican batteries. As the Río Grande flowed between them, Riley remembered Bragg's nativism, and found himself pleased to be the West Pointer's opponent. Could he have forgiven himself if he'd fought on the same side?

"How many left?" John Little asked.

Riley handed him the field glasses. "About five hundred infantry and artillery forces. He's left Major Brown in charge. Do you see that vile fella, Braxton Bragg, up on the redans?"

"Aye, he's lookin' our way now," Little said, handing back the field glasses to Riley. "Looks as if someone stuck a thornbush up his arse."

Riley trained his field glasses on Bragg, taking pleasure in the disappointment the Yank must have been feeling that his light artillery couldn't be employed in an artillery exchange across the river. His 6-pounders didn't have the range needed, nor could they be maneuvered on the ramparts as they were on the field. What did he feel at seeing the Irish gunners under Riley's command pointing Mexican cannons right at him?

"When do we strike?" Flanagan asked. "When do we cut the Yanks to pieces?"

"Hold your hour," Riley said, panning to the east with his field glasses, but he could see nothing but the dense thickets of cane growing along the river. He wished he could be there to witness General Arista's army intercept Taylor. It was only a matter of time. After weeks and weeks of a standoff with the armies eyeing each other from opposite sides of the river, both forces were now on the same side, in proximity of each other, ready to be put to the test.

"Arrah, I loathe waitin'," Quinn said. "Makes me nervous everythin' will go arseways on us."

Riley looked at his gunners eagerly awaiting his orders, most of them scarcely drilled and unaccustomed to fire. He wished there had been more time to bring them to a higher standard of instruction and better precision, but they were strong, capable men who had learned to work well. Riley patted Quinn on the back. "Faith, ye'll light those matches soon enough," he promised.

Two days later, on May 3, at the first tinge of sunrise, Riley's battery, along with the rest of the Mexican artillery, rammed round shot down their muzzleloaders, lanyards at the ready. The Yankee fort was hushed and still, its bugles not yet sounding reveille.

The day before, news reached them that General Arista's plans had gone awry. With insufficient boats at their disposal, it had taken his troops twenty-four hours to cross the river, and by the time all his forces and artillery pieces had landed on the opposite side, Taylor's troops had already gotten past them. Now that Taylor had reached the safety of Point Isabel, General Arista had no choice but to wait for Taylor's inevitable return to Fort Texas, and this time the Mexican forces would be ready to intercept his advance. In the meantime, to lure Taylor out of the depot and force him to countermarch, Arista had ordered the bombardment of the Yankee fort to commence.

The officers pointed their swords at Fort Texas and gave the order everyone had been waiting for: "¡Fuego!"

Thirty Mexican cannons belched and recoiled as the crews jumped to the side. Round shot screeched across the river, shattering the tranquility of the early morn. Riley watched the first shots slam into the walls of the fort, sending the Yanks scrambling into the shelters. Through the haze, he could see the residents who remained in Matamoros coming out to cheer heartily from their rooftops and on the streets. "¡Viva México!" they shouted. The church bells began ringing and bugles joined in with their calls as the Mexican cannons showered metal rain on the Yankee fort.

"¡Fuego!" Riley and the other officers shouted again. Just like he'd taught them, Riley's crew swabbed the cannons, reloaded, and fired away. After the first shots, the Yankees recovered from the surprise and hastened to reply to their fire. Now it was Riley's crew's turn to duck as Braxton Bragg's gun belched. Through the grayish haze and fragments of twigs and leaves swirling about, Riley trained his field glasses on Bragg's gun, took the range, and yelled, "¡Fuego!"

The exchange of fire was thunderous. Riley winced as he heard the Yankees' shots crashing into the town, tearing their way through the houses, blasting the streets. His crew returned fire on Bragg's battery again, determined to unseat his cannon.

The bombardment continued for another hour, with one Mexican cannon being taken out of commission and three of its crew members killed. Riley's battery suffered one injury from Bragg's cannon—Flanagan was wounded in the crossfire by an exploding shell that ricocheted from the ground and tore into his abdomen. He was rushed to the makeshift hospital.

General Mejía ordered some of the cannons to be repositioned and better protected. The Yanks, unable to take out another of the Mexican cannons, attempted to set Matamoros ablaze. Riley watched as they hurled hot shot at the heart of the town, the shells tearing through the terracotta-tiled roofs, the adobe and stone walls, but to his relief the buildings didn't ignite. The Yanks had failed to heat the shells to a high enough temperature. Riley took great pleasure in seeing Bragg's disappointment.

Six hours after the bombardment began, the Yankee guns went silent, and Riley assumed they were being careful with their limited supplies. The Mexicans continued to deliver their iron shower with little damage to the Yankee fort. Two of their guns had been dismounted, but not Bragg's. As Riley had predicted, most of the Mexican shells got lodged into the earthen walls, causing little injury. Other shots fell short of their targets. The shots that landed inside the fort exploded upward, so the Yankees simply dropped to the ground to avoid being injured. But it was the noise they were after, not carnage, and thus the firing continued. Riley hoped by now Taylor had decided to leave the depot and make haste to the fort.

But it was not to be.

An express was received from General Arista that Taylor still remained at his depot. Firing on the Yankee fort would resume the next morning. It was almost fifteen hours before the firing finally ceased. The troops' eyes were red and burning from the day's smoke, the air reeking of exploding gunpowder. Riley was grateful that because of the smoke, at least they hadn't been attacked by the mosquitoes that tormented them day after day. With no time to waste, he accompanied General Mejía and the engineers to conduct an inspection of the damage. The general ordered the troops to repair the sandbag fortifications and breastworks. The night was hot and humid, and the mosquitoes returned in swarms, but the troops labored incessantly. Beyond repair were three of the guns the Yankees had knocked out of commission, and one howitzer that had cracked during firing. Riley could hear the Yankees making their own repairs. He knew their fort had sustained little injury, but he hoped they'd at least suffered a good number of casualties.

Before succumbing to exhaustion, Riley and Maloney made their way to the makeshift hospital to look in on Flanagan. Taking out a handkerchief, Riley wiped the smoke and grime off his face. His ears were still ringing.

"You believe the lassie and her grandmother can save poor Charlie?" Maloney asked. He coughed for a spell before continuing on. The smoke from the cannons was still heavy and hovered over the town in a stinking cloud, making the air taste like burnt gunpowder.

Riley thought about the rush of blood pouring out of Flanagan and how he'd hastened to press on his stomach to stop the flow. "His life is in God's hands. I don't know. I saw the unlucky fella get hit."

Even before they entered the hospital, they heard the groans of those who'd been wounded during the cannonade. Luckily, there were few, and their injuries didn't seem grave, not like Flanagan's. They found him on a nearby cot being tended by Ximena, with padre Felipe standing on the other side giving him his last absolution. Flanagan was drenched in sweat, speaking in the Irish tongue, "*M'iníon, is cailín maith thú agus sól'as do d'athair.*"

As he listened, Riley realized the poor man thought the young woman was his daughter. Of course, she didn't understand a word he said, but she spoke to him tenderly, as a daughter would speak to her ailing father. Her back was to Riley and Maloney, but sensing their presence, she turned around. Her eyes were wet with tears, and she wiped at them with her soiled apron, leaving a streak of Flanagan's blood on her face.

Maloney went to her and wiped the blood off with his handkerchief. "Och, lassie, let me sit here with my friend. You deserve a bit of rest."

She nodded and stepped away from the cot. "I'm sorry, teniente Riley," she said as she came to talk to him. "I do what I can, but the shell cut his . . . intestinos. So I sent for the padre."

Her teary eyes were amber-colored, with flecks that glistened like shards of sunbeams. Riley tore his gaze away and looked down at Flanagan's abdomen, where blood soaked through the bandages.

"Thank you, lass. We will sit with him then," he said. "Stay with him 'til the end."

"I am sorry," she said again, looking at Riley and Maloney. "I wish I do more."

"You've done enough," Riley said. "You gave him peace."

She excused herself and went to help her grandmother with the other wounded.

"John, Jimmy, is that ye, boys?" Flanagan said. His voice was hoarse, and Riley leaned closer to his cot, taking his countryman's hands in his. They were cold and limp, his life draining out of him.

"Whist. Don't exert yourself, Charlie, be easy. We shall do aught we can to save ya," Riley said.

Flanagan shook his head. "My time has come. I'm ready to meet God. But you keep fightin' those Yanks, John Riley. Show them what we Irish are made of. Make them regret what they did to us, and to Franky."

"I'll never stop fightin', not until we win this war."

"You're a credit to your countrymen, John Riley. Don't let anyone—" Suddenly, Flanagan began shaking and Riley called for Ximena. Together they witnessed him take his last breath.

Padre Felipe made the sign of the cross over his body and prayed for him in Latin.

"*Ar dheis Dé go raibh a anam.* I won't let his death be in vain," Riley said.

"Heavens be his bed," Maloney said, then broke forth in tears.

Ximena put an arm around the old man. She looked at Riley, and for a moment, he wished to feel her arm around him as well, for her intoxicating scent of sweet green herbs and smokey incense to wrap around him. He wanted to bury his face in the nook of her neck and cry with abandon, the way Maloney was doing now.

"I appreciate your kindness," he said, taking a deep breath. He was a lieutenant and couldn't indulge in sorrow and lamentation. This was war, and he was bound to lose good men. He couldn't fall asunder with every loss. But hadn't it been he who had convinced Flanagan to risk life and limb for Mexico? *And yet, couldn't the same thing have happened to him with the Yankees?*

The bombardment continued for the next two days, with the Mexicans unable to lure Taylor out of the depot. Word from Arista arrived informing them that Taylor had sent a group of Texas Rangers to sneak past the Mexican troops to reach his garrison at the fort. The Rangers had shot their way past the Mexican sentries guarding a post near the camp, killing six. Although Arista couldn't be certain if the Rangers had managed to return to the depot, judging from Taylor's refusal to leave, it appeared they'd accomplished their mission. Riley

was sure they had succeeded and that intelligence the Rangers delivered to Taylor was the reason why he was in no haste to rush to Fort
Texas. By now Taylor must have been well appraised that the Mexican
guns were scarcely causing damage to his fort, making him confident
the garrison could hold out.

"What does General Arista order us to do now?" Riley asked General Mejía.

"We are intensifying our attack on the fort. He is sending General
Ampudia with some forces and four field pieces to bombard it from
the north bank while we continue shelling it from the south."

The crossfire continued, with Mexican artillery firing on the Yankee fort from several directions, but it remained unbreachable. Riley
had warned his men to prepare for a long siege, but he could tell their
spirits had deflated, bombarding the foe when they didn't have enough
firepower to cause any damage. If only General Arista would stop
waiting for Taylor to make his move so he could intercept him on
the road. Riley believed that if the general brought the entire force of
his troops upon the Yankee fort instead of having General Mejía and
General Ampudia attacking from two sides, perhaps then they could
capture the fort and conclude the standoff.

But as Riley feared, news arrived that a shipment of supplies and
new recruits had arrived at Point Isabel. Taylor finally had the numbers he needed to feel confident about emerging from his shelter. On
May 8, when they received word that Taylor was on his way to Fort
Texas with his troops and supply trains, General Ampudia abandoned
his post and took his infantry, sappers, and two cannons to offer Arista
support in intercepting Taylor along the road.

The battle was soon underway on the prairie of Palo Alto. Riley
and the cannoneers, on their end, continued the bombardment of Fort
Texas, making as much noise as possible. When there was a break in
their fire to let the cannons cool down, the deep booming of large guns
eight miles distant could be heard plainly, like the roar of an approaching thunderstorm. Judging from Arista's gloomy reports to General
Mejía and his request that they send more ammunition, Riley knew

the odds were not in their favor. If Arista had led the attack with his infantry and cavalry, there would have been a chance. As long as the battle was dominated by artillery, there was little the Mexicans could do against Taylor's murderous cannonade, especially out in the open prairie where the flying artillery had all the space it needed to maneuver and fire its grape and canister on the Mexicans. Unless Arista could find a way to silence the Yankee cannons, the enemy would continue to blast their way through the Mexican ranks. Hand-to-hand conflict would have evened the odds.

The next day, the battle between Arista's and Taylor's forces had changed location to Resaca de la Palma, four miles distant. By the afternoon, the command "Hold your fire!" rang out from the Mexican redoubts. Riley knew the outcome of the second battle when he and his crew watched from their batteries as Arista's troops appeared on the other side of the river, running as if the very devil were chasing them. So desperate were they to retreat, they tried to escape one danger by attempting another—defying the dangerous currents of the Río Bravo to reach the safety of Matamoros. They threw themselves into the water, whether or not they could swim. Others tried to cross on horseback, and Riley watched in horror as both men and horses succumbed to the voracity of the river.

Behind them, Taylor's dragoons were in hot pursuit. Riley and his men stood by their cannons, yet not pulling the lanyards lest they kill both friend and foe. They watched as Arista's disordered, panic-stricken soldiers attempted to cross the river. General Mejía ordered those closest to the water to help the retreating troops, but there weren't enough boats to ferry all the men, and hundreds dove into the river with their weapons, drowning in the attempt to get away from the mounted riders. Local ranchers appeared with their own boats to help, but they weren't enough, and the weight of too many men and horses pulled some of them under. Then fights erupted on the river-bank as the disorderly masses argued among themselves for the right to get on the boats. The last words of the drowning men were either a plea to God or a curse for their enemies. As the miserable fugitives were swept up by the current, Riley could hear the Yankee's shouts of merriment from the ramparts as they waved their flag.

"Merciful Father . . ." Maloney said, looking at the frightful whirl of dismay and confusion. Riley could see in his eyes the terror of the night he almost drowned. He needed to get Maloney away from the hubbub in the river. "Go to the barracks!" Riley commanded him. Knowing the day was lost, he ordered his crew to abandon their batteries, and they all rushed down to the river to save as many as they could from a watery grave.

15

May 1846
Matamoros, Río Bravo

Ximena had never seen so much blood. It covered the ground and splattered her legs as she rushed from one cot to another tending to the wounded being brought from the battlefield in supply wagons. They supplicated for water, for mercy, they asked for the priest, la Virgen de Guadalupe, their mothers. As blood oozed from their wounds, they cried in her arms, clutching her so tightly she had to bite her lip. But it was her ears that hurt the most—for the shrieks of the wounded were as terrible as those of the cannons bombarding the fort across Matamoros. It was through these men that she learned the outcome of the battles. Their shattered limbs, disfigured faces, and charred skin told stories the soldiers later confirmed. Among their cries and groans, these mutilated men revealed their woeful two days of fighting in the prairie of Palo Alto and in the chaparral of Resaca de la Palma. Again and again, it was the enemy's artillery they spoke of—the shower of exploding shells that dismembered and killed with impunity. They told of finding body parts in the thorny bushes, burying their dead in the dark, being unable to drink from the water hole tainted red with the blood of their fallen comrades, and vomiting at the smell of burned human flesh as the prairie grass fires spread, consuming the dead and the wounded lying helpless on the ground.

After the hasty retreat of the second battle, she tended to those nearly drowned but fished out of the river just in time. Yet the soldiers' delirium and fevers, their nightmares, were as difficult to cure as their battle wounds. The makeshift hospitals were so overcrowded, the injured came to die, not to heal. She and Nana Hortencia did as much as they could to show their female aides to make and administer poultices and ointments, soothing washes, and healing salves. She organized the women into rotating shifts so the men were looked after properly. But they soon resigned themselves to the indisputable reality that not enough could be done to alleviate the suffering of all their patients, and what the men needed most from them, beyond their infusions and soporific teas, were the words of comfort they could offer to a mangled soldier as he took his last breath.

She didn't need to leave the hospital tent to know chaos also reigned throughout the city. The defeated troops stumbled through the dimly lit streets and gathered in the plaza. The darkness couldn't hide their fear and confusion, their terror that at any moment the enemy forces would make their way across the river and attack once again. Some of the inhabitants barricaded themselves in their homes while the hungry soldiers spent the night sitting on the ground, leaning against walls, lying under trees. Later that night, General Arista himself staggered into the city.

For the following days, stragglers wandered into the town in groups, some too tired to talk, others too frightened to be quiet, their wild, haggard eyes constantly looking behind them. From the fragmented stories she heard in the overcrowded hospital tent, and from what Cheno told her when he paid her a visit, Ximena learned of the questionable decisions General Arista had made.

"Honestly, Ximena," Cheno had said, "Why would he allow Taylor to prepare for combat at his leisure before attacking? The pinches Yanquis even had time to refill their canteens! And then, when Arista finally did attack, he opened fire when the enemy was out of range."

She learned about the general's rotten luck and how his plans had gone awry, but the rumor most damning to his reputation—because it was true—was that when Taylor's troops attacked on the second day of battle, Arista wasn't even at the front lines but in his tent writing letters. Ignorant of the chaos reigning in the chaparral, the general had allowed the enemy to take him by surprise. Once his troops had abandoned their weapons and ran for their lives, Arista fled as well, leaving behind his belongings to be ransacked by the enemy—including a detailed map of the area that Taylor would surely use to his advantage.

Now only half of Arista's troops remained, including the wounded and distressed. The bloated corpses of the drowned were washing up on the riverbanks. No one could pass by the river without coming upon at least a dozen dead soldiers and rotting horses.

They were all waiting for the Yanquis to attack the town, to take advantage of Arista's broken army and damaged morale. They knew it would be foolish for General Taylor not to press on and take Matamoros. It wasn't a question of if the Yanquis would attack, but when. As the days passed, everyone held their breath, eyes fixed on the river.

When teniente Riley stopped by the hospital tent one afternoon to check on his wounded, he coaxed Ximena into taking a break. "You look weary, lass. When was the last time you had some rest or nourished yourself?" he said with a firm tenderness, offering her his arm.

"There is much to do, teniente Riley, and I can eat later when it is done," she answered, even as she allowed him to guide her out of the tent into the daylight.

Closing her eyes briefly, she felt grateful for the heat of the sun warming her skin. Ever since she'd been working with the injured, tending to shrapnel wounds or assisting with amputations, she couldn't stop shivering. It wasn't from cold, but fear. And even the sun's warmth couldn't help her with that. She held onto the lieutenant's steady arm, realizing how comforting his strong physical presence was at that moment.

"It is a noble service you are doin' for your countrymen—and mine as well," he said, "But if you aren't careful, you'll be lyin' in that tent with the sufferers instead of takin' care of them."

She could see the concern in his eyes, and she wanted to tell him she was fine, but she couldn't deny the truth. She *was* overextending herself. Depleting her spirit. As was her grandmother.

She led him under the canopy of an ebony a few paces away from the hospital tent and took a deep breath of its creamy flower puffballs. Their fragrance could not overtakethe metallic stench of blood and putrid human flesh that had soaked into her clothes, her hair, her very being. When the breeze shifted, she caught another scent, a wisp of burnt gunpowder. She looked at the exploding bomb symbol embroidered on the red collar of the lieutenant's uniform to denote his company, and she remembered the most horrific sounds she'd ever heard.

"This war," she said, "I pray to God that it . . . terminar pronto."

"I pray for the same," he said. "We Irish know what 'tis like to be oppressed by an aggressive neighbor. May God save Mexico from a similar fate. But for hostilities to end, your people must remain united."

"I have heard bad talk of General Arista," she said. "Is what you mean, teniente?"

"Aye, the officers aren't pleased with our commander. They blame him for his blunders, which led to us takin' that whippin' from the Yankees." He looked at her, his mood suddenly somber. "General Ampudia is none too pleased at playin' second-in-command to Arista and is leadin' the dissension. But the commander is right in pleadin' his subordinates to present a unified front to our troops. As he said, 'How can we fight the Yankees if we are too busy fightin' each other?'"

Upon hearing him repeat Arista's words to her, all Ximena could think of was that this handsome Irishman didn't know her country well. He didn't realize fighting each other was what Mexicans did best.

"What happens now?" she asked, swatting at the flies tempted by the blood on her apron.

"General Arista wants to preserve the city at all costs," he said. "If the Yankees take Matamoros, Taylor will use it as his base as he goes on to attack the next city and the next."

"And you believe is possible? To save Matamoros?"

The lieutenant took off his leather shako and ran his fingers through his hair as he gazed at the river and the enemy fort beyond, the dark feathery brown curls at the nape of his neck unfurled in the breeze like tender fern fronds. "'Tis true, lass, what the general said. Matamoros ought to be defended. But I'm afraid we haven't got the means. The equipment we have left is mostly broken , and so are our forces. The troops have been decimated and those who remain have low morale. If the general can't reenergize the will of his dispirited troops and get them back on their feet, I see but little hope in savin' the city."

"Especialmente now that Taylor has more cañones."

"Aye, right you are. I see Sergeant Cortina has paid you a visit. The Yankee general has already positioned those eighteen-pounders on the bastions of his fort ready to pummel us."

She pointed toward the growing pile of amputated limbs the surgeons carelessly tossed near the hospital entrance and said, "And we know now what his cañones can do."

"The general understands that we don't have the resources to repel an assault," Riley said. "And the ammunition at our disposal, we would be lucky to make it last four hours."

"And with our port in the hands of the Yanquis, there's little food." Ximena couldn't remember the last time she'd eaten. She hadn't been hungry until this moment when, all of a sudden, the last of her energy gave way to a ferocious gnawing in her stomach, and the memory of fresh corn tortillas cooking on a hot stone tormented her. "So, we die of hunger or suffer defeat?"

He looked away and said nothing.

Then she realized there was another potential outcome.

If the Yanquis attacked and captured the deserters, teniente Riley and his men would be shot to death.

A few days later, Arista sent out General Requena with a flag of truce to request an armistice from Taylor. The Yanqui general refused, stating that the capture of Matamoros was inevitable, though its occupation could be accomplished without the violence and chaos that had been required on the battlefield. If Arista wanted to avoid any more bloodshed, he must withdraw his troops and abandon the city at once.

Without the reinforcements promised by the Minister of War, Arista had no other choice and ordered his troops to prepare for the retreat. Ximena knew there were not enough mules and wagons to carry the supplies, let alone the three hundred sick and wounded. Would Arista dare to leave his injured soldiers and officers behind at the mercy of the enemy?

The more she thought of it the more she was sure of the answer. The lives of the poor, illiterate Indian peasants in their ranks were of little value to the criollo generals. Hadn't she seen how the Indian soldiers were poorly clothed, barely fed, and ill-trained? Didn't the officers speak to them in voices dripping with contempt? It reminded her of what teniente Riley had told her about how the Yanquis and the English treated the Irish. These Mexican Indians, like the Irish, were once a powerful people who were now oppressed and treated as foreigners in their own land.

On May 17, Cheno and the other scouts returned to Matamoros to alert them that Taylor was on the move. Their time had run out. As the troops prepared to evacuate the city and march south to Linares, Cheno came to the hospital.

"I've secured a place for you and your grandmother in one of the wagons," he said. "We don't have much time. Taylor now has all the boats he needs to cross the river and his troops are coming across as we speak."

"But what about all the infirm? There are hundreds of mutilated men in the hospital tents!" Ximena said.

"We're leaving them here. The general has moved his injured officers to private residences. The rest are to remain in the tents and Captain Berlandier will stay to ensure their safety."

"These men deserve better than that, Cheno. How can Arista abandon his wounded compatriots?"

He looked at her with resignation. "I agree with you, but it can't be helped, Ximena. We have no wagons and no oxen to pull them. We have been ordered to leave our personal equipage behind. Those who can still walk will rely on their own two feet to carry them away from the Yanquis. Those who can't, will have to pray that the enemy has mercy on them." He grabbed her hand and pulled her into the tent where Nana Hortencia was burning sage over each patient to ward off evil energies. Despite Ximena's insistence, the old woman refused to rest and continued to minister to the pain and suffering in the makeshift hospital. Ximena grew uneasy, knowing that her grandmother was giving too much of herself without taking the time to replenish her strength.

"I hate to disrupt the ceremony, but we must make haste if you don't want to lose your place in the wagon," Cheno said.

Ximena looked at Nana Hortencia. Tending to the wounded of the two battles had been too much for the old woman. A hasty retreat across barren land with little water would surely kill her. But she couldn't leave her grandmother behind, just as she couldn't leave these mangled men. She looked at the hospital tent, at the mutilated soldiers lying on the naked ground or palm petates. "My nana and I will be staying here, Cheno. She's too old to travel, and I won't abandon her or these men who have sacrificed so much for our country."

"It's not safe for you to stay here. The minute the Texas Rangers arrive, all hell will break loose, and you know what they're capable of."

"We'll take our chances. We could go to the rancho if we had to."

"Don't be foolish, Ximena. Two defenseless women alone on a burned-down rancho? The Rangers will be roaming wild, not only here in the city, but in the countryside, too, where you'll be isolated. And if they don't get you, the Comanches will. Listen to me. You know I'm right."

She wrapped her arms around him. "We'll stay here with the invalids and hope for the best," she said. "Take care of yourself, my friend."

Ximena and Nana Hortencia stood watching the troops march out of the town. The columns stretched as far as the eye could see. After losing their shoes or huaraches in the river, many of the troops were marching barefoot. Those in the hospital tents that could manage to walk crawled out of their cots and lined up with the columns, preferring to take their chances on the arduous retreat than with the barbarians from the North. The lancers whose horses had been killed in battle carried their saddles on their shoulders. Some of the cannons were thrown into the river, and the troops' belongings and weapons were left behind in the plaza. They were all hungry, weak, demoralized, and much fatigued before the march had even begun.

"Mi niña, are you sure you want to remain here?" Nana Hortencia said.

"No, but we can't abandon our patients. You've taught me that, Nana."

Teniente Riley and his men lined up in the rear of the infantry columns, and the carriages carrying the only cannons they could take with them lurched forward. The Irishman waved goodbye as he passed by on his caisson. "God bless you both," he said. Like Cheno, he'd tried to convince her to go with the troops, but he understood she was doing her duty and wished her well.

"I'll keep you both in my heart," Maloney said as he waved goodbye.

Nana Hortencia started back to the hospital, but Ximena stayed by the road watching the troops march away. The soldaderas walked or rode on humble donkeys behind the columns, some of them pregnant, others with their babies tied to their backs with a rebozo, their faces shaded by palmetto hats.

Ximena took one last look at the dusty road and went to join her grandmother.

16

May 1846
Matamoros, Río Bravo

Everyone was gone by the following day. All the troops, all the camp followers, and almost a thousand residents of the town disappeared into the cloud of dust the army had left in its wake. Ximena and Nana Hortencia lay on their cots listening to the whispers of the men. "They will kill us," they said. "The enemy will show no mercy." Their fear was palpable. Many of the wounded had died in their sleep, as if they had preferred the certainty of death over the uncertainty of the Yanqui occupation.

But when Taylor appeared and the local authorities informed him of the army's evacuation, there was no bloodshed. He honored the promise he'd made to Arista. Still, the pain of watching the Mexican flag, which flew over Fort Paredes, being lowered and replaced by the enemy's banner felt like a bayonet piercing Ximena's heart. And perhaps she shouldn't have been so shocked when the citizens of Matamoros welcomed the Yanquis into the city, lining up to offer food and liquor to the enemy, gladly taking their money. When Taylor removed the Mexican governor and put General Twiggs in his place, the possession of Matamoros was complete.

Ximena and Nana Hortencia stayed in the hospital tents as much as possible, the safest place for them to be. To her surprise, Taylor ordered his own medical team to help with the Mexican infirm, and there was soon a makeshift hospital on every street. Ximena was relieved to see that the Yanqui surgeons and their staff didn't mistreat her wounded compatriots, as she'd feared. She and Nana Hortencia worked side by side with the Yanquis, and although Ximena pleaded with her grandmother to slow down, that there was plenty of help, she refused to leave their side. Luckily, when the soldiers realized they weren't going to be killed while lying helpless on their cots, their morale improved, and with that, their will to live.

In the meantime, Taylor had the balance of his troops ferried across the river to the city. His officers occupied private residences, and most of his soldiers set up their canvas tents in the outskirts. Wasting no time, the whiskey merchants, gamblers, and harlots who'd been following Taylor's army descended upon the city, and places of ill repute sprang up—gambling halls, saloons, and dance halls. The norteamericanos roamed around Matamoros as if they owned it, especially the Texas Rangers swaggering about with their pistol belts and bowie knives, their wild eyes hidden under slouched hats, their untrimmed dirty beards and mustaches hanging from their face like Spanish moss. Everyone knew they couldn't be controlled, not even by the Yanqui general or the new governor. They were either drinking, playing monte and gambling, or out in the streets raping, beating, or murdering the townspeople. There wasn't a day when a murder or theft was not reported, especially after more Yanqui volunteers—including more Texians—began arriving to reinforce Taylor's troops.

At the end of May, Ximena heard the news that the US government had officially declared war against Mexico, claiming that "American blood had been shed on American soil." Ximena seethed with rage at that baseless claim. The land between the Río Nueces and the Río Bravo was *not* American soil. Their war was based on a false premise, and the Yanqui soldiers pouring into the city were there to defend that lie.

Soon, steamboats were brought up the river, and the inhabitants of Matamoros lined the banks to watch them going back and forth with their puffs of black smoke, transporting Taylor's troops and supplies. It was such a novelty to see those vessels, one of which was named *Colonel Cross*, even Nana Hortencia liked to watch them go by, scattering the birds with their shrill whistles. Then one day the remains of Lieutenant Porter were found. The Yanqui that Joaquín had killed two months before had been eaten by wolves, so it hadn't been easy to identify him. After she watched his funeral service, Ximena asked padre Felipe to say a mass for the murdered Yanqui, hoping that his soul would now rest in peace.

The summer rains began and with that, the river swelled until its waters overflowed its banks, turning the area into a swamp. The rains also brought swarms of mosquitoes, and sickness soon spread through the city. If that wasn't enough, the new Yanqui recruits were carrying diseases, such as measles, from up north. The pestilence spread through their regiments and through the region. Hundreds of Taylor's men had fallen sick and were being tended to in the makeshift hospitals in the city. The death march played all day long as the Yanquis buried their dead. Soon, an outbreak of measles took the lives of many of the local children. After long days and nights ministering to them, Nana Hortencia eventually contracted the disease as well. The battles had taken a heavy toll on her. She'd given so much of herself that her body had no strength left to fight.

Ximena tended to her grandmother, who seemed to be withering before her eyes. She prayed for divine intervention to stop the approach of death, to give her, just this once, miraculous healing powers so that with one simple touch, she could rid her grandmother of the fever ravaging her body, the infection in her lungs, the rash that had spread from her face to her feet, as if consuming her one piece at a time.

" You will feel better soon, Nana," Ximena said as she placed a chamomile compress on the old woman's inflamed eyes.

Nana Hortencia coughed and shook her head. "Let me go, child," she whispered, her voice hoarse and feeble. "The Creator is calling my spirit to Him."

"No. You can't leave me, Nana. What will I do without you?"

The old woman removed the rag from her reddened eyes to look at Ximena. She took her hand and smiled weakly. "You won't be alone, mijita. Have faith."

But how could Ximena hold on to faith when God seemed intent on taking away everyone she cared about? And what good was her healing gift when it couldn't keep alive the only person left on earth who loved her?

The next day, Nana Hortencia told Ximena that she wanted to depart this world under the canopy of the sky. Knowing that her grandmother would be unable to bear the brightness of the day, Ximena wheeled her out of the makeshift hospital that evening on a borrowed wheelbarrow. In the twilight glow, she took her nana to the river's sandy banks, where she could listen to the night songs of the birds. Through the treetops, they watched as the moon climbed, Ximena sitting on the damp ground beside the wheelbarrow where her grandmother lay wrapped in a woven blanket, lulled by the gurgling of the free-flowing waters of the Bravo. Toward midnight, when the moon was approaching its highest point, the old woman's soul entered the spirit world. Her last ragged breath of life became part of the breath of the wind stirring along the river and whispering through the moonlit trees. Ximena stayed there with her grandmother until morning's first light. She beheld Nana Hortencia's face, noble and serene, all traces of the rash gone. Her eyes, as clear as moonlight, raised to the sky.

After she buried her grandmother, Ximena felt like a tumbleweed, defenseless against the whim of the high winds rolling her across the plains. She had nothing to hold on to now. No one to cling to.

These thoughts were weighing on her as she walked to church for evening vespers a week after Nana Hortencia's burial. She passed by a vendor selling fruit outside the plaza and would have kept walking if he hadn't stopped her. It took her a moment to realize who it was.

Juan Cortina. He was wearing a sarape and a palmetto hat and selling cantaloupes out of a small cart pulled by a donkey.

"Cheno, what—?"

"Pretend you don't know me," he said, picking up a cantaloupe and offering it to her. "Here, señorita, please, taste this delicious melón straight from my farm," he continued. "I'll meet you in the church," he whispered, and then turned to the crowd and shouted: "Melones, melones, get your melones, ladies and gentlemen!"

She walked across the plaza to the church, careful not to look suspicious. There were Yanqui soldiers patrolling the area, and she knew Cheno would be in trouble if they suspected him. She had no doubt he was here to spy on the Yanquis. Every so often Taylor's men had captured spies and imprisoned them at the fort across from Matamoros, which had been renamed Fort Brown in honor of their fallen major. Another spy, Jerónimo Valdez, was locked up there now.

She sat on one of the pews and waited for Cheno. Mass was beginning, and as she listened to the priest, Ximena couldn't stop looking at the shattered walls of the church with its statues and crucifix missing. The stench of horse dung infected the air. The Rangers had desecrated the church, robbed it, and had even used it as a stable before Taylor forced them out. Then they turned to looting and destroying private property instead, burning ranches, especially preying on the vulnerable peasants living in jacales on the outskirts of the city where Taylor had no surveillance.

Cheno finally appeared toward the end of the service. Taking a seat next to her, he said, "I was very sad to hear of your grandmother's passing. I'm sorry, Ximena."

After the priest finished mass, they left the church together. It was sundown, and the Yanqui soldiers were wandering the town looking for dinner. Cheno helped her onto his cart, and the two of them rode outside the city, where they hid among a cluster of gnarled mesquites. The sweltering heat radiated off the ground, and the humid air vibrated with the songs of the cicadas. The canícula, the dog days of summer, would soon be upon them.

"I'm sneaking out of here tonight to deliver intelligence and catch up to our troops," Cheno said, confirming her suspicions that he was in town to spy on Taylor. "They're on their way to Monterrey. Come with me, Ximena. Taylor is leaving Matamoros soon to confront our forces. We need you at our next battle. The rancho will still be here waiting for you."

She thought of her home. Now that the enemy—especially the Rangers—were leaving the area, she could return there, rebuild it, and do her best to coax the land to yield a new life for her. But for what? She was all alone, and she had lost her spiritual guide. Knowing this made her feel so empty, like the husk the cicada leaves behind. Emptiness was the worst kind of sickness, her grandmother had often said. But how could she replenish her spirit when there was no laughter, no joy, no love left in her life?

A screeching in the sky made them look up. Two eagles were quarreling in midair, chasing each other across the fiery sky. As their threatening screams cut through the humid evening, Ximena saw something swirling down. She got off the cart and ran after it.

"Careful!" Cheno said as she forced her way through the thorny shrubs.

The spines on the twigs of a lime prickly ash clawed at her, but she managed to reach the fallen object on the branch where it had landed.

"What is it?" he asked.

"A feather," she said, "from a golden eagle."

In the afterglow of the setting sun, she could barely see the blood that covered the feather. Ximena thought of her grandmother. Nana had told her to look for the sign. She held the bloody golden eagle's feather and wondered if it was a portent of wounds yet to be inflicted upon the sacred soul of Mexico.

Was the eagle that once devoured the serpent now being itself devoured?

Part Two

Beyond
the Bravo

17

Upon the parapets of the citadel, twenty feet above ground, Riley was inspecting the placement of a cannon while scanning the road below. Any day now, the Yankee troops would march into view, and he and his gunners would be ready for them.

After the loss of Matamoros, the troops carried the burden of disappointment with them on the two-hundred-mile retreat across the desolate terrain, the weather alternating between blazing heat and cold, heavy rains. Many men had perished on the dusty roads from starvation, exhaustion, or suicide before the Mexican Army of the North—or what remained of it—finally stumbled half-dead into the city of Linares. Just the thought of it made Riley's blood boil. They lost good men on their retreat. After spending three weeks in Linares recovering from the ordeal, the troops, under General Mejía, trudged another hundred miles northwest to Monterrey, in the state of Nuevo León, while General Ampudia went to Mexico City to gather reinforcements.

General Arista had been court-martialed and dismissed from the army, and President Paredes had been overthrown. When Ampudia returned to Monterrey with three thousand more troops and sixteen artillery pieces, he also brought an order from the new government reinstating him as commander-in-chief of the Army of the North and authorizing him to make a stand in Monterrey against the approaching Yankee army. To Riley, the best part of Ampudia's trip to the capital was the chest of gold pieces he brought with him to finally pay the troops. Through the priests of the city, Riley was able to send Nelly his largest remittance yet, which would see them through the approaching winter.

His battery had been stationed at the citadel under the direction of General Tomás Requena, Ampudia's second-in-command. The citadel was, in fact, an unfinished church about half a mile north of the city in the middle of an open plain. Its weathered walls of blackened stones gave the fortification an eerie look. It was supported by twelve massive pillars and could hold a garrison of four hundred.

"When the Yankee fools finally show themselves, any of them tryin' to get into the city from this direction will have to get past our fire," John Little said proudly as he patted the cannon he was polishing.

Riley and his unit had put eight cannons up on the embrasures, though there was room for twenty-eight more. Riley's favorite was an 1842 brass 18-pounder made in Liverpool, etched with the words *República Mexicana*. It was unfortunate that the bulk of the cannons the Mexicans possessed were old brass relics from the War of Independence from Spain earlier in the century.

"Aye, Monterrey should be defended at all costs," Riley said. "It would be a dishonor to surrender the city without a fight." Not only was Monterrey the center of culture and commerce, it was also the major city connecting the northern frontier to the capital. Riley knew its defeat would be a huge blow to the country.

"We will defend it," Murphy said. "Have no doubt of it."

"This is a fine city," Quinn said, looking over the parapets. "Wouldn't you want to live here, Lieutenant?"

"Aye, 'tis a magical place, to be sure," Riley said. "Nature was not stingy bestowin' charm and fertility upon it." He loved the picturesque location of Monterrey, in the foothills of the Sierra Madre range, which wrapped around it on three sides, each massive mountain carved in distinctive shapes by the elements. The one to the east looked like a horse's saddle, the mountain on the west like bishops wearing miters. Two high hills on the west side, Independence and Federation, served as the gateposts to the city, with Fort Soldado on the peak of one and the Bishop's Palace on the other, which the engineers had also fortified. He could see the giant tricolored Mexican flag waving above the Bishop's Palace. The glittering blue Río Santa Catarina embracing the city's southern and eastern perimeters served as a natural moat offering protection from a siege. Past the white city wall, the cathedral's spire soared above the terracotta roofs, and by the cluster of trees, Riley could identify the central plaza where he loved to stroll in the evenings.

"When we can finally send for our families, I hope they love this city as much as we do." Quinn said.

"Aye, I'll warrant they will," Riley said, patting him on the back. "I told my wife all about Monterrey in my letters. And about the haciendas over yonder. One day, should it please God, we will have one of our own."

As the men gazed at the noble haciendas in the outskirts of the city, they fancied themselves living there, surrounded by rich corn and sugarcane fields and orchards bearing figs, pomegranates, and avocados. Riley knew that, just like him, his men were tired of never being able to own fine arable land. The English had taken it all.

The fresh air of the early morn was sweet and crisp. He inhaled deeply, realizing that soon they would be smelling nothing but burnt gunpowder and the stench of death. The bells of the cathedral rang the hour, reminding him of the work to be done. "Now men, the day is wearin' on. That ditch won't dig itself. On ye go."

Down below, the troops were in the process of fortifying the black fortress, digging a ditch around it where a drawbridge had been installed and finishing an eleven-foot wall all around to protect it from artillery shot. When the battle began, the gunners in the citadel would face the enemy on their own with no hope for reinforcements.

Riley took out the writing materials he'd brought with him and set out on a new task. The previous day, General Ampudia had asked his assistance in composing another letter to the Irish and other foreigners in the enemy's ranks. As soon as Taylor's forces got close enough to the city, the Mexicans would flood his encampment with new leaflets.

"Is that the letter to our countrymen?" John Little asked as he came back up to the ramparts.

"Aye, 'tis," Riley said.

"Will they come, you think? The Irish."

"And the Germans, and the Scots, and maybe even the slaves who wish to have their freedom."

"I wish the whole lot of them would come and leave Taylor with half his army," Little said.

"I don't wish to point our guns at our own countrymen," Riley said. "We're givin' them a choice. 'Tis up to them if they wish to remain in the ranks of the Protestant heretics, sufferin' from little thanks and scanty pay."

Riley inspected the guns, gleaming in the sunlight and loaded with canister shot. He surveyed the vast plains below for any signs of the enemy, but there was nothing out of the ordinary in the horizon, just a herdsman with his flock of white goats. Riley read his words once more. *It is well known that the war carried on to the Republic of Mexico by the government of the United States of America is unjust, illegal and anti-Christian, for which reason no one ought to contribute to it* . . . He tossed the white paper up in the air and watched it flutter, being carried by the wind over the fresh green of the planted fields. Soon more of his countrymen would come, and he'd be ready to receive them. His eyes returned to the road ahead, scanning the horizon.

Once they were done for the day, Riley and his men made their way back to the city, Riley on his horse, the men clattering behind him on mule-drawn carts. At the bridge over the arroyo Santa Lucía, which marked the entrance to the city center, they paused before the statue of Our Lady of Guadalupe, the patroness of Mexico. She was a comforting sight to behold. It was fascinating to him how similar and yet so different the Catholic faith was in these lands. They combined Catholicism with the spiritual beliefs of the ancient native tribes, just like in Ireland, where old Celtic beliefs had been incorporated into Catholicism. Seeing this offered Riley a sense of home and familiarity.

Once they crossed the bridge into the city, Riley was pleased to see the troops building breastworks and redoubts, digging trenches, fortifying civilian homes and public buildings. All the streets were being barricaded. The flat roofs of the stone houses were perfect for snipers to shoot anyone exposed on the cobblestoned streets, and sandbags had been piled on the housetops for protection. Even the cathedral was playing a role by serving as the army's main magazine, though Riley disliked the thought of God's holy house being filled with cases of gunpowder and musket balls. The whole city was being turned into a fortress, though none of that took away from its magnificence.

As they passed by the apothecary, they spotted Ximena and Maloney emerging from the shop. When she arrived a few weeks earlier, the old man had asked to be removed from the artillery crew and detailed with the hospital corps to work with the infirm along with her. He and the lass had now become inseparable.

"*Dia dhuit*!" Maloney said, waving hello.

"Hop in," the men said as they pulled the wagons to a stop. "Ready for some grub?'

Riley dismounted from his horse and took off his shako. "Buenas tardes, señora Ximena. May I carry that for you?" he said, pointing to the large basket she carried in her arms.

"Oh, is very kind, but is not heavy," she replied, lifting the lid. "The botánica not have big quantities of what I need."

"That's unfortunate. And you, ould fella? You seem in fine spirits," Riley said, happy to see Maloney back to his old self.

"Faith, I'm as happy as the day is long, no doubt of it! The lovely air of this city and the company of this darlin' creature has rejuvenated my spirits!"

"Will ye join us for dinner?" Riley asked them both.

Ximena looked at Maloney and said, "You go. I will take care of this."

"You can't go gatherin' plants on your own," Maloney said. "'Tis not safe, jewel. Not with the Yankees about to make an appearance any day now."

"Let me accompany you, my lady," Riley said. "If you don't mind."

She nodded. "Gracias, teniente."

They retrieved her horse and her tools and rode out of the city, beyond the corn and sugarcane fields and into the shrublands.

"Is not like Irlanda here?" she asked as they trotted along on their horses. The country stretched out before them, miles and miles of semiarid land covered in plants he had never known existed until he found himself in this part of the world, so far from thes misty rolling vales and hazel glens of Ireland. There was but little timber, mostly stunted shrubs, yucca and palmetto, and all manner of cacti—from impenetrable hedges up to twenty feet tall to tiny ones that scarcely peeked above the soil. Almost everything that grew in the sun-drenched northern frontier of Mexico was armed with vicious thorns and spikes. Even their lizards had horns!

"Aye. 'Tis nothin' like the Green Isle, to be sure," he said with a smile. "It couldn't be more different."

"I imagine my country is not beautiful like Irlanda is to you," she said as she halted her horse. "Too many things that prick or sting you."

He laughed and said, "Well, 'tis true, lass. We have no snakes in Ireland, if you can believe it."

"¿Cómo es posible?"

"We have Saint Patrick to thank. He drove the venomous reptiles into the sea with nothing but his faith." He dismounted his horse and extended his arms to help her down. Although she was an excellent horsewoman and didn't need his help, Riley was glad she didn't reject him. Instead, she reached out for him. The few seconds when he held her aloft in the air, when their arms were intertwined and their faces came so close to touching, stirred something deep within him. He wished he could hold her, feel her body against his. Ever since she arrived in Monterrey, he'd been enjoying her company more and more, but it led to such guilt afterward, to sleepless nights where he reprimanded himself for the pleasure he'd felt.

She grabbed her walking stick and handed one to him. "I bring one for you too. *Fe* . . . faith . . . will not save us from a bite." She looked at him from under her straw hat and grinned.

He followed behind her, noticing how her colorful skirt and petticoats swayed gently as she scouted for plants. When she found one she needed, she knelt down and began to dig with the knife she always carried.

"This plant is good to stop blood," she said as she tried to yank it out.

"I hope we won't need too much of it." He pulled on the plant until it came out. She chopped off the roots and the leaves and put them in her basket.

"Ampudia only cares of his victory," she said. "Does not think of the soldiers to be killed. He will sacrifice many."

"But your country's freedom is worth the sacrifice, is it not?"

"Sí, for freedom. But not for vanidad or hunger for glory. Joaquín, he gave his life to protect our home. Ampudia, he—"

"Is not like your husband and never will be. But we have the numbers. And Monterrey has been well fortified. Let us give our commander the benefit of the doubt. We all have our failings to be sure."

"I pray you are right, John Riley."

To his embarrassment, his stomach growled, and he hoped she hadn't heard it. She seemed not to have and started making her way to a thicket of spiny cacti with small red balls sticking out of them.

"You have tunas?" she said.

He shook his head. He'd seen this cactus—nopal as the Mexicans called it—everywhere since he marched down to the Río Grande with Taylor's army. Growing up to fifteen feet high, it had been blooming with splendid yellow, red, or white flowers—and some of his hungry comrades had tried to eat the pads and gotten spines stuck in their tongues. He had seen this cactus on the coat of arms on the Mexican flag and wondered if it was, symbolically, what the shamrock was for the Irish. Since he switched sides, he'd eaten a lot of it and learned that only the young succulent pads were good for eating, but he'd yet to taste the queer-looking fruit. Ximena put on her gloves and began to twist the tunas off the pads and put them in her basket. "You be careful with the espinas," she said. "Come, we will build a small fire and you try the tunas, ¿está bien?"

"Don't you fret about me, lass. I'm not that hungry."

She gave him a look and sent him to gather twigs and branches while she made a circle with stones. When the fire was ready, she passed each prickly pear over it to singe the spines on the fruit. She yelped when they pricked her through a hole in her buckskin glove.

"Nothing comes easy in this place, does it?"

She shrugged. "Vale la pena," she said. "The effort . . . is good, I promise."

She looked at him then, and their eyes locked for a few seconds. Her gaze made him burn inside. He looked away and wiped the sweat off his forehead with his sleeve. He felt lightheaded, and he hated the feeling of losing control of his senses, his feelings, his body. His brain was in a mist whenever he was around her. Intoxicated by her scent, the sound of her voice, the sunrise in her amber eyes, and there was naught he could do about it.

"Tunas are good for aches of the head, from too much drink," she said. "Tell your men to eat before the pulquerías."

"Aye, they've taken a fancy to pulque and mezcal." Riley had tried pulque, a milky spirituous liquor the Mexicans relished, and hadn't cared much for its odor or taste. Maloney, on the other hand, drank it as if it were the best thing that ever went down his throat.

"You see there?" She pointed to one of the plants in the distance, though Riley wasn't sure which. "The one with spiky leaves?"

"The one with spiky leaves, let me see, which one could that be?" They laughed, and she pointed again to the green-gray plant with long, narrow leaves, thorny edges, and wicked spines on the tips, saying it was called a maguey. Although he'd seen local ranchers use hedges of maguey to fence in their property, and had seen it cultivated in large tracts of neat rows, he hadn't known its use.

"That's where pulque and mezcal and tequila are from, and agua-miel." She took out her knife and returned her attention to the prickly pear. "Ahora, teniente, atención, por favor." She sliced off both ends and then cut along the skin in a vertical line up the length of the fruit. "You remove the tough skin." As she peeled it back, he gasped at seeing the flesh of the prickly pear—so red and shiny and moist. She offered it to him, and he put the fruit in his mouth, enjoying the combination of sweet and tart, similar to the raspberries growing wild in the brambles near his childhood home.

"Some people no like the seeds. Spit them out, if you wish," she said as she ate her fruit.

"I don't mind them," he said. "I don't mind the thorns either. Right you are, lass, they *are* worth the effort."

She laughed and shook her head and then tossed him another one. He peeled it the way she had taught him and ate it, relishing the flavor of the fruit. The sun was beginning to descend, and the delicate shadows of the shrub and cacti were lengthening around them. Cerro de la Silla rising majestically above them, was becoming tinged in red. He was loath to return to the city. He wanted to stay here in this open land eating prickly pears with the lass by the campfire, watching the sun's inevitable surrender to the moon on the other side of the sky.

They made their way back in the dim twilight at a delightful gallop across the plain. The civilians were beginning to congregate in the public plaza for the night's festivities. The following day was the twenty-fifth anniversary of Mexican Independence, but the celebrations would begin that very evening with a speech by General Ampudia, followed by a mass. Together they rode past the cathedral fronting the plaza where vendors were selling food—tacos, roasted corn, and baked yams. Flower arches in red, white, and green adorned the entrance to the cathedral. Colorful paper hanging on strings floated above the plaza where a band was playing, and the wind carried the music over to them.

Riley accompanied her to the door of the Hospital de Nuestra Señora del Rosario, a couple of blocks east of the cathedral.

"Thank you for the help, teniente," she said as he helped her untie the baskets of supplies.

"Anytime, lass. Anytime. I'll see ya in a bit."

He watched her go into the hospital and went in search of his men.

18

September 1846
Monterrey, Nuevo León

Later that night, Riley and his men were sitting around the fountain in the public square with Ximena, eating tacos de cabrito and machito as they watched the city folk stream in.

"'Tis a joyous occasion, the independence of your country," John Little said to Ximena.

"Pray tell us, lass, tell us about your country's independence," Maloney said.

"Well, thirty-six years ago, a priest—his name is Miguel Hidalgo—he gave the cry for revolución. For the people to fight Spain. His cry for independence is called 'El Grito de Dolores.'" She finished her taco and continued, "There was eleven years of fighting. So much blood. So much death. But in the year 1821, this is when I was born, we took our country back from the Spanish. New Spain was now los Estados Unidos Mexicanos, or Mexico."

"'Twas a lucky year to be born, in an independent country," Riley said.

"One day, we shall have our own 'El Grito,'" Mills said, looking at his comrades.

"One day, we'll be the Republic of Ireland!" Little said.

"Aye, one day, my brave fellas, it shall be so," Maloney said.

They raised their clay mugs of pulque and drank a toast to the future of their beloved land. Riley noticed the worried look on Ximena's face. "You don't look too happy about your country's independence."

"Perdón. I wish freedom for your homeland, I do. But I now remember, four of our five leaders, they died . . . ejecutados."

"Executed?" he said. "By firing squad?"

She nodded. "Yes, executed. They pay big price for freedom."

"Freedom comes at a cost," Little said.

"Aye, I would give up my own life to set our unhappy country free," Riley said.

"A toast for Ireland's freedom then," Maloney said, raising his mug again. "And if die we must, then may we all die in Ireland and meet merrily in Heaven!"

The men raised their mugs and shouted, "*Bás in Éirinn!*"

The bells began to toll, and Riley took his leave from his friends. He walked over to the sacristy, which was serving as the general's headquarters, to take his place alongside the officers gathered by the cathedral. They stood at attention in front of the sacristy and watched as Ampudia was escorted out by his staff who were carrying torches. Riley and the other officers followed behind their commander-in-chief in a parade that made its way to the center of the plaza where the troops and townspeople had congregated. The color guard led the way, and the military band played a battle song as civilians and soldiers alike saluted the flag as it passed by them. Once they arrived at the plaza, the tricolor was handed to Ampudia, who raised it high into the air and turned to address the crowd standing before him. Thousands more had flooded the streets and the balconies and rooftops of the surrounding buildings. He rang a bell several times, and a quiet descended upon the crowd as they waited for him to begin El Grito.

"¡Mexicanos!" Ampudia yelled as loudly as he could. "¡Vivan nuestros héroes que nos dieron paz y libertad! ¡Viva Hidalgo! ¡Viva Morelos! ¡Viva Allende! ¡Viva la independencia nacional! ¡Viva México!"

The crowd cheered and shouted, "¡Viva!" and "¡Bravo!" again and again. Ampudia rang a bell, and soon, all the bells in the city—from the cathedral down to the smallest chapel—began to toll. Rockets were launched into the air and burst above them. Ampudia waved the flag from side to side whilst the band played another battle song, and the people sang as loud and proud as they could. Riley couldn't take his eyes off the green, white, and red banner. By now he'd learned what the colors meant—the green for independence, the white for the purity of the Catholic faith, the red for unity, the eagle and the serpent for their Aztec heritage. He fancied what Ireland's flag would one day look like—perhaps a tricolor banner as well, one made of the finest silk—with green for the land, white for the peace that would follow English rule, and pale blue for Saint Patrick. And in the center, perhaps a shamrock and the Harp of Erin. He hoped he would be there when the flag finally flew above Irish soil.

The general finished his speech and the crowd cheered once again. Riley couldn't understand all of the general's remarks, but from the little he did grasp, he knew the commander spoke of protecting Monterrey at all costs. His speech aroused the people's patriotism and fueled their enthusiasm for revenge and their desire for glory. The cathedral couldn't fit everyone in the city, and so the priests came out to give mass in the open air. Thousands knelt and prayed, civilians and soldiers side by side. Riley loved the sound of their voices rising together to the very heavens, to ask God for His protection and His blessing in the battle to come.

After mass, a fandango was held in the main plaza. Gleams of moonlight shone through the palm trees, and torches and lights illuminated the whirl of figures spinning to the fiddles and guitars Riley pushed through the throng until he finally spotted his men dancing away with the local women. He saw Maloney twirling Ximena round and round, his cheeks flushed and his eyes bright with glee. Riley smiled at the delightful scene. He had never seen Maloney this happy. He had a light heel, and so did Ximena, dancing with the same indefatigable vigor she did everything else. Listening to the sounds of mirth, Riley knew this night was a gift to be treasured. The following day they would go back to fretting about the war, but at least for this one moment, the music and laughter was a gentle shower washing away their worries of the coming strife.

A lively waltz began, and Maloney spotted Riley and waved him over, "There you are lad, come and take my place. These old bones can't keep up with my lovely partner. Off with ye and enjoy the music!"

Riley hesitated before he took Ximena in his arms, and guilt soon pricked him. Nelly loved to dance. He was as graceful as a sheep dancing on its hind legs, but she had always managed to pull him out to dance whenever there was a bagpipe or fiddle present. Ximena noticed his hesitation and smiled in understanding.

"We go sit?" She turned to walk away from the dance floor to the bench where Maloney waited.

Riley grabbed her elbow and said, "I'm not very good at this, but I'd like to try for a bit, if you don't mind me steppin' on ya?"

She laughed and came willingly into his arms. She didn't make a fuss when he trod her tiny feet or when they collided against other couples. He was too nervous to concentrate, whereas she was graceful and swaying like a nocturnal desert flower unfurling in the sultry night. He could feel the warmth of her body, see the delicate curve of her neck, the valley between her breasts peeking through the lace-trimmed ruffles of her white blouse, the torchlight casting a silver glow on her black plaited hair. He became warm and flushed, as if he'd eaten a handful of piquín peppers, and as she looked at him with her lovely honeyed eyes, the burning glow spread through his body from the inside out. *Forgive me, Nelly.* He tried to recall what his wife looked like, and for a moment, just a brief moment, all he could see were the cold swirling mists that had enveloped her that cheerless morning he'd walked away. He'd turned to look back and seen nothing but white.

He let go of Ximena so quickly, she well-nigh lost her balance.

"Beg your pardon, lass. I didn't mean—"

"No worry, teniente Riley," she said, composing herself. She wrapped her rebozo over her head and shoulders, her face in shadow. "It's a nice evening, but I go to sleep now. Buenas noches."

Upon hearing the hurt in her voice, he reached for her and said, "Wait a blessed minute, lass." But she disappeared into the throng, and he didn't have the courage to follow.

Maloney came to stand beside him. "Och, small blame to you, laddie. You're only human after all."

Riley turned to look at his friend. "Let's have a drop together, ould fella. I'm buyin'."

He had avoided the taverns, but that night, he and Maloney found an empty table at the cantina across from the plaza. As the musicians played their sorrowful ballads and laments, Riley took a shot of tequila. And then another. A liquid ray of Mexican sunshine.

"Easy now. You'll get tipsy, you will," Maloney said, putting the bottle on his side of the table.

"'Tis Independence Day, a day to celebrate!" Riley held his mug out to Maloney and kept it there in the air. The old man refused to refill it. Riley put his empty mug down and sighed. He knew his friend was right, and he was ashamed the tables had turned. It was now Maloney who was keeping him from getting deep in liquor. "'Tis a drop of comfort, isn't that what Franky used to say?"

"Poor creature you are, John Riley, that your whole soul is tortured by what couldn't be helped," Maloney said. "Faith, even a blind fella would take a fancy to that lassie. The sight of her fills one with the same delight as the first shovel of upturned earth after a hard winter."

Riley knew what he meant. Like the breath of spring, her voice, her smell, her very essence, made him feel t there was hope in the world. He shook his head. "I left a wife back home, left her to shed many a bitter tear for me, I did. And now I'm disrespectin' her. Betrayin' her. Fightin' someone else's war. Hankerin' for another woman—Arrah!" Riley grabbed the bottle from the old man and refilled his mug, but midway to his mouth he stopped and threw the liquid over his shoulder in defeat and stood up. "I best stop makin' a holy show of myself and turn in. I'll see you in the morrow."

He avoided Ximena for the next few days. He didn't have courage enough to see her, so he gave up his quarters in the private residences where the officers were lodging and stayed in the citadel with the other gunners. Using his canteen as a pillow, he lay stretched beside the cannons, rolled in a coarse multicolored Mexican blanket damp from midnight dew. The night was keen, and he shivered as he looked at the sky above, trying to find answers written in the heavens. He wrote letters to Nelly by a lantern's feeble glimmer but tore them up and let the pieces flutter in the wind. What could he tell her that wouldn't be a lie? That he missed her, that he longed for her? Even as he wrote down those very words, his eyes kept drifting to the steeple of the cathedral in the distance, knowing Ximena was in the hospital nearby. It took every ounce of willpower to not climb down the citadel and ride his horse the half mile into the city, down the cobblestones that would lead to her. No, he couldn't write to his wife and tell her half-truths. What manner of man had he become? One that betrayed his soul and suffered his wife to hold on to false promises? He couldn't be that manner of man.

"Forgive me, Nelly," he said again as he tore up yet another letter and watched the pieces swirl away in the wind toward the peaks of the dark stone mountains scratching at the sky. He looked at the moon and fancied himself in Clifden, walking through a dark misty field upon a solitary lane. His cottage stood against a slope at the bottom of the glen, and guided by the stars glowing above him, he traversed the land of his youth, jumping across a stream whose silvery waters disappeared into the depths of the winding valley and the rolling hills beyond, and just as the sleepy cottage came into view, he paused to look at it, the stone walls softened in the moonlight, splendid in the quietude of the night. He continued down the slope until he found himself standing before the door. Placing his hand against it, he hesitated, too much of a coward to open it just yet. He fancied Nelly sleeping inside, Johnny in his cot by the hearth, the turf fire popping. What would Riley say to them when he saw them? What would they say to him?

He opened his eyes and fixed his gaze upon the pale Mexican moon being swallowed up by a mass of rain clouds thickening above him. He couldn't allow himself to fancy his first reunion with his family. It all depended on what manner of man he was by then. An accomplished one or a broken one.

He couldn't believe how grateful he felt when, at length, a cloud of dust rose in the distance, and he knew the hour had come to fight. It was only then that he could put Ximena out of his thoughts, when, at the blaring of the bugles and the beating of the drums, the soldier inside him took over, his unsettled mind gathered focus, and all he could think of was how to carry out the absolute defeat of the enemy.

"Yonder come the Yankees!" the gunners yelled.

The troops in the citadel fixed their gaze upon the road, at the growing cloud of dust. Through his field glasses, Riley spotted Taylor's forces marching toward them. He watched as they came to a halt and a reconnoitering party led by the Yankee general left the main columns and approached the city to get a closer view. The general, his staff, and the Texas Rangers had stopped out of range of the citadel's guns, but even so, Riley yelled the command for his crew to fire in their direction. "Let's give them a warm welcome, fellas," he said. He ordered another round and another, his guns spitting fire, followed by the boom of the cannons as loud as thunder, echoing against the mountains. It was a warning. A challenge. A defiance. Through the white smoke rolling out of his cannon's mouth, Riley could see Taylor's party turning around and heading back to the rest of their army.

That afternoon, Juan Cortina returned to the city and stopped at the citadel to give notice that the Yankees were camped three miles distant in the grove of pecans at the Bosques de Santo Domingo. Cortina had scattered the new leaflets around the campground to be found and read the next morning. Ampudia had posted sentries along the roads with instructions to escort any deserters seeking to join the Mexican ranks. Riley was pleased to see Sergeant Cortina return safely back to the city. The body of another Mexican spy, Jerónimo Valdez, had been found in the chaparral earlier that day, and Riley knew Ximena would have been devastated if anything had happened to her friend.

Throughout the afternoon, he and his battery spotted the enemy forces making reconnaissance, and the Texas Rangers roaming the periphery of the town. Later, the Rangers, always the daredevils, galloped toward them at full speed. Riley suspected they would dodge his fire, but he still gave the command. He'd seen them ride before and knew how fast and agile they could be. Riley's guns roared warnings, and the Mexican snipers directed their muskets at them, but the daredevils escaped unscathed, circling the citadel, yelling their Texas cry, before racing back to rejoin the troops.

The next day, September 20, Monterrey would be celebrating its two-hundred-and-fiftieth anniversary, but on the eve of such an important event, instead of the customary fandangos and celebrations, more families fled the city in haste. Those who remained gathered silently with the troops in the central square to pray for victory. Riley remained in the citadel, avoiding Ximena. He wouldn't go into the city that night. It was his punishment.

The priests came to bless the guns and to give the garrison their benediction. Riley and his men couldn't sleep that night. From the ramparts of the citadel, he watched the city, eerily silent, as if holding its breath as it waited for the combat to ensue. He thought of Ximena in the hospital. He should have gone to see her, to make things right between them. If anything happened to either of them . . . No, he refused to think those thoughts. He made the sign of the cross and said a silent prayer, for himself, for Ximena, for his wife.

19

September 1846
Monterrey, Nuevo León

After the first day of battle, Ximena was up all night supervising the care of the wounded. Toward morning, when her spirit and body could take no more, Dr. Iñigo, the head surgeon, bid her to retire. "Rest, señora, recuperate your strength."

Ximena and the other soldaderas and local women volunteering as hospital aides had spent the early part of the day preparing bandages, cleaning tools and sponges, and making poultices and ointments. Later they were tasked with washing and dressing wounds, comforting the living and the dying. So, by the time she was sent to bed, Ximena didn't argue. She knew she had reached her limit.

She dragged herself to a cot in the corridors not far from the patients in case she was needed. But no sooner had she closed her eyes than she was startled awake by the explosions. The local women had displayed incredible stamina preparing for the battle, and yet many ended up huddled in a corner, crying and praying for the bombardment to stop. Ximena wanted to offer them a word of comfort, but she hadn't the strength.

The first day, there hadn't been many casualties. But on the second day, she knew the tide might change. Maloney rolled over in his cot, covering his ears to block out the sound of the shells raining down. He would have never made an artillerist, he'd said. But Ximena knew it was more than that. It was the agony of war itself the old man couldn't endure, and she wished she could take him far away from the chaos. She went over to him, coaxing him to get up and help take out those who'd died in their sleep. She feared they would need every cot and blanket available by day's end.

As she listened to the sounds of the raging battle, she was unable to distinguish whether the roar of the muskets and the booms of the cannons were coming from the Mexican Army or the Yanquis. She thought of John Riley, and as she rushed from one wounded man to the next, cleaning and dressing their injuries, her mind again and again kept turning to their outing in the country eating tunas. Or dancing at the fandango, his strong arms wrapped around her. These memories helped her get through the day.

She encouraged Maloney to think of happy moments as well, but he claimed he couldn't. Whenever he was asked to hold a man down for an amputation, Maloney would close his eyes and cry as if the limb being sawed off was his own. But he also cried when he was sent to load the dead onto the wagons, their glazed eyes fixed upon him as he buried their mutilated bodies in shallow graves. Still, Ximena was thankful for his help. Every able-bodied man was out on the battle-field and only the women were here assisting the two surgeons.

Throughout the day, more wounded were brought in, their shrieks and moans merging with the lamentations and supplications of the others until Ximena felt that her head was going to explode. There weren't enough bandages to staunch the blood, not enough gauze or sponges. When she knew Maloney couldn't take the blood and misery anymore, she sent him outside for some fresh air and to see if he could learn any news of the battle. He liked going to the cathedral where he could watch the fighting from the bell tower along with the priests. The day before, he'd rushed in to tell her that Taylor's howitzers and mortars were having no effect on the citadel, and together they had rejoiced to know John and his men were safe and their guns were tak-ing down anyone who came within range. She remembered back in

Matamoros when she'd gone to the fields to watch the morning drills. She imagined him now, pointing his sword at the Yankee troops and yelling "¡Fuego!"

In the afternoon, however, Maloney returned from the cathedral with devastating news.

"Och, *acushla*. The Yanks have taken Independence Hill and the Bishop's Palace. General Ampudia best be retakin' that western position as soon as possible. It commands the whole city. Now that the palace has fallen, what's to stop the Yankees?"

"We will stop them," Ximena said.

In the evening, when the firing ceased and they went out with a cart to collect the wounded, Ximena saw the Yanqui flag flying over the Bishop's Palace and shivered. She didn't want to think about what that meant. Instead, she focused on not slipping on the pools of blood and splattered brains as she walked over the mangled soldiers strewn on the streets, some with their hearts or entrails exposed. It was a field of carnage. Limbs scattered about, heads without bodies, bodies without legs or arms, eyes hanging from their sockets. Crushed bones crunched under her feet. Flies swarmed in black clouds. Stray dogs fought over severed limbs. The soldiers who writhed and howled in agony didn't frighten her. The ones that filled her with dread were those who lay on the cold ground gazing serenely at her as life seeped from their eyes and their ghastly wounds. They had resigned themselves to their unhappy fate and seemed to welcome their approaching death with an appalling calmness. By now, she had learned to let them be, to ignore the impulse to help them.

The dead had different expressions on their countenance, some smiling, others full of defiance, some placid, others frozen in rage. "Please, a drink, a drink of water!" the Yanqui soldiers cried as they clutched at her skirt. "¡Agua, por favor!" her countrymen wailed. She lowered the water gourd she carried over her shoulders and tended to both friend and foe alike.

She heard a wail of despair different from the others and turned to see a group of soldaderas searching the rubble. One of them was bending over her dead husband, yelling his name. As Ximena was about to go comfort her, the soldadera picked up her husband's musket and rushed down the street to where the Yanquis congregated, screaming something in her indigenous tongue. Musket fire was heard from where she disappeared, and everyone rushed to take cover. Had she been shot down? Or had she shot someone?

"You oughtn't be here," Maloney said as they hid behind the wagon. He patted her shoulder. "Go back to the hospital. Leave the gatherin' to me and the others."

She shook her head. "I'm fine."

She looked at the citadel in the distance. It was silent now, and she wished John would come to the city so she could see for herself that he was alive. His absence these past few days had made her heart fold up its petals like a tulip on a rainy day. It was wrong, she knew. He was not hers to long for, and it was an insult to Joaquín's memory. But she had lost everyone she loved, and at times she felt there was no reason to carry on. It was only when the Irishman looked at her with the desire he tried so hard to deny, and her heart awakened, unfurling in the heat of his gaze, that she remembered she was still alive.

"Is it frettin' yourself after him, you are?" Maloney asked. "The big fella can take care of himself right enough. And up in the citadel, he's safer than we are here below."

"Is he angry . . . angry with me?"

"No, jewel. He's cross with himself, he is." He patted her hand in understanding. Looking back at the street, he frowned and said, "Wait here, lass." He stepped over the bodies strewn along the street until he stood before a Yanqui soldier leaning against the wall of a house. "Begorra! If 'tisn't Kerr Delaney himself!" Bending down to touch the soldier, he let out a yelp when the soldier opened his eyes and asked for water.

"He's alive! Quick, give me a hand, lassie."

"Faith! Is that you, ould rascal?" the soldier said. "Heard ya went over to the other side,"

"Aye, I sure did. Don't talk now, Kerr, *a chara*. Let me tend to ya first."

After they loaded him onto the wagon and were walking back to the hospital, Maloney told Ximena about his friend. "He was in the hospital tent with me when the Yankees did this," he said, touching the HD on his forehead. "When he recovers, he'll join our side, he will."

"I hope it is so," she said.

When they got back, she and Maloney took care of the soldier, who was weakened from the loss of blood. A musket ball had pierced his thigh, but it had a clean exit and there had been no major injury to the muscle. "Och, you're one lucky Irishman!" Maloney said, giving his friend a sip of mezcal from his flask.

Ximena turned to leave so that they could chat while she tended to the other men, glad to see Maloney laughing again.

"Don't go, lassie, come listen to this story. Riley is goin' to get a good laugh when he hears this."

Delaney was a big, hairy man, his bushy beard as red as terracotta tiles. After Maloney presented her to him, Ximena listened to his story. He said that two nights before, while camping out at the pecan grove near the city, he and his comrades had sneaked into Captain Bragg's tent while the man was sound asleep. Ximena remembered that John and Maloney hated this man.

"We thought we'd have ourselves a bit of a bonfire, so we lit the fuse of an artillery shell," Delaney said. "We rolled it through the flap of Bragg's tent and ran away."

"Now, I know you didn't get him because I just saw the rascal firin' his guns upon the city," Maloney said, laughing. "But *ma bouchal*, tell us what happened next."

"Well then, after a minute or two, the shell exploded and his tent was blazin'. His friends came runnin' to the rescue and pulled him out, all covered in soot, his hair and furry eyebrows singed. His face looked as if he'd been sweepin' a chimney, I tell ya!"

Both men laughed. Ximena smiled, but she couldn't help feeling bad for the Yanqui officer. To be hated so much that his own men would try to kill him.

"By my soul, 'tis a great pity that all we managed to do was give the captain some wee cuts and a hole or two on his nightshirt," Delaney said, his eyes changing from dark to light green like leaves flickering in the wind.

"I bet he took it out on all of ye rapscallions," Maloney said.

"Aye, plenty of us got the gag put in our mouths."

"Faith, 'tis plain as plain the heart of that vile creature is blacker than bog water," Maloney said, shaking his head.

Ximena continued on with her duties, leaving the men to their stories, until finally, the wounded man was snoring away on his cot. Maloney, still sitting on his stool, kept watch over his friend.

On the third day, having lost the outer defenses and making no effort to recapture the strongholds, General Ampudia ordered his troops to fall back to the center of the city and abandon their positions, thus allowing the Yanquis to move in from the east and west completely uncontested. The only fort that hadn't fallen into the enemy's hands was the citadel. The shooting intensified and came so close that even the cries and moans of the wounded couldn't drown out the musket fire raging outside.

"The Yankees are blastin' through the houses!" Maloney said when he came back from the cathedral. Everyone listened as he told about the Mexican snipers up on the rooftops shooting at the Yanquis as they tried to make their way through the streets. But the enemy was smart. They eluded the snipers perched on the roofs by forcing their way through the houses, making holes on the adjoining walls from one house to the next with heavy pickaxes and crowbars, and thereby avoiding the streets—and the sharpshooters—altogether. "The city folk are gatherin' in the cathedral and the main plaza now," Maloney said. "They have nowhere else to go. But the Yankees have positioned two howitzers and a six-pound cannon on the rooftops and are pointin' them straight at the crowds."

Suddenly, an explosion shook the building. Before she could stop him, Maloney rushed out of the hospital to see what had happened.

"Let us pray," said one of the priests who was giving the holy sacraments to the dying. He dropped to his knees, and everyone else soon followed. Ximena pressed her hands together in prayer as the wailing of the people outside grew louder and louder. Then Maloney came in, his hat clutched in his hands, his face pale.

"Well, what ya waitin' for, ould fella? What in tarnation is happenin' out there?" Delaney yelled from his cot.

"The Yankees have damaged the cathedral with their mortar," he said, fighting back tears. "The fallin' stones crushed some of the civilians gathered there. They're buried in the rubble."

"But the cathedral has gunpowder!" Ximena said.

"One more blast and they'll blow us to smithereens," Delaney said.

"There is no safe place left in the city. Our Lord have mercy on us," Dr. Iñigo said. "General Ampudia is in the sacristy. I will plead with him to put an end to this madness." He hurried out of the building while everyone else braced themselves for what might come.

With their cannons bearing on the cathedral and the plaza mayor, the Yankee troops were in position to attack at first light. The firing ceased at dusk, and when Ximena left the Hospital del Rosario to see the damage for herself, rain was pouring down on the city, making it difficult for the locals to dig through the fallen stones for their dead and wounded, most of them women and children. The monks gathered in the San Francisco Temple next to the convent prayed and sang hymns. Their voices echoed against the buildings, and listening to them, Ximena found a little peace.

Around three in the morning, when things had finally settled down, they heard the distant sound of a bugle. Maloney rose from his cot and ran to see what was happening outside. When he returned, Ximena and Delaney were awake waiting for him. The three of them went to sit outside the hospital doors. The rain had ceased, and the air was cold. Ximena wrapped her rebozo around her tightly. Delaney had shed his Yanqui uniform and now wore a Mexican jacket that Maloney had taken from a fallen soldier. It stretched too tight on his burly frame, but at least it kept him warm.

"I saw Captain Moreno comin' out of the sacristy and bein' escorted to Taylor's headquarters with a flag of truce," Maloney said.

"Is possible Ampudia send him to . . . ?" Ximena didn't possess the English word for what she knew in her heart was about to happen.

"Surrender?" Maloney said.

"Surrender," she repeated, hating the taste of the word in her mouth, as foul and bitter as creosote tea.

20

September 1846
Monterrey, Nuevo León

In the end, the battle lasted three days.

Through his field glasses, Riley bore witness to the surrender of the citadel. After the capitulation of Monterrey, it was decided that he and the other Irish volunteers should abandon the black fortress. They came into the city and hid in civilian homes, out of sight of the Yankee general. Though the terms of the capitulation had protected Riley and the others from falling into the hands of the enemy, it was better that they not be present during the surrender of the strongest position in the city. Taylor might demand that every deserter be turned over to him at once. So now, at eleven in the morning, Riley and his gunners, along with the city's inhabitants, were obliged to watch from the rooftops as the Mexican flag was lowered and eight cannon blasts cut through the air, a final salute to the Mexican colors. The smoke rose in the wind and was carried off across the plains toward the towering mountains.

When General Ampudia had called back the troops two nights earlier, ordering that they abandon their posts and retreat to the main plaza, Riley knew it was folly to concentrate all his forces in the center of the city. His fellow foreign soldiers, as well as his Mexican comrades, believed that the army could hold off the attack and defend Monterrey. But the general wouldn't give ear to them.

Being a half mile away in the citadel, Riley didn't get to witness the fighting within the city, he only knew what he and his battery had done on the plains where they were stationed. For three days, Riley and his gunners had fired the cannons from the citadel relentlessly, tearing into the blue columns marching double-quick time toward Monterrey. They killed or wounded many who came within range, forcing the Yanks to march over their fallen comrades as they rushed to attack the city. With his own eyes, he saw the dozens and dozens of mangled bodies scattered across the plain, soldiers that he and his gunners had literally stopped dead in their tracks with their canister shot. The Mexican lancers finished off whatever troops Riley's men had managed to disperse, spearing the enemy while Riley's guns kept sweeping the plains, raining metal on those who tried to hide in the cornfields. The vultures and the coyotes did the rest.

But Taylor's troops had pushed past into the city through the other points of entry, taking the northeastern part of Monterrey the first day, the western part the second. They took possession of the higher ground—Fort Tenería, Fort Diablo, and the Bishop's Palace—and the Mexican troops had fled, their own guns turned against them. On the third night, orders came to the gun crews at the citadel to hold their fire and hang the white flag from the ramparts. Dismayed that Ampudia was seeking to arrange a twenty-four-hour armistice with Taylor, the batteries in the black fortress didn't silence their guns immediately. The citadel cannons had been the first to open fire, and they were the last to grow silent. Riley's only consolation was that the Yanks never took the citadel.

Later, after General Ampudia had sent one of his officers to solicit a parley, he claimed that in doing so he was putting an end to the distress of Monterrey's citizens and preventing their slaughter. The cathedral was filled with ammunition and one more blast from the enemy's cannons would have blown it to pieces, killing countless innocent people. Ampudia claimed it was for their sake that he was compromising Mexico's honor. The truth was that the general had greatly underestimated the Yanks and had been outwitted.

Now here they were, witnessing this humiliating moment when the enemy's colors were hoisted up on the staff to fly over Monterrey. A cannon was fired by the Yankees, then another and another. All around him, cannons belched and recoiled in salute of the twenty-eight states that were part of the American constellation. Riley watched as the Mexicans marched out of the citadel and the Yankee troops marched in shouting their hurrahs and playing their patriotic tunes. He could scarcely hear the music, but in his head, "Yankee Doodle" played again and again, mocking him.

Afterward, Riley made his way to the hospital to check on his wounded men and speak with Maloney. Questions swirled in his head. What would his countrymen say about the capitulation of Monterrey? Would they regret joining the Mexican ranks? Would they blame him? As his horse forced its way over the rubble littering the streets and shell fragments, Riley couldn't help but mourn the injury inflicted upon this beautiful city, the white stone streets stained red, the fallen trees, homes with crumbled walls and doors riddled with bullets, shattered windows and ruined balconies. The grief-stricken civilians were walking about, searching for their loved ones while others were loading what they could of their possessions onto their mules or their own backs. Riley wished to close his eyes to the devastation. What had been gained from these calamities—a premature surrender of the city?

At least the terms of the surrender had spared him and his men from their worst fear—being captured by the Yanks, which would have meant sure death. General Taylor had agreed that all Mexican forces would be allowed to withdraw from the city with their arms and a six-gun battery. He agreed to not pursue the Mexican troops for eight weeks. So Riley and his men would be allowed to march out of the city in the ranks of the Mexican Army of the North. At least for now, the deserters were safe.

As he neared the cathedral, a crowd of civilians were gathered around it. Riley winced at the sight of destruction inflicted upon this holy place of God, with its damaged clock tower and marred facade. But then he realized what the crowd was looking at. The Texas Rangers, violating the terms of the truce, were committing atrocious acts, filing in and out of the cathedral on their horses as if it were nothing more than a stable. They came out carrying crucifixes, sacred vessels, wax figures of the Virgin Mother and Child, and religious paintings . One of them was dressed in the sacred vestments, another was banging on the organ inside, pealing forth the most grotesque sounds. The townspeople pleaded for them to stop. The priests and monks on their knees, with a crucifix in hand, begged them to cease their barbarity and respect the house of the Lord. But they simply laughed and continued their plundering.

Riley now knew how his people must have felt when Oliver Cromwell invaded Ireland two centuries earlier, desecrating its churches, using them as stables. The seething rage. The impotence. He heard someone shouting.

"Ye infernal scoundrels! 'Tis sacrilege what you're doin'! May the curse of God be upon ye!"

Even before he turned to look, he knew who it was. Maloney emerged from the crowd with a musket in hand and rushed at the Rangers. Riley tried to stop him but couldn't get through the onlookers quickly enough. Before he could reach his friend, Maloney fired at the Rangers, killing one of them. The Rangers all trained their deadly six-shooters on the old man, pouring their bullets into him until they were spent. Riley halted his horse and watched as Maloney's blood spread over the ground. The Rangers reloaded and pointed their Colt revolvers at the onlookers.

"Who's next?" they yelled. "Who wants to try to stop us?"

The crowd fled, and Riley took advantage of the chaos to try to turn his horse around before the Rangers spotted him. Suddenly, Ximena was there, and seeing Maloney slain on the ground, she screamed. She pushed her way through the crowd, rushing to where he lay, but Riley hastened to intercept her. The Rangers would kill her. He knew it, and when he blocked her path and she looked up at him, she seemed to know it, too, for she reached for his hand. He pulled her up onto his horse and together they galloped away.

When they reached the Río Santa Catarina, they dismounted and she broke down, sobbing.

"Whist, lass, Whist. We'll make them pay for this. I swear it."

They sat by the riverbank and leaned against a boulder, the Sierra Madre range towered over them. Riley realized he no longer wished to live in this city, never wanted to return. Ximena stopped crying, but she wouldn't utter a word. She stared at the river in dreary stillness and scarcely seemed to breathe. It affrighted him so much that he cupped her chin and turned her face to his.

"Look at me, lass," he said. "I know you loved the ould fella. He loved you as well, and he wouldn't be happy to see you fallin' asunder on account of him. He'd want you to be strong, to carry on. You hear me?"

She nodded gently. He pulled her into his arms, and it was as if he were gathering an armful of wild lavender and other fragrant herbs, for her delicate aroma was a healing balm on his spirit. They sat there by the river watching the current swirl and glide past them. A crane swooped overhead and fluttered over the surface of the water, and Riley felt the gust of its flapping wings stirring the air. They beheld its flight as it ascended once again, weaving through the clouds tinged in gold from the afternoon sun until it was just a speck in the sky.

"We will lose the war now, yes? The land is lost. And my husband and grandmother are gone, and now Jimmy is gone too."

"Nay. We've lost a battle, not the war. We will carry on, keep fightin' in their honor."

She turned to face him, and he took out his handkerchief and wiped the lingering tears on her face. Her eyes red with sorrow. Her hair disheveled. And yet, she shone with a fierce beauty that over-whelmed him.

She cupped his face, her fingers caressing his cheeks, tracing the outline of his bottom lip. With a groan, his mouth fell on hers, and she responded with the same ardor. He could taste the salt in her tears, the bitterness of her grief, then it all faded into the honeyed sweetness of her desire for him. And he wanted to drink more of her nectar.

But he tore away from her, suddenly gasping for breath. "Arrah! We mustn't. 'Tis wrong—"

She took out the red rosary beads she wore around her neck and put her fingers over them, her voice serene and comforting, like a warm embrace. "Creo en Dios, Padre todopoderoso, creador del cielo y de la tierra . . ."

He leaned his forehead against hers, and he took her hands and the beads into his. "*Et in Iesum Christum, Filium eius unicum, Dominum nostrum, qui conceptus est de Spiritu Sancto, natus ex Maria Virgine . . .*"

They held each other in mutual sorrow, whispering their prayers over the rosary, until they could feel Maloney's spirit take flight. A peace settled over them. He held her in his arms a little longer until finally they found the strength to get up and bury their dead.

21

The following day, Riley joined the two-hundred-plus gunners lining up in columns at the rear of General Ampudia's 1st Brigade as they prepared to leave the city. Over the course of the next few days, a division would march out of the city to San Luis Potosí, three hundred miles distant, where they would meet their new commander—General Antonio López de Santa Anna. News had reached them that the former president of the republic had returned from exile and taken command of the army. Ampudia was to assemble what remained of his troops and join Santa Anna. Once again, Ampudia had been demoted, and this time, Riley had no doubt that he deserved it.

Riley was desperate to get away from the citadel and from the sight of the Yankee flag flying over it, from the graveyard where they'd buried Maloney rolled up in nothing but a blanket for want of a coffin, from the plains still littered with rotting corpses of humans and animals, from the shattered homes and ruined cathedral. He walked past the columns and took his place on one of the horse-drawn caissons carrying the six cannons they were allowed to take with them. They were leaving behind twenty-five field pieces to the Yanks. Thinking about Ximena in the rear of the columns among the surgeons' wagons, Riley wished she was here by his side so that he could watch over her.

As the artillery waited for their turn to move out, Riley looked at the main plaza and the rooftops where thousands of civilians stood to see them off. They had lost their homes and possessions, their loved ones and their city. What cruel indignities would Taylor's troops commit upon them, especially when those devils, the Texas Rangers, would be free to roam wild in the city and murder and plunder as they pleased? He could sense the fear of the wretched inhabitants, or perhaps it was his own fear at the thought of the Yankees lined up outside the walls of Monterrey to watch the defeated Mexican troops evacuate the city.

The bugles sounded the advance and the infantry and the cavalry moved out. Then, finally the artillery rolled out down the cobblestoned street to the rhythm of drums and the blaring of trumpets. Riley kept his eyes looking forward and tried not to look at the people as they wept and waved goodbye. "¡Adios, Colorados! God be with you," they said as they waved their handkerchiefs at Riley and his men. Los Colorados, the red ones, was what the civilians had called them ever since Matamoros due to the men's red hair and ruddy complexion.

As they approached the outer edge of the city, the Yanks came into view. Riley held himself erect and kept his eyes glued on the sierras up ahead. But from the corner of his eye, he could see them. On either side of the Saltillo road, the Yanks stood, watching as the artillery columns marched past. At least half of the Mexican artillery was composed of deserters from the US Army, and Riley heard the Yanks hissing insults at him and his countrymen. Fear gripped him. If the Yankees offered them some violence, would he be able to protect his men?

Riley did his best to ignore their reproaches. As he took in the Yanks' disheveled appearance, their dirty, tattered uniforms, the fatigue and shock in their eyes, he cursed General Ampudia's rash decision to give up the city. They could have beaten the Yanks, he was sure of it. And now, here they were in full retreat. There was nothing he could do about the insults being hurled at him as the Yanks realized that he—John Riley, a deserter—had been behind the cannons pouring grape and shell on them from the citadel.

"You goddamn traitors!"

"God damn you, turncoats!"

"Irish sons of bitches!"

He recognized some soldiers from his old unit, Captain Merrill standing beside them. Riley looked away then, not wanting to make eye contact with his former commanding officer. But he heard someone, perhaps even the captain himself, yell, "I'm gonna shoot this cowardly cur!"

He fought the impulse to lower his face and hide his eyes beneath the brim of his shako. Instead, he thought of Ximena, her soft lips, her warm breath on his face. He clung to her image even more when, on the other side of the road, Braxton Bragg, James Duncan, and the other artillery officers stood by. From the looks they were now giving him, and the way they gripped the hilt of their swords, Riley knew that they would gladly bury the blade into his heart if given the chance. He thought it was unfortunate that during the battle, Bragg's crew had been fighting within the city, too far from the citadel and Riley's guns. He would have loved to have had another shot at the pompous Yankee.

Bragg spat toward Riley, "I should have run you through when I had the chance back in Matamoros, Mick!"

And I you, Riley thought as the columns left the Yanks and their maledictions behind in a cloud of dust.

The interminable days passed one after the other, as they toiled along through dry country to San Luis Potosí, half-dead from starvation and exhaustion, ravaged by illness and despair. Vultures circled above them. Soldiers fainted beneath the weight of their weapons and knapsacks and fell out of rank to be left behind on the roadside. Some tossed aside their arms and cartridge boxes, discarded their useless equipment, their clothing. Cases of ammunition and supplies were abandoned when one by one the pack mules and the oxen pulling the carts broke down from the rigors of the miserable march. The road was littered with dead or dying soldiers, ruined horses and mules. But the worst sight was of the women and children accompanying the men. They remained on the ground where they collapsed, Riley could hear their wails of sorrow and despair, see their hands reaching out as the artillery troops marched past them, their features distorted in a painful surrender to death. He willed himself not to look at their woebegone expressions, their tongues, blackened and swollen. He'd wished they'd stayed home, that they hadn't followed their husbands only to suffer a miserable fate. But by now he'd learned that Mexican women—mothers, wives, daughters—accompanied their men whithersoever they went, even if it meant dying of sunstroke, hunger, or thirst alongside them.

Choking on dust and grit, he kept his mind fixed on the road ahead and the city that lay beyond, as his fair skin blistered under the unforgiving sun. They trudged past dry arroyos and uncultivated land, arid landscapes lacking pasturage for the animals. With dust devils swirling around them in the hot wind, Riley searched for a patch of greenery to rest the eye upon, something to break the dreary sameness. His mind tormented him with images of raindrops sliding down blades of clover, morning dew quivering on cabbage leaves, ice glittering on yew boughs.

At about sundown, bugles sounded the halt and the exhausted columns dispersed and settled in for the night off the side of the road. Riley went in search of Ximena at the rear, where the wounded and the weak struggled to keep up. He wished he could have spared her the march through this parched desolation. He found her wrapping cactus pads sliced in half on the wounds of those being carried in the wagons, but they were too numerous, dying by the dozen each day from lack of medicine and from other privations. Some, driven by desperation, had committed suicide, but most were succumbing to hunger and thirst. She had neither food nor water to give them. None of them did. And his canteen was empty by now.

When he saw Ximena, his concern grew. Despite her large straw hat, her face was dusty and begrimed, her eyes red and sunken, her lips parched and blistered. He could see the remnants of a trail of dried tears on both cheeks.

" 'Tis no point in cryin'," he said as he untied the buckskin strings and removed her hat. Then he gently wiped her face with his handkerchief. "Water is a precious commodity at the moment, and you shouldn't give your tears to the desert."

She wrapped her rebozo around her, and the anger and defiance he usually saw in her eyes had been replaced with resignation. He carefully folded her into his arms. She was so thin now, he was afraid he might break her. He wished he had something to give her that would erase the haunted look in her eyes.

"It is a terrible way to die, John," she said. "This hunger, I feel like a . . . a zopilote is eating me inside."

"Zopilote?"

She pointed in the distance, where the sky was thick with buzzards circling over the dead they had left behind.

"Hang in there, lass. We will soon arrive in the city."

"Ampudia gave up Monterrey to protect the people and the soldiers. But this is hell. Too much death. Here on this road. Not in battle, with honor."

"Aye, it would've been better. No soldier ever wants to die in a humiliatin' retreat. I had always hoped that when my time came, I'd die fightin' for my country, in the glory of death on a battlefield. Not like this, fatigued beyond conception and on the verge of starvin', so close to despair. No, not like this." They looked at the setting sun, the silhouettes of the shrubs and cacti stark against the crimson sky. Up and down the dirt road, he could see the flickering campfires of each corps, a short distance from one another. The fires were small, for there was not much firewood to be found except for clumps of scraggly sagebrush. The cavalry had been forced to burn their lance handles and the infantry the butts of their muskets.

"Walk with me?" he asked her.

They made their way beyond the camps, deeper into the vastness of the land. A colony of bats flew across the sky looking for food. Riley wondered if they would have better luck finding nourishment from the arid brushland than the troops would. Ximena took a deep breath and sighed. She turned to him, caressed his face, and he winced at her touch, his scorched skin not able to bear it.

"The sun has no mercy for you," she said.

" 'Tis a hard place for us Irish to be sure. I've never seen so much of the sun as I have seen in the time I've been in your country."

"Come." She led him to a nearby spiky plant and took out her knife. He'd seen her use this aloe to treat the burns of the wounded. She cut off a leaf and sliced it open, revealing a clear gel inside, which she rubbed on his face and neck. Instantly, the burning on his skin was soothed. He licked a drop of the gel by his mouth and quickly spit it out. It was so bitter.

"You can eat it," she said. "But I need to wash."

She cut more of it and put them inside her bag. She turned to look back at the wagons full of sick soldiers, at the unsheltered troops sleeping off the side of the road. "If my Nana was here, she know how to save them."

"Nay, she wouldn't have attended to them better than you are under the circumstances. Those men are in want of nourishment and drink." He thought about the small parties that had been dispatched to search for water. "Word is tomorrow we will finally reach a well. We can satisfy our thirst. Water our horses. You can wash wounds and make your remedies."

"I hope we get there," she said. "So many men give up and die. This is like Matamoros?"

"Aye. 'Twas a dreadful march. But this one is worse—we're carryin' the heavy burden of a second defeat and humiliation. 'Tis twice as hard. And what distresses me more is the heavy sorrow of havin' lost yet another friend, of havin' buried him—uncoffined, poor fella!—in a place I'll never return to and where he'll remain forever in a forgotten grave. Who will say a prayer for him? Who will bring him flowers?"

She took his hand in hers and squeezed it. "He watches over us. His spirit is here with us. His body is in Monterrey, not his soul."

He contemplated her words for a moment. They looked at each other, and they sought each other's lips. Their kiss was tender at first, soft, and cautious, but then, Ximena gripped him closer to her with a strength he thought she no longer possessed. Her breasts pressed against his thick uniform. He growled under his breath as his mouth matched her hunger for hunger, want for want. She tasted as if she'd been drenched in seawater, her lips parting for him like the shell of an oyster, beckoning him inside. He wanted to take her, right here, in the middle of nowhere. Instead he tore away.

"Ximena, listen to—"

"Shhh," she put a finger on his mouth to silence him. "When the war is over, you be with your wife and son, and I go to my rancho. I promise. But now, there is a war, and I am alone. And you are alone, too, no?"

"I don't want to hurt you, lass."

She spread out her shawl on the ground, and then pulled her blouse down beyond her shoulders, her breasts illuminated with the silver glow of the stars above. *Sweet Jesus*. His knees weakened, from desire or hunger or both. He groaned and pulled her blouse back up and held her. That was all he would allow himself to do. The noises from the camp faded away, and all that remained was the two of them under the brilliance of the night sky. If only he could love her as she ought to be loved, but he was not free to do so.

Part Three

The Eagle and the Shamrock

22

October 1846
San Luis Potosí

It took three brutal weeks for the Army of the North to cover the three hundred miles from Monterrey to San Luis Potosí, and the troops staggered into the city scarcely alive. But there was no time to settle down and recover from their toilsome journey. The remnants of Ampudia's army were lined up at the plaza for review. There they were greeted by the new commander of the Mexican Army—General Antonio López de Santa Anna, who was back in the country after being exiled in Cuba.

Riley observed Santa Anna as he surveyed the troops, seated on a handsome stallion, proud and erect, his silver stirrups and high saddle inlaid with gold glinted in the sunlight. He was dressed in a resplendent blue and red uniform embroidered with gold thread and decorated with epaulets and medals. From what Riley had heard, Santa Anna had not only led the Mexican Army against the Spaniards, the French, and the Texians, but had also been president of Mexico eight different times. A hero to some and a scoundrel to others, he was in his early fifties, with his entire career marked by intrigue and corruption. But the one thing everyone agreed on was his valor on the battlefield, and he had a wooden leg to prove it.

After the review, Santa Anna called a meeting with his council of war, where he berated Ampudia for the loss of Monterrey. General Mejía didn't translate for Riley all that was said, but there was no need. The commander was in a furious passion. Ampudia spoke quickly and, from what Riley could catch of the Spanish, was simply repeating what he'd told the troops back in Monterrey—that he'd surrendered to prevent further injury to innocent people. Though Riley believed his words had merit, he suspected that Ampudia had not been worried solely for the people's safety. No, first and foremost, the general had saved himself.

"It was an honorable capitulation," Ampudia insisted.

"¡Basta! There's nothing honorable in a capitulation, ¡imbécil!" Santa Anna spat, ripping off the gilded epaulets on Ampudia's uniform, proceeding to chastise him further. Ampudia swallowed his words and lowered his head.

Riley had learned from General Mejía that their new commander was drafting the men in the city and the surrounding areas and had sent an order out to all the states to send him their forces. Santa Anna planned to build the biggest army Mexico had ever seen. "The next time we face the enemy, we will run them off our land once and for all," he said. The boundary between Mexico and the United States will be determined by me—and the muzzles of our cannons."

Throughout the following days, Riley learned more about the general from Juan Cortina and Ximena. Neither of them liked or trusted the man. They talked about the Texas Rebellion that Santa Anna had failed to suppress and the bitter times that followed. Later that week, Riley found himself being observed by the commander-in-chief during morning drills. In the days that followed, Santa Anna would come out to watch him training the artillery crews to man the cannons. Riley wasn't surprised when, by the week's end, he was summoned to the government's palace and escorted to the general's headquarters.

"His Excellency, the commander-in-chief, will see you now, teniente Riley," Santa Anna's aide-de-camp said to him. As he walked into the room, General Mejía smiled and beckoned him over.

Santa Anna stood by his desk wearing a white uniform covered in gold—gold galloon, gold epaulets, gold silk sash, and gold buttons engraved with the Mexican eagle. His black hair was perfectly groomed, and despite his sallow complexion, the general was quite a striking man—elegant, poised, and taller than many of his compatriots. He was sporting a walking cane with a golden handle in the shape of an eagle with ruby eyes.

The general didn't speak English well, but General Mejía was there to offer his services.

"I have heard great things about you, teniente Riley," Santa Anna said, giving Riley a wide smile and a firm embrace. Riley was taller than the general by four inches, and yet he felt dwarfed by the man's stance, full of confidence and regal authority.

" 'Tis an honor to fight for you, General," Riley said. By now he knew that many of the officers in the Mexican Army were men of fortune who had gotten their commissions through family ties or political connections, not because of their skills and knowledge of the military profession. He'd heard that some generals had attained that rank without ever passing through the lower ranks. But the man who stood before him was different. Santa Anna began his military career at fourteen as a cadet and saw action as young as seventeen. He had risen in rank through sagacity and savage determination. Despite what anyone said were the general's failings, Riley believed Santa Anna was likely to prove to be a formidable foe to the Yankee generals. With him, Mexico might stand a chance.

The general poured himself a glass of brandy and another for Riley. Then he said something and waited for General Mejía to translate. "The commander wants to know how you are liking our country."

Before Riley could answer, Santa Anna interjected in his limited English. "Good food, no? Pretty señoritas?" He laughed.

Riley thought of Ximena, the gleam of starlight upon her breasts. It'd taken every ounce of willpower to resist, but the image had haunted him every night since. He shook his head to free himself of it.

General Mejía and Santa Anna chuckled and exchanged glances. "Ah, I see that our women have made a great impression on you already."

Riley took a drink of the brandy and felt his throat burn. He let the alcohol relax him and said. "I have eyes, and I've had occasion to observe the beauty of which you speak, your Excellency. I cannot deny there are many beauties in your country. But I have a wife back home, and I won't forget my duty as a husband."

"And so you won't. Wives are meant to be treasured, but we must not deny ourselves a little pleasure once in a while, especially when we are at war. When you live your life one day to the next not knowing if you will live or die, a woman's arms can be of great comfort. Don't you agree?"

"The love of a woman is indeed a great gift."

The general took a seat behind his desk and placed his cane beside him. He motioned for Riley to take a seat as well. General Mejía came to stand behind the commander to continue translating for him. "Tell me, Lieutenant, what made you desert the Yanqui army? Why are you here in Mexico?"

Riley was surprised at the commander's bluntness, but he knew that the general had every right to ask. He, too, would be wary of foreigners in his ranks. "I assure you, General, that even though I'm a turncoat and I have violated my oath to the United States, I'm not a man who easily abandons his obligations. My loyalties are with Mexico."

Santa Anna waved his words away. "I understand, teniente Riley, believe me, I do. I've been a turncoat as well, several times in fact. I've been a royalist and an insurgent, a federalist and a centralist, a liberal and a conservative, but I always had a reason. Still, that's not why I'm asking. Your countrymen intrigue me. We've never had so many deserters in our ranks. We have a tradition of welcoming foreigners into our army—British, French, even the damn Yanquis fought in our War of Independence against Spain, but they were not deserters, as you are."

"I don't speak for my countrymen, but for myself—though most of my men share the same sentiments—I believe Mexico could turn into another Ireland, sir, and be forced to suffer under the oppression of an invading Anglo-Saxon Protestant nation. I wasn't able to help my country. I desire to help yours in its hour of peril."

"I see. And I'm grateful for your service, Lieutenant, and your loyalty. Mexico has had its share of wars. There have been other countries that have come here to try to plunder her riches and her beauty. I myself have led my country against invaders before, and as you can see from my mutilated leg, I have purchased my country's freedom with my own flesh." The general poured himself, Mejía, and Riley another glass of brandy before continuing. "Now once again the national honor has been entrusted to me, and I assure you that we will defeat the Yanquis. Just like we defeated the Spaniards and the French. Mexico belongs to the Mexican people. Perhaps one day you can say the same about the land of your birth."

"May I live to see that day, sir, if that is God's will." Riley left his drink on the desk, hoping he didn't insult his host by declining a second glass, and waited for the general to reveal why he'd been summoned.

"I've received a letter from the Yanqui general. He's terminating the armistice he negotiated with General Ampudia. So it won't be long now before he advances to San Luis Potosí. My generals tell me that you and your countrymen did an outstanding job in Monterrey. And based on what I've seen with my own eyes during your daily drills, I want more men like you in our ranks. There are many foreigners in the enemy's ranks with military experience, and we need to get more of them to join us. Enough to form an artillery unit of foreign soldiers under Irish leadership. Think of it, John Riley and his battalion. What shall we name it? And, as befitting a unit, you shall have your own banner."

Riley sat forward at the edge of his seat and glanced up at Mejía, who seemed as surprised and pleased by the news as he was. A unit of deserters with their own colors? No, he had never considered such a possibility. So far, he and his men had been serving in regular army units, though he had been given free rein in training them. He put his hand in his pocket and took out the shamrock Franky Sullivan had whittled, and the image of a banner appeared in his mind's eye, the same banner of freedom that he wished to see unfurled over his native soil. It would be as green as the fields of the Emerald Isle, with a shamrock on one side and its patron saint on the other. "The Saint Patrick's Battalion," he said. "That shall be the name."

"¡Excelente! El Batallón de San Patricio," Santa Anna said. Mejía nodded his approval.

"We'll need more men for what you propose, sir," Riley said, keeping his excitement in check.

"That is where you come in." Santa Anna caressed the golden eagle on the hilt of his cane and said, "You will make sure that your countrymen learn of the Saint Patrick's Battalion. When they hear of you—its Irish leader—it will inspire them to abandon their ranks in the Yanqui army and come fight for us. Do you think you can achieve that, teniente Riley?"

"Aye, sir, I believe I can." A unit composed of only foreign soldiers would be a powerful attraction to his countrymen and others in the Yankee ranks. If he put out the call, the men would come. Hadn't some of them done so back in Matamoros and Monterrey? The plan to organize a foreign legion composed solely of deserters was brilliant. Riley had no doubt that the men would listen to his call. He only prayed the Mexicans would win the war, for otherwise, he would have his men's blood on his hands, turning out to be nothing but a Pied Piper who led his own countrymen to their deaths.

"¡Excelente! It is settled then," Santa Anna said, standing up. "I will designate capitán Moreno as your commander. He'll allow you to organize and train el Batallón de San Patricio as you see fit. Once the battalion proves its worth, I shall personally see to it that you're promoted."

Riley liked Moreno, who had been born and reared in Florida. He could speak English as well as Spanish, and they'd become friends. "I understand, sir. And I feel much obliged to you, sir, for the faith you have placed in me."

"I assure you, teniente Riley, Mexico won't disappoint you. We're a republic of fighters and aren't afraid to stand up to oppressors. We will defeat the Yanqui invaders, even if I have to lose my other leg. Or my very life. Defending Mexico is a sacred cause, and I thank you for your services to this great nation. Together, we shall put an end to the national agony."

"Perhaps one day, your Excellency, you will help Ireland attain its freedom," Riley said.

"Of course. We are brethren, are we not? Our Catholic faith is a bond that is as strong as blood."

Riley saluted his commander with newfound appreciation. Cortina and Ximena had warned him to be careful, and he would be, but it was difficult not to believe in him. The Saint Patrick's Battalion—he loved the sound of it.

When he was dismissed, Riley headed to the Temple of Our Lady del Carmen a few blocks distant, made of Mexican cantera stone that glowed pink in the afternoon sun. Ximena had taken to praying there in the afternoons and though his schedule rarely allowed him time to join her, that day, he was desperate to see her. He wanted her to be the first to hear the news of his meeting with Santa Anna.

As he traversed the plaza fronting the palace, he fancied himself there with Ximena, listening to the ballads being played by the musicians on the kiosk, the Spanish lyrics a string of sighs. Men and women out for a stroll dressed in their elegant finery greeted him—the dons in their embroidered jackets, tipped their broad-brimmed hats at him; the doñas lowered their lacy fans to reward him with a smile. "Buenas tardes, teniente," they said.

"Buenas tardes," Riley responded. Even after all these months, he was still shocked at how the Mexican aristocrats treated him. Previously, a man like him knew only scorn and disdain from the higher classes, but now he found himself being treated like a human being. And it wasn't for his skills, he knew that. Mexico was a land where skin ranged in colors, from the deepest brown to the palest pink. He'd not seen anything like it. His fair skin and blue eyes had never afforded him either privileges or admiration before.

He passed the busy cafés, fondas, and shops. Unlike the Río Grande region, this old city, surrounded by mountains with gold and silver mines and a population of sixty thousand souls, had pleasant weather year-round and, best of all, no dreadful humidity. This is why Riley was not surprised to see the streets teeming with people. As he stood before the doors of the temple, stone angels hovered above him, carved into the intricate facade. He entered the temple and was at once overwhelmed by the ornate gilded retablos rising high above him, the decorated pulpits, and the glassy eyes of saints watching him from their pedestals. He wasn't used to so much opulence and grandeur. For a moment, he missed the humble chapel in Clifden, whose stones were covered in moss, not gold leaf.

Making the sign of the cross, he waited for his eyes to adjust to the dimness inside before searching for Ximena among the kneeling figures. Silently, he made his way to the front until he spotted her before the golden altar of the Virgin. Like all Mexican women, she wore a long shawl over her shoulders, and her black hair was woven into an intricate braid that wrapped over her head like a crown. Not wanting to disturb her, he knelt a few paces behind, but she must have sensed him staring at her because she turned around and her eyes widened in surprise.

"John!" she said, a little too loudly. Her voice—his name—echoing against the golden walls of the church. She blushed, and he could tell she'd forgotten where she was. *Methinks the lass is happy to see the likes of you, John Riley*, he thought, and despite himself, he grinned like a lovesick schoolboy.

"I beg pardon for distractin' you from your prayers," he whispered.

"You aren't," she said. "I was thinking about Jimmy, about how much he loved to pray."

"Aye, he was a pious man. A true believer." Suddenly he no longer wanted to be in there, especially not under the watchful eyes of the saints and Jesus. Though he had not acted upon his longings for Ximena, just having them was sinful enough. "Would you like to take a stroll in the square?"

She nodded, and he offered her his arm as they headed out into the sunny afternoon. A flock of doves was circling above the church. Riley took in the beauty of the temple domes, with their tiles of blue, green, yellow, and white glinting under the Mexican sky.

"It's a beautiful church, isn't it?" Ximena asked as they walked toward the plaza. More people were coming out now to enjoy the afternoon breeze.

"Aye, 'tis truly magnificent, but even more impressive is the cathedral yonder," he said, pointing to the Catedral Metropolitana just a block away. "I've never seen so many majestic churches in my life. Nay, I have never seen so many churches, to be sure!"

"You do not have in Ireland?"

"Many of our ancient churches and temples were destroyed and defiled. And several of our cathedrals were stolen from us by the Protestant sassenachs during the Reformation." He told her about the Penal Laws against Catholics, and how it'd been only seventeen years since the last of them were ended by the great Daniel O'Connell's campaign for Catholic Emancipation. With the Irish people stripped of their rights and persecuted for practicing their faith, not many large stone places of worship had been built until recently. "But one day, I hope, the Green Isle can once again become a land of cathedrals, shrines, and convents, just like Mexico. And be restored to its days of glory."

"I pray for it, John."

He took his eyes off the cathedral and turned to look at Ximena. "I had a meetin' with General Santa Anna, lass. He's givin' me my own company—the Saint Patrick's Battalion. I'll be fightin' under my own banner now!"

Ximena listened attentively as he relayed the details of the meeting, but he could tell she had reservations

"Are you not pleased for me?"

"Perdón. I do not wish to ruin your happiness. To have your own company is important to you, I know, and you deserve it. But be careful with Santa Anna. Do not sacrifice your honor for him."

"I appreciate your concern, Ximena. Truly, I do. And I shall be careful. But for now, the commander has afforded me this opportunity, and I won't lie to you, 'tis the best thing that has ever happened to me in my military career. I believe in my soul I can prove to him 'tis not folly to put his trust in me."

"I understand. Now, tell me, your banner."

"Will you sew it for me?"

She laughed. "My grandmother taught me to stitch flesh. Fabric not so much. Don't worry, the nuns at the convent have excellent sewing. I will ask them to make for you."

"You think they'll help me? I have the design already. I can see it plain in my head." He closed his eyes and said, "There . . . it flies over my cannons!"

"Tell me, tell me what it looks like!"

"It is green, as green as my isle, and embroidered on it are the words that will forever be etched on my heart: *Erin Go Bragh*."

"What it means, John?"

"Ireland forever!"

Unable to control himself, he lifted her aloft and twirled her around. She let out a yelp of surprise, and some of the passersby stopped and gave them disapproving looks, but he didn't care.

23

Over the course of the weeks, Santa Anna's army began to take shape. Many states of Mexico, including Jalisco, Michoacán, Guanajuato, Aguascalientes, and San Luis Potosí provided all the troops and supplies they could. But Riley was surprised that other states hesitated to fulfill their duty in supporting the campaign; some, such as Durango and Zacatecas, refused to send reinforcements altogether. It baffled him that instead of uniting and cooperating to defeat the enemy to the north, some state leaders were allowing their animosity for Santa Anna to cloud their judgment, looking for any pretext to oust him. The governor of Zacatecas, a rival of Santa Anna, had even tried to get a group of states to form an alliance against him, going so far as to proclaim that he would rather see the Yankees win the war than to see Santa Anna triumph. Riley was perplexed. This was their chance to defeat the invaders and get them out of their country. Why couldn't the Mexican leaders see that and put their squabbles aside to unite for this single cause?

With the federal government providing a minimum of resources, Santa Anna had been compelled to mortgage his own properties to have enough funds for his army. Yet, there wasn't enough food, clothing, weapons, or ammunition to train the men, so progress was slow.

Santa Anna forced a loan from the Church, and due to great opposition from the clergy, he only got a part of what he'd requested. Still, the general persisted in his efforts to raise an army. Riley couldn't help but admire him, for in no time at all, he had built up his troops to more than twenty thousand men.

As Riley and Santa Anna had predicted, once news of the Saint Patrick's Battalion got out, deserters flocked to its standard. Every day foreign soldiers arrived in San Luis Potosí after having separated themselves from Taylor's forces still stationed in Monterrey and Camargo. Santa Anna put out the call to all Mexican civilians to aid these foreigners and deliver them to him. Rancheros and priests were largely responsible for guiding the deserters safely across the deserts and mountains to San Luis Potosí. Riley soon had more than one hundred and fifty men in his unit—mostly Irish, some Germans, with a sprinkling of Scots, French, Poles, Italians, and Prussians, three runaway slaves, and even an Englishman. Capitán Moreno and Riley welcomed the new recruits together, but trusting Riley's gunnery skills, the captain allowed him to organize and train the gun crews and wagon teams to man the caissons and the 16- and 24-pounders that Santa Anna had turned over to them. With the brand-new Saint Patrick's Battalion banner— which he'd taken to the church to be blessed—flying in the breeze, Riley drilled the recruits daily until he was satisfied with their speed and precision. He shouted his instructions in English, Irish, Latin, and even German, using the few phrases he'd learned, and timed his crews as they hitched the cannons to the horse-drawn wagons, hauled them to specific spots, and fired practice rounds. As he watched the drills taking place under his green banner, Riley couldn't have been prouder of what he'd accomplished.

And yet his mind was troubled. General Santa Anna had secured 21,553 men for his army, but that gave him an advantage only in numbers. The Mexican rank and file was, by and large, composed of prisoners or barefoot and ragged Indian conscripts armed with machetes or discarded muskets purchased for almost nothing from the English. Santa Anna had managed to acquire twenty-one pieces for his artillery to command, but the quality of the weaponry and the ammunition was inferior to what the Yanks had in their possession. Riley knew that the superb training of his crew couldn't overcome the poor caliber of the cannons, which had a third of the range of the Yankee guns.

"We might not have the quality, but we have the quantity," Santa Anna reassured him when Riley brought up his concerns. Taylor had a third of the troops Santa Anna now had at his disposal. Riley hoped the general was right, that their superiority in numbers would supersede the Yanks' superiority in weaponry. But past experiences had taught him otherwise—thus far, the Yankee general had beaten the Mexican forces in spite of his deficiency in troops.

Despite the challenges, Santa Anna's Liberating Army of the North would soon be ready to leave this beautiful city. Meanwhile, Riley wasted no time drilling the battalion. After a hard day's work of training, they'd go out and enjoy all the pleasures San Luis Potosí had to offer. His men preferred visiting the cantinas, frolicking with the Mexican señoritas, and attending the bullfights or Santa Anna's cockfights on the weekends. Riley relished the fandangos and strolls around the public square with Ximena, their dinners of enchiladas potosinas, or the delightful rides out in the country where they would gather her plants and enjoy the open skies. He treasured these outings, but it was getting more and more difficult to spend time with her. His body ached with desire. She haunted him in his dreams and when he was awake. No matter how black his sinning soul became, he remained faithful to Nelly, regularly sending her a letter and his pay. But was it a lie when he told her he would never betray his duty to her?

One November afternoon, Riley was summoned by General Santa Anna to his headquarters, where he was introduced to a newly arrived deserter. "Teniente Riley, please come in, come in," the general said through his interpreter, smiling as he motioned Riley to approach. Riley saluted his generals, but his gaze lingered on the wiry, sandy-haired man standing next to him, whom he immediately recognized as a fellow Irishman.

"I'd like you to meet Patrick Dalton," Santa Anna said. "Like you, he served in the British Army and is a skilled artillerist, or so he tells me," he said with a laugh.

Dalton saluted Riley respectfully.

"At ease, soldier. And where in the Green Isle do you hail from?" Riley asked.

"County Mayo, sir," Dalton said in a confident voice.

"I'm also a Connacht man myself, from Clifden. A pleasure to meet you," Riley said as he shook his countryman's hand.

"Tell me, Private Dalton, how did you come to join us?" the general asked.

Dalton told them how, after hearing about the Saint Patrick's Battalion, he'd separated himself from the Yanks while they were stationed in Camargo. His sergeant had taken him and a few other soldiers of Company B to the Río Grande to wash their clothes. Dalton had finished quickly and was given leave to return to camp. But instead, he sneaked into a cornfield and hid there until nightfall. Before anyone could come looking for him in the field, he plunged into the river and swam to the other side.

"'Tis a mighty river," Dalton said. "But I would've rather died swimmin' across than to spend another blessed day sufferin' the Yanks ridicule and contempt."

Dalton had been helped by two rancheros who, following Santa Anna's orders to help deserters from the Yankee army, had escorted him safely to San Luis Potosí. "I came here because I desire to serve under one of my own," Dalton said, looking at Riley. "It would be a great honor to join the Saint Patrick's Battalion and fight under your banner, sir. We Mayo men have a special affinity for our patron saint, as you well know, Lieutenant Riley," he said with a smile. "Our holy Mayo mountain bears his name."

"Well, then it's settled. Welcome to the Saint Patrick's Battalion, soldier," Santa Anna said. His manservant entered the room and said something in Spanish to the commander. Santa Anna smiled and turned to Riley and Patrick Dalton. "Well, gentlemen, it seems my carriage awaits me. Would you do me the honor of being my guests tonight? I've organized a private cockfight with some of my compatriots to raise more funds for our cause, and I'm sure you will enjoy it. Teniente Riley, I've not seen you at one of my cockfights yet, and I hate the thought of you missing out on the greatest sport in all of Mexico!" He grabbed his cane and gestured for them to follow him.

Riley looked at Dalton and smiled at seeing the surprise on his face. Though he had yet to attend one of the fights, by now Riley knew—just like everyone else—that the commander had a relish for the blood sport. "Another thing the Mexicans have in common with the Irish, no?"

Dalton nodded. "Aye. Course the Mexicans got all the sunshine, and we the rain."

The cockfight was held at the private residence of one of the city's wealthiest citizens. The pit had been specially constructed for this occasion in the splendid courtyard, and chairs had been placed on three sides of it. Judging by the presence of the most distinguished gentlemen and ladies, along with army generals and officers, Riley deduced that in Mexico, cockfighting wasn't looked down upon as a vulgar sport of the poor as it was in Ireland.

He'd just joined the British Army when the Cruelty to Animals Act in 1835 had banned the sport. As a young soldier, Riley had observed with his own eyes the hypocrisy of the law, for when it came to cruelty to animals, only the Irish poor were punished and charged with misdemeanors while the upper class was left to enjoy their hunting sport unmolested. The Irish still patronized the cockfights despite the ban, and his own father and brothers loved the sport. When Riley became a redcoat—and a stain upon his family—he was no longer invited to go with them deep into the fields where makeshift cockpits were built for a day of gathering with neighbors and friends.

Presently, the master of ceremonies walked into the center of the pit and recited the cockfighter's prayer, "Ave Maria purísima, los gallos vienen." As the games got underway, Riley observed Santa Anna, as merry as could be, standing by the pit with a beautiful woman on each arm. The commander had brought six of his best fighting cocks, and like their owner, the game fowl demanded respect and admiration. Watching as the spectators—including the fine ladies who didn't find it beneath them to support their favorite animals—placed their bets with the brokers in nothing but gold coinsRiley thought that were he a betting man and had the gold, he would've placed a wager on every one of the commander's cocks. In less than thirty seconds after the fighting commenced, Santa Anna's first fowl emerged the victor. With its opponent dead at its feet in a pool of blood, the cock puffed up its chest and crowed, causing the people to cheer and Santa Anna to take a bow. When Riley saw the heaps of gold being wagered, it struck him how orderly and well-behaved the crowd was compared to those in his homeland, where his boisterous countrymen would be swearing and quarreling throughout the games. As much as he liked the decorum of the higher classes, Riley missed the jesting and good-natured fighting of the peasantry.

"Are you an admirer?" he asked Dalton as they watched the games unfold.

"*Ní maith liom é*," he said, shaking his head. "But my ould fella enjoyed it very much. He would take me to the taverns or barns to see them."

"*Mise freisin*," Riley said. "My father believed that the sport was not cruel. He said the cock can quit the fight at any point he wants. 'Tis his choice to run or to stay."

"Aye, I never knew if 'twas bravery or foolishness that makes most cocks fight to the death," Dalton said.

"There's a fine line between bravery and foolishness, to be sure," Riley replied.

When Santa Anna won every single match, his generals and officers stood and saluted him. By then, the man was half gone with brandy, but he still managed to give the crowd a rousing speech. Riley couldn't understand everything the commander said, but judging from all the times the crowd shouted "¡Viva México!" and "¡Muerte a los gringos!" he knew the general's remarks had inspired them.

Abandoning his female companions for a moment, Santa Anna approached Riley and Dalton. He said something to the crowd about el Batallón de San Patricio and proposed a toast, whereupon everyone raised their glasses as the general shouted, "¡Viva la República Mexicana! ¡Viva Irlanda! ¡Vivan los San Patricios!"

Over the next few days, Riley became acquainted with the newest recruit of the Saint Patrick's Battalion. Since Dalton too had donned the hated redcoat back in Ireland, Riley found in him someone who was just as haunted by his service to the sassenachs. They had the same stain upon their souls. In Dalton, he also found an artillerist who matched his own skills and passion for gunnery tactics. At Riley's recommendation, Santa Anna promoted Dalton to second lieutenant and made him Riley's second-in-command. After donning his new officer's uniform, Dalton put an arm around Riley and said, "One day, Lieutenant Riley, we will take the Saint Patrick's Battalion to Ireland and continue to fight for our sacred cause. We shall be like the Wild Geese, the sons of Ireland coming home to set it free."

24

Early one morning, Ximena found herself being escorted to Santa Anna's private quarters. When she entered his chambers, he was on a large four-poster bed reclining on fancy feather pillows trimmed with lace, a glass of brandy in his hand. John had told her that the previous evening after the nightly junta of officers, the commander had been feeling ill, and General Mejía, who had heard of her skills, recommended that Santa Anna send for her. John had no choice but to second Mejía. Although Santa Anna had his own personal physician, he'd followed their recommendation and now here she was this morning, in the presence of the man she'd wished to avoid.

When the servant pulled back the mosquito curtains, she could see his face flushed and sweaty from fever, with large beads of perspiration gathered on his prominent forehead. He bid her closer, watched her approach with his dark, penetrating eyes. His lower lip protruded naturally, making him seem as if he were permanently pouting. Ximena was taken aback by how he looked without his elaborate uniforms and gold cane. He seemed more like a sickly schoolmaster than the army's general-in-chief.

"Forgive me for not greeting you properly, señora Ximena, but as you can see, I'm obliged to keep to my bed, very much indisposed.

Thank you for agreeing to minister to my injury. Teniente Riley and General Mejía speak very highly of your skills as a healer."

"I'm at your service, your Excellency," she said, almost choking on the words.

She placed her supply basket on the table in the center of the room where a large porcelain bowl overflowed with pomegranates. Unwrapping her frayed rebozo from her neck and shoulders, she hung it on the back of a scarlet velvet chair. The servant coughed his disapproval, but she left it there, requesting a pot of hot water and clean bandages and towels to be brought to her. When the servant took his leave to fetch the items, she found herself alone with the general.

Despite the fever and fatigue, Santa Anna's gaze remained just as intense as when he was healthy, perhaps, even more so. Previously, she'd observed him from a distance, and thus far had managed to stay out of his way. The manner in which he looked at her made her even more uncomfortable than she already felt in his luxurious surroundings, replete with silk draperies and marble floors, alabaster candelabras and crystal lamps, papered walls and gilded mirrors. Under his piercing gaze, she felt even more self-conscious of her threadbare blouse and worn-out sandals, the faded skirts Nana Hortencia had dyed with wild indigo and goldenrod. But her apron was clean, and her hair was braided neatly and fastened together with new ribbons. Those and her gold hoop earrings were the only nice things she owned, and the best she could do to make herself presentable. Besides, she was here to cure this pompous caudillo, so what did it matter what she looked like? She wasn't here to please him with her looks. He was just another patient, wasn't he? No, the devil lurking behind his feverish eyes reminded her that he was no ordinary human being.

She took a deep breath to steady herself and approached him. "May I?" She took the glass of brandy, setting it on the night table, and peeled away the sweat-soaked sheets to expose his left leg. The stump was red and inflamed, with pus and blood oozing from open sores. If it had an unpleasant odor, she couldn't tell, for it was overpowered by the general's plumeria-scented perfume, which he'd applied too generously.

"The surgeons that tended to me butchered my leg. It has never healed properly. ¡Imbéciles!"

As she assessed the wound, Ximena noticed how clumsy the amputation had been. The surgeons hadn't left enough muscle and skin flap to pad and cover the amputated bone, leaving a few centimeters of it exposed just below the knee joint. He told her it caused him excruciating pain when he walked. The wooden leg couldn't fit properly, since it rubbed against the protruding bone, and the skin had been stretched so much when it was stitched at the closure that sometimes it broke open, making the stump prone to chronic infection.

"The infection is superficial," she said. "It hasn't affected the flesh or bone. You'll soon be on your way to recovery."

"¡Nunca! Those incompetent surgeons condemned me to a life of pain. They should've left me to die instead." His lower lip stuck out more than usual, making him look even more like a petulant man-child.

"The general is fortunate to still have his life," she said, opening the window to allow the fresh air to circulate. "In my time now in this army, I've seen half of the soldiers whose limbs were sawed off perish from the operation, botched or not."

"It's an honor to die for one's country," he said. "And I would gladly give my life for the motherland. If I had died from my wounds in the battle against the French, I would have had a sublime death with the sweetest taste of glory. To die for Mexico, to go down in history as a martyr!"

She took some supplies from her basket and busied herself with preparing the herbs she needed to make a paste to treat his wound. She could hear her grandmother whispering in her ear—hierba del pollo to staunch the bleeding, gobernadora to discourage infection, calendula to soothe inflammation, florifundia to ease the pain. As she crushed the petals and leaves in her mortar and pestle, Ximena thought about those who'd already perished in this war and how they would never be celebrated as saviors or martyrs. Most who'd given their lives for their country, or who had yet to do so, would be forgotten, as if they never existed. And now this foolish man was speaking of being grateful for a chance at martyrdom.

"Teniente Riley said that you're a widow. Your husband was killed by the Rangers, was he not?"

She nodded. She didn't want to talk about Joaquín with this man.

"¡Esos Rinches malditos!" he said. "Death and damnation to them!"

The servant returned with the supplies and set them on the table for her before leaving the room. She put malva leaves into the hot water and let them steep before washing his wound. Glancing up, she found him watching her intently. "Tell me, señora Ximena—if it isn't impertinent of me to ask—where in the República do you hail from? I detect a familiar accent in your voice."

"San Antonio de Béxar."

"¿Una bexareña? You don't say. And your family—did they fight with me or against me during the Texan insurrection?"

She looked him in the eye and didn't hesitate to say, "Against." Then she held her breath as she waited for his reaction. His eyes, the color of roasted tobacco leaves, revealed nothing. She almost wished he would throw her out of his chambers so she could get away from him.

Finally, he shook his head and shrugged. "It doesn't matter now, does it? It comforts me to see that you're on the right side of the war *this* time."

She turned back to the table, her body throbbing from the sting of his words. She took her time finishing the paste, mixing some of the hot water into the crushed herbs until it was the right consistency. She remembered so vividly the day Santa Anna and his troops arrived in San Antonio. Many of the townspeople had tried to flee into the country as soon as the rumors reached them that he was on his way to the town. Lieutenant Colonel William B. Travis and his small force barricaded themselves in the old Alamo mission, including her father who was under the command of Captain Seguín. The wagon her father sent to take her and Nana Hortencia to their ranch fifteen miles from the town was unable to get past the Mexican troops, and so they'd locked themselves up in their house and were forced to witness the siege. Santa Anna hung a red flag from the towers of San Fernando Church—a sign that no quarter would be given, no mercy for the rebels—and she and Nana Hortencia cried for the fate of her father and prayed for his safety. When the Alamo fell, they both rushed out to search for him among the fallen and didn't find him anywhere. They later learned that he'd left the Alamo one night with Seguín under orders from Travis to bring reinforcements.

Santa Anna, denying the insurgents a Christian burial, incinerated their bodies in pyres. Ximena watched from the terrace of her home as the smoke rose over the buildings. The fire burned for two days, and the stench of burnt flesh permeated the air, lingering permanently in the collective memory of its citizens. A few days later a letter arrived from her father with news that he was alive and with General Houston's forces.

The executions in Goliad soon followed. Almost four hundred captives—Texian and Tejano alike—were marched onto a field and shot dead on the orders of the vile man before her. As she observed him lying prostrate in bed, Ximena saw not an invalid or an amputee, but the monster who had committed such atrocious acts of violence from which her homeland had never recovered. Did he have any idea how the destruction he'd wreaked in Texas had incited the Texians' fury and loathing for all Mexicans? She wished she could shake him and make him see how his mishandling of the Texas Rebellion had set the stage for what was happening now. She turned away from him and placed the rags to soak in the hot water.

"You know, they call me the butcher of the Alamo, but it was the troublemakers themselves who chose their fates. I gave those malcontents the opportunity to surrender—seven times, in fact. They made their choice."

She turned back around to look at him. How had he known what she was thinking? Had he noticed the accusation in her eyes?

He smiled at seeing the surprise on her face. "You're not the only Tejana I've met. Juan Seguín has looked at me the same way you just did, as if I were a bloodthirsty, barbarous villain and not a president-

general fulfilling his duty by suppressing the rebellion of those foreigners who were intent on taking Texas from us. You blame me for
the way the ungrateful Texians have treated Tejanos ever since. After
the revolt—which too many of you supported—you became second-
class citizens in your own homeland. So much unnecessary bloodshed,
isn't that what you accuse me of? But as I said, I gave the wretched
adventurers the opportunity to surrender, and they didn't, at least, not
until it was too late. Now they are venerated as martyrs. Travis, Bowie,
Crockett . . . Those lucky scoundrels. But it is only those Yanquis who
will be remembered and beloved—not the native sons of Texas who
were in the fort with them. Only the white defenders will go down
through the ages as the heroes of Texas Independence, whereas their
Tejano allies, like Juan Seguín, were run out of Texas in shame and
disgrace. That's Yanqui gratitude for you."

She remembered the moving eulogy Seguín had delivered at the
funeral service of those who were killed at the Alamo. Burying the
ashes from the pyres, he'd lauded the heroism of the defenders. "*Yes,
my friends, they preferred to die a thousand times rather than submit themselves to the tyrant's yoke.*" He'd called them valiant heroes and worthy
companions. Her father had wept as he listened to Seguín's moving
speech.

"And what about Goliad?"

Santa Anna shrugged. "I was merely upholding our existing laws.
Our government had decreed that foreigners bearing arms in Mexican territory were to be treated and tried as pirates, which, as you may
know, is punishable by death. The law was unjust, but the law commands, and who am I to violate it?"

So that was how he justified having almost four hundred prisoners
shot in cold blood.

"They weren't all foreigners," she said, realizing she was entering
dangerous territory. "Some were Mexican citizens."

His skin turned redder and his feverish eyes flashed with anger.
"When you Tejanos took up arms against the motherland, you for-
feited your rights as Mexican citizens! You committed treason against

your own people. How else should I have treated the rebels who dared
betray our nation?"

His accusation hovered in the room like a swarm of screeching
grackles darkening the sky. She turned away from his anger, her hands
shaking. The mortar and pestle were suddenly too heavy and she set
them down on the table. She wished she could simply leave instead of
tending the wounds of this man whose actions were responsible for so
much bloodshed and for the plight of the Tejanos. If instead of brutality he had shown mercy and treated his prisoners in an honorable
way, maybe then in the eyes of the Texians, not everyone of Mexican
descent would be looked upon as an enemy.

She breathed deeply, letting the aromatic oils of the crushed plants
calm her. Then she took a rag from the pot, squeezed it out, and began
to wash his stump vigorously. Hearing him wince, she stopped and
willed herself to be gentler. He was, above all, her patient right now.
She couldn't let her personal feelings and bad energy get in the way of
her healing.

Suddenly, he grabbed her arm and said, "I'm not angry at you, señora Ximena. Your family might have betrayed me once to ally yourselves with the Yanquis, and you paid for your disloyalty. But now here
you are, fighting alongside me. Instead of trying to kill me you're here
trying to heal me so that I can do what I was put on this earth to do—
to bring honor to Mexico."

He released her and let her continue working. She patted his skin
dry, lathered the poultice on a clean bandage and applied it to his
stump, saying nothing. But she felt his eyes still on her. The anger
was gone, replaced by something else. His gaze roamed her body, as if
undressing her. She glanced at her rebozo on the back of the chair and
wished she could wrap herself with it.

"You're a beautiful woman. I can see why teniente Riley is so be-
witched by you." His voice was deeper now, overtly sensual. And she
realized that she preferred his anger.

His eyes were lingering on her breasts, so she cleared her throat and
to distract him asked, "How did you get this injury?"

"Have you heard of la Guerra de los Pasteles?"

She shook her head. Her plan had worked. She did in fact remember the Pastry War of 1838. She'd been seventeen when the French invaded Mexico and set up a blockade of the ports. Santa Anna, reclining on his pillow, began recounting for her the dispute between the French and Mexicans that began over a bakery owned by a Frenchman that had been looted and destroyed by Mexican soldiers. France, demanding reparations for that and other debts owed to its citizens, had attacked Vera Cruz. When Santa Anna rushed to defend his home state, the French fired a cannon loaded with grape, killing Santa Anna's horse, two of his officers and some of his troops, and shattering his left leg.

"It cost me dearly," he said, "But it was worth the price. Ah, you should have seen us charging the enemy with our bayonets, driving them back into the sea. Our country's flag remained in its place, flying triumphantly over Mexican soil. That day, I brought victory to la República Mexicana. And I will do so again, with the Yanquis."

When she finished dressing his wound, she massaged his stiff leg muscles and knee joint with a salve she'd made from árnica mexicana simmered in lard. She'd wanted to redirect his attention and she had, but now she had to suffer his bragging.

"It was worth it, you know."

"What was, General?"

"The loss of my leg. The people thought it was a national tragedy. They offered prayers for my life, held parades in my honor. They came to watch my leg being interred at the cemetery of Santa Paula. What a glorious funeral it was. You should have seen the celebrations, the magnificent monument that was to be the home of my lost limb. I think about that on the days I cannot bear to put on the prosthetic because of the pain. My people know I am but a selfless warrior, a good Mexican. A soldier of the people."

She wished she could hurry out of there. The man was intolerable. His arrogance and egoism were irritating, but she knew that healing required patience, good energy, and faith on her part. So she pushed her frustration aside and massaged the pain and stress from the leg muscles until they were relaxed and supple. He sighed with pleasure and closed his eyes. "Ah, don't stop. Por favor. My wife chose to remain in the capital instead of accompanying me on the campaign. But I'm glad you're here to minister to me," he said, his voice deep with arousal. Then he took her hand and placed it over his manhood.

Without hesitation, she slapped him across the face. Startled, he opened his eyes but was too shocked to speak. She could see the terrible ferocity in his eyes, the violence raging in their dark depths, but she refused to be intimidated by it and matched it with anger of her own.

"If you wanted a whore, General, you should have called for one instead of a curandera." She got up and tossed her supplies into her basket.

"My apologies, señora Ximena," he said. She turned to look at him. The expression on his face had changed, the savage ferocity replaced by repentance. His lower lip protruded even more. "Please, forgive me for committing such indelicacy. My fever has led me astray."

He was lying. Fever or no fever, she could see who he was—vile, despicable. And what if he retaliated against her or John?

She nodded. "I'm done for today. I'll have your servant bring you fresh sheets for your bed and a light dinner. As soon as you eat and drink the seven blossoms tea I will have him prepare for you, you should rest, and please, stay away from alcohol."

"Will you return in the morrow?" He looked beseechingly at her, his voice nauseatingly sweet, like overripe fruit about to spoil.

What would he do if she said no, refusing to treat him again? Was she ready to find out? Could a healer refuse to heal?

"If you promise me there will be no more disrespect toward my person, I will tend to you until the infection is gone. You have my word."

"I shall eagerly await your return, my lady Ximena. You have my sincerest appreciation for your tender care, believe me. Teniente Riley was correct. You have a great gift."

That afternoon, as she and John walked around the busy mercado, she recounted her visit with Santa Anna. She thought about telling him how he had disrespected her, but decided against it. The thought of it sickened her.

"Beggin' your pardon, Ximena," John said as they sidestepped the vendors who offered them their produce, insisting that they try the freshest melons, the ripest tomatoes. "'Tis compassion that I had for the general, when I saw him agonizin' from the pain on his leg, worse than usual last night. I knew you could help him. He doesn't trust surgeons anymore. Since they mangled the amputation, he's had no faith in them."

"I do not trust them either," she said as she stopped to buy a bag of zapotes. "Some are incompetent with the saw. And they go from one patient to another with dirty tools and sponges. If the pacientes survive, it is because of their stamina and intervención divina."

"Forgive me?" he picked up some guavas from a nearby fruit stand and clumsily juggled them, dropping one on his head.

She laughed as he massaged his scalp and paid the vendor for the bruised fruit. "I know you meant well, John, but the man is insoportable!" As they made their way to the stalls that sold fresh herbs and spices, she accepted that John and General Mejía had not meant to put her in harm's way. But this wasn't going to be a one-time thing. The general suffered from chronic pain. Even once he healed, there would be the next time, and the next.

"You think it's true, what people say about him?" she asked as she inhaled the earthy tang of oregano. They had both heard rumors that Santa Anna was secretly collaborating with the Yanqui president, which would explain why he'd been allowed through their naval blockade of the port of Vera Cruz and permitted to disembark and make his way to the capital.

"The commander has many enemies," John said. "He claims the rumors of his treachery to Mexico are poor attempts to turn the people against him, to discredit him."

"And you believe him?"

"I believe what I see. He has fulfilled the promise he made to the people when he returned from exile—he's leadin' the Mexican Army against the Yankee invaders. Those who are heapin' calumnies upon him are the ones who are *not* here preparin' to go to battle and willin' to die to avenge the insults to their country."

"Santa Anna made a treaty with the Yanquis before—when he was capturado after the Battle of San Jacinto. He gave Sam Houston all he asked. Why he not do the same now with Polk?"

"He was a prisoner of war, wasn't he? A captive president forced to enter into an agreement with the enemy, which the Mexican government later disavowed."

"El daño—the damage—was irremediable by then," Ximena said. As she paid the Indian woman for the herbs she needed, she thought of what a cruel joke destiny had played on her—to have her use her healing gift on the very man her father had once fought against.

As they returned to the barracks, Ximena turned to John and said, "My father fought in the Battle of San Jacinto. He'd be disappointed to see me here, tending to Santa Anna. He was wrong to betray Mexico, this I know. But when I was with the general today, all I wanted was to defend my father from his ire." She sighed and looked away. "My poor father . . . he wished to be a hero of Texas independence, but instead he died seen as a traitor by both sides."

John put an arm around her and looked at her in understanding. "When I joined the British Army, my people saw me as a traitor as well. I pray to be given the chance to redeem myself one day. Your father didn't have that chance, but you are here now in his stead. It is through you he will get his redemption."

25

A few days later, the city was abuzz with news of the latest presidential elections—once again, Santa Anna was president of the republic. Cannons fired a salute from the Palacio de Gobierno, rockets were launched into the air, and the people cheered from the streets and terraces. Even Ximena celebrated but for a different reason—she hoped this meant Santa Anna would head to the capital and leave the army to be led by a different commander.

But it was not to be.

Santa Anna proclaimed that his duty was to defend Mexico's honor, and so he designated his new vice president, Valentín Gómez Farías, to hold the reins of the government during his absence from the capital and serve as acting president. Meanwhile, he was staying put in San Luis Potosí to continue preparing for battle.

Just as she had expected, he sent his servant to fetch her again. It would be the third time she tended him, and she hoped it would be the last. As she and the servant arrived at his private quarters, Santa Anna was preparing to go out, immaculately groomed as always. "Ah, there you are. Come with me," he said, grabbing his golden cane.

"Where to?"

"Mi gallinero. I haven't been out to visit my gamecocks. I'm organizing a cockfight to celebrate the great news."

"I need to inspect your leg, make sure it's healing properly."

He waved her words away. "I'm feeling fine. In fact, I've never felt better. I think your treatment is working. Now, come." He held out his arm for her.

She shook her head. "I'm sorry, your Excellency, but I have other patients to tend to. May I take a look at your leg and take my leave? I won't be long."

In response, he grabbed his hat and walked past her. "Leave your basket," he ordered.

They made their way to the pens he'd built for his prized game fowl. He winced as he limped along but assured her it was only a minor discomfort. He refused to spend another day in bed, he said. And there was much to be done. As usual, he'd bathed himself in too much plumeria perfume, but out in the open air, the scent was not suffocating. When they arrived, she noticed the familiar smells of dry hay, feathers, and rooster droppings, and she thought of home. For a moment she could almost feel herself back at the rancho, listening to the roosters crowing, the mules hee-hawing, the dogs barking. The chatter and laughter of the ranch hands' families. She shook those memories away and looked at Santa Anna's gamecocks. The trainers were busy trimming around their cockscombs, shaping the tails, clipping the wing feathers to give them a straight edge.

"The wings need to be done very precisely," Santa Anna said. "They have to be trimmed exactly alike, otherwise the gallo will be out of balance when he engages in battle with his opponent."

He ordered the trainers to bring his favorite. Taking a seat on a bench, he clasped the rooster close to his chest. "This gallo is my pride and joy. His name is Libertador. Isn't he magnificent?"

She tried to not roll her eyes. She wondered if his other roosters were named the Savior of the Motherland, the Soldier of the People, and the Napoleon of the West.

Santa Anna gently spoke to Libertador. He rubbed oil on its beak, cockscomb, and sharp spurs, then massaged more of it into its red and green feathers and long flowing tail. "The oil keeps the beak and spurs from getting brittle," he said as he wiped down the rooster with a rag. She thought of Joaquin and remembered him brushing his horses with sweeping strokes and patiently detangling their manes and tails with a comb. How was it possible this vile man could have something in common with her beloved husband?

When Santa Anna was done, the cock's plumage was gleaming in the light. She was struck by the beauty of the creature.

"People think they're pets that I pamper too much," he said. "And that I waste my time with cockfighting. But to me, these gallos are combatants, warriors. A fighting cock doesn't retreat, doesn't surrender. The instinct to flee has been bred out of them, and if they flee, they don't deserve to live. Many a bird has ended up on my dinner table."

Ximena sat on the bench next to him and watched as the sparring began, starting with the lightest cocks and so on to the heaviest. It was like a dance, the birds leaping into the air, turning, kicking, pecking, at times in perfect synchronization, feathers floating down like autumn leaves. In the sparring, she was glad to see that the birds didn't use sharp razors. Instead, their spurs were covered with pads.

"Right now, it's not a matter of killing or being killed. It's about improving one's stamina and getting stronger. Quicker. Better!"

She marveled at how focused Santa Anna was on every move the game fowl made, his eyes so alive and alert, carefully assessing and missing nothing. "Each gallo has his own particular way of fighting, can you tell? See how the red one likes to attack by flying high, and the brown one attacks from the ground?"

To her, the cocks' movements seemed a blur, too complex to take it all in. But as he walked her through it, she began to notice the individual ways each bird attacked.

"Is it strange that they make no noises?" she asked, thinking of her roosters back at the rancho, who'd certainly always had plenty to say.

"No. The only time they'll make a sound is if they are losing. God help you if your cock emits a squawk. Because they rarely make sounds, you have to learn how to judge the damage your cock is making and receiving through keen observation. And you have to know the rules thoroughly, so that you can break them or abide by them, depending on what is most advantageous to you."

"Like in Goliad?" she asked and immediately regretted it. But it was true. He'd used the absurd Mexican laws against foreigners with arms and piracy to justify the massacre. That was certainly an occasion when abiding by the rule of law had been advantageous to him.

He laughed but didn't take his eyes off the roosters. "Sí. Exacta-mente, querida."

The birds were allowed to spar for no more than five minutes and separated before they caused any serious injury to each other. Libertador went last. Had the metal blade been attached to his spur, he would've killed his opponent within seconds. Instead, he pecked out its eye. The unlucky opponent let out a squawk and tried to flee, but the pit was en-closed with hay bales and wooden boards, so there was nowhere to run.

"Get that pinche runner out of my sight!" Santa Anna said, waving his cane around. "Send it to the kitchen!"

He turned to her and the rage in his eyes was immediately replaced by a smile. His shifting moods discomfited.

"Didn't Libertador do well? He turned his opponent into a squawk-ing sissy!"

When the sparring was over, Santa Anna took his winning rooster back from the trainers to tend to him, checking for injuries, especially on his neck. He sipped a drink of water and sprayed some mist on the bird to cool it down, speaking sweetly to it, then pressed it against his face to relax it and slow its heart rate down. Again, Ximena found herself amazed at Santa Anna's tenderness, at the way he stroked the bird before handing it back to the trainers.

"You forgot to kiss it goodbye," she joked, as she'd often teased Joaquín about his horses. Too late, she realized she'd forgotten who she was speaking to.

Santa Anna looked at her, surprised, and then laughed. "Gallos can't be trusted, querida. They aren't loyal creatures. You can't let your guard down around them." He pointed to a small scar near his eye and said, "This one bit me one time. He was aiming for my eye. He likes to peck eyes out, as you've noticed. When I look at the scar, I remember to be careful about whom to trust or not to trust. Too many people around me are like my gallos—they won't hesitate to hurt me, no matter how well I treat them. That's one of the many lessons they've taught me."

The trainers took the birds in to bathe and retire them for the day, each in their own enclosed pen with dividing wooden walls to keep them from seeing one another. The general got up, and she followed him back to his quarters.

"Do they have to be kept separated?" she asked.

"Yes, otherwise they will kill each other. When I first got into cockfighting, my favorite gallo killed himself."

"How?"

"He saw his own reflection in the water trough and attacked it, thinking it was another gallo. The fool was so intent on killing his opponent, he drowned himself."

"Well, he succeeded then, didn't he?" She stopped and turned to him. "He was his own enemy."

He smiled and made as if to kiss her. When she took a step back, he grabbed her hand and kissed it instead. "So you think I'm my own worst enemy, is that it? Quizá tenga razón, señora Ximena."

When they got back into his private chambers, he served himself a glass of brandy from a crystal decanter and offered her one, which she declined. He sat on the chair by the window and watched her roll up his pant leg, detach the wooden leg, and remove the soiled bandages. His stump was bleeding slightly again, though at least the infection and swelling had mostly subsided.

She glanced at him and shook her head. "You must take care not to overuse it. Stay off the leg as much as you can for another day or two. Give it time to fully heal."

"This thing will never heal. But I shall abide by your recommendations. I would hate to lose the rest of my leg."

"Well, you could have a glorious funeral for it, bury it in that magnificent monument where the other part of your leg is interred."

Her sarcasm made his smile vanish, and in his eyes appeared the familiar flash of rage and indignation. But then, to her surprise, a certain sadness registered on his face. It was so unexpected—his naked sorrow—that she forced herself to apologize to him. He said nothing, and she thought that perhaps he hadn't heard her apology. His eyes had a faraway look to them, lost in a bitter memory.

As she dressed his wound, he watched her in silence, and she wondered if her words had upset him. Losing a limb was a deeply traumatic experience, she knew, and she reprimanded herself for her rude remark. Her grandmother would have been disappointed in her behavior. This was no way for a healer to behave. *This man brings out the worst in me, Nana.*

"My leg is no longer interred," Santa Anna said at last.

She looked up at him. "Where is it?"

"Vanished. Right before I was forced to go into exile in Cuba, the mob in the capital took it out of its tomb, dragged it through the city streets in protest. Imagine, having the limb I lost so gloriously in service to my country treated in that manner. And it wasn't just my leg that received such treatment, but my statue, my theater, robbed and defiled, my portraits burned! They would've pecked my eyes out, had I let them."

Two years before, after he'd made a mess of the country, he had been overthrown. Joaquín had talked about it for weeks, asking Ximena to read to him every newspaper article that covered the revolution in the capital. Santa Anna had tried to regain control of the government, but it was too late. The revolution couldn't be stopped. The people, fed up with the oppressive conditions he had them living under, protested and rioted in the streets, not just in the capital but in other cities, including in his home state of Vera Cruz. The president general was captured while trying to escape and thrown in prison for months before being exiled.

"Well, it doesn't matter now. Fortune turned its back on me in '44, but it has smiled upon me again," he said, his somber mood suddenly lifting. "The people have thrown the city gates open to me once more and have hailed me as their savior. My return to the capital was a day of celebration. I wish that you'd been there to witness how the people entrusted the destiny of Mexico to me, how they saluted me once more with the title of Soldier of the People! And look at me now— señora Ximena—I have once again been reelected as president of this great republic!"

Yes, he was back in power. Somehow, he'd gone from being the most hated man in Mexico, deposed and exiled, to being president again and the commander-in-chief of the Liberating Army of the North. She wondered how he had pulled that off. How did he get past the blockades the Yanquis set up in Vera Cruz? How did he take back the reins of the Mexican government, with the support of the same political and military rivals that had imprisoned and exiled him? How did he get the masses that had so gleefully dragged his limb across the public streets to hail him once again as their liberator and president? Could the rumors of his secret dealings with the Yanquis possibly be true?

Ximena knew he could see the questions in her eyes, but he didn't answer them. He puffed up his chest and gloated instead. For a second, she almost expected him to crow.

26

January 1847
San Luis Potosí

7, Sep' 1846

Dear beloved husband,

I pray that this letter reaches you wherever you may be in that far land. I think too many of me letters seem to have miscarried. I received your remitance, which we were verry much wanting afther we ate our last potato. It soothed my sowl to know God has spared you and kept you safe, a stór. We are doing our best to keep going, but life is getting harder and harder. It looks like the praties are rotting in the fields again, God help us. Scarcely a house has escaped the hunger or the terrible faver. There are dead lying in homes, in the ditches, in the fields, and everyone is too hungry and weak to bury them. And you couldn't believe the stench of it all, John. Anyone who has the means to escape is laving. My dear frind Molly and her family jist up and left and went over to America a few days ago, widout even a farewell. I pray that you can send for us soon, a stór. Mammy and Daddy talk about us going to the workhouse. We oughtn't to do that! They would take Johnny from me, sure enough. We would all be separated. At laist for now, thanks to you, we still have a roof over our heads and a bit of food in our bellies. What you send keeps us alive, but most important, it keeps us still together. I regret not having betther tidings from home. Sometimes I'm afeard God has left us widout Him. I know it isn't thrue. God is good, and I must have faith.

I remain your loving wife,
Nelly

The letter had arrived at the cathedral in late December. Riley hadn't received new correspondence from his wife since Matamoros, but he suspected, even before she'd confirmed this to be true, that whatever letters she'd sent since had been lost. Her words weighed on him, but he found comfort in knowing that at least his letters were reaching her, and most important, the remittances. At times of crisis, the price of food was inflated to outrageous amounts and money was needed more than ever. He finished his next letter to her just when marching orders were given, and once again sent her everything he could. With a heavy heart, Riley prepared himself to do his soldier's duty, hoping that this would be the last campaign. Mexico needed to win this next battle. Then he could finally have the land that was promised him, and he could send for his loved ones.

It was with this thought that Riley took his place among the columns on January 28. As the San Patricios and the Mexican troops formed ranks in the public square and along the street leading north, the potosinos cheered for them, waving and tossing flowers from their balconies. It was time to face the enemy.

Riding on his caisson alongside capitán Moreno and Patrick Dalton, Riley held his green silk banner high as the people chanted "¡Viva México! ¡Vivan los San Patricios!" He turned to look at his men. Their eyes glittered from beneath their caps as they waved back at the residents of San Luis Potosí who throughout the last three months had treated them with generosity and respect.

The journey north to the town of Encarnación de Guzmán would be long and arduous. Two hundred and sixty miles, most of it unsettled land. The army had little in terms of provisions, but Santa Anna's plan was for them to seize the supplies the Yanks had with them. Riley was ill at ease about the risk the commander was taking, for the consequences would be great. If they didn't get their hands on those provisions, it could prove their undoing.

Bugles announced the arrival of Santa Anna, and Riley turned to see him approach on horseback and making his way through the ranks as the men parted for him. He was there to see the lead units off and give them a few words of encouragement until they met up again. He himself would be leaving in a few days with his staff and the rest of the infantry and cavalry, and he'd insisted that Ximena ride with him in his handsome carriage, along with his chaplain and secretary.

"¡Soldados!" Santa Anna addressed them. "The independence, the honor, and the destiny of the nation depend at this moment on your decisions! My friends, what days of glory await us! Hurry forth in the defense of your country. The cause we sustain is a holy one. Never have we struggled more for justice, because we fight for honor and religion, for our wives and children!" As he delivered his speech, he galloped up and down the columns, waving his hat. The troops received his remarks with enthusiasm. "¡Vencer o morir!" the commander yelled, concluding his eloquent speech. To conquer or die. The cheers of the civilians and the troops echoed among the buildings, and Riley cheered along with them. Their banners floated in the wind, and the military bands struck up an inspiring tune. Then Santa Anna brought his horse before Riley's caisson to examine the glittering green banner. He smiled in approval. "Teniente Riley," he said, "la victoria será nuestra."

"Así será, mi general," Riley said, saluting his commander.

"¡Libertad para la República Mexicana!" Santa Anna said, as he read out the words on Riley's banner. Then in a louder voice, he said it again, and Riley and the San Patricios shouted along with him.

"Liberty for the Mexican Republic. *Erin Go Bragh*!"

Amid the cheers from the crowd, Santa Anna gave marching orders and the troops began to move out. While the Saint Patrick's Battalion waited their turn, Ximena emerged from the crowd and approached Riley. Her troubled look made him get down from the caisson and go over to her side. She'd been behaving queerly the last few days but wouldn't tell him what was wrong.

"What's unsettling your mind, lass?"

"Take care of yourself, John," she said, her voice grave, her eyes heavy with worry.

"I will. Don't fret about me none. I'll be grand."

She shook her head, and as she looked intensely at him, her face paled and her eyes widened, as if she were seeing something no one but she could see. Grabbing his hands, she blurted out, "Keep your eyes open!" Then she turned and disappeared into the crowd.

As the columns began to move out, Riley wondered what she'd meant by that.

They left the city behind, and the cheers grew fainter and fainter. Riley's cannons glinted in the sun as the horse wagons that carried them lurched forward, across the terrain. He turned to look behind him. It was hard to see the city through the cloud of dust the army had left in its wake, but the steeple and tower of the cathedral and temple rose high above San Luis Potosí. Riley said a silent prayer and thought of Ximena, of the strolls they'd taken around the plaza, of how she'd been by his side as he formed the Saint Patrick's Battalion. That she would be following a few days behind him in Santa Anna's carriage eased his worries. At least this time, she wouldn't suffer a brutal march.

They trudged northward past cultivated fields, then miserable desert. There hadn't been enough carts and mules to transport all of the food supplies, and so each man had to carry his own week's worth of rations. Some quickly ate through theirs. Others, not knowing any better, had thrown some of their rations away at the beginning of the march to lighten their loads. They soon regretted it when they were forced to subsist on half-rations of corn biscuits and strips of dried beef, pilo-

ncillo and pinole, and whatever the camp women could forage in the
brush as their days turned into weeks.

When they were finally nearing the town of Encarnación, a
norther came roaring upon them one night with furious speed, and
the soldiers and camp women, tentless and exposed, huddled together
seeking protection from the keen winds and freezing rain which soon
turned to snow. The little wood they had gathered was wet, and what
few flames they managed to coax from it were suffocated by the snow.
The commanders and officers who had tents didn't fare any better. As
Riley lay inside the tent he shared with Dalton, buttoned up to the
neck, numb from the intense cold and wishing he had an overcoat, the
canvas flapped and whipped all around them. He felt that at any moment the wind would yank the tent off the face of the earth and hurl
it into the heavens with the two of them still inside. As the norther
raged unabated, he wondered if the dire weather was an omen. Was
God trying to tell them something?

Drifting in and out of a troubled slumber, he dreamed he was back
in Clifden, trudging through the frozen field down to his snow-dusted
cottage. This time when he opened the door, seeking the warmth inside, the turf fire had completely gone out, and the winter winds were
moaning through every corner. He stood by the door watching Nelly
asleep in their straw bed, and she turned to look at him, her gray eyes
as dreary as the wintry sky. Her bluish lips opened and spoke to him
in a mournful voice. *"Come here, avourneen. Come lie with me."* She
opened her arms and Riley wanted nothing more than to put his head
on her bosom and sleep. He slid into the bed beside her, seeking comfort from his wife's warm body, but she was cold, so cold, like a maiden
made of ice. She gripped him fiercely and wouldn't let go. *"Sleep now,
avourneen,"* she said, and her breath was an icy blast of wind.

Then, he heard another voice. From far away.

"Open your eyes, John!"

He groaned in his sleep, but Ximena's voice was calling him from
somewhere in his dream. When he awoke, he found tears frozen on
his cheeks. Felt a cold he'd never felt before. His joints were stiff, and

he couldn't feel his legs. He huddled closer to his second-in-command, who was also awake and clutching the ridge pole holding up their rattling tent while the storm howled about and beat against the canvas walls.

Dalton handed Riley his flask of mezcal and said, "Have a drop, Lieutenant. 'Twill keep your soul from freezin' on ya."

They sat vigil for the balance of the night, praying for the fury of the tempest to subside and for the blessed light of the sun to shine on them once more.

Morning broke at length, and Riley was one of the first out of the tents. The trees glistened with ice glitter. Dry frigid air stung his face. The norther had abated altogether, but as he walked around the encampment, he realized that his nightmare had been nothing to what other men had suffered during that night of agony. As the troops shook off the snow from their colorful sarapes, they found four hundred Mexican men still squatting on the ground, wrapped in their sarapes, their eyes closed, their arms tightly wrapped around themselves. Eternal sleep had claimed them.

"Heavens!" Dalton said as he approached him. "These poor wights, freezin' down to the very marrow in their bones."

Riley nodded, blowing some warm air into his hands. "Did we lose any of ours?"

"Two," Patrick said. "Cooney and O'Brien."

"Cooney from Cavan and O'Brien from Tipperary?"

"Aye, the very ones."

Riley shook his head. "Two good soldiers, and O'Brien was a great man to tell a story." He made the sign of the cross. "May God keep their souls."

"Perhaps they didn't suffer. Just drifted off to sleep and didn't wake."

Riley thought about his dream. Is that why he'd heard Ximena's voice urging him to wake up? If she hadn't, would he now be one of those stiffened corpses?

By February 17, when the troops finally arrived in Encarnación, having covered two hundred and sixty miles in three weeks, they'd lost about a quarter of the army to hunger, thirst, fatigue, exposure to the elements, or desertion. Riley mourned the loss of four more of his men, whom he and Dalton buried on the side of the road, covering their graves with cacti to keep the wild beasts from digging up their bodies. Three days later, when Santa Anna arrived in his carriage and ordered the troops to line up for review, he was not pleased with their reduction. Riley was glad to see that the commander set out to raise the morale of the soldiers that were still standing. What the men needed, besides rest and food, were words of encouragement from their leader.

"¡Soldados! The enemy is waiting for us in Agua Nueva," Santa Anna said to his troops. "The operations of the enemy demand that we should move at once upon his principal line. Privations of all kinds surround us due to the neglect shown toward us by those who should provide your pay and provisions. But when has misery ever debilitated your spirits or weakened your enthusiasm? The Mexican soldier is well known for his frugality and patience under suffering. My friends, let us purge from our soil the stranger who has dared to profane it with his presence. Let us show the North Americans that Mexico will always be ours. ¡Viva la República!"

"¡Viva!" the troops cheered. Despite the harsh conditions the men found themselves in, they were ready for a fight.

That evening, while he and Ximena had supper together, Riley told her about the storm and the frozen men. "I heard you calling me," he said. Then, remembering the expression on her face before he left, he asked, "How did you know that was going to happen?"

"I wish to know," she said. "I almost died from cólera when I was twelve, and my Nana saved me. Since then, I have strange dreams sometimes. Visions of things to come."

"In my dream, Nelly was frozen. What does that mean, lass? Have you seen her in your visions?"

"No," she said. "I only dreamed of the storm. Men frozen. That night I knew I needed to wake you before it was too late."

When he retired to his tent, he lay awake, his mind uneasy until the day finally dawned.

In the morning after they broke camp, Santa Anna addressed his troops once again to lift up their spirits. It was his fifty-third birthday, and with great enthusiasm, he led his army forward on the march to Taylor's camp, thirty-five miles away. Riley was once again impressed with how fast the Mexican soldiers could march.

The Saint Patrick's Battalion lagged behind, their artillery caissons bouncing along the uneven roads full of gopher holes, the wheels sinking into the sandy soil. The crew had to constantly help the mule drivers pull the wheels out, and Riley and Dalton and the other officers were walking behind the heavy field pieces with their men to spare the mules the extra weight.

At the end of the day, as they trudged along the mountain pass, everyone's enthusiasm dropped with the temperature. They continued past nightfall, and by the time they gained the summit, Riley thought that the men around him no longer looked alive. They headed down the slippery slope on the other side of the mountain, the path treacherous for the artillery caissons and supply wagons, and it wasn't until a few hours before dawn that Santa Anna called for a halt. They were six miles away from the enemy troops.

"You will need all your strength today, boys," Riley said as he and his men huddled together around the small fire they managed to get going. With no supper to be had, most had drifted off to sleep as soon as they came to a halt. The night was well advanced to pitch his tent, and Riley was too haunted by his dream to allow himself to close his eyes. As he listened to the icy wind whispering around him, he thought of Nelly. Wrestling with the gloom trying to take possession of him, he glanced at Dalton, sitting on the ground a few feet away. He was one of the few who was still awake. He was a sturdy fellow and even now, despite what they had just gone through, Dalton seemed to be doing better than the rest of them. But upon careful inspection, Riley saw the fatigue in his friend's eyes. He was fighting off sleep, just as Riley was.

"Rest now, Pat, *a chara*. Today you'll need to have your wits about ya."

"Aye, but you should do the same, eh?"

Riley nodded and put his head against his knapsack, but there was no wink of sleep to be had. Instead, he kept a careful watch over his sleeping men and thought of the fight that awaited them. Above all they must avoid getting captured. He would see to it that the Yanks didn't get their hands on the Saint Patrick's Battalion.

At dawn, even before the officers began shouting their commands for the troops to move out, Riley was ready. As the army advanced to the Yankee camp in Agua Nueva, they saw clouds of smoke on the horizon. It seemed that upon hearing of Santa Anna's approach, the Yanks had abandoned their position in the valley below and had set their stores of supplies on fire. Riley cursed under his breath. Counting on Taylor's food supplies to keep them going, they'd gone through the last of the rations. Now the meals they'd been hoping for had been burned to ashes.

Santa Anna seemed to have the same concerns and proceeded to rally the spirits of his men. But this time, the troops were too deflated to join the general in his cheers for the motherland. They observed the smoke in the distance, knowing that there would be no food coming, no nourishment for their fatigued bodies. Santa Anna claimed that the smoke was proof that the Yankees had fled in fear. "Let us make haste then! Victory is near!"

In his enthusiasm, the general ignored their wretched state and forced the half-starved army to take up the line of march without even a chance to refill their water gourds or water their horses. Instead, he gave the bugle call for a quick march. The army trudged ahead for thirteen miles due north, finally reaching the narrow pass known as

La Angostura, near an hacienda called San Juan de la Buena Vista, where the Yankees had decided to make a stand.

Riley scanned the defensive position the Yankees had taken on an irregular plain surrounded by the steep Sierra Madre range to the east and arroyos to the west. He surmised there were no more than five thousand troops. The Mexican forces had dropped to fourteen thousand, but the Yanks were well fed and well rested and had the advantage of having better positions on the broad plateau and in the hills. Old Zach knew what he was doing. Protected by the ravines, high ridges, and deep gullies crisscrossing the plateau, the Yanks were using the landscape in their favor. The narrow gorges prevented Santa Anna from spreading out his forces for maximum effect, squeezing them into a confined space only forty paces wide, with gullies on one side and bluffs on the other.

The commander sent out his officers with a parley flag to demand Taylor's immediate surrender, giving him an hour to do so. Riley knew the Yankee general wouldn't back down. Within the hour, his fears were confirmed when General Mejía read Taylor's note aloud and then translated it for the commander. "In reply to your note of this date, summoning me to surrender my forces at discretion, I beg leave to say that I decline acceding to your request."

"Be it so, then," Santa Anna said. Then the council of war set out to devise a plan of attack. "I know they have the weaponry and the ideal terrain, but we have the numbers," Santa Anna repeated when Riley and some of the officers pointed out the disadvantage of their position. "We will fight with our bare fists, if we must. But we will be victorious."

He ordered his officers to maneuver their regiments into position. Under the direction of the chief of artillery, Riley scanned the area and chose the best location they could find for the three heavy guns that would be manned by the Saint Patrick's Battalion. He and his men spent several hours dragging the three cannons—two 24-pounders and one 6-pounder—up the ridge. In shifts, his men worked the ropes tied to the cast-iron guns, each weighing a ton. By afternoon, standing on the high ground, Riley inspected the cannons and the cases of shot, shell, and canister. Peering over the rim of the ridge, where his cannons commanded the plateau, he beheld the Yankee army moving their eighteen artillery pieces into position and spotted Braxton Bragg's battery. At the sight of Yankee scoundrel, Riley hoped this time he could finally blast him to perdition.

"Are you ready for this, Lieutenant?" Dalton said as he came to stand beside him. Riley ran his hand along the cold metal surface of one of his cannons.

"Aye, indeed," Riley said. "I've been ready. *Fág an Bealach*."

Together, they stuck their banner in the ground and watched as the flag of the Saint Patrick's Battalion unfurled in the breeze, a vivid green against the azure of the sky.

27

In the morning, Ximena was awoken by the Mexican bugles calling the troops to fall in. The soldiers had not had any rations, for there were none. The military bands from each brigade played loudly as Santa Anna positioned his forces to begin the attack. Ximena knew the noise and fanfare were meant to intimidate the Yanquis. She watched the men drop to their knees as the priests walked along the lines to offer their blessings, incense wafting into the air. From far away she could see John and the San Patricios kneeling by their cannons, waiting for their benedictions. She spotted Juan Cortina with the cavalry, their lances lowered as the priests sprinkled them with holy water. Their prayers rose in unison to the heavens. Then Santa Anna addressed the troops, and she strained to hear his remarks.

"I glory in the consciousness of being at the head of an army of heroes, who not only know how to fight bravely but to suffer patiently both hunger and thirst, a sacrifice required of you by our nation."

The cheers went up into the air. "¡Viva la República!" echoed against the mountain range, and then one by one the units took their positions. When Santa Anna gave the order, the military bands sounded the charge and the fighting commenced.

Along with the other soldaderas, Ximena remained on the ridge overlooking the battle grounds. As the cannons and muskets crashed and roared, and the crack of the rifles and the clanging hooves of the cavalry reverberated over the battlefield, she thought of the worst storms she'd witnessed in San Antonio de Béxar and the Río Bravo region, when the clapping thunder and vivid flashes of lightning seemed to be splitting the heavens above. She'd never imagined she would one day witness storms even worse than those—with gunpowder flashes and bombs exploding, with a hail of cannon balls falling upon the battlefield. This darkening storm was more sinister and deadlier than any other created by nature. For this one was man-made, forged by greed, vanity, tyranny.

Finally, the soldaderas dispersed to forage for food and gather firewood, others to the makeshift field hospital. Ximena had seen enough of the battle as well, and yet, she couldn't pull away. She watched Cheno with his mounted riders charging at the enemy. He tossed his rawhide lasso at a Yanqui cavalryman, catching him by the neck, and pulled him off his horse and hauled him along until the man choked to death. She thought of the stories Joaquín had told her of the spring roundups out on the open prairie when branding calves, of him teaching Cheno everything he knew about roping until the day came when the younger man bested him in the skill.

When a Yanqui cannon tore into the Mexican cavalry, making a bloody mangled mess of horse and man, she could take no more. She returned to the hospital tent to get away from the horrific sights and sounds of the battlefield, from the sight of John shouting orders to his men, his cannons ripping into the North American ranks below on the plateau. From the hospital she could hear the incessant roar of the San Patricios' cannons throughout the day. Yes, the sounds could have been from the enemy, but in her heart she couldn't bear to think that the blood-curdling screams rising from the battlefield belonged to her countrymen and to the foreign soldiers who had so gallantly taken a stand on behalf of Mexico.

After many hours, the combat finally ceased when the sky broke open, flooding the terrain with a cold, heavy rain, turning the battlegrounds into a lagoon. Both armies took a respite to wait for the rain to pass. From the ridge, she could see the horror of the aftermath, with soldiers fallen in heaps everywhere, limbs interlaced. The hospital aides and burial parties went out to search in the muck for their injured and slain. The wheels of the wagons got stuck in the mud, and the hospital aides had no choice but to carry the wounded one by one in makeshift stretchers made of muskets. The wounded were laid upon the muddy ground of the hospital for want of cots and blankets, and there they remained stretched upon the bare earth, their uniforms caked with mud and blood.

Ximena, the surgeons, and the other hospital attendants did their best to ease the suffering of the wounded they had managed to bring in, but they had insufficient medical supplies and shelter to provide them and not a grain of rice or drop of clean water to offer.

The wind blew, like the wails of La Llorona. Ximena shivered under her thin rebozo as she listened to the eerie sounds. Two San Patricios came in carrying their comrade in their arms. Kerr Delaney's left arm had been blown off by an exploding shell. The surgeon ordered her to prepare the Irishman for an immediate amputation, and she wished she could save what was left of the arm from the surgeon's saw. But upon seeing the torn muscles, the crushed bones, the thin pieces of flesh hanging from the limb, she knew there was nothing she could do but help hold him down and give him strength. This time, he hadn't been as lucky as in Monterrey.

"It's going to be alright, Kerr," she said.

"Don't fret about me, lassie," he said. "And don't be alarmed about Lieutenant Riley. We've been giving the Yanks hell out there. Took two of their guns, we did."

After the operation, Santa Anna's manservant came looking for her. She changed her apron and cleaned herself as best she could and was escorted to his quarters. A war meeting was taking place, and they all turned to look at her. A hush fell inside the tent. Her eyes locked with John's, and she wished she could run to his arms, but she stood at the entrance of the tent, clutching her basket. On seeing her, Santa Anna dismissed everyone, and his chiefs and officers took their leave. John squeezed her shoulder as he passed and smiled encouragingly. His uniform was blackened with powder stains, and his eyes were irritated from too much smoke, but otherwise, he seemed fine. In the evening, she would prepare chamomile tea to rinse his eyes.

"Delaney?"

"He's alive."

"Good. I'll go see him now," he said. The flaps of the tent closed behind him, and it took every ounce of strength to remain inside the tent and not follow him out.

Santa Anna bid her closer to where he sat. "Ximena, please, I'm in need of your services." He winced as he removed his wooden leg.

"You didn't have to send your officers away," she said. "I can minister to your wounds while you conduct your meeting."

"No, no. They must resume their positions. And I can't have my subordinates see me in this state. I would lose my authority if they saw any weakness on my part."

His stump was bleeding again, the closure had broken open. But he also had cuts and bruises on his face, and as she watched him remove his uniform jacket and saw the blood on the shirt beneath, she understood why he had sent everyone away.

"Damn Yanquis killed my horse from under me," he said as she checked for broken ribs. "I barely managed to avoid being crushed to death by my own mount. That wouldn't have been such a glorious death, would it?"

While she cleaned and dressed his wounds, he spoke to her about the battle, how before the rain had forced a pause in the fighting, he had enveloped Taylor's left flank and gained his rear, had decimated three of his cavalry units and had taken two standards and three artillery pieces, two of which had been seized by the San Patricios themselves. Trophies of war, he called them. "My troops have secured an advantageous position on the plateau," he said. "As soon as this wretched storm passes, we will attack even harder. Victory will be ours by the time the sun sets tonight, and I shall present a new laurel to our nation."

She nodded enthusiastically, wanting to believe. Needing to believe. "You can do it, General. You can end this war today."

"I won't yield," he said as she reattached his wooden leg. "No matter how hungry or thirsty we are . . ." He stood up proudly and helped her stand up, then placed his hands on her shoulders. "We will stand our ground and fight to victory or death! Se lo prometo, Ximena."

As soon as the storm passed, the fighting recommenced, its brutality a dark contrast to the beautiful rainbow that painted the sky. Through the interminable hours, all she could do was pray, knowing that if Jimmy Maloney were there with her, he would've kept her abreast of the battle. But he was gone, and now the only thing she cared about, regardless of whether they won or lost, was that John and Cheno would be alive and standing when the last cannonball flew.

As dusk settled over the land, the two armies called for a cease-fire, twelve hours after the fighting began. The field was a marshland, the gunpowder too damp. Ximena and the other soldaderas went into the boggy field of carnage. So many mutilated bodies of both men and horses were scattered about that she couldn't even walk without stepping on a limb or slipping on a pool of blood. As the curses, prayers, and screams of the dying reached a crescendo around her, and she saw all the faces disfigured by death, she realized that the real winner in this battle was La Muerte.

Men and beasts shrieked in excruciating agony. Ximena forced herself to keep her eyes in front of her or she knew she would go mad. The wounded were slowly being carried out to the hospital tent, but the dead lay everywhere. The soldaderas roamed the battlefield anxious as they sought their men. Their wails mingled with the anguished cries of the dying. But sometimes, the cries were of jubilation when a wife found her husband in the muck still alive and well. Those were moments of ecstasy, and Ximena's spirit lifted briefly as she watched husband and wife embrace once again.

She knew that she needed to work quickly, find those who could be saved and leave the rest to their fate. *God have mercy on us all*, she thought. The night was closing in around them and, in the dim light with their muddy uniforms, she couldn't tell if the bodies belonged to the Mexican or the North American army, but it didn't matter. These were human beings who reached out to her, supplicating for help, asking to be held, men who in their last seconds of life, called out to their mothers, their wives. What could she do but kneel beside them, friend and foe alike, clutching their hands and praying for their souls as she watched them take their last breaths?

She felt a firm but gentle hand on her shoulder and turned to find John standing behind her. She fell into his arms, desperate to be held and comforted by him. At this moment, she wished with all her heart to never be separated from him again. Even if she knew that he could never be hers.

"I'm sorry you have to witness this desolation." He wrapped his arms tighter around her, and she could feel, by the way he gave into their embrace, his own need for solace. She kissed him then, and when he returned her kiss, his desire for her anchored her, gave her the strength to carry on with the task at hand.

"I will remember this until the day I die," she said.

"A third of my men have been killed or wounded today, and I shall forever mourn this loss. Let's hope 'twasn't in vain."

"We're winning, aren't we?"

"Wish to God that it be so. The battle isn't over yet. In the morrow, there will be more fightin'. Heaven help us. With no nourishment and no protection against the elements, 'twill be a long night tonight."

Ximena thought of what Santa Anna had said. They wouldn't yield, no matter what. "Have you seen Cheno? Is he alive?"

He took her hand and led her toward the spot where he said he had last seen his cavalry charging the Yanqui lines. "Prepare yourself, lass.

Bragg's guns ripped many of the lancers to shreds. That sonofabitch is the reason why Taylor's flank didn't collapse."

They stepped over severed limbs and broken weapons, the air smelling of roasted flesh and sticky blood. The darkness brought the wild animals out, and coyotes and cougars roamed the perimeter, ready to pounce on either men or horses. One coyote came too close to them, trying to pull an arm off a dead soldier. Ximena threw a broken musket at it to scare it away, but more would come, and she knew it was only a matter of time before the bloody feast began.

"Riley, Ximena, over here!"

In the dim light, she could barely make out the figure of Patrick Dalton, bending over a soldier who was leaning against his horse. The animal's entrails had spilled out, and yet, the horse chewed on the wet grass with indifference, oblivious to its condition.

"Cheno!" She and Riley rushed to their side. "Are you hurt?"

His leg was stuck under his stallion. "I think it's broken."

As Riley, Dalton, and Cheno's friends pulled him out and carried him away, stumbling in the dark toward the field hospital, a cougar growled, and Ximena turned to see the wild cat and a lobo facing each other, preparing to fight over the horse. *Don't they understand there is no need to fight? Don't they see there is plenty here for them all to gorge their fill?* Sensing the danger, the horse began to squeal. Ximena yanked a musket from a fallen soldier's hands and shot the animal dead.

After she set Cheno's broken leg and made him a cast with the pulp of crushed globe mallow roots, he succumbed to a deep sleep. Soon the rain started up again and it was too dark to see. The search for the wounded was called off for the night, and everyone sought shelter from the unrelenting rain and bitter cold. The soldiers and the camp women lamented not being able to light fires to lessen the evening chill, and most had neither a blanket nor a sarape to protect themselves from the elements. Not one piece of bread or tortilla remained for them to eat.

Wrapped in her frayed rebozo, Ximena busied herself with the injured and didn't allow herself to think about how cold and hungry she was. John came into the tent and, by the look on his face, she knew he was the bearer of bad news. "The commander has ordered the troops to evacuate the area and leave our dead and wounded behind."

"We are retreating?" Ximena asked incredulously. They had suffered severe losses, yes, but she knew they had won the day.

"We've exhausted our ammunition and our provisions. Our troops won't withstand another day of fightin'. Taylor, on the other hand, has just received two regiments to reinforce him and our spies have spotted forty wagons of fresh supplies on the way."

"So, we are running away? All those men died, and now we abandon the field and let the Yanquis win?"

"During the war council, some of us tried to dissuade our general from yieldin' the field to the enemy. To make him see reason. Death on the field of battle is a better destiny than to die strewn upon the road. But there were many others who were of the same mind as he. The general has claimed today's victory and given the order to withdraw. We're to pull back to Agua Nueva at once."

"How can we be victorious if we are the ones running away?"

"We can't." He clenched his fists. "The troops don't deserve this, I know. 'Tis an insult to all that we've sacrificed. Once we relinquish the field, Taylor will be the victor."

"Then we must not abandon it. We must stand our ground, just like Santa Anna said we would!"

"Believe me, lass, the man in me condemns his decision, but the soldier in me has to obey my commander. The only way out is to violate the oath I have made to your country. Would you have me be a deserter yet again?"

She could see the turmoil inside him, sensed his impotence. She felt the rage course through her as she hurried out of the field hospital.

"Lass, come back. Where do you think you're goin'? You won't reason with him, I tell ya!"

She broke into a run, not listening to anything but her own fury. Santa Anna's ornate carriage and baggage carts waited outside his tent, but she knew he was still inside. The guards knew her, and they didn't try to stop her from bursting into his private quarters. He was standing by his desk dictating a letter to his secretary while his staff finished packing his belongings. He seemed surprised to see her.

"You have something to say to me, I see." He motioned to his secretary and aides to leave and waited for her to approach.

"Didn't you say you would never run away?"

"I'm not running away. I'm protecting my men from being slaughtered. Their performance today was outstanding. They have done their duty, so let us rejoice in the blessings of today. Tomorrow, it'll be a different story."

"You're wrong. I've watched every soldier fight with strength and loyalty, even without decent weapons, without food and water, without proper shoes and clothing. They've fought on an empty stomach, and they've held the field. And now you're taking that from them? Turning them into cowards on the run, like the cocks you disdain so much."

"It's not for want of courage, it's for want of provisions that we leave. I'm saving the honor of our army by sparing them from the shame and certainty of a defeat. Let us claim victory while we're still ahead."

"Why won't you let them fight and die with honor like the brave men that they are? Are you afraid of being captured by the Yanquis . . . again?"

"Who do you think you are? I do not owe you an explanation for my decisions!" he said, shaking her by the arm. "I am the commander-in-chief of this army."

"You are the commander-in-cowardice. You don't deserve this army," she spat, yanking her arm from his grip. How could she have allowed herself to be fooled by him? "You don't deserve John Riley and the San Patricios, the eight hundred wounded in the field hospitals, the weary soldiers braving hunger and thirst, the thousands slaughtered in vain. It should be you out there being eaten by cougars!"

He raised his hand, as if to slap her. Instead, he pulled her to him and tried to kiss her. She turned her face, and his lips landed on her cheek. He laughed. "You have more cojones than my chiefs, querida. Your courage is truly admirable. One day, I shall make you a general."

He saluted her and yelled to his driver outside to prepare the carriage. He held out his hand to escort her.

"I'd rather walk," she said. Ignoring his outstretched hand, she left the tent and went out into the starless night.

28

The dispirited troops broke camp and undertook the inglorious retreat to Agua Nueva, from thence to San Luis Potosí. The weak and
the wounded were soon left to the buzzards. As the days progressed,
Riley was disheartened to see that they were taking further losses.
Soon the bulk of their dead consisted not of those who had fallen in
action, but of those who had crumbled on the road and were left to
blacken in the sun, or who crawled into the thicket to die alone. He
trudged along with the crippled battalions, many of them shoeless
and their clothes in tatters, trying not to walk over the bodies of the
fallen or trample upon those who had yet to take their last breaths.
He turned his eyes from these images, which only increased his feelings of helplessness. He regretted bitterly once again that they had
not been allowed to die honorably on the battlefield and had instead
abandoned it to the enemy. By committing the folly of this tragic retreat, Santa Anna had compromised the national honor he had sworn
to defend and undermined the morale of his army, increasing its misery and hardship.

Without a drop of rain to swallow the choking dust, the camp
women left the columns to make fruitless forays into the brush to lo-
cate fresh water. The best that could be found was stagnant and foul-

smelling, and if it hadn't been for Ximena, Riley might not have been able to resist. Those too thirsty to care had thrown themselves into the puddles to drink, only to collapse from dysentery hours later, convulsing horrendously in pain. Ximena had filled his water gourd, thrown a chopped nopal into it, and waited hours until the water had been purified before allowing him a drink of it. Several times, he went with her into the brush, and she managed to find enough food to keep them alive for one more day—a small barrel-shaped cactus she carefully peeled and sliced before feeding him the green pulp inside, chia sage seeds she shook off the plant, which he licked right off the palm of her hand, roots she pried from the stingy soil and he nibbled on with relish. Another time, he lifted her high onto his shoulders so she could reach the flowering stalk of a towering yucca plant.

He wolfed down the precious creamy-white flower petals she handed him. They weren't enough to appease the hunger consuming them. "Perhaps tomorrow, we will find something more . . . If tomorrow comes," he said, savoring the last of the flowers. He looked at the vast barren land in resignation, imagining his unmarked grave in this lone desert, a coyote howling over it. "We're going to die here, aren't we?" The utter defeat in his own voice affrighted him.

She heard it too, and she wrapped her arms around him. He crushed her against him. "Don't give up on me, you hear?" he pleaded. "Don't leave me to the buzzards."

"¡Nunca! I will not leave you behind, soldier." She stood on her toes and reached for him, nibbled on his earlobe as delicately as she'd nibbled on the yucca flowers, and the bolt of desire that ran through his body jolted his heart, made it palpitate with renewed strength, breathed life back into him.

"I want you, Ximena," he growled, pulling her against him. "May God in Heaven pity me, but if I'm goin' to die, then let it be in your arms." He lowered her onto the ground and pulled up her skirt, and she tugged at his trousers. She clung to him with all her strength, matching his rhythm, both of them consumed by another kind of hunger.

For two weeks, half-dead with fatigue, he and Ximena trudged on, along with the remnants of Santa Anna's army, braving hunger and thirst, freezing rain and scorching sun, sickness and despair, but each night, they found solace in each other's arms, their lovemaking urgent and desperate, as if it were their last day on earth. But mostly they simply held each other, making sure they were both still breathing come dawn. Finally, the city of San Luis Potosí came into view. With barely enough strength to stand, on the verge of desperation, Riley looked upon the beautiful domes of the Templo del Carmen in the distance. For a moment he allowed himself to rejoice, but his elation turned to fear. Was his mind playing tricks on him again? Was he seeing a mirage? The scorching sun beat down on him. His brain was a potato crisping on a gridiron. His tongue was swollen, and he could no longer spit. He scarcely knew what to think—was he alive or burning in hell, paying for his infidelity? As he squinted at the bright light, the city blurred and the ground opened beneath his feet. He heard Ximena calling his name, but his tongue was too heavy to speak. The last thing he remembered was the sound of the cathedral bells and the sight of pigeons taking flight. He wanted to follow them, let his spirit soar into the clouds above . . .

When he woke up, he didn't know where he was. He was lying on a cot in a corridor, amid rows of other cots and straw mats filled with the living skeletons of Santa Anna's troops. They were coughing and moaning, crying and praying. Ximena was sitting by his side, dozing on a chair. She seemed utterly fatigued, her skin sunburned, her lips parched.

"Ximena?" he whispered, hating to wake her. She opened her eyes. They were swollen, her cheeks pale and hollow.

"How do you feel, John?" She reached to grab his hands. Hers were calloused and rough to the touch, but he clung to them, let the warmth of her skin seep into his. He felt faint and had a pain in his head.

"Where am I?" he said, rubbing his eyes, struggling to recover his senses.

"In the convent." She handed him a cup of tea, and he sipped from it. Between the march, the battle, and the retreat, fifteen thousand men had perished or vanished, she told him, and the nuns had taken in what remained of Santa Anna's army.

"How long have I been here?"

"Two days."

"How—?"

"We barely made it to the city. You were very deshidratado, cariño," Ximena said, brushing his hair back. "But you're better now."

He looked at her and the memories came rushing back, the two of them intertwined, clinging to each other out in the merciless desert. What had he done? She bent over him to give him another sip of tea, and when her breath fanned his brow, his body became as taut as the strings of a fiddle, and he knew he could never have enough of her.

"What news is stirring?" he asked.

"Santa Anna is leaving for Mexico City. There is a revolución in the capital. Can you believe it, John? While we were fighting for our lives, the caudillos began another insurrección. Blood is spilling on the streets of the capital, the moderados against the radicales. What madness is this? Even now, instead of uniting to fight our enemy, we are fighting each other!"

"And unite now you must," Patrick Dalton said as he walked down the corridor toward them.

Riley couldn't believe how happy he was to see his friend. "Pat, you are well! And the men?"

Dalton came to stand beside the cot. "We lost many, but you are alive, and so is the Saint Patrick's Battalion."

Riley peeled the blanket off and made to get up.

"You should rest," Ximena said.

"No, there's no time," Dalton said, helping Riley up. "The commander has called a council of war. Things have taken another turn. The Yankee general Winfield Scott has landed on the shores of Vera Cruz with nine thousand soldiers and is about to besiege the port city."

"Perhaps we deserve to lose," Ximena said. "Since our own leaders are incapable of creating peace, only disturbios, they deserve to have no country left to rule!"

"Whist, lass. Don't say such things," Riley said as he put on his uniform jacket. "Mexico is a young nation and not yet used to its newborn freedom. Twenty-five years of independence isn't sufficient time for your leaders to figure out the best way to govern. One day they'll realize that they must stand together, and that the blood of the Mexican people should flow only on the battlefield repellin' invaders, not takin' up arms against each other."

He made his way down the corridor, stopping to check on the twelve men who had spent the night in here with him. "They will be fine in a day or two," Ximena reassured him. She looked at the cot farther down the corridor and shook her head. "Cheno is there fighting for his life."

Even from where he stood, Riley saw plain enough that the sergeant's condition was grave. It was a miracle he hadn't perished during the retreat, considering his already weakened state after the battle. His comrades had managed to carry him on a makeshift litter, sometimes even on their shoulders, until they made it to the city. Juan Cortina was a fighter, and his stamina and willpower were things Riley most admired about him.

"Go mind your friend, lass," Riley said. "And I shall see you tonight."

He and Dalton left the convent. The brightness of the day hurt his eyes, and it wasn't long before his head was splitting. When Dalton urged him to stop and rest, Riley refused. No, he needed to be strong. He needed to be a leader. Dalton insisted and pushed him onto a bench in the public square.

"I'm fine, Pat," Riley said. "Let us go to the barracks. I must change and take this beard off me. See to the men."

"In a minute," Dalton said. He pulled out an envelope and handed it to Riley. "Tidings arrived for you whilst we were away. The priest at the cathedral asked me to deliver it to you. It was sent to him by another priest in Matamoros, he said."

Riley looked at the cathedral on the other side of the plaza. His hands shook as he took the letter. Dalton patted his shoulder and stood up. "I'll leave you to it, then. Give me a holler if you need anythin', my friend."

With trembling hands, Riley opened the letter. He recognized the hand immediately. It was from his parish priest.

30, Oct' 1846

Dear John,

It is with a heavy heart that I must be the bearer of bad tidings. The typhus fever visited your family and came upon Nelly and her parents quite sudden and violent. God took pity on the afflicted and took them to His side without letting them linger in their suffering. God, in his benevolence, has spared Johnny. Let your mind be easy in knowing that I am looking after your boy and will do my best to help him survive this hunger and pestilence scourging the land. He will remain with me until you deem ready for him to embark on the voyage to Mexico, if that is still your desire. The state of the country is such that I do not recommend you return yet awhile. My condolences to you, my son. I imagine your heart must be torn in pieces, but do not despair. Put your trust in our Lord.

I send you my blessings,
Rev. Aidan

Riley stumbled into the cathedral with barely enough strength to make it to the nearest pew. He sat in the cool, dim interior surrounded by candles and wanted to cry, but no tears would come, as if the arid landscape he had barely survived had gotten inside him, and his dreams, his hopes, his very being had dried up and withered. Jesus hanging on his crucifix looked down upon him, and Riley wished to be punished for his betrayal of the most sacred oath he had ever made—

to care for his wife. He'd nothing to give her when they married but an uncertain future. And now, Nelly was dead, she'd been dead for more than five months. And if Father Aidan hadn't taken in Johnny, the lad would probably be dead by now too.

He had never felt so alone. So far from his homeland. So far from its gentle rain and rolling mists. So far from the son he'd left to seek his fortune on the other side of the Atlantic. He ought never to have left. Now he found himself adrift, a stranger in a strange country, without a way home. He'd failed his wife and now he was a man with the burden of another broken oath upon him. He fell to his knees and shook with violent grief.

29

March 1847
San Luis Potosí

At the council of war, Riley didn't hear much of what was said. General Mejía, as usual, translated for him, until he noticed Riley's state of mind. "Are you unwell, teniente Riley?"

"I'm grand," Riley said, not wanting to distract him from the meeting. There was no point in him being here anymore. What was he doing oceans away from where he should've been all this time—back in his homeland with his loved ones? Hadn't he well nigh died of thirst and hunger in Mexico? He'd been braving death here, so why not do so back home?

He'd admired the Mexicans for doing what the Irish couldn't—gaining their freedom. In his folly, he'd believed he could help them keep it. But what if Ximena was right? What if they didn't deserve it? Santa Anna had literally marched his troops to their deaths. The general still stood by his decision to abandon the battlefield and dared to continue to declare a false victory for Mexico, claiming as proof the colors and guns he'd taken from his foe and the Yankee corpses he'd left on the battlefield. Could the general live with the falsehoods he was making to his own people just to preserve his image as their liberator?

Riley could still taste the bitterness of their shameful defeat. And now, without even giving the troops a chance to recover, Santa Anna was planning to march them all the way to the city of the True Cross—Vera Cruz—to confront General Scott. Since Mexico had no navy, Scott had been able to sail down the Gulf of Mexico completely uncontested.

"I will drive the Yanquis back into the water to drown like I did with the French," Santa Anna boasted. "The French took one of my legs, and the Yanquis might take the other, but we will send them back into the Gulf where they can feed the sharks."

Applause erupted in the room. The general ordered the chiefs to prepare their units for the march. He was departing the following day with his staff and a small detachment. He was leaving half of his forces in San Luis Potosí to reorganize and the other half was marching out by the week's end under the command of Generals Ampudia and Vásquez. The Saint Patrick's Battalion was to be part of this group. Riley thought of his men who were still lying on the cots at the convent. What would they say when he told them that in a few days, they needed to be up and ready to follow him to the coast to join the Mexican Army of the East? What would they say when he told them that he had lost his desire to fight? That perhaps it was time for the Saint Patrick's Battalion to be disbanded and its green banner lowered from its staff. He was tired of seeing his men suffer all manner of privations and enjoy none of the glory he'd promised them.

He decided that, after the meeting, he would ask to be relieved of his duty to the Mexicans, thereby being spared of any further indignity. He would ask for his back pay and all that was promised him, though he feared those glorious acres of Mexican soil wouldn't be his if he left. But did it matter anymore? Nelly was gone and her feet would never walk upon their own land, as he'd promised her.

But at the conclusion of the meeting, Santa Anna called Riley forward. "Teniente Riley, por favor." He motioned Riley to stand beside him, along with Captains Moreno and Álvarez, Bachelor, and Stephenson. Riley wondered what was happening as applause erupted in the room once more. Riley was shocked to learn that Santa Anna was awarding him and the others a medal of honor, a promotion, and with that, a pay raise.

"Captain?" Riley looked at General Santa Anna, at the chiefs and officers around the room, unable to believe what he'd just heard.

"For your courage and daring bravery in La Angostura," General Mejía said, translating for the general. "Thank you for your service to la República Mexicana, Captain Riley." Santa Anna pinned on the medal in the shape of a white cross. As Riley shook his hand, he wondered if perhaps he'd misjudged his commander. Had Santa Anna truly believed in good faith that in yielding the field to the Yankees he was saving his men? Instead of an act of weakness and cowardice, had it been one of honor? He looked into the general's eyes, searching for an answer. He wanted to believe, to renew his faith in his dreams and believe that they were not simply foolish fancies. But after the council meeting ended and he returned to the barracks, the burden of doubt and regret returned to weigh heavily on him.

He didn't go to Ximena that night as he'd promised he would. He remained in the barracks with his men, Patrick Dalton by his side. It was only with Dalton that he could be completely honest.

"I've deserted once. I could do it again," Riley told him. They were seated on a bale of hay, observing some of the other San Patricios who were gathered around campfires, roasting maize and singing Irish airs while drinking pulque and mezcal. "I could leave tonight. Ride into the darkness, find a way to get back to my son."

"Do not speak of resignation, Captain! You would betray the oath you've made to this country? This country which has welcomed you—us—with open arms?"

"We're on the losing side," Riley said.

"Both here and back in our homeland," Dalton replied. "At least here, they've made you a captain. If that is what losin' looks like in this country, aren't you better off stayin' here, then?"

"Aye, I've dreamed of this day ever since the British put me in their muster rolls. It took three armies for it to finally come true, but what price must I pay for military glory?"

" 'Tis mournin' your wife you are. And you mustn't let your guilt unsettle your mind. There's no blame to you, John, *a chara.* You were a responsible husband and did your best to maintain her. It's the English who are starvin' our people so they can finally be rid of us Irish. Even if you were there, you wouldn't have been able to save her. Besides, if your wish is to go home, our general has given you the means to do it."

Riley looked at his friend. "What are you sayin'?"

"He's marchin' us to the east coast, isn't he? To the water, the port. There are ships there! The Yankees have blockaded all of the Mexican ports, so if you wish to get back to Ireland, then fight them you must. Once they are defeated, you'll be that much closer to home. You see, Captain, there's no need to desert. No need to quit the Saint Patrick's Battalion in despair." He put an arm around Riley and said, "And, as your friend and second-in-command, I refuse to believe that all your mettle is truly gone."

In the morning, he sought Ximena in the convent. They stepped out into the sunny courtyard, away from the foul smells of the makeshift hospital and the wretched sounds of human misery, and sat on a bench under the orange trees where the white blossoms cascaded around them, releasing their sweetness into the spring breeze. The murmur of bees was the only sound to be heard, and they sat there for a spell in silence, the air thick with the scent of nectar. Riley wished they could stay there forever.

It was Ximena who broke the silence. "You are leaving. Without me," she said, matter-of-factly. There was no reproach in her voice.

Only a quiet acceptance. For a second, he wished she would yell at him, sting him with hateful words.

He reached into his pocket and handed her the letter from Father Aidan. He had no voice to say, "My wife is dead." So he let her read the letter and see for herself the graveyard of woe he was carrying in his heart.

After she finished reading, she handed it back to him and fixed her gaze upon the ground. "I know you blame yourself for her death. But you did the best you can, do you not see?" She looked tenderly at him and said, "John, you must not permit your guilt to eat at your soul. You are a good, honorable man. And I—"

Her voice choked, and she swallowed the words. Instead, she cupped his face with her hands and kissed his cheek, sighing in resignation. She stood to leave, but when she began to walk away, he grabbed her hand and pulled her back to him.

"I love you," he said. "Perhaps 'tis cruel of me to say it, when I have to leave you, but I want you to know that I do love you, Ximena."

Tears welled in her eyes. "I love you as well," she said, her voice raw. But then she pulled her hand from his and wiped her eyes. "But if you think to love me is a sin for which you must do penitencia, then I prefer you do not love me, John Riley."

With that, she left him to his grief, and as he listened to the buzzing of the bees around him, the ache in his heart pulsed and throbbed as if he'd stumbled upon their hive, and the tears finally came.

During the days that remained in the city, Riley did nothing but prepare the San Patricios for the march ahead. To his surprise, new deserters from the Yankee ranks arrived—despite their loss at Buena Vista—and he replenished his unit. The enthusiasm of the new recruits made him realize that he was honor-bound to the Saint Patrick's Battalion. He gave himself completely to his busy schedule, avoiding Ximena as much as he could. He could always count on Patrick Dalton to do the daily drills, but he was captain now, he told her, and he had his duties to fulfill. Yet she was never out of his mind. Even as he shouted orders to his men, he would think about when he had made love to her out in the open land as dusk faded into night, and he longed to have her in his arms again. But then, he would think of Nelly, of not being there by her side when she took her last breath. What right did he have now to happiness?

Giving up his love for Ximena would have to be his penance. How else could he atone for what he'd done?

30

March 1847
San Luis Potosí

Ximena sat under the shade of an orange tree in the convent's court-yard, listening to the sounds in the plaza as the troops prepared to march out of the city. When she heard the bugles ordering the regi-ments to move out and the potosinos cheering and shouting their fare-wells, she closed her eyes and held back the tears. She pictured John at the head of the columns, rolling out on the horse-drawn caissons as the Saint Patrick's Battalion moved on, their banner high in the air.

After a time, an eerie silence fell upon the city, even the persistent buzzing of the bees disappeared, as if all life had come to a standstill and there was no one left in San Luis Potosí but her. She was startled by the sudden tolling of the convent bells calling the nuns to eve-ning vespers and sending swallows darting through the courtyard. She wrapped herself in her rebozo and followed the melancholy sound.

The hours, days, weeks passed in a blur, one after the other, until she no longer knew what day it was. She busied herself tending to the invalids, and little by little the convent's corridors emptied out as they left—either walking out on their own or carried out feet first through the door.

One day she received a letter from Santa Anna at the convent, with news confirming the rumors that had reached them—the port city of Vera Cruz had fallen after sustaining a four-day siege from Scott's forces. Day and night the Yanqui cannons, howitzers, and mortars had bombarded the city until it finally succumbed. Scott refused permission to evacuate once the siege began and hundreds of the city's residents perished, mostly women and children.

Now that Santa Anna had put an end to the revolution in Mexico City, he and his forces were marching to Vera Cruz, ready to confront Scott. Another battle would soon ensue, and though the general told her he was confident that this time the Mexican Army would be victorious, Ximena wasn't going to fall for that again—only God knew for certain what the outcome would be. If Scott defeated Santa Anna's army, he would then advance to the capital, the heart of Mexico. The general concluded his letter with a copy of his proclamation to the Mexican people, which had been distributed to the masses.

I pray you heed my call, querida Ximena, he'd written on the margins of the copy he'd sent her.

López de Santa Anna
President Ad Interim of the Mexican Republic,
to his compatriots.

Mexicans! Vera Cruz is already in the power of the enemy. It has succumbed, not under the influence of American valor, nor can it even be said that it has fallen under the impulses of their good fortune. To our shame be it said, we ourselves have produced this deplorable misfortune by our own interminable discords.

The truth is due to you from the government; you are the arbiters of the fate of our country. If our country is to be defended, it will be you who will stop the triumphant march of the enemy who now occupies Vera Cruz. If the enemy advance one step more, the national independence will be buried in the abyss of the past.

I am resolved to go out and encounter the enemy. My duty is to sacrifice myself, and I well know how to fulfil it!

Perhaps the American hosts may proudly tread the imperial capital of Azteca. I will never witness such an opprobrium, for I am decided first to die fighting!

Mexicans! You have a religion—protect it! You have honor—then free yourselves from infamy! You love your wives, your children—then liberate them from American brutality! But it must be by action, not by vain entreaty nor barren desires, with which the enemy must be opposed.

Perhaps I speak to you for the last time! I pray you listen to me! Do not vacillate between death and slavery; and if the enemy conquer you, at least they will respect the heroism of your resistance. It is now time that the common defence should alone occupy your thoughts! The hour of sacrifice has sounded its approach! Awaken!

The nation has not yet lost its vitality. I swear to you I will answer for the triumph of Mexico if unanimous and sincere desires on your part second my desires. Mexicans! Your fate is the fate of the nation! Not the Americans but you will decide her destiny. Vera Cruz calls for vengeance! Follow me, and wash out the stain of her dishonor!

ANTONIO LÓPEZ DE SANTA ANNA
Mexico
March 31, 1847

"I've had enough of this damn war, enough of Santa Anna," Cheno said after Ximena read him the proclamation. His leg was healed enough that he could walk around the convent's orchards without the use of the crutches, though he still needed a cane. Every day Ximena had accompanied him on his morning exercises so that he could strengthen his leg, and she was happy to see that very soon he would be able to ride a horse without too much discomfort.

"I'm not going to follow him anymore. I've done my duty. I almost paid with my life to wash away the stain of Mexico's dishonor. But that won't happen as long as that caudillo is in command." Out of breath, he took a seat on one of the stone benches and massaged his injured leg.

"So you are giving up the fight?"

"Never! I will always offer my country my blood and never stop defending the Mexican name. One day, if I must, I shall start a war against our oppressors and fatten the land with their own gore. For now though, it's time for me to return to the Río Bravo and tend to the honor and interests of my family."

"How?"

"General Canales and his guerillas are heading north, and I'm going with them," Cheno said. "Come with me. If we run into any Yanqui patrols along the road, Canales will be able to handle them. It's the safest way to get home."

Even though General Scott and most of the Yanqui forces were now in Vera Cruz, Taylor was still in Monterrey, holding possession of the city, probably until the war came to an end. The norteamericanos were still roaming Mexico's northern lands and the skirmishes between them and the Mexican guerillas continued to leave a trail of corpses and burned-down homes.

"When will you leave?"

"Next week. I've asked Canales to secure us some horses, in case you desire to go home as well. Or have you other plans?"

"Do you mean will I go in search of John?"

"If I didn't know the Irishman, I would say he was a fool. But I understand that his grief has blinded him, led him to believe he doesn't deserve you. Being the good Catholic that he is, he will self-flagellate to kingdom come."

"I can mend his body and do my best to mend his wounded soul, but what can I do for the anguish of his guilt-ridden heart?"

"Santa Anna then," he said, taking the proclamation out of her hands to look at it, though, like Joaquín, he did not know how to read. His bad temper had gotten him in perpetual trouble at school. "Will you heed the caudillo's call, as he implores you to do? I can see in your eyes, querida amiga, that you still haven't given up on him, or your Irishman for that matter."

She covered her face and sighed. "Perhaps I am the one who is the fool, Cheno."

For the balance of the day, Ximena thought about Cheno's proposal to join him on his return home. Part of her wanted to go back to the rancho, though without Joaquín, she wasn't sure how she could make it prosper again. The survival of the rancho had depended on the wild mustangs Joaquín caught and broke and the good mules he bred by using his best mares and jacks. She knew that Cheno would offer assistance, but he had his own family to take care of, and she didn't want his charity.

Another part of her wanted to follow John. She understood his grief, his guilt, and she shared in his sorrow. Although she had never met his wife, Ximena felt compassion for her and yes, even guilt for being able to enjoy John's presence, to receive his love and attention, while Nelly had been suffering thousands of kilometers away. They hadn't meant to hurt anyone, especially that poor woman. Was being apart the price to pay now?

As for Santa Anna's proclamation, she felt as Cheno did, that she had done her duty to her country. But she also hoped that their compatriots would answer Santa Anna's call, especially those who had the means to do so. She hoped they would rouse from their apathy, to unite and chase the invaders off their land once and for all.

If she was now going to let go of everything—the rancho, the war, and John—there was another option for her to consider, one she'd tried not to think about until now. She could remain here with the nuns. They treated her kindly and took great interest in everything she was teaching them about the healing arts and the uses and spiritual powers of each plant. She enjoyed working in the convent's gardens and had begun helping the nuns add more medicinal plants. Inside the convent's high walls, Ximena felt safe, and she loved the solitude and

tranquility of being away from the world, from its violence and heart-
ache. What if she took the veil? What if she remained inside these
walls forever and gave herself up completely to God ? The convent
could be a place of refuge for her. She could seek asylum here from
all that had befallen her, and she could finally rest her weary body and
soul. The nuns could be a new family for her, she could have sisters
with whom to share her joys and sorrows, sisters who would nurse
her when she was sick, offer her a kind word or a smile. She could
grow old here in this cloister, contentedly surrounded by her medicinal
plants and flowers, in her small cell in peaceful meditation, and perhaps one day, God willing, she could die in her black robe peacefully in
her sleep, surrounded by her sisters, and take her last breath amid the
sweetness of their prayers and tears.

"We would gladly take you, hija," the old Madre said to her when
Ximena shared her thoughts with her the following day. "But your
heart belongs to capitán Riley, and it will always be so. Especially now
that you're carrying his child."

Ximena was taken aback. She put a hand on her belly and looked
at the Madre knowing she spoke the truth. In her distress, she hadn't
paid attention to the signs—the queasiness in her stomach, the retch-
ing in the mornings, her missed cycles.

"Yes, hija, I've been watching you," the old Madre said. "The babe
belongs with its father as well. But above all, it cannot be brought into
the world out of wedlock. You can't suffer the poor creature to pay
for your sins. Some of our priests will be traveling to Mexico City by
the week's end to visit the archbishop. I can inquire if they have a seat
in one of the carriages for you, perhaps you can travel with their attendants. And with your skills as a healer, they might not protest the
presence of a woman."

"Thank you, Madre. I appreciate your kindness. But I don't yet
know what I will do."

Afterward, Ximena sat in the courtyard, thinking about what she'd
just learned. When she was a child, she'd watched from afar as a wild-
fire, started by lightning, had spread across the prairie and burned ev-

erything in its path. She still remembered the breath of heat on her skin, the odor of scorched earth, the crackling grasses and screeching wildlife. Seeing the sky choking on smoke, she'd cried at the catastrophe before her. Nana Hortencia put an arm around her and told her not to cry. *"Don't you see, mijita, this is how the Creator renews the prairie. The fire gives it new life."* After the fire passed, and Ximena looked at the blackened earth, the piles of cow dung still smoldering, the carcasses of rabbits, coyotes, prairie dogs, and other small animals littering the scorched land, she'd doubted her nana's words. How could there be life when all she saw was death everywhere? It wasn't until a few weeks later, when the new grasses and plants returned with vigor, that she'd understood. The fire had burned everything to the ground to give new seeds and overcrowded roots a chance. She imagined her baby as a seed burrowed deep within the sacred ground of her womb. Her home had literally been destroyed by fire, the war had all but consumed her, her loved ones had been taken from her. She was as scorched and barren as a burned prairie. But now life had sprouted within her.

A new beginning.

She dreamed of him that night. She saw herself in a plaza, with rain falling and trees swaying in the wind. On bare feet, she walked across the wet cobblestones, slippery and cold, the rain soaking into her nightgown, her hair sticking to her face. And there before her, hanging from the gallows, were the San Patricios. Some had their backs to her, others faced her with dead red eyes, tongues thrust out of their foaming mouths, hands clenched into fists. One of them turned with the wind and now she could see his face, and she blinked and blinked, wiping the rain from her eyes, but every time she looked, it was him. It was always him.

She woke suddenly, bathed in a cold sweat and choking down a scream. After she caught her breath, she lit a bundle of sage and gave herself a barrida, the smoke soothing her mind and steadying her as

she swept her body with it. She lay down, trying to push the images of
the hanging men out of her mind. But every time she closed her eyes,
she could see John hanging from a rope.

At sunrise the following week, Cheno appeared with Canales along
with the other guerillas. Furnished with a mount, Ximena grabbed the
reins and climbed willingly upon the saddle. Soon she would be back
to the Río Bravo delta, back to the rancho and her new life with her
child. The old Madre and the nuns stood outside the convent to see
her off, some crying their farewells. They handed Ximena a box with
sweets and fruits for her journey.

   "Gracias, madre. Gracias por todo."

"God be with you, hija."

Canales gave the order and the group rode out. Ximena didn't turn
to look behind. She stared straight ahead until they reached the city
limit and the convent bells began to toll, as if calling her back. Then,
very faintly, she heard the nuns singing their daily hymns.

As they left the city behind them, she listened as Canales told
Cheno about his adventures and misadventures fighting Taylor's
forces, including all the Yanquis he'd killed and the men he'd lost to
the Rangers who roamed wild in the area, committing atrocities from
village to village. He told of how he'd lassoed a Ranger and dragged
him through the cacti where he stripped and castrated him in retalia-
tion for killing two guerrilleros.

"Well done, amigo. They thought they would come here to kill
Mexicans and go unpunished? No, señor," Cheno said approvingly.

When Canales told the story of another band of guerrillas who'd
killed dozens of Mexican muleteers whom Taylor had hired to transport his supplies, Ximena thought about the carnage she'd witnessed
and the stories from the wounded she'd tended to. In the ranchos and
haciendas from San Luis Potosí all the way to the Río Bravo, Mexican
families had been forced to flee because if they refused to help the
guerilla bands, the guerrilleros would destroy their homes, and if they

helped the guerrillas, the Yanquis would destroy their homes. They were caught, as the saying went, entre la espada y la pared, between a sword and a wall .

This war was taking place not only on the battlefield, but also on the roads, in humble villages and isolated ranchos, in the chaparral and prairies, in deserts and mountain passes. She thought of Joaquín, of what had been asked of him.

She wondered what kind of journey lay before her. Would they be plundering and killing their way home? What atrocities would she be forced to witness? If more slaughter and devastation awaited her, wasn't she heading the wrong way? She turned her head to look at San Luis Potosí, but only the steeples and bell towers of the churches were visible now. She thought of John, of how he had almost lost his life right at this spot from sunstroke and the fatigue of that nightmarish retreat. But he had lived. He was still alive. Then she thought about her dream. How could she not warn him? He'd made it clear that there was no future for them anymore, and she might be foolish to go look-ing for him, but how could she start a new life with her child when its father's life was in peril? Didn't her child deserve a father? Shouldn't she at least try?

"I'm sorry," she said to no one in particular. "I'm heading the wrong way."

They all turned to look at her. She dismounted the horse and handed the reins back to Canales.

"Take it," he said. "It's one of the horses Joaquín gave us."

She nodded her thanks, then looked at Cheno, who approached her on his horse. He squeezed her hand and smiled. "I'll look after your rancho, Ximena, and when you're ready, it will be there waiting for you."

"Adiós, Cheno." She looked at the guerrillas and said, "Vayan con Dios."

She remounted the horse, turned it around, and cantered back to the city, her eyes fixed upon the cathedral steeple where the priests were making preparations for their visit to Mexico City.

Part Four

The Heart
of Mexico

31

The Port of Vera Cruz had surrendered to the Yankees at the end of March, and in April, Santa Anna's armies collided with Scott's at the Battle of Cerro Gordo in the hills of Vera Cruz. Though the Mexicans managed to inflict a good deal of damage, the Yankees still bested them in battle, and Riley had found himself once again on the run with his men and his Mexican comrades-at-arms, leaving behind more than one thousand of their dead on the battlefield, thirty-three field pieces, ammunition, and a chest with twenty thousand dollars from which the soldiers' wages were to be paid.

To Riley, Cerro Gordo had been a clearer defeat than Buena Vista—this time, there was no doubt that the Yanks had emerged victorious, forcing Santa Anna to abandon the battlefield at panic speed on horseback after his personal carriage was riddled with bullets and his spare wooden leg fell into the enemy's possession. Scattering in every direction in a disordered mass, Santa Anna's Army of the East had then made its way to Mexico City. Riley had no choice but to follow, since as long as the Yankees had possession of Vera Cruz and its port, there was no way to get home but to keep on fighting.

In Mexico City, Santa Anna occupied himself with arrangements to defend the capital, but he faced the same obstacles as before—insufficient funds, limited supplies and munitions, and lack of support from the Mexican states and the clergy. After his disastrous defeat in Vera Cruz, he'd also lost the confidence of some of his followers, and his enemies, especially Generals Ampudia and Valencia, wasted no time in renewing their intrigues and sowing dissent. Riley watched as Santa Anna, undeterred by his subordinates' plotting, took the reins of the presidency once again and made the defense of the capital his priority. Soon fortifications were being constructed and martial law imposed, forcing males between the ages of sixteen and sixty to report for military duty. Riley was not surprised when in no time at all, Santa Anna had accumulated twenty-five thousand soldiers under his command. Now he was focused on raising funds and support, invoking the patriotism and zeal of the city residents, urging them to devote their fortunes and their honor in defense of Mexico.

On his end, Riley welcomed more deserters into the Saint Patrick's Battalion, including a few foreigners who'd been residing in the capital, but he needed more men. Aware that many of the prisoners of war in the Mexican prison cells were Irish, Germans, Poles, and American deserters, he decided to seek them out and recruit them. At the Santiago Tlatelolco Prison, Riley and Patrick Dalton went from cell to cell, observing the men before addressing any of them. The Yankee prisoners would most likely not heed his calling, and though Santa Anna had given him a written order empowering him to take any American prisoner into the Saint Patrick's Battalion, he wanted only men he could trust, who would become San Patricios of their own free will.

Eighteen of the foreign-born prisoners had petitioned the British consul general in Mexico to help them. These were the ones Riley most wanted to talk to. Since the British consul would do nothing for them, joining the Mexican ranks was their only hope for now, and he would make sure they understood that.

At the third cell, Patrick Dalton stopped and pointed to one of the men sitting on the ground. "That's one of the eighteen," he said as he pointed, "Matthew Doyle. And there's Patrick Casey over there, Henry Ockter, and Roger Hogan."

After glancing at the men, Riley decided to address them. "Good afternoon, brave fellas," he said in a deep, loud voice, so all the prisoners could hear. "I'm Captain John Riley, and this is my second-in-command, Lieutenant Patrick Dalton. We're here to offer ye assistance."

One of the Yankees spat on the ground, "I want nothing from the likes of you, traitors."

Undaunted, Riley pressed on. "This is no place for fine soldiers such as yourselves. I can offer ye food, lodgin', clothin', and fair wages, but the best thin' I can offer is this—a chance to live a life with honor and dignity, a life where ye'll be respected and recompensed for your skills and bravery. Join the Saint Patrick's Battalion, and I promise ye your merits shall be recognized. This isn't like the Yankee army. Here with the Mexicans, ye'll be promoted for your skills and your contribution to the war, as ye deserve."

"Leave us be, John Riley. A bigger coward never set foot in this prison," an Irishman said.

"Listen to me, fellas. The Americans will soon be makin' their way upon the National Highway. Ye all know what's goin' to happen to ye when they get here. All of ye are already doomed men. But if ye stand with us and fight for Mexico against the wicked invaders, the Mexican government will reward ye—"

"That's all very fine talk, Captain," another prisoner said. "But how do we know to believe ya?"

Riley pulled out the paper he'd brought with him and waved it before the men. "I have negotiated a contract with the Mexican government, signed by President Santa Anna himself. At the war's end, they will give you lands to cultivate. Or, if you do not wish to settle in this country, you shall be embarked for Europe at the expense of the Mexican government at the conclusion of the war with all your pay."

Riley saw some of the men nodding in approval. But others refused to look at him. He directed his words at them. "'Tis better to stand up and fight than to sit in a cell and wait for death to come to ye, brave fellas. There's no honor or glory in that. Ye must decide if ye are goin' to wait for the Yanks here, sitting helpless, or come and man one of my cannons."

He let his words linger in the air, and he and Dalton waited for the men to make their choice. When they left the prison, they had twenty-three men enlisted in the battalion. Riley expected them to report the next day, and he put Dalton in charge of the new recruits.

After his errands, Riley made his way to the barracks up the wide principal streets, relishing the sights of the metropolis. Mexico City was unlike any city he'd ever seen. It was breathtaking. The capital boasted the finest houses, churches, and public buildings, especially el Palacio Nacional which stretched for an entire city block. Then there was the glorious beauty of the Catedral Metropolitana in Gothic style, with its interior decorated with gold, silver, and copper. At fourteen acres, the main square, la Plaza de la Constituci√≥n, was the largest in the country. The private residences nearby were two or three stories high, with terraces on their roofs and high windows and balconies decorated with intricate ironwork and brilliant flowers.

He would have loved to have seen the city with its normal hustle and bustle. Now, the movement in the streets was mostly that of the troops, priests, and monks, and the Indian vendors and their droning cries. In anticipation of the impending battle, little by little families were leaving the Valley of Mexico to avoid the hostilities. Every day, Riley would see carriages or carts loaded with all manner of possessions, horses, and mules packed with boxes and crates, men, women, and children making their way on foot with baskets and whatever else they could carry. Those who remained, secluded themselves in their homes and only emerged to purchase their necessities from the shops that were still open and from the ambulant peddlers with clay pots of charcoal, lard, cheese, or baskets of tortillas hanging from their backs.

There was a multitude of Indian beggars and lepers, a bundle of rags and deformities and squalid misery. When he saw their arms stretching out for alms, asking him for "un tlaco, por favor, niño," Riley handed out some copper coins and thought of the mendicants back home, and how Mexican and Irish poverty were not so different at all. Having this glimpse of another country's misery made him feel less alone. What could he do to help the destitute escape their condition, this degrading poverty that seemed so similar in both lands?

When he passed by an old Indian woman selling herbs from a basket, she looked so much like Ximena's grandmother that Riley almost did a double take. She gave him a gap-toothed smile and handed him a bunch of epazote, which Nana Hortencia and Ximena used for cleansings. He bought the herbs from the old woman and brought the bundle to his nose. For a moment, he was back in Ximena's arms. He leaned against a wall, the yearning for her so intense his knees weakened, and he could not take another step. He buried his face in the herbs, reeling from the smell of her. He'd been an utter fool, he knew that now. And he'd probably lost her forever. What if he went in search for her? She was perhaps back in the northern frontier, back in her beloved ranch and too busy restoring it to think about him. He wanted to imagine her happy. Even if he could never forgive himself for losing her, he prayed to God He would at least grant her some happiness.

When Riley finally reached the battalion's barracks, which were in an abandoned monastery near the Alameda in the outskirts of the city, the Mexican guard handed him a note. "Capitán Riley, this arrived for you while you were gone."

"Who left this here for me?" Riley asked, his heart pounding as he read it. "¿Quién dejó la carta?"

"Una mujer, mi capitán," the guard said. "No dio su nombre."

He turned on his heel and took off running to the park. No. It couldn't be. Had she truly come all this way? After all the suffering he'd put her through, could it be true that she was here and not where he'd imagined her? He hurried down the stone-paved sidewalk, sidestepping the peasant women selling pottery, wooden toys, and corn husk dolls, and the peddlers carrying bundles of colorful sarapes and blankets.

He finally gained the Alameda and spotted her sitting in the shade on one of the stone benches by the large water fountain, feeding the pigeons. In the dappled light beneath the poplars, Riley paused for a moment, catching his breath and listening to the falling waters of the fountain. The sight of Ximena was like a sunbeam penetrating the dark brooding of his heart. He could scarcely trust his eyes to believe she was truly there. That he wasn't just imagining her. But then, he began worrying, uncertain as to what he should say. *Forgive me . . .* He would start with that.

As soon as she saw him, she ran to him. He held her aloft and swung her around, his body thrilled at being able to embrace her once more. Then she cupped his face in her hands and kissed him, and he responded in complete surrender.

He bought her a lemonade from a peddler selling refreshments, and they strolled around the verdant gardens on shady paths lined with flowering shrubs, sharing what had transpired in their lives while they'd been apart. He concluded by telling her about the deserters he'd recruited at the prison that morning. "The Saint Patrick's Battalion is still strong," he said. "When the Yanks get here, we'll be ready for them."

"And our child will be born in a country free of invaders," she said, putting a hand on her belly.

He stared at her, wondering if she was jesting. She hadn't mentioned a babe, but then, he lowered his gaze and confirmed what she'd just said. Her Mexican skirts nearly hid the swell of her belly.

"I'm sorry, I should not have surprised you like this. I thought—" she put a hand to her mouth and bit the tender flesh of her knuckles.

He gathered her into his arms and felt her body tremble.

"Should I not have come, John?" she whispered.

"No, lass, don't say that," he said. "I've dreamed of having you back in my arms every night, though I was too much of a coward to seek you out. But just give me a minute to get over my shock, will ya?"

He held on to her, afraid to let go, not knowing what to make of this news. A child. They were going to have a child. Would the conflict between Mexico and the United States be over before the birth? He wished to God it was so. He raised her chin so that she could look at him.

"I love you, Ximena, and I love our child. Have no doubt of that. But I loathe the thought of this innocent creature being born in a country ravaged by war, you understand? Don't I already have another child living in a land scourged by hunger and misery? Is my lot in life to subject my children to such a sorrowful existence?"

She wiped her eyes and took a deep breath. "Do not think this way, John. The Yanquis haven't won. Not yet. When we win this war, our child shall be born in a new Mexico. One ready to be the great nation it is destined to be."

He smiled and pulled her against him, trying to share in her fancy for the future. "Aye, and we shall send for my son. And we can be a family. The four of us. Would that be alright, darlin'? He would make a fine brother, my Johnny . . ."

"I can't wait to meet him," she said, holding tight to him.

He kissed the top of her head and looked up at the cloudless sky. He wanted to believe in the future they envisioned, but hadn't he learned by now that a windy day was not a day for thatching? The Yankees would soon be marching their way. The upcoming battle would be the defining moment—the moment that could turn the tide of the war once and for all. He prayed with all his heart that the Mexican eagle would be the victor.

32

August 1847
Mexico City

After mass one Sunday , Riley hired a carriage to take them on a ride around the city. With the invasion of the capital looming over them, this period of calm was sure to be brief, and he wished to spend it doing things that they might have done had her country not been at war. The carriage ride was enough for now, but someday, perhaps they could visit the museums or the Botanical Garden, the Shrine of Nuestra Señora de Guadalupe, the famous Chinampas, floating gardens, the pyramids in Teotihuacán. He wrapped his arm around her and held her close to him, enjoying the beautiful trees and lush plants and flowers on either side of the road, the sharp outline of the two volcanoes in the distance, rising above the plains of the Valley of Mexico, and the stone arches of the two aqueducts that bisected the city. As the carriage rumbled past Chapultepec Hill, he looked at the formidable castle on the summit, which was visible through the trees, and at the Mexican flag flying from its ramparts. The castle was home to the country's military college, the Mexican West Point, and he wondered if there was still time for him to obtain permission to visit it.

As they traversed the Paseo de Bucareli, the driver told them how in times of peace, there were a thousand carriages out on the avenue in the evenings, full of people dressed in their finery out for a bit of fresh air and socializing. But the city was about to be under siege, and so even though the day was perfectly brilliant, the Paseo was mostly deserted. The driver pointed to two of the mountains surrounding the city and asked if they wanted to hear the story of their creation, according to the Aztecs. These snow-covered volcanoes dominated the horizon and were named Iztaccíhuatl and Popocatépetl.

With Ximena translating the driver's words, Riley listened to the ancient myth of the beautiful princess, Iztaccíhuatl, who was deeply in love with a warrior under her father's command. This great warrior Popocatépetl was sent to fight a war by the emperor, who promised him he could marry the princess upon his return. But Iztaccíhuatl died of grief while he was gone after believing the malignant rumors that the brave warrior had perished in war. When Popocatépetl returned, and upon finding his beloved dead, he took her body out to the plains where he knelt by her side. The gods, taking pity on them, transformed them into volcanoes—she, sleeping peacefully covered in her white mantle of snow, and he, waking once in a while to rain fire upon the land to release his sorrow and rage.

Gazing at the mountains, Riley thought of Nelly. Would that the gods took pity on her as well. Would that she could sleep peacefully, transformed into a beautiful snow-covered mountain to join the others—Fionn mac Cumhaill, Cú Chulainn, Queen Maeve—that kept watch over their beloved land.

When they returned to the barracks and went up to their quarters, Ximena prepared them a bath while he sat down to compose a letter that would be smuggled into the Yankee camps a few days hence to entice deserters. They had been invited to a dinner party hosted by Santa Anna later in the week, and he wanted to have it ready for the general's approval.

Irishmen—Listen to the words of your brothers, hear the accents of a Catholic people. Could Mexicans imagine that the sons of Ireland, that noble land of the religious and the brave, would be seen amongst their en-

emies? Well known it is that Irishmen are a noble race, well known it is that in their own country many of them have not even bread to give up to their children. These are the chief motives that induced Irishmen to abandon their beloved country and visit the shores of the New World. But was it not natural to expect that the distressed Irishmen who fly from hunger would take refuge in this Catholic country, where they might have met with a hearty welcome and been looked upon as brothers had they not come as cruel and unjust invaders?

. . . Many Mexicans and Irishmen, united by the sacred tie of religion and benevolence, form only one people.

The dinner party with the general was at the Palacio Nacional, which occupied the entire eastern side of the great public square. And as Riley and Ximena stood before the imposing building, they felt overwhelmed by its immensity.

"This is where the palace of the great Aztec emperor, Moctezuma, once stood," Ximena said. " The Spaniards tore down his palace and used the tezontle stones to build this one."

"This is what conquerors do to the conquered," Riley said. "They build their empires on the stones and bones of those they defeat."

Above them, masses of dark clouds were gathering. The rainy season was in full swing, and Riley was surprised by how every night the heavens would pour down on them while they slept and the next day the sun would come out in all its splendor and everything would be sparkling with raindrops, the air pure and refreshing. He was certainly loving the cool, wet summers of Mexico City.

He gave Ximena his arm and together they walked into the palace. One of the guards guided them to Santa Anna's private quarters, which occupied a small section of the palace itself, the rest being devoted to government offices, such as those of the Minister of War, the treasury, and the House and the Senate, and the chief courts of justice. There were beautiful quiet courtyards and gardens throughout. As they walked up a flight of stairs, Riley noticed soldiers loitering about the galleries wrapped in their cloaks, and when they reached the landing, Santa Anna's aide-de-camp was already waiting for them. They were escorted to an ornate room with sumptuous furniture and French ceramics, splendid red draperies, and fine oil paintings, where other guests were mingling, brilliantly illuminated by golden candelabras. Riley saluted the Mexican generals in attendance—Bravo, Valencia, Anaya, Rincón, Álvarez, Mora y Villamil, Lombardini, and a few others.

When they were introduced to the generals' female companions, he felt Ximena stiffen beside him, and he knew the source of her discomfort. The general's wives were in their finest evening dresses of silk, velvet, and satin and bedecked with splendid diamonds and pearls. It seemed to Riley they were wearing all the ornaments in their possession, and even their heads hadn't escaped, laden with glittery diadems and large silver hair combs. His beloved Ximena wore nothing more than a modest muslin dress dyed with the cochineal insects harvested from cacti, simple black satin shoes, her gold hoop earrings, and a fresh red rose stuck into her silky hair. To him, she seemed more lovely than ever in her humble simplicity. It was a sacrifice she'd made for his son. Instead of spending his wages buying expensive apparel, Ximena wanted the money to be sent to Johnny, and with padre Sebastián's help, that is what he'd done.

Though the women were cordial, Riley saw plain enough they were judging his beloved's appearance, not just her attire but her bronze skin, which in their eyes betrayed an impurity of blood. Luckily, Ximena was spared exchanging more than a few pleasantries with them when the president general made his entrance.

"Welcome, my dear friends and compatriots," Santa Anna said as he stood at the door in full uniform. With his colossal epaulets and the numerous medals covering his breast, he was more bedizened than any of the ladies in the room. Riley saluted his commander when it was his turn to greet him, thanking him for his hospitality.

The general kissed Ximena's hand and proceeded to flatter her as he did the other ladies. "My lady Ximena, you look lovely in carmine. It is a perfect color for you, indeed."

The servants rang the dinner bell, and they were escorted to the adjacent room where a handsome mahogany table had been set with French porcelain dishes, alabaster trays, and crystal bowls trimmed with gold and silver. There were a series of platters laden with meat, fish, and fowl, cheeses and summer vegetables, and goblets of wine and champagne.

Riley's military uniform and rank, his fair skin, and blue eyes gave him an advantage in this country he'd never had before. The Mexican elite prized such things above all else, and looking at his blue eyes, they didn't see a man who had more in common with the Mexican landless peasant than with the higher born. Under their admiring glances, Riley's hands shook once dinner began as he reached for the solid silver flatware next to his plate. He'd never in his life had a silver spoon in his mouth, and he stared at it for too long, admiring the intricate details etched on it. Very demurely, Ximena coughed into her napkin to get his attention and stop him from making a fool of himself. He mimicked her movements and smiled at her as she ate her soup daintily, her gestures as elegant and refined as the other ladies in the room. And once she had a little wine in her, Riley watched her transform into a Tejana belle, as Ximena once told him her mother had hoped she would be. She chatted amiably with the ladies with ease, her impeccable Spanish revealing her good breeding, and little by little, he noticed that the women put their prejudices aside.

"A toast to the great República Mexicana," Santa Anna said, and everyone stood and raised their glasses. "Today, my heart palpitates with joy in these happy days in which we have come together for combat in defense of our firesides and our outraged rights. The national dignity has been condemned, justice derided, our holy rights trodden under foot. War to the invaders! Liberty or death should be the cry of every generous bosom in this city!"

"Liberty or death!"

After dinner, a lavish spread of sweetmeats, cakes, custards, fruit, and ices were served. Riley could no longer stuff anything into his mouth but out of politeness partook of a meringue, which melted heavenly on his tongue. Then the gentlemen retired to Santa Anna's office to drink and smoke Cuban cigars. He could see Ximena's reluctance to go off into another room with the women to talk, perhaps, about trivialities.

In the president's office, the men soon pulled out their cigars while Santa Anna's attendants filled their glasses with the finest brandy Riley had ever tasted.

"Now, gentlemen, we have important matters to discuss," General Santa Anna said. "I have received intelligence that after all these weeks in Puebla, General Scott has finally given the order to his troops to advance on the capital. His vanguard has left the city of Puebla today."

Riley listened carefully, grateful that Ximena had helped him learn enough of the Spanish tongue to get by, yet he struggled to keep up with the rapid and heated conversation. The generals spoke quickly and angrily, critical of the state of Puebla for not putting up a fight against the Yankees in May. The second most important city in the country, Puebla de los Ángeles was the last defense before Mexico City and had so easily come into the possession of General Scott, without the inhabitants firing a single shot at his troops, that now there was nothing standing between the Yankees and the capital.

"There are eighty thousand poblanos in that city!" Santa Anna said. "Enough to defend themselves from the enemy. Instead, those egotists handed it to Scott on a silver platter."

"If the poblanos hadn't betrayed the republic," General Anaya said, "this war would have been over by now."

"They will rue the day they welcomed the enemy with open arms," General Rincón added.

"Scott is on his way to us now, and I aim to confront him at El Peñón," Santa Anna said.

"¿Perdón, mi general? Do you mean to permit him to approach the capital completely unopposed?" General Valencia asked. "Are we no better than the poblanos then?"

Once again, the generals began to shout among themselves, and Riley could see that Valencia was getting more and more agitated, his countenance reddening as he and the commander had a shouting match.

"Give me twelve thousand men and see if I don't have the Yanquis running back whence they came with their tail between their legs!" Valencia insisted.

Santa Anna berated him for his insolence and threatened to court-martial him if he didn't change his tone.

"I will not leave the capital undefended!" Santa Anna said. "We will all go to meet Scott and his troops once they reach the Valley of Mexico, and we will bury their corpses there."

Valencia scoffed and shook his head but held his tongue. Instead, it was Ampudia who challenged the commander. "Ask him," Ampudia said, pointing at Riley. "Ask capitán Riley what happened when Taylor was allowed to march down to Matamoros."

They all turned to look at Riley. He fixed his gaze upon his commander and said, "With all due respect, your Excellency, there is truth in what your generals say. General Taylor was given a great advantage when he encountered no opposition on his way down from Corpus Christi, and even when he settled across from Matamoros, he was unmolested, uninjured, and allowed to build up his defenses as well as he pleased. Perhaps it would be wise to consider a different course of action with General Scott."

Santa Anna nodded and lamented the lack of funds and provisions and his untrained troops, and once again cursed the poblanos for not helping to defend their nation's honor. "Very well, I will give it some thought," he said, rising to his feet. "Now, gentlemen, enough with the bickering. Let us conclude with an act of celebration, shall we?"

"Major?" Ximena said, embracing him.

"Aye, can you believe it, darlin'?"

As they returned to the barracks in the rain, the carriage making its way along the slippery cobblestoned streets, he told her how at the conclusion of the meeting, Santa Anna had called up a few of the men to his side, including Riley, and bestowed new promotions. And so he had walked out of the Palacio Nacional with a rank no other foreigner in Mexico's army had ever attained. Finally, he informed her about the most important news of the evening—that Scott had given marching orders to his troops to move against the capital. Taking her hand, Riley asked, "Will you marry me, Ximena? Before the battle ensues, will you unite yourself to me?"

She kissed him tenderly and put his hand on her belly. "I love you, John. To call you husband, for our child to have you as a father, makes this wicked war less so."

"I wish I could give you a proper weddin', with flowers and a grand celebration, but there is no time, and I must go off and fight your country's enemies. But after, my darlin', when the war is over, I shall plant you roses, build you a home."

The carriage pulled up to the barracks, and as they walked along the path toward their chambers, they held onto each other, laughing while the heavens poured down on them. He kissed her hungrily, urgently, tasting the rain on her lips.

"My shoes are soaked through," she said, bending to take them off. But then, as she began walking barefoot over the wet cobblestones, her smile disappeared and her eyes became blank, as if in a trance.

"What's the matter, lass?" he asked.

"Time is running out," she said.

33

August 1847
Mexico City

The dream came to her again, longer and clearer this time. The wet cobblestones, the gallows, the men hanging from their necks, twisting and jerking in a dance of death. John's body whirling in the wind, his tongue protruding, his bloodshot eyes staring at her. *John!*

"Ximena! Wake up, darlin'. Wake up," he said, lying beside her. She sat up abruptly and he lit the candle by the bedside, then gathered her into his arms. "Was it the dream again?"

She nodded, afraid to look at him, as if she might see rope marks on his neck.

"You're shiverin'," he said, pulling the covers up to her chin. He held her as if she might break. He kissed her forehead, her eyelids, her mouth with exquisite tenderness. Her breathing slowed, and she took in the comforting smell of his warm skin, like damp fallen leaves and tendrils of smoke.

"I don't want you to go," she said at last. "Not you. Not your men."

"There is a battle to be fought, a war to be won. Until that happens, we must obey orders."

"No, you mustn't go. Please, John."

His eyes bore into her, and she thought of her home, of the blue lupines growing wild in the prairie. She wished that she was back there again, that she could take him far away from this city. Away from the plaza where the nooses waited.

"I see plain enough you're lettin' those visions get the better of you," he said. "But nothin', you hear me, nothin' will keep me from your side."

"You were hanging from the gallows. Patrick, Auguste, Thomas, Francis, and so many of the others. And you, John, you!"

"This might be one of those dreams that prove false, my love," he said reassuringly, "or you would have dreamed us facin' the firin' squad. Be that as it may, I promise to be careful. The blessed Saint Patrick will watch over us."

She kissed him savagely, hungrily, with a passion so fierce, so demanding, she scared herself. She pushed him down on the bed and climbed on top of him. She held onto him, just as the dawn was breaking, just as the day—their wedding day—was beginning. They would only have one day as a married man and woman. One day before he was gone. And so she needed to take him inside her, join him to her, keep him safe and alive.

"Is this a wedding or a funeral?" Santa Anna asked when he came to escort her to the barracks chapel, which had previously been part of the abandoned monastery. Ximena was startled by his voice, being so lost in her thoughts, she hadn't heard his uneven footsteps approaching or his knocking at the door of her chamber.

Now he stood before her, magnificently dressed as usual. Upon hearing the news of the wedding, he'd insisted on walking her down the aisle, and she couldn't refuse him. But now that he was here, grinning at her, she wished he hadn't come at all. He was to blame for what was about to happen.

With a flourish, he presented her with a velvet box from his pocket and said, "A wedding gift for you, querida Ximena." He opened the lid, and she leaned closer to look. He turned slightly so that the sunlight streaming through the window would fall directly on the brooch nestled within. Her breath caught in her throat—the Mexican coat of arms sparkling in all its glory, the serpent inlaid with tiny rubies, the cactus inlaid with emeralds, the golden eagle of smoky quartz, its eye a perfect yellow topaz.

"I can't accept this gift," she said. "Thank you but—"

"But nothing," he said, taking it out of its box and pinning it on her cream-colored mantilla, a simple wedding gift from John, but one that she would treasure more than any jewel. She was afraid to look at it. Never had she received such an extravagant gift. She wanted to hate it, but as she glanced at it, the golden eagle resting against her bosom, it gave her an immense pride to be wearing the Mexican crest.

But then, upon seeing his satisfied smile, she remembered her anger, her fear. She walked over to the window to put some space between them.

"You must order John to not go to battle with you."

His grin was immediately replaced with a scowl. "¿Perdón?"

"It won't end well for him and his battalion. Have him stay here and guard the Catedral Metropolitana, or the Palacio Nacional, or your own private residence, or your favorite brothel, I don't care! Just don't take him with you."

He limped to where she stood by the window and took her hands in his. "It's your wedding day, and I'm sure you're nervous and getting the jitters, so I shall forgive your strange behavior. But I must confess, this is not like you. Not like you at all."

"It's not jitters!" she snapped. "Por el amor de la Santísima Virgen, General, you need to believe me. Something is going to happen to the San Patricios. They will be hanged at the gallows unless you put them out of harm's way, as far away from the Yanquis as possible."

"I cannot do what you ask. General Scott is marching to this city as we speak, and I need John Riley, and I need his men. I understand he will be your husband now, and no wife wants to see her husband go off to battle, but my lady, if you cannot handle it, may I suggest that you not marry a soldier?"

"I will hold you responsible if anything happens to my husband," she said, and then, unable to stop herself, she burst into tears. He held her in his arms and whispered words of comfort to her, and though she knew they were lies, she listened to them. His voice was kind, gentle even. He spoke to her with the same tenderness as he did his precious gamecocks.

He sighed and took out his handkerchief to wipe her face. "Basta. Stop crying now," he said, changing his voice, the sweetness gone. "You don't want to get married with tear-stained eyes, do you? Now come, I will deliver you to your betrothed and after the ceremony ends, I shall take my leave. The battle is nearly upon us, and I need to prepare to face our enemies."

She put her arm through his, and he guided her out of the room.

Ximena and John had chosen to have an intimate wedding in the small chapel at the barracks, and though its walls were crumbling, its pews falling apart, she didn't care. The San Patricios got to their feet as she and Santa Anna entered. She avoided looking at them, trying not to think about her dream, about the nooses around their necks. She simply smiled and forced herself to keep her eyes forward. John was up front with padre Sebastián and Patrick Dalton. He smiled as he watched her walk toward him. He stood proudly before her wearing his new uniform, the dark blue of a man of his rank, major in the Mexican Army. If truth be told, she would have rather seen him dressed in regular clothes, at least for today, their wedding day. She would rather not think about the war and the fact that at this very moment General Scott and his army were heading down the National Highway to the Valle de México and soon the battle would ensue.

"Mayor Juan Riley, aquí está su amada," Santa Anna said. John saluted his commander and then took Ximena's hands in his. As padre Sebastián began the ceremony, they both knelt on pillows. They kept their heads bowed as the priest united them by wrapping a white cord from Ximena to John. The soft Latin prayers of padre Sebastián echoed against the old stone walls. Finally, it was time for their vows and they rose to their feet.

"Señor Juan Riley, ¿acepta a Ximena Salomé de Benítez y Catalán, aquí presente, como su esposa, según el rito de la santa madre Iglesia?" padre Sebastián said.

John looked at her and smiled. "Sí. Acepto."

The priest turned to her and said, "Ximena Salomé de Benítez y Catalán, ¿acepta a Juan Riley, aquí presente, como su esposo, según el rito de la santa madre Iglesia?"

Just then, a cannon from the ramparts of the citadel boomed, shaking the fragile walls of the chapel. Ximena looked at John, at Santa Anna. The San Patricios stirred in the pews, whispering among themselves. John clutched her hand and didn't let go, but they both knew what that sound meant. The Yanquis had reached the valley. They were a mere twenty-five miles away. She could hear the drums summoning men to their posts, the bugles sounding the alarm. Why couldn't they have today, at least today, to enjoy their wedding?

Padre Sebastián looked at her tenderly and asked if she wished to continue. She looked at John.

"Lass, do you desire to stop? D'ya not wish to go on?" he whispered into her ear. "I would understand if you've changed your mind." Yet his eyes were pleading for her to not give up on him. Not now when he was about to put his fate in God's hands once again. She thought about her dream of the San Patricios hanging lifeless from the gallows and turned to look at Patrick Dalton, the best man, standing by John's side, watching her with puzzlement. She looked at the men on the pews—Lachlin McLaghlin, Elizier Lusk, John Appleby, John Benedick, and that big lovable bear of a man, Kerr Delaney. Was their fate sealed? Was there anything that could be done to change it?

Padre Sebastián coughed, bringing her back to the chapel, to her betrothed looking beseechingly at her. She couldn't let her dream ruin their wedding day. When the priest repeated the question, this time she didn't hesitate. "Sí, acepto," she said softly. John sighed in relief and bent toward her. As she felt his lips upon her own, her lips parted, and she kissed him as she had never done before. She wrapped her arms around him and held him close. No, they didn't have much time left, but the hours that remained, she would make sure they were the best hours they could have together.

The next morning, she watched Riley and his men gather at the Plaza de la Constitución as Santa Anna's army prepared to march out and confront the enemy. Ximena stood among the thousands of city residents that had come to bid them farewell. Her eyes scanned the troops and spotted her husband upon his horse at the head of the columns. Her eyes lingered on the faces of the foreign soldiers clad in their blue uniforms and red tasseled caps. She could feel John's eyes looking at her from beneath the visor of his shako. She wished to shout out to him, to tell him that she loved him, no matter what, to beg him not to go. But she knew he wouldn't hear her above the patriotic music meant to give courage to the men as they headed to battle, and so she only returned his gaze in silence and tried to be strong, for him, for his men. As John and Patrick Dalton rode alongside the other officers, the troops marched out of the plaza and the crowd shouted, "¡Vivan los San Patricios!" The distance between them grew bigger and bigger, and she could no longer see him, but she could still see his pride and joy flapping in the morning breeze above the columns—the green banner of the Saint Patrick's Battalion.

She turned and pushed her way through the throng. In her hand she carried a handwritten letter John had composed the night before. She'd watched him sitting by candlelight, trying to find the right words as he put ink to paper, and she sat nude under the sheets, her lips throbbing, her body ravaged by their insatiable lovemaking, her mind struggling to speak no more of her visions, of what she knew to be true.

John had bid her to take this letter to the printer's that day and have the pamphlets delivered into the hands of General Scott's foreign soldiers.

To My Friends and Countrymen in the Army of the United States of America, the letter began. She hurried out of the plaza, and read it once again before taking it to the printer.

Actuated by nought but the purest motives, I venture to address you on a subject of vital importance . . . The President of this Republic, once more offers to you his hand & invites you, in the name of the religion you profess, the various countries in which you first drew the breath of existence, of honor and of patriotism, to withhold your hands from the slaughter of a nation whose thoughts or deeds never injured you or yours.

My countrymen, Irishmen! I call upon you for I know your feelings on this subject well, for the sake of that chivalry for which you are celebrated, for that love of liberty for which our common country is so long contending, for the sake of that holy religion which we have for ages professed, I conjure you to abandon a slavish hireling's life with a nation who in even the moment of victory treats you with contumely & disgrace. For whom are you contending? For a people who, in the face of a whole world, trampled upon the holy altars of our religion, set the firebrands upon a sanctuary devoted to the blessed Virgin, and boasting of civil and religious liberty, trampled in contemptuous indifference all appertaining to the dearest feelings of our country.

My Countrymen, I have experienced the hospitality of the citizens of this Republic; from the moment I extended them the hand of friendship, I was received with kindness; though poor, I was relieved; though undeserving, I was respected, and I pledge you my oath, that the same feelings extended toward me await you also.

34

They marched ten miles up the National Highway to confront Scott's army as it approached from Puebla. Santa Anna distributed his forces to block Scott's path, focusing the bulk of his troops on strengthening the main position at El Peñón, a fortified hill that commanded the road to Mexico City. But when his scouts alerted him that Scott had chosen to avoid the National Highway and had taken a circuitous southern route, Santa Anna quickly set up a new line of defense south of the city and positioned his three units around the villages of Churubusco, San Ángel, and Coyoacán, all of which were situated around an impassable, desolate field of volcanic rock known as El Pedregal. Each unit was strategically placed within five miles of each other for quick reinforcement. Along with the Bravos and Independence Brigades, Riley and his men were positioned at an old Franciscan monastery in the village of Churubusco eight miles southeast of Mexico City. Under the command of Generals Rincón and Anaya, the Saint Patrick's Battalion and more than a thousand Mexican soldiers were to protect the fortress. Rincón divided up the troops, placing some on the heights of the monastery and its right flank and the San Patricios and the Bravos Brigade up on the parapets, front and left flank of the monastery.

After scanning the area, Riley and Patrick Dalton gave orders to the men to position the seven cannons on the parapets. It was a good place to make a stand. The monastery had walls four feet thick and twelve feet high made of solid stone, as were the parapets on the roof. The Río Churubusco ran alongside the monastery, and the bridge across it was well fortified and guarded by three Mexican regiments. From the parapets Riley had a good view of the cornfields surrounding the monastery and the two roads leading to it, so they'd be able to see the Yanks coming.

On the evening of August 19, Riley stood on the parapets peering through the sultry darkness. Earlier that day, they'd heard an exchange of artillery fire and later learned that General Valencia had engaged the enemy. According to the expresses from General Santa Anna, Valencia had disobeyed orders and had taken it upon himself to confront the Yanks two miles beyond his assigned position at Padierna. Santa Anna ordered Valencia to pull back to San Ángel and send his artillery to Churubusco. Valencia refused, opting instead to stay put. That evening, word reached them that the outcome of the duel between Valencia and the Yanks had ended with the withdrawal of the enemy. Now everyone was cheering and getting drunk. But as Riley watched the lightning flash across the sky and heard the thunder rumble as loud as a cannonade, he felt uneasy.

He turned northwest, in the direction of Mexico City, and thought of Ximena. She'd followed him here with the hospital corps, and he wished she had stayed in the safety of the city. He had pleaded with her to sit this battle out, despite knowing he was being a hypocrite. When she'd asked him to do the same, he'd said he was honor-bound. *So am I*, she'd replied.

"The calm before the storm," Dalton said as he came to stand beside him. "Gives me the jitters. I'd rather be fightin' already."

Lightning burst above them, illuminating the two empty roads leading to the monastery. Riley gave an involuntary shudder when the thunder slammed against the monastery walls. He patted Dalton on the back and said, "Be patient, my boy. The battle will get to us soon enough, and you'll get your chance to give the Yankees thunder."

"And God willin', we will carry the day," Dalton said.

"Aye, indeed," Riley said, leaning against the parapets. The wind picked up, and the rustling of the cornfields put him on edge. "Tis late, and you should get some sleep."

"I can't sleep. Not with the racket the sky is makin'. But come inside. The rain's startin'."

"The rain doesn't bother me none," Riley said. He took a deep breath, inhaling the familiar scent of wet earth and stone.

"I would be a happy man to lay my eyes upon the green fields of Erin again, wouldn't ya?" Dalton said.

"Aye. Perhaps one day we will finally be able to go home. Help set it free."

"And Ximena? What if she isn't happy there, findin' herself in an unfamiliar land, sufferin' the dismal winters, so far from her country where the sky is brighter. Don't Mexicans and cactus flourish best in sunshine?"

Riley forced a laugh. "Aye. But as long as we're together, we will find happiness wherever we are. Ireland needs us, Pat. When this war is over, we have to go back and fight for her."

"It would be an honor to fight there by your side," Dalton said.

"Go willin', Pat. Dismissed, Lieutenant," Riley said. He turned his eyes to the road below, as Dalton walked away with brisk steps. The storm finally arrived in all its violence. Riley stood there in the howling wind and pelting rain, and as the strikes of lightning scattered across the sky and the thunder gave a long roar, he knew that no one could possibly be out and about in this torrent, not even the Yankees would be stirring this evening. Thankful that at least tonight there was nothing to fear from the enemy, he turned to go indoors, cursing under his breath as he became aware of how drenched he was, how heavy his uniform felt, with its thick, sopping fabric wrapped so tightly around him, suffocating him. For the first time in his life, he wished to be free of it.

He made his way to the interior of the monastery, where some of the chambers had been turned into a makeshift hospital. Ximena was there now, preparing for the carnage that would soon ensue. He should have been selfish, forced her to stay away from the battlefield this time and remain in the city. She was now his wife, and she was with child, and it was his duty to protect them both.

When she spotted him, she ran out of the room to him. There in the darkened corridor, he took her in his arms and held on to her with all his might.

"You're wet," she said. "Come, you must change out of your uniform."

"I love you, Ximena," he said, kissing her. "Come what may, know that I will always love you."

"And I, you," she said, returning his kiss.

She grabbed his hand and walked them both to the window. Mexico City was there, beyond the wet darkness. A vivid flash of lightning illuminated her face and he could see she spoke in earnest when she said, "We could leave tonight. There's still time."

He stood behind her and wrapped his arms around her thickening waist. They stood there looking at the incessant rain befouling the roads, knowing full well that they would both stay and fight for the future of Mexico, a future they might not live to see.

In the morning, Riley awoke to the sound of cannon fire in the distance. The smoke billowed over Valencia's location, but they were too far away to know what was happening. The firing didn't last, and Riley and the fourteen hundred men positioned at the monastery anxiously awaited news of the confrontation. They didn't have long to wait. During the night's deluge, with the rumble and thunder of the sky masking their movements, the Yanks had found a way to cut across the field of sharp volcanic rock, which the Mexicans had insisted was impassable, and had led a surprise attack on General Valencia's forces at first light, surrounding his entire command from three different directions. His position had collapsed in less than twenty minutes and his twenty-three guns had fallen into the hands of the enemy. Santa Anna was furious and had given the order for Valencia to be shot on the spot for disobeying orders, so Valencia was now on the run and his army was no more. After Valencia's defeat, the Yanks had raced northeast to attack the main Mexican force. According to Santa Anna's express, the Yanks had taken possession of the main roads leading to and from Churubusco and would soon be closing in on his troops.

Later in thethat morning, Santa Anna himself appeared. Unable to repel the invaders, he was pulling his troops back within the walls of Mexico City, and the men in the monastery were to hold the Churubusco bridge and the monastery at all costs to give his forces the chance to retreat across the river. With that, he returned to oversee his men.

General Rincón ordered the troops at the monastery to their positions. "The Yanquis must not get past us," he said.

There were a little more than a thousand Mexican soldiers inside the monastery, plus Riley's battalion up on the parapets. He glanced at the four 8-pounders and wondered how long they could hold out against the Yanks. Santa Anna's orders were to hold the position at all costs—and fighting to the death was what he and his countrymen would be obliged to do. Getting caught by the Yanks was not an option, not for them.

At around noon, they watched as hundreds of Mexican soldiers ran toward them, and then past the monastery, fleeing as fast as their feet could carry them across the Churubusco bridge, trampling each other in the horrible disorder. They were Santa Anna's troops, which meant the Yanks were not far behind.

A few moments later, the San Patricios started yelling, "The Yankees are comin'!" as they pointed at the enemy charging up the road toward the monastery in pursuit of the Mexicans. Riley glanced at his men. They knew full well what the sight meant for them. The Yanks were winning, and if the battle were lost, the San Patricios would be captured in this monastery.

But he wouldn't let them.

He raised his banner high above his battery, in plain sight of the Yanks. He made the sign of the cross and prayed a quick Hail Mary.

"Steady men," he said as he and his men watched the Yanks get closer and closer.

"We fight to the death," Patrick Dalton said.

"To the death!" the men repeated.

"Hold your fire," Riley said. Down below, across the rain-soaked fields, the Yanks charged the monastery at full speed, General Twiggs in the lead. When no more than sixty yards stood between them and his guns, Riley finally opened fire upon the enemy. Their aim was true and steady, and they didn't waste a single shot. All around him were the screams of Twiggs's men below, the shrill of the musket balls as they whistled through the air, the roaring of the cannons, the cries of the enemy's horses and the moans of the dying. The Yanks returned fire, and bullets whistled past Riley. From the parapets, his men fell over the railings to their deaths, but he kept his eyes on the troops below and kept firing, tearing into the columns of the enemy. At the sight of General Twiggs, Riley thought about Franky Sullivan. This was the day when he would avenge his tentmate. "Aim for the officers!" he yelled, turning his gun in the direction of Twiggs. To his disappointment, Braxton Bragg was not part of the Mexico City campaign, but he spotted James Duncan and the other West Pointers that had made his and his countrymen's life hell, and turned a gun on them, too. Without their leaders and no one to give the orders, the enemy troops would be lost.

He watched as the Yankee soldiers dispersed, some diving into the boggy cornfields surrounding the monastery, but the Yankees returned fire and Riley saw more of his men fall. Wasting no time, he ordered his gunners to fire against the Yankee artillery and maintain the cannonading. He had them pinned down. As long as he had ammunition, the Yanks were going nowhere.

Three hours later, Yankees lay dead in heaps in the muddy fields below. Everywhere Riley looked there was blood. Though they had managed to repulse General Twiggs' division, the Yankees had taken the bridge and were now turning all their guns and musket fire toward the monastery. The Mexicans, running out of ammunition, had sent a request to Santa Anna for more, but when it arrived, it turned out to be the wrong cartridges. The powder and musket balls fit only the .75 caliber muskets of the San Patricios, but not Rincón's and Anaya's brigades. Riley knew that it wouldn't take long for the Yanks to realize the situation.

Sure enough, the Yanks lost no time. As soon as they noticed the lessening of fire from the Mexican side, they renewed their attack from all sides. From up on the parapets, Riley could see the Yankee cannons being moved to a better position and aimed directly at him and his men.

"Everybody down!" Riley yelled.

He took cover just in time. After the blast, more San Patricios lay dead and three of their four cannons had been rendered useless. His green banner flapped in the wind, ripped and stained with smoke and powder. He would need a new one made.

"Riley, get us inside!" Dalton yelled through the noise. He had reached the last of his ammunition, and so had his men. But Riley wouldn't give up, not until he loaded up the last of the cannon with grape and fired his last shot. Suddenly, a spark ignited the last of their powder and burst into flames. Captain O'Leary and three other San Patricios were enveloped in flames. Riley and the other gunners rushed at them with blankets, wet from last night's rain.

"Take them inside, quick!" Riley ordered. He turned back to the remaining working cannon and ordered his gunners to load it with the last of their grape. The blast shook the walls of the monastery. Several more Yankees fell in a heap, but still they kept coming, their bayonets at the ready. Then his cannons finally went silent. Riley tore down the green banner riddled with bullet holes and blackened with smoke. This banner might very well be his shroud. Tying it around his waist, he yelled, "Inside!"

He and his men grabbed their muskets and rushed into the monastery to join the soldiers inside. They pushed furniture to barricade the doors, but the Yanks were not to be stopped and soon pushed their way in, crashing through the doors, surging past the last bullets of the Mexicans' muskets. They were too many, and as Riley fired his musket, he knew that there weren't enough bullets to stop the Yanks. Seeing some of his officers mortally wounded, General Rincón yelled, "Retreat!", and the Mexicans and the San Patricios ran up to the second floor, with the Yankees at their heels, shooting at them from behind.

One of the Mexican soldiers raised a white flag. Riley raised his musket and without thinking twice shot the Mexican soldier's hand, splattering the white flag with blood.

"We're not giving up, you hear me?" Riley yelled at the Mexican soldiers. "If you have no valor to fight with, then fight from the shame of cowardice. But fight, we must, to the death. ¡Hasta la muerte!"

Only a few had anything left to fire at the Yanks, and when that was spent the only thing to do was to fight with whatever they had. Riley charged at the Yanks with nothing but his bare fists, and his men did the same. Dalton fought bravely by his side, but they were pushed back, retreating up the steps of the monastery. The Mexicans raised two more white flags, and the San Patricios quickly tore them down. "To the death!" they yelled. "To the death!"

Panic-struck, the Mexican soldiers rushed past them to seek a way out of the monastery. The battle was over, and Riley knew they weren't going to stay around to be killed. Santa Anna's orders to fight to the death be damned. They disappeared down the corridors and left the San Patricios to their fate.

"Go!" Dalton yelled at Riley. He pointed to a door in the back hall, where some of the Mexicans were making a dash to the river. "Go to her! Grab her and get out of here!"

Riley hesitated.

"Go to her, now!" Dalton said.

Thinking of Ximena, Riley did as his friend said, hastening to the makeshift hospital. There was a way out of the monastery there, and he knew this was his only chance to take it.

"John!"

He saw Ximena on the other end of the corridor, calling to him. But as he was dragged down the corridor with the throng, he turned and saw his countrymen being felled one by one by the Yankees charging at them with their muskets and bayonets, yelling like demons. And how could he, John Riley, their leader, save himself and leave his men in their moment of need? What manner of man was he then? He looked back at her. *Forgive me, Ximena*, he thought, then turned his course and ran back to Dalton's side just as a Yankee was aiming at his friend. As he pushed Dalton out of the way, a bullet tore through Riley's leg, and he dropped to the ground on his knees.

"John!" Dalton yelled, rushing to help him move out of harm's way. A bullet whistled past Riley's ear, and then another.

"Leave me!" Riley said, blood soaking through his uniform. "Go! Save yourself." But Dalton wouldn't move, and then it was too late.

The gunshots finally stopped. Riley turned to see a white flag in the air. It was being raised by a Yankee officer. *Why would a Yank raise the white flag for them? Why not just kill them all?*

"Enough!" the captain said, raising the flag even higher. He ordered his men down and then looked at the eighty-four San Patricios and the Mexican soldiers lying on the floor and leaning against walls. "I, Captain James Smith, hereby declare that you are now all prisoners of war of the United States Army."

General Twiggs then entered the monastery, and Generals Rincón and Anaya both lowered their swords in surrender. "Where is your ammunition, Generals?" Twiggs asked.

General Anaya looked at him and said, "If we had ammunition, you wouldn't be standing here now."

The Yankee general ordered his men to search the premises and as he looked around the monastery, his eyes fell on Riley. As recognition set in, his eyes filled with hatred and disdain.

"The jig is up for us," Riley said, looking up at his friend.

"There's a fine line between bravery and foolishness," Dalton said, repeating Riley's words from long ago. "I do believe we've crossed that line, Major. We should have run."

It began to rain again later that evening, and Riley was thankful for the raindrops. After disarming them, Twiggs had forced the San Patricios and the other prisoners out into the monastery's courtyard and for hours they had sat on the hard ground suffering from want of food and water. Riley stuck out his tongue and savored the bit of moisture that soothed his parched throat.

He couldn't move, sitting on the ground in irons while the wound on his leg continued to bleed through the handkerchief he'd tied around it. He could feel his strength fading away. He wasn't the only one that was injured, all around him were incapacitated San Patricios with varying degrees of injuries. He could hear their moans, their cries. Their prayers grew fainter and fainter as their bodies weakened and a gloom settled over them as they pondered their uncertain fate. A few feet away from him, Francis O'Conner lay on the ground, unconscious and groaning. Both of his legs had been blown off by enemy cannon. Twiggs refused to give O'Conner medical treatment, and Riley feared that his countryman wouldn't live to see another day.

But perhaps it was better that way. The Yanks had them now, and they would show no mercy. Not after today's battle. Not after all the Yankee soldiers and officers Riley and his gunners had killed.

Sentries walked among the prisoners, kicking them, mocking them, enticing them to try to escape. They needed a reason to shoot them in cold blood. But Riley and his men were spent and none of them moved. Instead, they sat under the rain, and Riley wondered if they knew they were doomed. The Mexican prisoners would probably be exchanged, but what would happen to him and his men? The Yanks would never forgive them for switching sides and would always consider them traitors. But hadn't the Yanks betrayed them first?

"What's this you're hiding?" one of the Yankees said. "Hand it over, Mick." He pointed his bayonet at Riley and held out his hand. When he didn't move, the Yank pressed the tip of his bayonet on Riley's breast. "Now, Mick!"

Reluctantly, Riley untied his bloodstained banner from his waist and handed it over. He closed his eyes, not wanting to see what the Yank was going to do with the colors of his battalion.

The sound of their laughter nettled him. Unable to contain himself, he opened his eyes to see the Yankee maggot waving the green banner around, and then pretending to wipe his arse with it. Riley tried to scramble to his feet, but the pain in his leg and the irons made him fall back to the ground.

"Arrah, ignore the scoundrel," Dalton said.

But Riley couldn't. "You sonofabitch! Curse you to hell!" he yelled at the soldier, seething at the man's disrespect for the holy banner of Saint Patrick.

The Yank threw the bloodstained banner to the ground and marched toward Riley with his musket pointing straight at him. "What did you call me, Mick?"

"I said you're a sonofabitch," Riley yelled again. An officer standing watch ordered the soldier to lower his weapon.

"Death will come to them soon enough," the officer said. "But it'll be in a place where everyone can watch."

"Just kill me now," Riley said. "And let my men go. 'Tis me you want, is it not?"

The officer sneered. "It isn't just you we want, John Riley. Every single one of you will pay for what you did to our comrades."

Riley glanced at the monastery, wondering if Ximena was still inside. As part of the hospital corps, the Yankees wouldn't harm her, that he knew. He closed his eyes and willed himself to sleep, but he couldn't. Instead, he spent the night listening to the rain, and the moans of the wounded and dying. He looked at his men, lying on the ground under the torrential rain, yielding to their fatigue, and said, "Forgive me."

In the morning, Riley was roused by the clattering of horse's hooves at a brisk trot. He watched as a Yankee officer rode into the courtyard, dismounted, and disappeared into the monastery where the Yanks had camped out in the night, sheltered from the rain. Later, the man emerged and approached the prisoners.

Riley nudged Dalton to wake up. "They've come for us."

"I'm Captain George Davis," the officer said as he stood before them. "You're hereby under my custody. You're to remain as prisoners of the United States Army and will be transported to your prisons under my supervision."

On the captain's orders, the prisoners were divided into two groups and then chained. Riley watched as his men were separated, one column on its way to Tacubaya, and the other heading to San Ángel. Riley contented himself knowing that Patrick Dalton would be coming with him. He sighed in relief when Francis O'Conner was finally loaded onto a wagon on his way to get medical treatment. As for him, he knew that his wound wouldn't be treated. The Yanks wouldn't show mercy to him, and he accepted that.

Captain Davis gave the order to march. As his column was led forth to the village of San Ángel, Riley turned to watch the other column and said a silent farewell to the forty-three men being taken to Tacubaya to await their fate. He doubted he would ever see them again. "God be with you, my brothers, until we meet again. *Erin Go Bragh!*"

"*Erin Go Bragh!*" they replied and gave Riley their final salute, and then all he could hear was their heavy chains clanking as they were taken away.

35

"His Excellency will see you now," the attendant said. Ximena stood up, smoothed her skirts, and followed him down a large hall of the Palacio Nacional. He paused before two huge wooden doors and knocked softly.

From inside, a voice said, "Enter."

At hearing that voice, the anger that she had been trying to suppress flared up. She took a deep breath to calm herself and walked into the office. Santa Anna sat before his desk and watched her approach. There were several men in the room, all of them dressed in their finest military uniforms, their numerous metals glinting in the light. Here they were, clean and well fed, drinking brandy and puffing on their Cuban cigars while her husband and his men were locked up in prison, hungry and thirsty, cold and miserable.

"Ximena, querida, come in, come in," Santa Anna said. Grabbing his cane, he stood up and came over to embrace her. Ximena didn't look at the other generals, some of whom she'd met at the dinner party, others on the battlefield or the hospital tents. Their imposing presence shook her confidence, and she couldn't lose that now.

"General, I apologize for disrupting your busy schedule," she said. "Thank you for agreeing to see me."

"Of course, my dear. How could I not make time to see you. Now, you know my generals, don't you? Gentlemen, may I present señora Ximena, wife of Major Juan Riley."

"I am sorry about the fate that has befallen Major Riley and his men," General Ampudia said.

"Don't worry, señora Riley," General Bravo said. "It should be a consolation for you to know that our commander will make sure we get the San Patricios back."

"Thank you, sirs. Thank you for your words of encouragement." She turned to Santa Anna and said, "May I speak with you in private, sir?"

"Of course, of course, my dear. Come, have a seat."

The men excused themselves and closed the door behind them. Santa Anna served himself another glass of brandy and offered her one as well. She shook her head no. She was thirsty, and she wished she could ask for a glass of water, but she was tired of pretending. She had come here to talk about John's fate, not to waste time with formalities.

The general was quiet. He made his way to his desk, set his cane aside, and then sat down. The smile and the pretense were all gone now, replaced by a frown.

"You've come to say 'I told you so'?"

"No."

"Good. Because I am in no mood for your reproaches and bitter recriminations. I will take responsibility for the fate of my most loyal officer, and I can assure you that I will do my best to get him back. I promise you that."

She nodded, not knowing what to say. She wouldn't believe it until she saw it, until John was back home with her, until she could hold him in her arms again.

"If I had a thousand men like John Riley, we would have won this war by now," he said, finishing the brandy in his glass.

"What happened? How did they get captured?"

He looked at her, and she could see that he was debating whether or not to answer her question. He sighed, pushed his empty glass away, and said, "If my damn officers had obeyed orders, this wouldn't have happened! You have General Valencia and his blind ambition to thank for the outcome of this battle. The insubordinate imbecile!"

Perhaps it was the alcohol that was getting to him, loosening his tongue, but he reclined in his seat and told her more than she had expected. She sat quietly and listened as he described the battle, how, hungry for glory, General Valencia had disobeyed his orders and left his assigned position, deciding to confront the enemy alone. When Santa Anna ordered him to withdraw to the village of San Ángel and join forces with him, Valencia had decided to stand his ground, not expecting the Yanquis to pull off a surprise assault on his camp and wipe out his division.

"I watched it happen through my field glasses," Santa Anna said. "I was there with my troops, a mere two thousand yards away. I could hear the screams of his troops being cut to pieces. The blasts of the cannons. I saw everything. I could have gone to his rescue. And I should have. But instead, I ordered my men to withdraw. In seventeen minutes, the fool Valencia was defeated. I meant to teach that imbecile a lesson for disobeying my orders. Who does he think he is? There is only one commander-in-chief of this army!"

Ximena remained silent, unable to believe him. She had previously tried to piece together the details of the battle as she remembered them. She remembered seeing the Mexican troops on the run, being chased by the Yanquis. Then Riley and the San Patricios fought for hours until their ammunition ran out and she saw the enemy breaching the monastery. She remembered running down the corridor, hearing the awful fighting going on throughout the convent, and there was John, running toward her, until he stopped and turned around and ran back into the fray. She remembered begging the Yanquis to let her tend to the San Patricios out in the courtyard, but they refused to let her near them. She had watched from the window when they lined up John and his men and took them away. That was the last time she saw him.

After she and the rest of the Mexican hospital attendants were released, they had made their way back to the city with their wounded. Judging by the number of wagons bringing the men back to the city, even before the official numbers were released she knew they had sustained heavy losses . She heard that at least a third of the twenty thousand soldiers in the Mexican ranks were killed, injured, or captured, and those who remained were demoralized. In addition to the San Patricios, eight Mexican generals had been taken prisoner, including Generals Rincón and Anaya, and most of the ammunition and artillery pieces were lost to the Yanquis.

"You wanted to teach General Valencia a lesson for insubordination," she said. "So you abandoned him and his men to their fate. But you didn't think about the price to be paid once they were on the run, and how the criminal abandonment of your general and his troops would affect the rest of your army. Was it worth losing the battle?"

"It was Valencia's error, not mine. If it weren't for him, those perfidious Yanquis would now be buried in the Valle de México!"

"What will you do now, General?"

"I'm negotiating a truce with General Scott to buy me some time—"

"And meanwhile John and his men have been marched to two separate villages to be imprisoned while they await trial. And you know what the outcome of that trial will be."

"Once the armistice is duly ratified, we will exchange prisoners, and of course I shall do everything in my power to get your husband back." He stood up and came to stand behind where she sat, caressing her neck with his cold fingers. His touch made her cringe.

"Ximena, the war isn't over yet. Have faith in me. I will save Mexico from the Yanquis and prevent her dishonor. I will save Juan Riley and the San Patricios. I shall bring peace to our country. I am the Liberator, am I not?"

"If you say so." She stood to take her leave, not waiting for him to walk her to the door. "Thank you for seeing me, your Excellency. I won't take any more of your time."

Once outside, she finally let the tears come, and before long her body began shaking with rage. Poor Mexico. To be in the hands of vainglorious caudillos who allow their wounded pride to control them. Corrupt men who cared only about their reputation, whose souls were darkened by their twisted desire for wealth and power and glory. They were like Santa Anna's gamecock who was drowned by his own reflection—intent on taking themselves, and all of Mexico, to their doom. What kind of future could her country have when ruled by men like that? And what would become of John and the San Patricios?

36

September 1847
San Ángel, Outskirts of Mexico City

They imprisoned Riley and twenty-eight of his men in a dank warehouse that smelled of sewage and rot. As soon as the door closed, he gathered his men around him, Dalton by his side.

"Come now, my boys, this isn't over yet!" Riley said. "There ought to be a way out of our present calamity. Let us not despair."

"They're going to kill us, kill us all," Dennis Conahan said.

"No, Major Riley is right," Dalton said. "Have faith men, have faith."

"Faith in whom, him?" Alexander McKee said, pointing at Riley. "Isn't he who got us into this sad scrape?" He looked at Riley and spat. "*Go hIfreann leat!*" He struggled to his feet and made his way across the room.

"Listen now, McKee, I will not tolerate—" Dalton said.

Riley put a hand on his friend's shoulder. "Let him be. He's right."

"We can tell them the truth," John Bowers said. "Those sonsabitches treated us worse than animals. After all the abuse we tolerated, the insults, the mockery, the harsh discipline, they left us no choice but to desert."

"The infidels mocked our religion and didn't allow us to worship our Creator in our own manner," Edward McHeran said. "Heavens know 'twas reason enough for us to do what we did."

"They won't give ear to that," Riley said. "Especially our religion. They'll throw the Articles of War in our faces."

"We can say that their laws don't apply to us Irish," Thomas Riley said. "And you Germans, and you Scots," he said as he glanced around the room.

"We can say we were much bewildered by liquor to know any better," Hezekiah Akles said. "I've got proof, right here on my forehead." He touched his forehead where the letters *HD* had been branded by his commanding officer.

Riley nodded, remembering that, according to general order, drunkards would be allowed back into their ranks after going absent without official leave. Besides, hadn't the Yanks just won the battle at Churubusco? Surely they were feeling generous right now. There might be a chance they would forgive the San Patricios if they claimed to be nothing but drunks. Paddy the drunkard, isn't that what the Yanks called them?

"Hear me," Riley said. "Let us tell the Yanks a good cock-and-bull story, then. Claim drunkenness when ye stand afore the judge. Say the drop led ye astray. At any rate, they've always accused us of being nothin' but drunken brutes, haven't they? So tell them they spoke truth."

"D'ya really think that will work?" John Bartley asked.

"'Tis worth takin' the chance," Riley said. "Besides, the Yanks have another battle to fight. 'Twon't be long afore they have to face the Mexicans again, so they've got no time for trials. They need to focus on their strategy to win the war. The trials will be over afore ye know it." Riley paused and looked at his men. He hoped they believed him. He wanted to believe it himself, but deep down, he knew the Yanks would show no clemency. Especially not now. He knew Scott would make an example of them in order to stop more soldiers from deserting. But what else could he say to his men to give them hope? "If that story fails to convince, claim that ye were spirited away from your ranks by rancheros and were forced to fight with the Mexicans, that they threatened ye with death if ye didn't fight for their cause." He knew that under the Articles of War, their only valid defenses would be drunkenness and coercion.

"But they didn't," Dalton said, "We made our choice, and now we must abide by it."

Riley nodded, "I know, but 'tis plain our Mexican friends are about to lose this war, and they won't be able to give us succor when they can't even help themselves. 'Tis up to us now to defend our cause and save ourselves from the bitter fate that's upon us, ye understand?"

The men nodded.

"If that story fails, then say that ye were beaten until ye had no choice but to give in. Blame it on me, if ye must. Say that it was John Riley of County Galway who forced ye all to fight under his green banner."

"*Níl!*" Dalton said, standing up. "We will do no such thing."

"If there is blame to be passed around, I will bear my share," Riley said, hitting his breast with his fist. "*Mea culpa.*"

"I'll just say that I was a prisoner of love," Dennis Conahan said. "That my head was unsettled by the love of my Mexican sweetheart, which compelled me to put on the Mexican uniform."

The men chuckled.

"Let us pray," Edward McHeran said, putting his hands together in prayer. Knowing they were past the help of men, they bowed their heads in unison to ask for God's mercy. Even Alexander McKee returned to the group and knelt with the rest, the sound of their voices drifting out into the wet night.

Throughout the next few days, news reached them in their cell. The trials of the San Patricios held in Tacubaya had begun, and an armistice had been agreed upon, forbidding either country from fortifying their defenses and strengthening their armies. The exchange of prisoners and the wounded would soon be carried out, but Riley knew without a doubt that Santa Anna wouldn't be able to negotiate with Scott for their freedom. No, Scott would be sure to make examples of them.

Then their own trials began. One by one, the San Patricios imprisoned in San Ángel were sentenced to hang—not death by firing squad as defined by the Articles of War—but to hang at the gallows as if they were lowly spies or rapists. Every single one of them received the death penalty. None of the claims they had made in their defense had swayed the Yankees. When Patrick Dalton received his sentence, Riley was close to tears. He needed to be strong, for all of them, but after that, he couldn't look his friend in the eye.

On September 5, Riley was the last of the men to be summoned. As the guard was placing the chains around his hands, Riley observed his men, who were leaning dejectedly against the walls.

The guards pushed him out of the warehouse, and even though Riley knew the verdict that awaited him, he still said a silent prayer. "God, have mercy on me. Let me live long enough to see my son once more and my unborn child."

He took a deep breath and tried to hold himself together as best he could, though the pain in his leg caused him to limp and his forehead broke into a sweat. When they pushed him into the room that had been turned into a courthouse, and Riley faced his judges, the wound on his leg had opened up again and blood was seeping through his already bloodstained Mexican uniform.

Riley could feel the room's gaze on him. He spotted Duncan sitting in the front row and saw the blatant hatred in his eyes, the same contempt with which Braxton Bragg would have looked at him if he were here. Colonel Bennet Riley was serving as judge. Riley hated sharing a surname with this man, a child of Irish parents but born and reared in America. A Catholic, but a Yank through and through. Riley knew not to expect any sympathy from the colonel. He knew the colonel would be harder on a true Irishman like Riley. Many American-born Irish were like that—turning against their own kind, pretending they had nothing in common with the folk from the ould sod. General Scott knew what he was doing when he appointed Bennet Riley to oversee the trials. On the outside, it would seem like the San Patricios were getting a fair trial, presided over by someone of Irish descent, but that couldn't have been further from the truth.

Sure enough, Colonel Bennet Riley stood and looked him up and down, taking in his major's dark-blue Mexican uniform, the braided epaulets, the medal of honor, the insignia of his rank. The colonel sneered with contempt and called the trial to order.

Riley kept his face impassive as Captain Ridgely read the accusations against him.

"Private John Riley of K Company, Fifth Infantry, you have been accused of deserting service to the United States on the twelfth of April, 1846. You are accused of joining the Mexican ranks and taking up arms against the United States Army in the battle of Churubusco. How do you plead?"

"Not guilty," Riley replied. His voice sounded sure and steady.

Murmurs broke out and many in the audience yelled, "Liar!" and "Traitor!"

The Colonel called the courtroom back to order. Several men were called to testify on Riley's character, among them his former commander, Captain Merrill. Riley remembered that rainy Sunday morning, the day after Sullivan's death, when he had made his decision to desert. He had thought Captain Merrill would be resentful that it was under his watch that Riley had deserted, but he saw no hatred in the captain's eyes. If anything, what he saw was respect, maybe even a hint of pity because he too seemed to know what the verdict would be.

"Private John Riley was a man of good character and an excellent soldier," Captain Merrill said. "I don't recollect ever having to punish him in any way."

Riley nodded a silent thanks and prepared to give his own statement. He knew full well that nothing he said would turn their hearts, but he wasn't going to make it quick and easy for the Yanks to sentence him to death. No, he was going to make them wait, and he was going to give them a piece of his mind.

"On April twelfth, after my tentmate, Franky Sullivan, was murdered in cold blood, I was in need of comfort from the Lord and his

Holy Mother, so I asked the good Captain Merrill here to give me permission to attend mass. On my way there, I was thereupon taken prisoner by Mexican lancers who dragged me across the Río Grande against my will." He heard the hisses, saw the shaking of heads. Of course they didn't believe a word he was saying, but he continued. "There in the town of Matamoros I was imprisoned, and for nineteen days I lived on nothin' but bread and water and the good grace of my Lord and Savior, Jesus Christ. Finally, General Ampudia came to my prison cell and gave me three choices." Riley stopped then and looked around the room. "The Mexican general said I could die by facin' the American firin' squad or his own firin' squad, or I could join his army. I, of course, refused to take up arms against the United States, not after I had been treated *so* kindly and respectfully by my American comrades and superiors. Not after bein' promised the opportunity to move up in rank. And especially not after bein' recompensed with a whole seven dollars in wages to send back home every month. So the Mexican general said to think things over. I was kept prisoner, with my hands tied behind my back all the way to the city of Linares."

He went on and on, describing the ordeal he had suffered. He was actually beginning to enjoy himself, his lies becoming more outlandish. He'd never told a better cock-and-bull story before. He saw the people in the audience squirming, the judges's faces turning redder and redder . Finally, during a pause in his storytelling, the colonel said, "Are you ready to close your statement, Private?"

Riley still wasn't ready to give them the satisfaction of sentencing him to death and being done with the trial so they could enjoy their dinner. And how dare he call him *private* when he knew damn well what his rank was? Riley shook his head and continued with his story. "And so 'twas, that many days later—after much sufferin' and anguish—I was sentenced to be executed by Ampudia's firin' squad, after which, I was to have my head fried in hog's grease and hung at the public square. But just when I was about to face death itself and put my defeated soul in the hands of the Lord, the other Mexican general, Arista, arrived to halt the execution. He gave me one more chance to take up arms in defense of Mexico." Riley heard the audience's whispers. The words traitor, liar, coward made his blood boil, and so he gave up the performance and brought his statement to a close.

"So I was given a choice, and I made it," he said, his voice louder, his tone serious. "I decided that instead of bein' sentenced to death and have my head fried, I would rather serve as a commissioned officer in the ranks of the Republic of Mexico. There, as you can see," he said, standing proudly and showing off his gilded epaulets and medal of honor, "I obtained the rank of major because of my skills and bravery on the field of battle—and because the Mexicans valued me and respected me in a way you Goddamned Yankees sonsofbitches never did!"

The audience was in an uproar. The colonel called the court to order but no one paid him any heed. He banged his gavel again and again. Riley tried to keep his face expressionless, but he couldn't help himself, and a grin spread across his face. He watched as the judges shouted among themselves.

Then Captain Ridgely stood, waited until everyone quieted down, and said: "After much deliberation, the court finds the prisoner Private John Riley, of Company K, Fifth Infantry, guilty as charged, and does therefore sentence him to be hanged by the neck until he is dead!"

37

"He is going to hang, hija," padre Sebastián said, coming to sit beside her in the pew. "They all are."

He had gone out that morning seeking news of John and his men. Every day he'd inquired on Ximena's behalf because no one would tell her when John would be court-martialed. And now it had finally happened, that very day, and like everyone else, he'd been given the death sentence.

She looked at the altar, at la Virgen de Guadalupe, at the shafts of broken sunshine streaming through the church's stained-glass windows. "Hang? Hanged by the very men who have called Mexicans barbarians and savages? Who are the savages now? Damn them. Damn them all to hell!"

"Lo siento, hija," padre Sebastián said. "But please, do not blaspheme in front of la Virgen."

Ximena took a deep breath and composed herself as best she could. *No, no, he couldn't be hanged, not after everything he had gone through, after everything they had sacrificed, fought for.* "I won't let them," she said. "I won't let that happen." She got up and took her leave. "Que tenga buen día, padrecito."

"Pero ¿adónde va, hija?" padre Sebastián called out.

She emerged from the Catedral Metropolitana into the bright day and pushed her way through the throng. Where could she go? Santa Anna was once again in the midst of political turmoil. Due to the armistice he agreed upon with the Yanquis, he'd been accused of being a traitor, not only by the people but also by government officials, including the governor of the state of Mexico. Although the armies had exchanged prisoners, Santa Anna didn't have Yanqui prisoners of high enough rank to exchange for his own officers, let alone John. Scott wouldn't give him up, even if Santa Anna had had a Yanqui major in his possession. Who could save John and the other San Patricios from that horrible fate? When she finally reached the Alameda, she was assailed by memories of strolling hand in hand with John. As they listened to the rustling of the trees and felt the caresses of the cool breeze, they had planned a future together that now would never happen. Not if the Yanquis got away with murder.

No, she wouldn't allow it!

She hired a coach to drive her to the British consulate. She had little money to spare, but her feet were swollen from all the walking and she needed to sit. Surely the British would help. After everything they had done to the Irish, surely they would have mercy now and do what they didn't do for them back in their homeland—save them. She wished now she had gone home to fix her hair, changed into her muslin dress, and exchanged her old rebozo for the mantilla John had given her on their wedding day. Appearances determined whether you were listened to or not. As she climbed up the steps to the consulate, she stopped and pinched her cheeks for some color, then licked her lips and smoothed her hair. She wished she had gloves, a parasol, anything that would elevate her in the eyes of the consul. What would he think of her coming into his office in such disarray? She should have also donned the beautiful brooch Santa Anna had given her, but this was a matter of life and death, gloves and brooch be damned.

The guard held the door open for her and she forced herself to slow her pace as she entered, pausing to thank him. She gazed at the ornate walls, the marbled floors, the imposing pillars.

"May I help you, madam?" a kind-looking older gentleman said as he approached her.

She forced a smile.

"Yes, please, sir. I must see the British consul. I have a matter of great importance to discuss. Please, it's very urgent."

"May I ask who is calling?" he said, guiding her to the waiting area.

"Señora Ximena de Benítez y Catalán."

He motioned for her to have a seat while he headed through a pair of wooden doors.

There were a few people sitting there, gentlemen reading the paper, smoking their cigars with such calm and ease that it made her angry just to look at them.

Finally, the doors opened, and the clerk motioned for her to follow him. He escorted her into an office where a middle-aged man sat behind a mahogany desk. His face was impassive, though she could see the curiosity in his eyes as he took in her disheveled appearance.

"Forgive me for interrupting your duties, sir," Ximena said, grateful that in the time she had known John, she had much improved her command of the English language. "But I must speak to you about a matter of great importance."

"Percy Doyle at your service. Please, madam, have a seat. Your English is excellent, though clearly you are not a British citizen. I am afraid I might not be able to assist you in my capacity as British consul."

She sat down, grateful to get off her feet. Taking a deep breath, she said, "I'm here to speak on behalf of the Irish soldiers imprisoned by the United States Army, sir. They have been sentenced to hang."

There was no response from the man, and Ximena could tell by his demeanor that he already knew. He looked at her, as if wondering how she fit into all of this.

"They are citizens of the United Kingdom," she said, "and as such, is it to be assumed that the British consul will solicit a pardon from the North Americans?"

He pulled his seat back, as if to stand up, but didn't.

"Yes, madam, the British government is well aware of the situation regarding the Irish soldiers, and I assure you, if I could be of assistance, I certainly would offer it. But as it is, alas, there is naught to be done for them."

"They are going to hang, sir," Ximena said, feeling her body shudder.

"It is a rather complicated situation, and one cannot expect a . . . ah . . . lady of your station to understand. Rest assured that I would look into the matter if I knew there was anything that could be done. At the moment, I do not believe there is."

"They're British citizens," Ximena said again. "Does that mean nothing to your government?"

"They are wild and reckless," he replied. "Those soldiers gave their word to the Americans, just as many of them gave their word to the English. They went back on their word and now it has come to this. You cannot expect the British government to support those who show no honor or loyalty. Now, if you excuse me, madam, I have another matter to attend to."

Ximena stood. She could see that he didn't care at all about the fate of John and his men. They were not worth his effort. John had told her how the English had treated them back home. Now she understood the hatred in his voice whenever he spoke of them.

"You must know, sir, that one of them is my husband." There, she said it. She had thought it best not to reveal this, but it was the only thing she could think of.

He looked at her and frowned. "I beg your pardon, madam?"

"John Riley, sir, is my husband. We were wed here, in this city, before the battle."

"I assume it was a Catholic wedding, madam. Do you have legal proof of this wedding?"

"Padre Sebastián—"

"Forgive me, madam, but I don't think marriage to a Mexican citizen will save your husband from the gallows. The Americans will not care."

He didn't say it but she heard it clearly. *And neither do we.*

"I am with child, sir. I'm carrying John Riley's child. Please, will you not speak in his favor for my child's sake!" She allowed her shawl to drop off her shoulders and stood so that he could see her protruding belly.

He coughed in discomfort at her lack of propriety and looked away. "I will see what I can do," he said, but she knew he would do nothing. "Now, if you will excuse me . . ." He picked up a stack of papers and motioned for the clerk to guide her out.

The old man held out his hand to her and she was grateful. Her legs were shaking, her body throbbed, as if she'd collided against a thicket of cacti. Suddenly, there was a kicking inside her. Her child, pressing its little elbows and knees against the walls of her belly. She stood outside the building and placed her hand over her belly, feeling the life she held inside her. Did her child know that its father was in danger? What was her baby trying to tell her? When Joaquin died, she'd dreamed of his death and just stood by, afraid of her visions. Not this time. She closed her eyes and said, "For you, my child, I'll do it for you." She rushed down the steps and hurried up the street. She would go to the archbishop and whoever else might help the San Patricios. She would not return home until she knew that John's life, and the lives of his men, would be spared.

38

September 1847
Mexico City

The next morning, Ximena went first to the private residence of señora Rubio in the village of Tacubaya, almost five kilometers from
the capital and near the Yankee headquarters. Padre Sebastián had ar-
ranged for her to meet there with señora Rubio and four other ladies
from the aristocracy who had created and signed a petition in defense
of Riley and his men. Together they were determined to deliver the
petition to Scott.

When Ximena and her five veiled companions were finally escorted to the general's headquarters, señora Rubio asked Ximena to
address the general since she was John's wife and spoke English. Ximena was surprised and nervous, but she tried not to show it. These
high society women were dressed in velvets and silks, delicate lace
mantillas fastened together with diamond brooches, their necks and
ears adorned with exquisite pearls. In truth, in her simple muslin dress,
Ximena looked more like their maid than the wife of the leader of
the Saint Patrick's Battalion, but she wouldn't let that intimidate her.
These women were willing to use their prestige and fortunes to help
her husband and his men.

"Come in, come in," General Scott said to the group. He was a giant
gray-haired man, large in height and weight, his uniform stretched

tightly across his girth. Ximena felt dwarfed by him. Extra chairs were brought into his office for the six of them, and confined in the small space with the imposing Yanqui general, Ximena was careful not to step on the ladies' fine dresses. When Scott requested an interpreter, she spoke up.

"There will be no need."

Scott seemed taken aback, not only by her English but that it was she, and not one of the elegant ladies, who spoke. Directing his gaze at Ximena, he asked, "How can I help you, ladies?"

"We are here to ask his Excellency to allow the members of the Saint Patrick's Battalion to be released on parole," Ximena said, speaking slowly and carefully. She handed him the petition that had been signed by more than one hundred Mexican citizens of great respectability.

Holding the paper in his large hands, Scott perused the petition, his deeply furrowed brows and sagging jowls becoming more crinkled with displeasure. Señora Rubio leaned over and whispered to her, "Dígale que le damos nuestra palabra de honor, que nosotras cuidaremos de los Colorados."

"Señora Rubio would like to assure his Excellency that you have our word of honor that we will watch over them during their parole."

"Forgive me, Mrs. . . ."

"Ximena de Benitez y Catalán, wife of John Riley."

"Ah, I see. I see. Look Mrs. Riley, I can't imagine what hardships you must be going through having your husband in prison, facing such a terrible fate. But the law is the law. John Riley and the other deserters broke their vows to the United States Army, and now, they must face the consequences of their actions."

"You broke your vows first, sir."

"I beg your pardon, my lady?"

"If the Yanqui officers hadn't mistreated and abused the foreign soldiers in your ranks, they would have faithfully kept their vows."

"There is truth in what you say—some of our officers and generals have exhibited unprofessional conduct toward our foreign soldiers.

But it is also true that some of these men were malcontents who abandoned our ranks in search of a better deal. Regardless of the reason for their betrayal, the law is the law and duty obliges me to deny your request." Scott didn't look at her when he said, "Desertion is punishable by death."

"Tenga piedad," señora Rubio and the other ladies said. "¡Nuestros héroes irlandeses no se merecen la muerte!"

Scott looked at Ximena and waited for her translation. She didn't want to beg. She wanted to yell at him and make him see reason, demand that his government own up to their responsibility in the desertions of Riley and his men. But controlling herself, she said, "My companions beg for your mercy. Our Irish heroes do not deserve to die."

"Heroes? They are *not* heroes! At worst they are traitors without honor, at best they are cowardly drunks!"

"Or perhaps they are victims, yes?" Ximena said. "Victims of your country's contempt and forced to fight in an unjust war." Then she added, "Call them what you wish, but we ask the general to please consider a prisoner exchange. Now that the truce between the countries—"

"What truce? There is no more truce. You can thank your general-in-chief for that!" Scott furiously pounded on his desk, his face turning as red as an old turkey vulture. "He didn't keep the good faith that was due. Therefore, as of today, I have terminated the armistice and shall be renewing hostilities."

"¡Dios mío!" señora Rubio said, "¿pero por qué nos grita así este Yanqui?"

Ximena translated Scott's words, and the ladies gasped. Of course, it was no secret that Santa Anna had ordered work to be made on the fortifications in the city and its surroundings, that he had sent church bells to the foundry to be turned into new cannons to replace the ones seized by the enemy, and he had tried to replenish his forces, all in direct violation of the armistice.

Seeing the women's frightened expressions, Scott lowered his voice. "My apologies. Mrs. Riley, General Santa Anna has exhibited dishonorable conduct by continuing to strengthen the city's military defenses, in gross violation of the terms he and I had agreed upon. Our armies will soon face each other in battle again, and now more than ever, I will need the loyalty of all my troops. Do you understand? If I release the Saint Patrick's Battalion, it will only encourage more desertions, especially of the foreign soldiers in our ranks, of which there are far too many. I cannot afford the continued spread of this contagion that has infected my troops for so long. And now, I must bid good day."

He stood up and waited for her and her companions to stand as well.

"If you won't free them, then don't free them. But you don't have to hang them," Ximena said as she and the other ladies collected themselves and headed to the door. "They made vows to your country, yes, but your country made vows to them too. And your government broke them first. Tell me, General, where was the good faith that was due to them when they enlisted in your ranks?"

More well-to-do Mexican citizens followed suit, appealing to Scott on behalf of the San Patricios. and Mexican newspapers published pieces in support of the foreign soldiers. Even padre Sebastián and the other priests helped her to convince the archbishop and prominent foreigners living in Mexico City to try to persuade the Yanqui general to spare the Irish soldiers. Padre Sebastián gave Ximena a copy of the letter that had been delivered to Scott, and in the dim candlelight, she read and reread it, wishing with all her heart that those words penned by the archbishop himself would touch Scott's heart.

We humbly pray that His Excellency the General in Chief of the American forces may be graciously pleased to extend a pardon to Captain John

Riley of the Legion of Saint Patrick, and generally speaking to all desert-
ers from the American service. We speak to your Excellency particularly of
Riley, as we understand his life to be in most danger, his misconduct might
be pardoned by your Excellency as we believe him to have a generous heart
admitting all his errors.

Your petitioners therefore repeat that their humble prayer may be granted
by your Excellency, and as in duty bound will everyone pray.

She placed the letter on her small altar, at the feet of la Virgen de
Guadalupe, and knelt on the floor, praying until her body was numb
and her eyes swollen from crying. Only when she felt the fluttering in
her belly did she finally get up. The innocent life growing inside her,
the product of their love, was reminding her that her duty was not only
to John. She needed to remain strong and not succumb to despair.

In the end, the begging, the threats, and the tears were not enough,
not enough to save them. Once Scott terminated the armistice, the
Mexican elite who had been willing to speak up for Riley and his men,
now fled the city in haste. The streets were choked with carriages taking the residents out of the capital to their haciendas on the outskirts.
She had no one else to turn to.

On September 9, Ximena received a letter from General Scott
himself bearing news both hopeful and discouraging.

Unfortunately, duty demands that I uphold the military code and have
sentenced the men of the Saint Patrick's Battalion accordingly. I trust that
you will rejoice in learning that in regards to your husband, the death sen-
tence has been rescinded.

Though he had pardoned some San Patricios for various reasons,
he had upheld the death sentences of fifty of them. He had also re-
duced the sentences of fifteen others, including John. Since he had
deserted a month before war was officially declared, John had thereby
been spared the noose. As she read further, Scott's words chilled her
to the core. Instead of being hanged, John's punishment would be a
public flogging and being branded on the cheek as a deserter. And
he would be kept a prisoner as long as the norteamericanos remained
in Mexico.

She read the letter again and was grateful that at least he had escaped the death penalty. Life was a precious gift. She and John and their child could still have a future together. But then she worried. Who could say that John wouldn't die in the process of being whipped or during his incarceration? And what about his men? What toll would their deaths take on his spirit?

39

September 1847
San Ángel, outskirts of Mexico City

Riley sat on the dirt floor of the prison cell, listening to the staccato sound of the pelting rain outside. This rain put him in mind of the mighty torrents that ever and anon swept in from the Atlantic over Clifden, and the thought of his homeland made him ache for his son. He had broken many promises, had made too many people suffer on his account. If only God would allow him to at least fulfill that one promise, just that one—to send for Johnny.

He looked at his men. Some sat on the floor, like him, with their backs against the cold stone walls. Their hands and feet were chained. No one spoke. They just listened to the rain and the sound of one another's breathing.

But in the spaces between the breaths and the rain, Riley heard another sound. It sent a chill up his spine because he knew what it meant. The sound of a saw cutting into wood. The echoes of a hammer punctuating the night. He got up and walked over to Dalton, who sat musing by the door. It was too dark to see his friend's face clearly, but Riley could smell his fear.

"I would yield my life for yours if I could, Pat," Riley said softly. "You know right well I speak in earnest, don't ya?"

"Nay, I'm a lucky Paddy. I'm going to die a quick death," Dalton said with a forced laugh. "I don't begrudge you your sentence, John. I've seen men bigger than you get flogged. 'Tis not a pretty sight, to be sure. And the brandin', well, I would rather swing than to be turned into a monster." Dalton laughed again, and though he had spoken in jest, Riley felt his breath catch in his throat. "Beggin' your pardon, John, *a chara*. I didn't mean that."

Riley said nothing. He had led his men to their deaths, and now he would be forced to watch them turned into rope dancers. would never be able to forget it, not if he lived to be a hundred.

"I shall die as a San Patricio ought to die," Dalton said, "with the satisfaction of having done my duty well under your command. That shall be my soldier's glory."

"Aye, that you have, indeed. You have fought bravely and loyally under the green banner."

Riley made out the glistening of tears in his friend's eyes. And his own chest throbbed as if his heart had been replaced by a handful of stinging nettles.

"You will make sure they bury me proper, won't ya?" Dalton said. At his trial, he had asked the court to be buried in consecrated ground, and his request had been granted.

But one never knew what the Yanks would do or not do in the end. Still, Riley nodded. "I will make sure of it, Pat, I promise."

The guards came for them early in the morning. Some of the men had drifted off into listless sleep. Others, like Riley, had sat vigil all night. He had prayed to every saint he knew, even Saint George, the patron saint of soldiers. He had begged God to spare the lives of his men but when he heard the footsteps outside the cell, he knew it was not to be.

"Rise and shine, Micks," one of the guards said as he unlocked the cell. "The day you have all been waiting for is here."

They broke them up into two lines, those going to the gallows and those meant for the muleteer's whip. Riley cringed at seeing how short his line was compared to the other one. Only seven in his line, sixteen in the other.

Riley pushed his way up to Dalton and the two men embraced. Dalton stifled a sob. "Promise me, John," he said, holding Riley tighter. "Promise me that when this is over, you won't think about this day. That you won't carry the burden of our deaths—"

"Move, traitors, move!" the guard said, hitting Riley with the butt of his musket so hard he had to struggle to regain his breath. "And you, fall in line!"

They marched them all out of their prison, down the corridors where the sounds of their shuffling feet and dragging metal chains echoed against the damp walls. They took them outside and proceeded to San Jacinto Plaza in the heart of San Ángel. Daylight had broken and the rain had ceased, but the cobblestones were wet and slippery beneath their feet. Riley held his head up but didn't look at anyone in particular. The square was full of people, even at this hour. Yankee soldiers stood around the perimeter, their faces filled with mockery and hatred, clearly looking forward to the grotesque spectacle that was about to unfold. He looked away and his eyes fell on the hundreds of Mexican villagers holding rosaries and chanting silent prayers, the women—young and old—wrapped in shawls and pleading for him, for his men.

"Perdónenlos," the women cried out at the soldiers, their arms raised in supplication. "¡Tengan piedad por los Colorados!"

He searched their faces but did not find Ximena's. And wasn't it better that way? Best for her not to see him like this.

"God have pity on us," Dalton said.

Riley turned his head at the sound of his friend's voice and there, looming before him, were the gallows with sixteen nooses hanging down, swaying in the morning breeze. There was no platform, no trap door. Eight wagons pulled by mules had been placed underneath the nooses, waiting.

"Courage, my brave brothers!" Riley said. "Courage!" But his own knees were already trembling.

Hezekiah Akles broke forth in tears.

"Curse ye, curse ye all!" James Mills cried.

"Quiet now!" one of the guards said, pulling on the chains and forcing them to continue their march forward. Riley winced as the wrist chains ate into his flesh, knowing this was only the beginning.

General Twiggs came out to the plaza on his horse, and at the sight of him everyone fell silent. "We'll start with you first," he said, looking at Riley but indicating his line with the other six men who were to be flogged. Riley could feel the horse's hot breath and saw a hint of his reflection in its glossy brown eye. He looked away. When this was over, he would never want to look at his reflection again.

"Thomas Riley, Hezekiah Akles, James Mills, John Bartley, John Bowers, Alexander McKee, and John Riley," General Twiggs said. "You have been found guilty of desertion and have been sentenced to receive fifty lashes and to be branded with the letter D for deserter. We will now proceed." He ordered his sergeants to take Riley and the six other men to the stand of ash trees where a small group of priests stood chanting prayers as they held a large crucifix high in the air.

One by one the seven prisoners were freed from their chains and stripped of their ragged shirts and coats, and with torsos now exposed, each man was tied to a tree. The muleteers came to stand behind each man, their rawhide whips at the ready. Riley caught sight of the whips, with their long-knotted tails quivering like rattlesnakes ready to strike. He took a deep breath as the muleteer behind him measured the distance between his bare back and the whip. *Saint Patrick, protect me.*

Then Twiggs shouted the order to begin. As the whips whistled through the air in unison and tore through human skin, the cries of the men echoed against the buildings.irds flew out of the trees and fled.

Riley had never known such pain. It felt as if he were being skinned alive. He bit his lip and tasted blood but didn't cry out. The flogging

was unendurable, and some of the San Patricios fainted, others begged
for mercy. Through the wailing and the praying, and the cracking of
the whips, Riley latched on to the sound of Twiggs's voice counting
the lashes one by one as they landed. Drifting in and out of darkness, he felt himself succumbing to the pain. He thought of his son
and could hear his voice calling him, *Don't leave me, Dadaí.* He willed
himself to come back.

At one point, Twiggs pretended to have lost count and nine long
lashes went by before he began to count again.

"Forty-one, forty-two, forty-three . . ."

Then, before his eyes, Riley saw Nelly. She was white, thin as mist,
and she held out her arms to him. *I've been waiting for you, John . . .*

He shook the apparition away, and felt the pain again, so excruciating he struggled to breathe, to not succumb to the solemn darkness.
He opened his eyes and saw the crowd around him, and then there she
was, Ximena, standing next to the priests clustered nearby. Was she
real? Was he imagining her as well?

"Forty-nine . . . fifty!" General Twiggs shouted. Riley sagged
against the tree, gulping for air. There was a roaring in his ears, and he
struggled to stay conscious. Wasting no time, Twiggs gave the order to
continue and seven soldiers approached the prisoners, each carrying a
branding iron heated a fiery red and glowing with the letter D. They
held them inches away from the prisoners' faces, and Riley could smell
the smoke, feel the intense heat.

"Hold them down!" Twiggs said.

"Mercy, have mercy!" Ximena yelled, her shawl flapping in the wind
like wings, and Riley thought he was seeing an angel, just as the left
side of his face was pushed against the rough bark of the tree and a soldier pressed the hissing hot iron on his right cheek. When it entered
his flesh, a searing pain, like a jolt of lightning, made his body jerk, his
muscles clenching in agony.

"Aaaaghhhhh!" The smell of burnt flesh, his own flesh. Riley
wished he could bash his head against the tree trunk and put an end
to his agony.

"Please, enough. ¡Basta!" said the priests as they rushed over to his side.

"Wait a minute," Twiggs said as he dismounted from his horse. He approached Riley and ordered his soldier to reheat the iron. "The D is upside down," Twiggs said. "Do it again and do it right this time, even if you have to burn his damn head off!"

"The man has suffered enough," padre Sebastián beseeched him. "Please, have mercy."

"Let him go!" Riley heard Ximena say. "His punishment has been carried out. Let it be enough, I beg you."

"I've been ordered to brand this traitor with a letter D—not an upside-down letter—and by God I will do it!" Twiggs said. "Now, bring the iron and do it right, man!"

Riley couldn't speak, couldn't get away. The Yankees grabbed him and pushed his burnt right cheek into the bark of the tree, and when the red hot iron was pressed into his other cheek, he bellowed in anguish until darkness finally overtook him.

When he came to, Riley realized he'd been dragged across the square with the six others and made to stand in front of the gallows. He was dripping wet, and a soldier stood above him holding an empty pail. "Wake up sleepy head. Wake up," he said.

Riley didn't shake off the water. He sighed in relief as the cold water soothed the burning on his face for a few precious seconds before it came back again in full force, the pain radiating from his cheeks, pulsing throughout his entire body and soul. The odor of burnt flesh drifted in the wind, and his face felt as if it were melting. He wanted to tear off his skin with his own hands, but he was back in chains and couldn't move.

As his face swelled, his vision blurred, and he could scarcely make out the figures of the men at the gallows, standing two by two on wagons. The mules in front of each wagon jerked side to side, the men almost lost their balance. Soldiers climbed up on each wagon and placed white hoods around the prisoners' heads. The nooses were secured on their necks just as the priests finished moving down the wagons offering the last rites to the unfortunate souls whose fate was to die so far from home.

Suddenly, Riley yelled, "*Erin Go Bragh!*"

"*Erin Go Bragh!*" the condemned men repeated.

Twiggs gave the order, and the mules pulled the wagons forward, leaving the sixteen men swinging violently in the air, their bodies twitching and jerking. Since there was no trap door, the fall hadn't broken the men's necks, denying them a quick death. One by one they asphyxiated and became still, all but Patrick Dalton, who continued to convulse for several seconds longer. Riley couldn't unfix his gaze from his friend as he choked to death. At last, Dalton stopped quivering and was still. The silence of death, of surrender, hung over the plaza.

Forgive me, Pat. Riley broke forth in tears which stung his burned, swollen flesh. *I'm sorry to the heart, I am, that your life should end with such little dignity.*

He could barely see as one by one the bodies were taken down. Seven of them, including Dalton's, were loaded into a wagon for the priests to bear them away and give them a proper burial. The other nine of his men were to be buried there, under the gallows, and Riley and the six other whipped and branded men were forced to dig their graves.

Some of the Mexican men demanded that Twiggs allow them to do the digging, that the prisoners had suffered enough. But Twiggs wouldn't listen. He could scarcely stand, but Riley dug fast and hard. He was the reason his men were dead. From the moment he had put out the call to his countrymen and the other foreign-born soldiers, he had sentenced them to their fate. Now his soul was stained by their blood. *Eternal rest grant unto them, O Lord. And let perpetual light shine upon them. May they rest in peace. Amen.*

To humiliate them further, the pipers on the opposite side of the square began to play "The Rogue's March" as Riley and the others were dragged back into the jail with an iron collar around their necks. He heard his name being called. Turning around, he saw Ximena only a few paces back, trying to get past the soldiers. He couldn't make her out, for his face had swelled so much that his eyes were closing up on him. But he would recognize her voice anywhere. She *was* here. He hadn't just imagined it.

40

Padre Sebastián had advised her to not go, that she had seen enough. But Ximena knew that if she didn't, she would always regret it. "Think of your child," he'd said. "Think of the distress." But she hadn't listened. She was John's wife, and since he couldn't be there to say good-bye to his men, she would go in his stead.

So the morning of September 13, she accompanied the priest to bid farewell to the remaining San Patricios who had been sentenced to death. The day before, four of them had been hanged in the village of Mixcoac, and now the rest would be as well, while the latest battle of the war was taking place on the grounds of Chapultepec Castle and at the toll gates of the city. Outlined by the golden light of dawn, the twenty-nine San Patricios stood beneath the gallows on mule-drawn carts. Unlike the sixteen men hanged in San Ángel, however, these San Patricios didn't have their faces covered by white hoods. Their feet and hands were bound, but their eyes could plainly see what the Yanks wanted them to see—Chapultepec Castle in the distance, under siege.

Colonel Harney said, "When the American flag flies above that castle, that is then when you will meet your fate."

"You can stick your filthy little rag where the sun don't shine," one of the condemned men said.

The San Patricios laughed. Ximena wanted to cry at the sound of their laughter. Even this close to death, the men could still find a reason to laugh, teasing the colonel, trying to rile him up.

Colonel Harney counted out the men. Eight would be facing the muleteers' whips, just like John had. The other thirty would be hanged. "There are twenty-nine here!" Colonel Harney said as he finished counting the men at the gallows. "Where is the thirtieth?"

"Francis O'Conner is on his deathbed, Colonel. He lost both legs at Churubusco," one of the officers said.

"My orders are to hang thirty and by God, I'll do it. Bring him out, now!" Colonel Harney said.

"Aren't we enough for you, Colonel?" Kerr Delaney said. "You want to see the poor mutilated creature dancing a pretty jig for ya, is that it? You sick scoundrel."

"Your country has a crow to pluck with us, true enough, but there's no need to subject the poor little fella to this manner of torture, Colonel. Let him be," another San Patricio said.

Despite the protests, two Yankee officers returned carrying Francis O'Conner on a litter. He was unconscious, for which Ximena was thankful. With his missing legs, he was the height of a small child. In horror, she watched as they placed him on a wagon and then lowered the noose around his neck after they lengthened the rope.

"Our Lord have mercy," padre Sebastián said as he placed a hand on Ximena. She reached to support the old priest. Feeling weak herself, her heart began to beat rapidly, making her dizzy, but she needed to be strong.

"And they say we are the barbarians, padre," she said.

Amid the protests of the San Patricios and the Mexicans who had come out to watch the execution, Colonel Harney read General Order 283. "And now we wait," he said as he finished. "When our beloved flag unfurls in the wind, I will swing you all into eternity."

"I can't bear this, padrecito," Ximena said.

"Be strong, hija mía. Now more than ever, we all need to seek strength from our Lord."

The morning mist dissipated, and the sun beat down on them. She could hear the blasting of cannons and the staccato of muskets in the distance. The wind carried the screams of the dying, and Ximena felt a pang of guilt as she remembered that her place should be at the castle, in the makeshift hospital, tending to the injured. But how could she not be here as well?

"The castle won't fall," she told padre Sebastián. They peered through the smoke of the cannons as the battle raged on. Chapultepec Castle was supposed to be an impregnable fortress, but as she watched through the trees as the Yankee bombs exploded on its roof, she realized that its soundness had been an illusion.

The priest patted her hand and said nothing. She could tell he was getting tired. Over an hour now they had stood, waiting for the fighting to cease. She had offered to lead him to some shade under a tree, but padre Sebastián had stayed put near the gallows. He would be administering the last rites, and his presence, along with those of the other priests in attendance, offered much comfort to the doomed men.

Another hour passed, and Ximena didn't know how much longer she could bear it. But the San Patricios were still standing at the gallows with the sun beating hard on them. They had been given no water. Flies and mosquitos pestered them, and they could do nothing about it.

And then, the outcome of the battle became clear. Mexican soldiers were escaping through the smoke, the Yanks in pursuit. Even from where she stood, Ximena could see that it wouldn't be long before the castle fell. The Yanks were scaling the walls with ladders, and soon, even the castle gates were breached.

"Padre, the cadets!" Ximena yelled, thinking about the boys in the military college, some as young as thirteen. "Will they be killed?"

Padre Sebastián looked at her and said nothing, but he was also clearly worried about the children inside the castle walls. What if the Yanquis showed them no mercy?

"It is time, my daughter," he said with a sigh. He left her side and walked down to join the other priests. They approached the men at the gallows and began to administer the last rites.

"Wait, not yet—" Ximena said. But then she looked toward the castle and as the dense cloud of smoke cleared, she knew that the priest was right. It was time. Above Chapultepec Castle, the Mexican flag no longer flew. Instead, she caught a flash of red, white, and blue flapping on the highest tower. Her breath caught in her throat, and her knees gave way. Now that Chapultepec Castle was lost, the Yanks were that much closer to taking the city.

As she collapsed to the ground, the Yanks around her, especially Colonel Harney, burst out in cheers.

When the colonel approached the San Patricios, she scrambled to her feet.

"Wait!" she said. "Please, have mercy!"

One of the Yanquis caught her and pulled her back. She kept on screaming. The men smiled at her and shouted a last farewell. Kerr Delaney said, "Take care of yourself, lassie. May God finally grant you some happiness."

"Long live John Riley!" they cheered with their last breaths. "*Erin Go Bragh*!"

And then, at Colonel Harney's orders, the wagons moved forward, and the San Patricios hung in midair, jerking in a macabre dance. Ximena did not look away, not until the very last man came to a standstill.

He came to her that evening. Disguised as a street peddler, rain dripping from his sarape, he walked into the little house she'd moved into when she could no longer bear to be in the barracks without John. He hung his sarape on a hook by the door and then looked at her. His hair was disheveled, his face haggard.

She had been praying at her altar, and before she got off her knees to see what he wanted, he stopped her. "No se levante."

He limped to her side and removed his wooden leg, using it for support as he bent down to pray with her. He groaned at the pain but knelt on the floor alongside her, lowering his head as his voice joined hers in prayer.

When their throats eventually grew hoarse and dry, she helped him get up. He sat on the chair while she tended to his leg. It was inflamed and the wound had opened again. She washed it clean. He sighed in relief as she applied her árnica mexicana salve, massaging it into his skin.

"Why have you come?" she asked as she finished dressing his wound.

"To take you with me," he said. "I depart at midnight. My council of war has decided to evacuate the city. I'm withdrawing my troops to Guadalupe Hidalgo."

"You're abandoning us? You're allowing the Yanquis to take possession of the capital?"

"For now. Until I replenish my troops. Until I figure out a new strategy to restore our country's liberty and honor."

"You've lost. There is no strategy that will change that. You have been defeated."

He hung his head and fixed his gaze upon the floor. And then, very quietly at first, he began to cry. As his sobs grew louder, she looked away, not wanting to witness the president of the República Mexicana bawling like a spring calf separated from its mother. She wouldn't comfort him nor join her sorrow to his. Instead, she grabbed the bottle of mezcal she used for her healing and poured him and herself a shot.

"Was it true?" she asked as she handed the drink to him.

He took the mezcal and downed it, then held out the earthen cup for another. When he asked for a third shot, she refused. He looked at her and nodded, finally admitting what she had always known in her heart.

"All this time, the rumors were true?" She served herself another shot and sat down.

He took out a handkerchief from his pocket and wiped his eyes dry. "While I was in Cuba living in exile, I dispatched my friend, Colonel Alejandro Atocha, to pay President Polk a visit and bargain with him on my behalf."

In exchange for thirty million dollars, Santa Anna had promised to give Polk the territory he wanted. But he insisted that Polk attack Mexico first so that it looked as if it was by force. It was crucial for the Mexican people to believe that their government had no other choice but to negotiate with the Yanquis.

"I was the one who told Polk how to attack us," he said. "I told him that the Mexican people would never yield unless forced to do so. I provided him with the plan of attack—to send his forces to our northern frontier, to send a naval expedition to Vera Cruz and take advantage of our scarcity of ships to guard the coast. I promised him that if he helped me return from exile and establish myself firmly in power, I would convince our government to make peace with the United States and give him what he asked for, the Río Bravo boundary, Alta California, Nuevo México—"

"This was your plan all along then, to sell us out? You were defeated on purpose? You sacrificed John and the San Patricios . . ."

"No!" He grabbed her hands, and when she tried to pull them away, he squeezed them harder, pleading. "Listen to me, Ximena. I lied to the Yanqui president. I never intended to despoil our country. I just wanted him to help me return from exile. My country *needed* me to save them, to have faith in me again. You understand? The minute I returned, I placed myself at the head of our army and spent every waking breath to restore Mexico's honor. I betrayed my agreement with Polk. Don't you see?" he said, kissing her hands. He laughed smugly and said, "I fooled him! The land-grabbing Yanqui believed me and restored me to power, whereupon I dedicated myself to make him understand that I would never consent to despoil Mexico of her northern territories. Ximena, querida, trust me when I say that I didn't take my troops—I didn't take Riley and his men—into the battlefield to lose. I meant to win. I meant to bring victory to Mexico. I meant to give us all a little taste of glory."

She yanked her hands away and shook her head in disbelief. "You handed our country over to the Yanquis. From the very beginning, you betrayed your people, your homeland. I watched the San Patricios hang in the gallows because they fought for you. I watched my husband flogged and his face defiled for defending a country not his own. So many soldiers lost their lives in this war. Even the cadets in Chapultepec Castle died defending it. General Bravo lost his life. Their blood is on your hands. The blood of the San Patricios is on your hands. You're a murderer! ¡Un vendepatrias!"

She slapped him once, twice, the third time he caught her hands by the wrists. "¡Basta! I am no murderer. And how dare you accuse me of selling out Mexico? I have suffered privations, insults, and calumny! I've risked my life to defend this ungrateful country. It is the people and their lack of patriotism you ought to blame. Where were they today? Where was their pride? The Yanquis were attacking their city and they simply watched with apathy. Only my soldiers and I fought while the masses stood by and did nothing." He grabbed his wooden leg from the table and struggled to put it back on.

"They have no weapons, what could they have done? Pelt the Yanquis with stones?"

"¡Sí! Hurling stones would have been better than just standing by. A lack of weapons has never stopped them before. When they rise in revolt against their own government—against *me*—weapons or not, they still put up a fight. Look what they did to my limb! Where was their outrage today when the Yanquis stormed the castle, when they seized the city gates? Where was their outrage when the Yanquis flogged your husband, when they hanged his men, our Irish heroes? If the Yanquis had fought the people as well as my soldiers, they would have been annihilated."

He ran a hand through his hair and shook his head. Then he stood to leave.

"Hágame caso, Ximena. It is in your best interest to come with me. I deeply lament saying this but it is true—Juan Riley belongs to the Yanquis now. There is no saying when he will be released—*if* he will be released. Scott won't exchange the San Patricios, you know that. He needs to make an example of them, especially of Juan Riley." He limped toward her and took her hand, his voice gentler now, shifting into a sweet seductive tone. She hated how he could do that, the capricious mood swings, the change in the tenor of his voice.

"Let me take care of you, querida. I will be good to you. To your child. Se lo prometo." He grabbed her by the shoulders and kissed her. When she didn't respond, he pressed her against him and tried to pry her mouth open with his tongue. She stood there like a statue, giving him nothing, not even this kiss he'd always asked for.

"You have violated the sacred soul of Mexico," she said when he at last gave up. "Adiós, Antonio." She handed him his sarape, and he draped it over himself and left. She knew this would be the last time they would ever see each other.

The next day the city was abuzz with the news that Santa Anna had broken his promise to the people to defend the capital to the bitter end and instead had fled, taking with him his remaining troops. Coming out of the Catedral Metropolitana, Ximena watched as General Scott marched into the city to take possession of the Palacio Nacional. She couldn't bear the sight of the invaders. Sitting atop a magnificent horse and surrounded by his escorts, Scott made his way past the citizens, who watched his entrance into the palace in horror.

On the eve of Mexican Independence Day, the flag of stars and stripes unfurled in the wind in full view of the city, to the sorrow of the Mexican people. Ximena remembered the first time she saw that flag at the Yanqui encampment across from Matamoros. Who would have imagined then that from Matamoros, it would go on to fly over other Mexican cities until it ended up here, piercing the heart of Mexico?

The following night "El Grito" should have been reenacted in the Plaza de la Constitución, the heroes that had given their lives for Mexican Independence honored and remembered. Ximena thought of how a year ago, she'd been celebrating the independence of her country with John and Jimmy Maloney in Monterrey. Now, Jimmy was dead and so were most of the San Patricios. John was in prison, and Santa Anna had abandoned the city that he claimed to love. She was alone, about to bring forth a child into this unstable world. Watching the Yanqui colors floating over the Palacio Nacional, she knew that the demoralization of the Mexican soul was complete.

Something snapped inside her at the same moment that a change happened in the crowd. Perhaps it was seeing the enemy's flag flying over the palace that woke the people from their culpable apathy. They realized that with Santa Anna's army and the government officials gone, no one was coming to defend them. Perhaps it was the realization that instead of celebrating their country's independence, they were watching Mexico return to its days of conquest and back in the hands of invaders.

Even stones would have been better than nothing, Santa Anna had said. Ximena picked up the stone by her shoe and hurled it at the Yanqui soldiers marching by. Others did the same, raising the cry for war, raining stones and bricks upon the invaders. A stormy riot broke out. The people—even the beggars, the lepers, and the peddlers—weaponless but full of indignation and hungry for revenge, fought with whatever they could, yelling "¡Muerte a los Yanquis! ¡Muerte a Santa Anna!" Then others joined in and, from the rooftops and windows of the nearby buildings, they discharged their escopetas upon the enemy. The Yanquis fell into ranks, loaded and fired their cannons upon the multitude. The crowds ran for cover, and Ximena barely kept herself from being trampled by the fleeing masses. Clutching her protruding stomach, she reached the doors of the Catedral Metropolitana just as another blast of cannon exploded outside.

41

October 1847
Mexico City

With Santa Anna gone, John's fate was even more uncertain. The commander-in-chief had made promises to the San Patricios, promises that would no longer be honored, not now and perhaps, not in the future. Ximena kept herself apprised of his movements. After a few skirmishes with the Yanquis from his base in Guadalupe Hidalgo, Santa Anna resigned the presidency and unsuccessfully attempted to besiege the Yanqui garrison in Puebla and retake the city. He failed. The new Mexican president, Peña y Peña, asked him to turn over what was left of his troops and retire to a place to await a court-martial. Terminating his futile harassment of the Yanqui forces, Santa Anna issued several proclamations, and everyone, including Ximena, paid no heed to his words.

Mexicans! I am a man, and I have defects, but never have I sinned against my own country; never has my breast harbored anti-national sentiments. To leave a good name behind me has been the aim of my ambition. I have earnestly longed for everything which is great and glorious for Mexico, and to obtain it I have not spared my own blood. You know this and you will do me justice.

His words had no weight to them, and his cry for vengeance was carried away by the wind. Facts were facts. Deliberately or not, he had allowed the Yanquis to occupy Mexico City. With the Mexican Army now decimated, the enemy claimed victory.

The bloody revolts of the Mexican people spread from building to building, street to street, plaza to plaza. The Yanquis suppressed the insurrection through force, breaking into homes, slaughtering and scattering dead bodies through the streets, until the noises of musket and cannon came to an end. General Scott published penal orders, threatening anyone who took up arms against his soldiers with severe punishment, ordering his soldiers to shoot any Mexican carrying arms in the streets. Ximena was disgusted when she realized that only the poor had rebelled against the invaders, while the "distinguished" citizens of the city had stood by, offering no support to the resistance, instead protectingtheir own wealth. Some even obtained positions of power from the Yanquis. White flags of truce hung from their balconies, as did the flags of the foreigners living in the city who wished to prevent the Yanquis from confusing them with common Mexicans.

The population now resigned themselves to the disgrace of a Yanqui occupation. Others abandoned their homes and left the capital, carrying with them their meager belongings. Ximena watched the Yanqui soldiers doing in the capital what they had done in Matamoros, sacking the churches, erecting whipping posts to punish any Mexican who rebelled. All night long, the Yanquis gambled, danced, and drank anywhere they pleased in the city. More taverns, billiard halls, and brothels opened up, where many impoverished Mexican women went to sell their honor to feed their families. Others took to the streets to ask for alms. Food and other necessities became scarce, and the people struggled to secure what was needed to survive, especially after the arrival of more Yanqui forces, including the vicious Rangers and other volunteers with their pistols, bowie knives, and rough manners.

Pushing aside her worries for the gloomy future of her country, Ximena focused on the only things that were just as important to her— her child and helping her husband and the surviving San Patricios.

To make matters worse, only a few days after taking possession of the city, General Scott had John and the other branded Patricios transferred to the Acordada Prison in the city. She was not allowed to see him, but in the Mexican newspaper *El Republicano*, she read about the ordeal that he and his men were going through. She read that they had been chained up by their arms, so that they couldn't lie down, with iron collars around their necks. And they were suffering from hunger, for the little food that they received was barely enough to sustain them. "We hope that General Scott won't be deaf to our request and will consider that not even the laws of war permit unhuman chastisement. The light of the age has proscribed all cruel treatment," the article read.

Ximena didn't stop asking for help. She swallowed her pride and went to higher officials, as well as to señora Rubio and the wealthy señoras who had shown their support to the San Patricios. She accompanied padre Sebastián and other priests to speak once more to the archbishop, who in turn put pressure on General Scott to ease up on the prisoners and permit visitations. As a result, Scott finally granted permission for the imprisoned San Patricios to receive visitors.

Ximena didn't know what to expect when she arrived at the Acordada Prison not far from the Alameda where she and John had often strolled. As she and the other visitors were escorted to the second floor where the San Patricios were, she had told herself that she wouldn't cry, not in front of John. But at the sight of him behind bars, she couldn't help the tears from welling up. She stood to the side as the other visitors passed her and went to the cells. John stretched out on a straw mat in the farthest corner of the second cell, hiding in the shadows. Unlike the other men, who seemed happy to receive visitors, John didn't look pleased. He kept his face hidden and turned to face the wall, taking no notice of the visitors. While the prisoners were not wearing the iron collars described in the newspaper, they were indeed shackled and dressed in rags, each with a straw mat and thin blanket offering no protection from the damp walls and floors.

After drying her tears, she finally approached his cell. Grabbing hold of the cold bars that stood between them, she called out to him. He turned slowly to face her. His eyes were hidden by his hair, which was getting long and shabby. Why wouldn't he come to her? Why was he just lying on his petate, unmoving? Wasn't he happy to see her?

"John," she said. "Please. We haven't much time."

He finally stood up and came over to her. He was thinner than he'd ever been, and though still tall, he seemed to have shrunk somehow. She'd never seen him so dirty and slovenly. He slouched as he walked, and he put his hands over his face as if to shield himself from an un-relenting wind. But there was no wind. Just her. Why would he need to hide from her?

"You ought not to have come, darlin'," he said at last, still hiding his face behind his hands, and she could see only his haggard-looking eyes. She felt the pain as his words registered in her mind. She had waited so long, fought so hard to make this moment happen. And now to hear him say those words to her. But she knew he didn't mean them. She could hear what he hadn't said, and she understood.

"Nothing has changed between us, John. I love you. No matter what they've done to you. I will always love you, come what may."

He finally dropped his hands, and he stood facing her. The room was dimly lit by the torches hanging on the walls, and there were sin-ister shadows everywhere, but as the torch light flickered on his face, she could see what he didn't want her to see—not his pallid flesh or his sunken cheeks, but the burns still red and scabbing, the two-inch D's marring his handsome face. The Yanquis had inflicted a great violation upon him. For the rest of his life, he would carry these scars, and in time the physical ones would fade, but the scars on his soul might not. She wouldn't let them win. She would help restore his traumatized spirit and guide him in feeling whole again.

She put her hand through the bars, reaching for him. She wanted to touch him, hold him, but he took a step back from her, and she had no choice but to retract her hand. "Don't be afraid of me, mi amor."

He got closer to her and put his forehead against the bars. He reached for her hand and raised it to his cheek. "Forgive me, darlin'," he said. "I don't want to hurt you more than I already have."

"Shhh," she said. "You don't need to apologize, John. What they've done to you—" she stopped herself. There was so much that she wanted to say, but she knew that time was brief and the Yanqui guards were listening to their every word. She reached for the parcel she had brought. She handed it to him and watched as he took out a jar of calendula salve she'd made for his wounds and a cotton shirt, the first she'd ever stitched with her own hands. He traced the shamrock embroidered over the left pocket with green silk thread.

" 'Tis truly a fine shirt," he said. "But they won't let me keep it."

"They will," she said. "The officer promised me they would."

He looked at her and smiled, as if she were a child. And what if she was being naïve to believe in anything the Yanquis said?

"Thank you, darlin'," he said. " 'Tis so good to see you. And how is the babe?" He put his hands through the bars to touch her huge belly, running his hands gently up and down. Suddenly, the baby kicked hard, as if saying hello to its father. Finally, his impassive face lifted into a genuine smile. There he was, her John. So he was not completely broken, as she'd feared.

"He's a fighter, this one," he said proudly.

"Just like his papá," she said.

"Time's up!" the head guard called out. "All visitors will now be escorted out. Please make your way to the stairs."

They reached for each other through the bars, clutching tight, afraid to let go. "Don't concern yourself about me, mi amor. I'll be fine. Our child will be fine. Just concentrate on staying alive. For me. For us."

He kissed her hands and then released her. A guard came up behind her and yelled at her to move. As she hurried out of the prison, she realized she hadn't told him about the Irish and German soldiers still deserting the Yanqui army and heading to Querétaro to join the San Patricios who had escaped Churubusco. Even with John in prison, even with so many of his men hanged at the gallows, the Saint Patrick's Battalion still lived on.

42

October 1847
Mexico City

Respected Sir,

I have taken the liberty of writing to you hoping that you are in good health as I am at present, thank God for it. I have had the honor of fighting in all the battles that Mexico has had with the United States . . . and have attained the rank of major. I suppose from the accounts you have seen in the United States papers, you have formed a very poor opinion of Mexico and its government, but be not obscured by the prejudice of a nation, which is at war with Mexico, for a more hospitable or friendly people . . . there exists not in the face of the earth, that is to a foreigner and especially to an Irishman and a Catholic. So it grieves me to have to inform you of the deaths of fifty of my best and bravest men who have been hanged by the Americans for no other reason than fighting manfully against them, especially my first lieutenant, Patrick Dalton, whose loss I deeply regret . . .

Riley put the pen down, unable to continue. Writing a letter to his former employer in Michigan, Charles O'Malley, had seemed a good recourse, but now he couldn't be sure. O'Malley was the only acquaintance Riley had in the United States, and surely, a man in his position might be able to speak on his behalf. O'Malley had always looked out for his countrymen.

In the solemn glow of the little piece of tallow candle he'd managed to procure, he reread the last sentence and thought of Patrick. He wished he hadn't witnessed the hanging. He wanted to remember his friend as he was before the gallows, a loyal and courageous fellow, a man that deserved better, so much better.

With a shaking hand, he resumed his writing.

You may possibly have thought strange at my not writing to you before, but there being no communication between Mexico and the United States, it was impossible for me to address you before now, but as I am at present a prisoner of war by the Americans, it is impossible for me to state facts as they are, but in my next letter, I will give you a full and true account of the war as it has progressed. If you will remember my last words to you and Thomas Chambers when last we parted, which was if God spared me I would again attain my former rank or die.

My situation is such that it is impossible for me to give you a better account at present but have patience for my next. In all my letter I forgot to tell you under what banner we fought so bravely. It was that glorious Emblem of native rights, that being the banner which should have floated over our native Soil many years ago, it was St. Patrick, the Harp of Erin, the Shamrock upon a green field.

The days turned into weeks. Every day, Riley and the other prisoners were let out at seven in the morning and put to hard labor. One day, one of his men, Roger Duhan, managed to escape from the prison. His wife smuggled him out by dressing him as a woman. Such a feat could only work on a little fellow like Duhan. He was slight enough to fit into the women's clothes his wife had smuggled in. With a Mexican shawl wrapped around his head and shoulders to obscure his face, he'd snuck past the Yankee guards. When his absence was discovered, they imposed further restrictions on visits, and Riley saw Ximena even less. It shamed him to admit, but he was glad that she wouldn't be obliged to look at his hideous face, his filthy body. He couldn't remember the last time he'd washed or changed his underclothes. Fleas and lice were bad bedfellows and tormented him every night. No, he didn't want his beloved to see him like this, such a poor excuse of a man. But on the first of December, padre Sebastián brought him the tidings of the birth of his daughter, Patricia. When they wouldn't let Ximena visit him to show him the babe, he cursed the Yanks once again, and wept with misery.

On December 22, the Yankees released five hundred Mexican prisoners, but they refused to release the San Patricios. Riley and his men were forced to spend Christmas in prison. They weren't even allowed to receive visitors on that special day, and Riley's hopes of finally meeting his daughter and seeing how she fared were dashed. Then, a few days after Christmas, the Yankees came for them. For a moment, Riley and the others thought that perchance their luck had turned. Perhaps the Yanks would let them go and they would be able to welcome the New Year as free men. But it wasn't to be. He and the other unhappy wretches were merely being transferred to another prison, to Chapultepec Castle where security was tighter and the prison cells more miserable.

Through the thick walls, Riley and his men could barely hear the sound of firecrackers and rockets, of music and cheering as the people welcomed 1848. The church bells in the city tolled heavily, and Riley felt the familiar desire to be once again inside his parish chapel. He betook himself to a dark corner and closed his eyes, but he could hear his men whispering among themselves.

"What will this year hold for us, ye think?" John Bartley said.

"Whatever it is, can it be worse than this?" Hezekiah Akles replied.

"Aye, it can. We miserable creatures can die within these prison walls and be buried in unmarked graves," Alexander McKee said.

Riley wished he could say something to his men—to encourage them, raise their downcast spirits, show them a way out of their despair. But he had lost his will to lead.

Someone came to sit beside him in his dark corner and said, "I know right well you're awake, Major. Is it ignorin' us, you are?" It was James Mills, the only one left of the men who'd fought alongside him since Matamoros.

That first battle felt so long ago, and there was nothing left but bygone hopes of glory and distinction.

"What in blazes is the matter with ya, John Riley? I know you're hurtin' over our dead comrades, but when will ya stop actin' as if we're all dead? Look around ya, Major. Some of us are still here."

"Leave him be, Mills," Peter O'Brien said. "'Tis plain that cock will never fight again."

"Hold your tongue, you eejit!" Mills yelled. He patted Riley on the back and whispered, "'Twill be a black day for us, Major, when we know for sure the Yankees have indeed broke your fightin' spirit."

Riley had lost all relish for fighting. The yearning of his heart was to get out of that damp prison and escape the darkness that was consuming him. With no reply forthcoming from Charles O'Malley, he set out to write another letter, this time to the British consul in Mexico City.

Your Excellency, with opportunity of . . . writing to you hoping that your honour will take compassion on me as a British subject as I am unfortunate to be here in prison, I write hoping that you will do your utmost with General Scott . . . on the conditions that I do not take arms against them. . . . I shall go to my home, that is the old country . . .

Weeks later, Riley opened the letter containing the British consul's reply.

I wouldn't fail to speak to the General on your behalf, were there any chance of my being of service to you, but I see none at the present moment.

Riley read those lines again and again. The bastards! Of course he'd known, even when he composed the letter, that it was useless to ask the British for help, just like it had been useless to write to his former employer. He leaned against the wall of his cell and crumpled the letter in his hand. Closing his eyes, he let out a sigh. Though he tried to block Patrick Dalton out of his mind, every time he closed his eyes, he saw his friend hanging from the noose like a marionette.

And all for what?

No, he mustn't think that. Even though the war was over, and he knew the Saint Patrick's Battalion had fought on the losing side, they had still fought on the right side and had proved their mettle. Long ago he'd dreamed that one day, he could take the Saint Patrick's Battalion to Ireland and fight for its independence. But like most of his dreams, perhaps that one was also destined to never be realized.

Their daughter was two months old when Ximena was finally allowed to visit him. The iron bars between them didn't permit him to hold Patricia, but he could touch her little feet, stroke her black wispy hair, feel her fingers wrap around his. The sight of his daughter was a great comfort to his flagging spirit. When he saw her yawn, he smiled at her little pink mouth formed in an O. Then she opened her eyes and gazed at him, and in the dim light of the torch, her eyes shone like two sapphires.

"My pretty jewel," he said.

Riley and Ximena stood watching their daughter as she fell asleep, rocking in her mother's arms. "Beggin' your pardon I wasn't there for you, Ximena," he said. "It grieves me I couldn't be there by your side to welcome our daughter into the world."

"I know," she said. "You don't owe me an apology, John. Soon, this will all be over and we will finally be together again. Now that Mexico has officially surrendered—"

"What do you mean, lass?"

"You haven't heard? It happened last week, on February second. It is done. The so-called treaty of 'peace and friendship' has been signed in the town of Guadalupe Hidalgo. Everything Polk desired is now his. Henceforth, we Mexicans must accept the Río Bravo as the legitimate boundary."

"So the Yanks now own all the land north of the river?"

She nodded. "And New Mexico and Alta California and its ports. Mexico is now half the country it used to be. Imagine that. My rancho is officially in the United States now. The border has crossed me."

"The land is still yours," he said.

She scoffed. "You believe they will let me keep it? The Yanquis will do anything in their power to take away the lands of the Mexican families living there, just like they did to us in Texas, mark my words. Those living in the stolen territory will be forced from their homes. We lost the war, John. The new map of Mexico will remind us forever of our staggering loss. Of our country devoured."

"And Santa Anna? What's become of him?"

"He's requested the government permission to leave the country and go into exile."

"With him gone, we'll be hard-pressed to get the new Mexican leaders to honor the promises made to me and my men." Riley said, "The war is lost and not one battle did we win. Not once did we taste the sweetness of glory."

She reached across the iron bars and grabbed his hand. "We have our love. Our future is the battle that matters most. As long as we have each other, we will win. We can rebuild our lives."

"I'm still in prison," he said, "What kind of future can I offer you and Patricia?"

"The treaty requires for the prisoners of war to be freed as soon as it's ratified. That means you and your men will be released! Do not despair, mi amor. I will wait for you, John Riley. The day you get out of here, our daughter and I will take you home. Soon, we will be together, and together we will decide what our future will be."

He thought of her words as time rolled on. In late May, when the Mexican government finally ratified the Treaty of Guadalupe Hidalgo and ceded its territory to the United States, he felt betrayed. Scott didn't consider him or the other San Patricios as prisoners of war, and although all other prisoners were released as mandated by the treaty, Riley and his men were transferred yet again to another fortress in the city—the citadel. A rumor was afloat that the deserters would be sent to New Orleans in due course, from whence they would be drummed out of service. Riley gave faith to the rumors. He wanted to be drummed out of service far away from this city, so that Ximena wouldn't see him being shamed yet again.

Finally, on the first of June, Riley awakened to the distant sound of marching footsteps. The door of the cell creaked open and Lieutenant Gibson, along with some of his infantrymen, marched in.

"On your feet, traitors."

Riley and the other prisoners scrambled to their feet. He couldn't take his eyes off the muskets the infantrymen held over their shoulders. "Whither are we bound?" he asked. Could it be true then, that they would be shipped to New Orleans?

"Well, if you aren't the luckiest Paddies I've ever seen," Gibson said with disdain. "Isn't that so, boys?"

The infantrymen nodded. One of them spat on the ground.

"If I were in charge, I would have left you here to rot," Lieutenant Gibson said. Taking out a letter from his pocket, he proceeded to read the men's names one by one. Hezekiah Akles, John Bartley, Thomas Cassady, John Chambers, John Daily, James Kelly, Alexander McKee, Martin Miles, James Miller, James Mills Peter O'Brien, John Wilton, Samuel Thomas, Edward Ward, Charles Williams, and John Riley. "The prisoners in confinement at the citadel, known as the San Patricios, will be immediately discharged."

Riley looked at the men and saw the glee in their eyes. He was the only one not pleased by the news. *Discharged immediately? Here, in Mexico City, not New Orleans*. He touched his cheeks, then let his long hair fall over his face. *Today, I will be released. Today, I will have to face Ximena and the world and whatever fate awaits us.*

"But first things first," Gibson said. He motioned to his men to step forward. They grabbed the prisoners, and Riley struggled to break free from their hold. "Get your filthy Yankee hands off me!" Riley said, his hands clenched in fists.

Gibson pulled out a razor and said, "Not yet. We wouldn't want you going out there looking like apes, would we?"

Riley was about to protest, but he didn't want to sabotage his men's chance to get out of the cells, and so he held his tongue and swallowed his pride. They pushed him down onto a stool and took scissors to his hair. He kept his eyes fixed on the ground and watched as his hair fell to the floor. There was no hiding behind it now. The first thing Ximena would see would be his branded cheeks, his marred face.

Gibson was deliberately brutal with the razor, and Riley bit his tongue when the razor nicked his scalp. "Well, what do you think, boys? Did I miss my calling as a barber?"

The Yankees laughed.

Riley glanced at James Mills, and by the expression on his face, he knew what he looked like. He rubbed his head, felt the sharp stubble, saw the streaks of blood on his palm. As if it wasn't enough that his face had been destroyed. Now he had to go out into the city with a bloody scalp. And Ximena, how could he go before her looking like this?

"Next!" Gibson yelled, pushing Riley off the stool.

After getting unchained, the prisoners were escorted out of the cell, down the hall, down the stairs, and out into the bright sunlight. Outside the citadel the American soldiers yelled and protested the prisoners' release. Riley squinted in the bright light as he and his men stumbled out of the fortress. The Yankee band played "The Rogue's March," which felt like a slap in the face as he was shamefully drummed out of service.

Poor old soldier, poor old soldier,
He'll be tarred and feathered and sent to Hell,
Because he wouldn't soldier well.

There were Mexicans everywhere crying and cheering for them. The Catholic priests stood in a line. "Come with us, Colorados," they said to the prisoners. "We will take care of you. Vengan." Then there she was with their daughter in her arms, standing next to padre Sebastián.

"John!"

He turned to look at her. He wanted, more than anything, to run to her side, scoop her up in his arms. Instead, Riley drew away from the priests and his men, away from the woman and the daughter he loved—for he was a stain upon them now.

"John!" Ximena said again, he turned to see her pushing her way through the throng. "Where are you going, mi amor?" she said as she caught up to him.

"You deserve more," he said. He had felt hideous in the dark, and he knew he was even more so in the bright light of day.

"All I want is you, John Riley, and nothing that has happened will change that. Now come, let me take you home."

The priests took in his men to give them shelter and food, and Riley allowed Ximena to take him to the small house where she'd lived alone during his time in prison. When Riley crossed the threshold, he scanned the room, not saying a word. It was a simple one-room adobe house with unplastered walls and a hard-packed earthen floor, a curtain hanging from the rafters that separated the bed from the rest of the house. A small kitchen table with two chairs was in a corner, next to a crude stove and a bucket filled with water. A small altar was tucked into a corner, with a bowl of water, flowers, and two candles burning feebly against the soot-stained wall. She had once been the proud owner of a ranch. Now she was barely surviving in the slums of this city where he had left her to fend for herself.

"Why don't you wash up while I make you dinner?" she said, handing him the bucket of water. The babe had fallen asleep and she placed her in a crate that was padded with a blanket. "You must be hungry."

As he washed the grime off himself with a cloth, he watched as she lit the coals in the brazier and set a clay pot full of beans to reheat. From a basket she took out a small ball of corn dough she'd prepared earlier and set out to make tortillas. He saw her knead the dough and form it into small balls, then picked them up one by one and shape them into disks with her hands, slap-slap-slapping them into perfect circles, before placing them on the hot griddle. He couldn't remember the last time he'd had a freshly made tortilla.

When he sat at the table, she placed a steaming bowl of beans and a basket full of piping hot tortillas in front of him. Then she cut a chunk of cheese and pieces of pork cracklings and served him those as well.

"Eat," she said.

He tore a piece of tortilla and used it as a spoon to scoop up his beans. She smiled and set out to eat her own food. He was grateful to her that she didn't ask him a million questions, that she let him be, that she respected his need for silence. But every time she looked at him, his cheeks burned, as if he were being branded all over again. Did she think him hideous? No, he didn't see disgust in her face. Compassion, yes. But not disgust. Still, the tortilla got stuck in his throat, and he could no longer take another bite. He looked around for a looking glass and saw there was none. Had she removed it so that he couldn't see his hideousness? Sensing his sudden loss of appetite, Ximena stood up and came to him. She took his hand and pulled the curtain aside where she forced him to sit on the small straw mattress she'd slept on alone all these months. When he sat, her humble bed sank under his weight. She kissed his forehead, the tip of his nose, his eyelids, his mouth, and then she placed a kiss on each of his disfigured cheeks. He turned away. "Don't soil yourself touchin' my face with your lips, lass."

"Shhh," she said, putting a finger on his lips, and she did it softly again and again. Her kisses on his face, a cascade of sweet-scented orange blossoms.

She took off her blouse and guided his hands to her breasts. She let out a moan, and that sound of pleasure helped him forget that he was a monster now. She wanted him. Despite everything, she still wanted him.

He lowered her onto her back, and she tugged at his pantaloons while he pulled off his shirt. He entered her hard, without holding back. She wrapped her legs around his waist and clung to him with all her might, pulling him deeper inside. Her body spasmed with pleasure just as his own body shuddered and emptied inside her, and he fell on her, breathing fast and hard. Then suddenly, his body convulsed again, but in tears. She wrapped her arms around him and held him as he cried on her bosom. He thought about his men hanging from the gallows, of Patrick's painful death. He thought of the guilt that was eating at him knowing that he, John Riley of County Galway, had led his men to their brutal deaths. He had robbed them of a future, of their families, of the love of a woman. What right did he have to such things? What right did he have to love and be loved? To have a future with Ximena? To have a family?

I ought to leave her, he thought as his tears finally subsided. He pulled away from her arms and turned away, sat up on the edge of the mattress and wiped his face dry.

"¡Madre mía!" She gasped, and he turned around to look at her, wondering what had affrighted her so, until he realized what it was. His bare back. The skin had been torn open and shredded by the muleteer's whip. She ran her fingers along, tracing every scar that zigzagged and crisscrossed like markings on a queer map, the geography of his pain and humiliation. The wounds of his lacerated flesh had healed, but they still rankled. As did the bitter memories of the Yanks.

She wrapped her arms around him from behind and kissed his back again and again as she cried. It was her turn now to convulse in tears, her body shaking from sorrow and helplessness. He wanted to gather her in his arms and tell her that she oughtn't cry, that he didn't deserve her tears, her anguish. But he didn't comfort her. He sat, unmoving, remembering that fateful day when General Twiggs gave the order to strip and whip him, to brand him like cattle—not once, but twice. Double was his hatred now for the Yanks.

He couldn't tell how long they sat like that, but she finally stopped crying and let go of him. She went to the altar in the corner of the room and placed fresh candles and copal incense before the statue of la Virgen de Guadalupe. She crossed herself and said a silent prayer. Soon, curls of incense filled the room with a piercing fragrance. She reached into her basket and took out herbs and jars and a few other things, and she came back with a tray and told him to lie down.

She rubbed his body with almond oil, her hands glided across his chest, his arms, his legs. His muscles relaxed under her healing touch, the knots unraveling. She mumbled prayers in Spanish, entreating the Virgin, the saints, God himself, to relieve him of his burden and restore the lost piece of his soul. He surrendered to the sacredness with which she caressed his body with her eagle feather.

She took an egg and rubbed it over his body, beginning with his head, down his chest, his arms, the palms of his hands, the soles of his feet. The coolness of the egg against his skin soothed him. He remembered her telling him that eggs absorb negative energy and harm inside the patient. He had a lifetime's worth of that. She gently swept him with the fragrant branches of epazote, and he inhaled and took it deep inside his being. She asked him to turn around and lie on his stomach. She was extra gentle on his back, touching him with compassion, and he wanted to tell her it no longer hurt, though he wondered if he might be lying. Perhaps his ragged wounds had healed, but he could still feel the pain as if he had been flogged yesterday. Her monotone voice rose above him in prayer, and he mumbled along with the words. He thought of the chapel where he'd received his first communion, his parents beaming with pride, Father Aidan giving him the holy Host. And after, his friends and relations had gathered for a modest meal but with plenty of poteen that his father had made, and dancing and singing, his uncle playing the fiddle for the last time before the English hanged him in the gallows two weeks later. No! He pushed the memory aside and returned to Ximena's prayers, to let her voice bring him back to the happy memories of his life. He wanted her words to take away the memories that hurt him, like thorns of a cactus buried deep inside. If she could yank them out, one by one, singe him over an open fire, peel him like a prickly pear, he could finally be free.

When she got to the last part of the cleansing, she rolled dried hemp leaves in a corn husk, lit it, and blew the smoke over him. As it hovered above him like a cloud, he thought of his cannons, of his gunners expertly firing at his command, the gunpowder smoke lingering over them, the cheers and hugs they gave each other when they hit their targets, decimating the Yankee ranks. That was how he would remember his men, Patrick Dalton by his side. All of them fighting under the green banner of Saint Patrick.

Exhaustion finally overcame him, and he felt himself drifting off to sleep. He felt comforted, reassured.

"I love you, John Riley," she said as she pulled the blanket over him. She kissed each of his cheeks and tucked him in.

"And I you, lass," he said, opening his eyes to look at her. "My heart will always be yours. Always."

He closed his eyes again, and let sleep take him. No, he couldn't leave her. As long as she wanted him, he would stay with her, do right by her and their daughter. He couldn't let the Yanks destroy their love, destroy his family. But he knew he could no longer stay in this country. He could not make a home upon the soil where his men had been so brutally killed.

No, he needed Erin's shores to heal his spirit and wash away the stain upon his soul .

43

The Road to Vera Cruz

They left the capital at daybreak. Ximena turned to catch the last
glimpse of it from the window of the diligence pulled by eight mules and
guarded by a hired escort, traveling along the National Highway. The
magnificent Valle de México, flanked by the two snow-capped volcanoes and enclosed by rugged mountains, was spread out under the pink-
tinged sky. She looked at the towers, domes, and spires of the churches
pointing to the heavens above, the numerous trees and gardens in and
around the city, their verdure contrasting with the red roofs of the buildings, the countryside dotted with sleepy haciendas and lakes as clear and
glittery as looking glass. Ximena elbowed John and pointed outside the
window to get him to look as well, but instead he turned up the collar
of his cloak to hide his face and closed his eyes, feigning sleep. He was
a big man, and no matter how small he tried to make himself, his long
legs took up too much of the insufficient space inside the coach. Ximena
couldn't miss the last glimpse of the valley's beauty and splendor. These
four hundred kilometers stretching out before them could be the last
she might ever see of her country. But her soul was Mexican and would
always be so, and even when her feet no longer touched her native soil,
she would always carry Mexico inside her heart. So while John and baby
Patricia slept, she poked her head out the window to take it all in.

She leaned back in her seat, trying to keep her teeth from rattling as she was jostled every time the stagecoach went over a rut or rock on the road. As she listened to the rumble of the wheels, she wished the driver would slow down, and at the same time, she wanted his mules to go faster so that the passengers would stop looking at John's branded cheeks with open curiosity. She knew he was feeling self-conscious about their stares, which was why he was feigning sleep.

But still, she was grateful to be on this journey, grateful they'd finally had the funds to pay for their travel expenses and had convinced the British consul to assist them with passage on one of the English vessels. After requesting his discharge from the army, it had taken John months to get the Mexican government to pay the wages owed to him and the surviving San Patricios and to provide him and Ximena with passports out of the republic. Once Santa Anna went into exile, the government vacillated in honoring the promises that were made to the San Patricios. The treasury was empty and the country in ruins, they said. The Yanquis had brought Mexico to its knees and who knew how long it would take for the collective agony and wounded national pride to recover. Nevertheless, the government finally gave John his back pay, made him a colonel, and thanked him for his services to the republic.

As the sun-kissed Popocatépetl and his sleeping lady, Iztaccíhuatl, faded behind them, another volcano appeared in the distance—Orizaba, the highest peak in all of Mexico, the most majestic mountain Ximena had ever seen. The volcano rose before her, cutting through the sky with its snowy crown that pierced the clouds. They passed by humble villages of cane huts and immense haciendas of stone and mortar, decaying chapels and ancient churches, large gray convents and small shrines to la Virgen de Guadalupe, white gleaming crosses off the side of the road or perched atop rocks, fields of volcanic rock and haystacks, vast plantations and sugarcane fields, arrieros with their loaded mules and shepherds with their flocks of goats or herds of pigs, Indians collecting cochineal from the cacti or siphoning the sap out of the maguey and into their pigskin pouches, but still Orizaba never got any closer.

In Puebla de los Ángeles they changed mules and spent the night in a modest inn and acquired a new escort. At sunrise the next morning, the stagecoach left the city behind and entered the state of Vera Cruz. When Santa Anna had talked to Ximena about the place of his birth, she'd thought that, like with everything else, he'd exaggerated its grandeur and beauty. And now, here it was before her, the most beautiful place she'd ever seen. Every shade of green—the fertile fields of waving cornstalks and plantations of coffee; forests of cedar, oak and pine; rolling hills carpeted in grass and wildflowers where cows and horses pastured; emerald streams meandering through the lush vegetation and falling in small cascades. This was the xalapeño's home, this paradise of eternal spring, with its verdant foliage, its tropical flowers and orchards heavy with papayas, its banana groves and fields of pineapples.

When they finally arrived in Xalapa at dusk and wound their way along the steep mountain road, Santa Anna was more present in her mind—the evening air smelled like him, the fragrance of plumeria amplified by the humidity. They stopped for the night in an inn near an old convent. Too tired and jolted to eat, they retired to their room where Ximena and Patricia slept on the bed, and John, unable to break his prison habit, slept on the floor. Ximena longed to feel his body next to hers, to make love to him under the light of the moon streaming through the bars on the window. But he had withdrawn inside himself once again, and she wondered how many limpias it would take to make his soul whole again, to lure his spirit out of the dark shadows of his prison cell. She had faith that one day, he would finally transcend his sadness, his guilt, and the disharmony within him would end once he remembered who he was.

They left the paradise that was Xalapa at the break of day. To the southwest, the snowy Orizaba enveloped in clouds tinged with the pink of dawn, and in the distance, beyond the lofty mountains, a glimpse of the Gulf of Mexico. It was only then that John's melancholy eyes brightened, like clouds lit by lightning. Soon, they would be traveling upon those waters, sailing to his beloved home, and the Atlantic breezes would blow away the somber darkness inside him.

"It won't be long now," she said.

He smiled and pulled her and their daughter against him.

Most of the land from Xalapa to the city of Vera Cruz belonged to Santa Anna, and so the stagecoach traversed his hacienda for kilometers. It was quiet and empty, not a peón in sight, not even a sign of cattle out to graze. The house itself was too far away from the road for Ximena to see it, but she'd heard that the Yanquis had plundered and destroyed Santa Anna's property with reckless abandon. As they left El Lencero behind, the scent of plumeria finally faded away.

Descending the mountain, John could not take his eyes off of the glittering blue stretching toward the horizon. And finally, as dusk fell upon them, a breath of salt water, the murmur of waves, and the Gulf of Mexico came into view, tinted with the fiery glow of the setting sun, with vessels, large and small, lying at anchor near its shores. The port of Vera Cruz spread out before them in a half-moon shape, surrounded by a high wall and barren hills of moving sands. Seagulls flew across the scarlet sky and over the flickering lights of the city.

No sooner had they gotten settled in their inn, than John wanted to go out and call upon the ship's captain to ensure the arrangements were properly made. Ximena wished to have a bath, to soak her body in hot water and wash away the toils of the journey, but she could see his desperation to gaze upon the waters and see to the ship that would bear him home.

"You go on, John," she said, as she and the baby lay down on the bed. "I will feed Patricia and request hot water to wash. I feel like a sparrow that was out dust bathing all day."

She was asleep before the door closed behind him.

In the morning, it was her turn to go out. "I will light a candle at the cathedral and pray for good weather," she said, kissing his cheeks. "If we are unlucky enough to get hit with a norte, it will delay our departure for days."

She left him to take care of their daughter and hurried out the door. As she walked down the streets, Ximena could see the remnants of the four days of bombardment the city had suffered at the hands of the Yanquis when over a thousand veracruzanos, a great many women and children, had been killed or wounded. Half of the city had been destroyed, and almost two years later, many of the houses and public buildings still had walls riddled with holes, while others had been turned to a pile of ash and ruins or left with only blackened walls. Zopilotes circled overhead, and two of the buzzards landed on the street to fight over a pile of refuse by an abandoned home. It made her quicken her step.

Upon her arrival at the cathedral, she sought the padre in the sacristy.

"Padre Bernal? I am Ximena, wife of coronel Juan Riley."

"Sí, hija. Come in, come in," the priest said. "I was just writing a letter to padre Sebastián. He'll be happy to hear you've all arrived safely."

"Is it done, then?" she said. "Are they here?"

"Sí, sí, no te preocupes, hija. Everyone's here now, and it's all taken care of."

She sighed in relief. "Gracias, padrecito. I thank you with all my heart for your help. Without you and padre Sebastián, and the archbishop, it wouldn't have been possible."

"Your husband has suffered enough for our country. And so have all the San Patricios. Mexico will not abandon its Irish heroes. Now, God be with you, child. And I will pray for a safe journey for you and your family across the ocean."

"Thank you, padre." She kissed his hand and took her leave, lighting a candle in gratitude before returning to the inn.

Two days later, they were waiting to embark on the ship which was first bound for Cuba. The wind tasted gritty from the sandhills surrounding the city. Ximena looked at the Gulf of Mexico, remembering that fateful day when she had stood on the shore, watching the Yanqui ships approach El Frontón de Santa Isabel almost a thousand kilometers to the north of Vera Cruz. Would her eyes ever behold the prairies and chaparrals, the solitary thickets of thorny cacti and twisted trees, the golden bells of esperanza glowing under the sun again? The wild mustangs running free in the prairie? Would she ever hear the vibrating songs of the cicadas, the warm breath of the wind whispering through the grasses, the chorus of the chachalacas and green jays once more? She was so far from the rancho now, from the pecan grove where Joaquín and their son were buried, from the cemetery in Matamoros where her father and grandmother lay in eternal rest, from San Antonio de Béxar where her mother and brothers had remained. *I'll always keep you in my heart*, she promised. She would be like a mesquite, dig her tap root deep into the entrails of this Mexican earth and never let go.

Little by little, the passengers arrived at the dock with their trunks and crates. John kept his eyes on the ship anchored in the harbor, anxious to board, oblivious to the activity around him. Ximena saw him startle when he heard the familiar voices behind him.

"At your service, Colonel Riley."

John turned around to find a group of grinning men saluting him. The surviving San Patricios, not all of them, but a dozen of them. Some, Ximena knew, had chosen to settle in Mexico.

"Faith, but what in blazes are ye all doin' here, fellas?"

They turned to look at her, with smiles on their faces. "Our lady Ximena found us. Told us you were going home," James Mills said.

"And here we are, going back with you, sir," Peter O'Brien said.

John looked at her. "But how?"

"The church," she said. "The priests helped find them and made sure my letters got to them. They forced the government to honor the agreement you made with them, that they would pay for passage of any San Patricio who may wish to travel home."

His frown deepened, and then, after her words sunk in, he burst into a laugh. "Jesus, Mary, and Joseph, woman, you sure beat all!" He took her and the baby in his arms and spun them around.

Then he embraced his men, one by one. "Ye are a glorious sight to behold, my boys!"

All of the men were branded on their cheeks, though John was the only one with the two brands. The Yanquis had tried to shame them by marking them like cattle, but Ximena hoped that one day, John would learn to see those marks as a badge of honor. Because that is what he was, an honorable man who had stood up for what he believed. The D was not for deserter. But rather defender.

"We're goin' home, my brave fellas!" he said. "And fight we shall for the good of Ireland."

Alexander McKee took out his flask and said, "*Bás in Éirinn!*"

The ship sounded its horn, and it was time for the passengers to be taken aboard on the rowboats. The locals gathered to watch them leave, and as she was being rowed away, Ximena waved goodbye to her compatriots. Would she ever see them again?

As they left the shore, Ximena stood on the deck, enjoying the spray of the waves breaking against the ship. Seagulls skimmed the surface of the waters, and pelicans plunged right in to pick up their breakfast. She took out her brooch and tenderly caressed the Mexican eagle as she watched Vera Cruz drift farther and farther away. The white houses, the churches, the sand dunes, the fortress San Juan de Ulúa, they all receded into the horizon until there was nothing left of her country but the blue of the Mexican sky and the lofty mountain of Orizaba peeking through the morning clouds that enveloped its snowy bosom like a lacy mantilla.

No, this was not an eternal farewell. Not adiós, but hasta luego.

John came to stand beside her and pulled her close. "A long time ago I crossed an ocean, and now this gulf will return me to that same ocean—the great Atlantic—and back to my son and my homeland. I shall be a wanderer no longer."

"No, you will be a brave son of Erin who has come home," she said. They looked at their daughter, with Mexican and Irish blood flowing through her veins. Ximena knew that she and John, haunted by the horrors of war, would always carry battle scars within them, but they had survived, hadn't they? One way or another, they would find a way to thrive as a family.

They walked along the deck to where the San Patricios stood watching the sailors work the ropes, the canvas sails bending before the breeze, and together they turned to face the future that lay before them, praying it would be as splendid and boundless as the golden waters rippling ahead.

Maps TK

Maps TK

Acknowledgments

TK